AN ORIGINAL GRAPHIC NOVEL

CAPTAIN AMERICA
THE GHOST ARMY

WRITTEN BY
ALAN GRATZ

ILLUSTRATED BY
BRENT SCHOONOVER
WITH **MATT HORAK** AND **ÁLVARO LÓPEZ**

COVER BY
DAVID AJA

COLORS BY
SARAH STERN

LETTERS BY
VC's JOE CARAMAGNA

graphix
AN IMPRINT OF
SCHOLASTIC

LAUREN BISOM, Senior Editor
CAITLIN O'CONNELL, Associate Editor
STACIE ZUCKER, Publication Design
JENNIFER GRÜNWALD, Director, Production & Special Projects
SVEN LARSEN, VP Licensed Publishing
JEFF YOUNGQUIST, VP Production & Special Projects
DAVID GABRIEL, SVP Print, Sales & Marketing
C.B. CEBULSKI, Editor in Chief

MICHAEL PETRANEK, Executive Editor, Manager AFK & Graphix Media, Scholastic
JEFF SHAKE, Senior Designer, Scholastic

Special Thanks to **GAVIN GUIDRY**, **TOM BREVOORT**, and **KATERI WOODY**

Captain America created by **JOE SIMON** and **JACK KIRBY**

ISBN 978-1-338-77589-1

10 9 8 7 6 5 4 3 2 1   23 24 25 26 27

Printed in the U.S.A.   40

First edition, January 2023

Art by Brent Schoonover, Matt Horak, Álvaro López, and Sarah Stern
Letters by VC's Joe Caramagna
Young Steve Rogers art by Dale Eaglesham & Andy Troy
Map by Mark Gruenwald & Rick Parker

For Greg Bunch.
Thanks for letting me read your comics.
— AG

To Brandon Terrell,
who always wanted his name in a Marvel Comic.
— BS

UNITED STATES ARMED SERVICES

DO NOT COPY/CONFIDENTIAL

Name: Steven "Steve" Rogers
Current Alias: Captain America
Status: Active
Place of Birth: Brooklyn, NY **Date of Birth:** July 4,
Race: Caucasian **Gender:** Male
Height: 6'2" **Weight:** 240 lbs.
Hair: Blond **Eyes:** Blue
Relatives: Joseph Rogers (father, deceased),
Sarah Rogers (mother, deceased)
Languages: English, French, Spanish,
German, some Russian and Italian

Military background: After being repeatedly
rejected as unfit for service in the U.S. Army,
Rogers was accepted into PROJECT REBIRTH, under the direction of Dr. Abraham Erskine. Using
a combination of Vita-Rays and a Super-Soldier Serum now lost since the death of Dr. Erskine,
Rogers became America's first and only Super Soldier. As a result, Rogers's physical and mental
abilities have been heightened to superhuman levels. After extensive physical and tactical
training by Colonel Rex Applegate and William E. Fairbairn of the British Royal Marines, Rogers
was sent into Nazi occupied Europe to battle

Steve Rogers
Captain America

TOP SECRET

UNITED STATES ARMED SERVICES

DO NOT COPY/CONFIDENTIAL

Name: James Buchanan "Bucky" Barnes
Current Alias: None
Status: Active
Place of Birth: Shelbyville, Indiana   **Date of Birth:** March 10
Race: Caucasian   **Gender:** Male
Height: 5'4"   **Weight:** 125 lbs.
Hair: Brown   **Eyes:** Brown
Relatives: George Barnes (father, deceased),
Winnifred Barnes (mother, deceased),
Rebecca Barnes (younger sister)
Languages: English, Russian, German,
some French
Military background: Barnes's father, a career
U.S. Army soldier, died in a basic-training accident
at Camp Lehigh when Barnes was a young boy,
leaving him an orphan. Rather than be sent away
to boarding school with his sister, Barnes persuaded his father's friends to keep him on as a ward
of the state at Camp Lehigh, where he became something of a camp mascot. At Camp Lehigh,
Barnes trained with U.S. Army soldiers, British Commandos, and Office of Strategic Services
operatives, becoming an expert in martial arts, marksmanship, and espionage at an unusually
early age. Now assigned as the partner to Captain America, Barnes

James Buchanan Barnes
"Bucky"

TOP SECRET

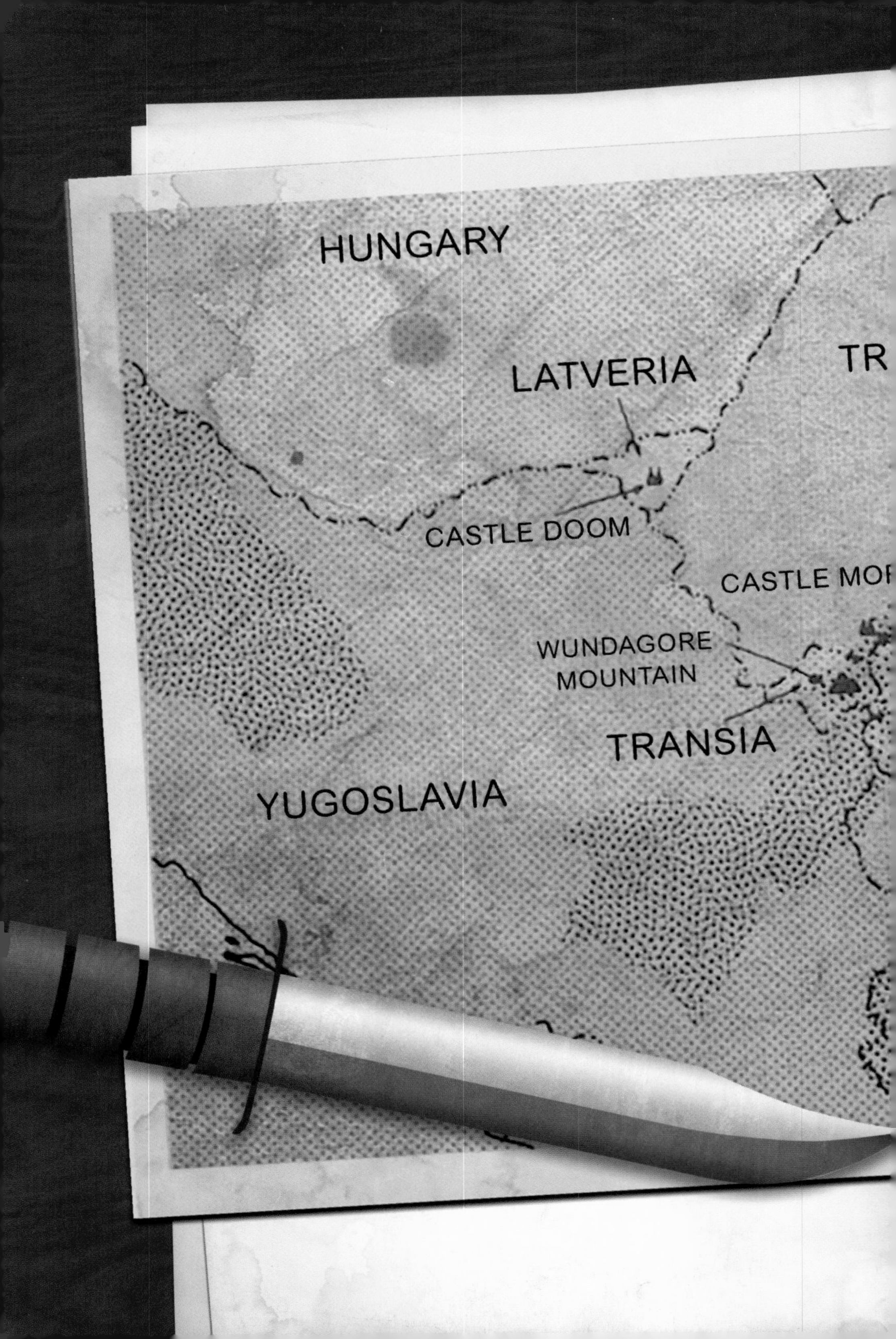
HUNGARY
LATVERIA
TR
CASTLE DOOM
CASTLE MOR
WUNDAGORE
MOUNTAIN
TRANSIA
YUGOSLAVIA

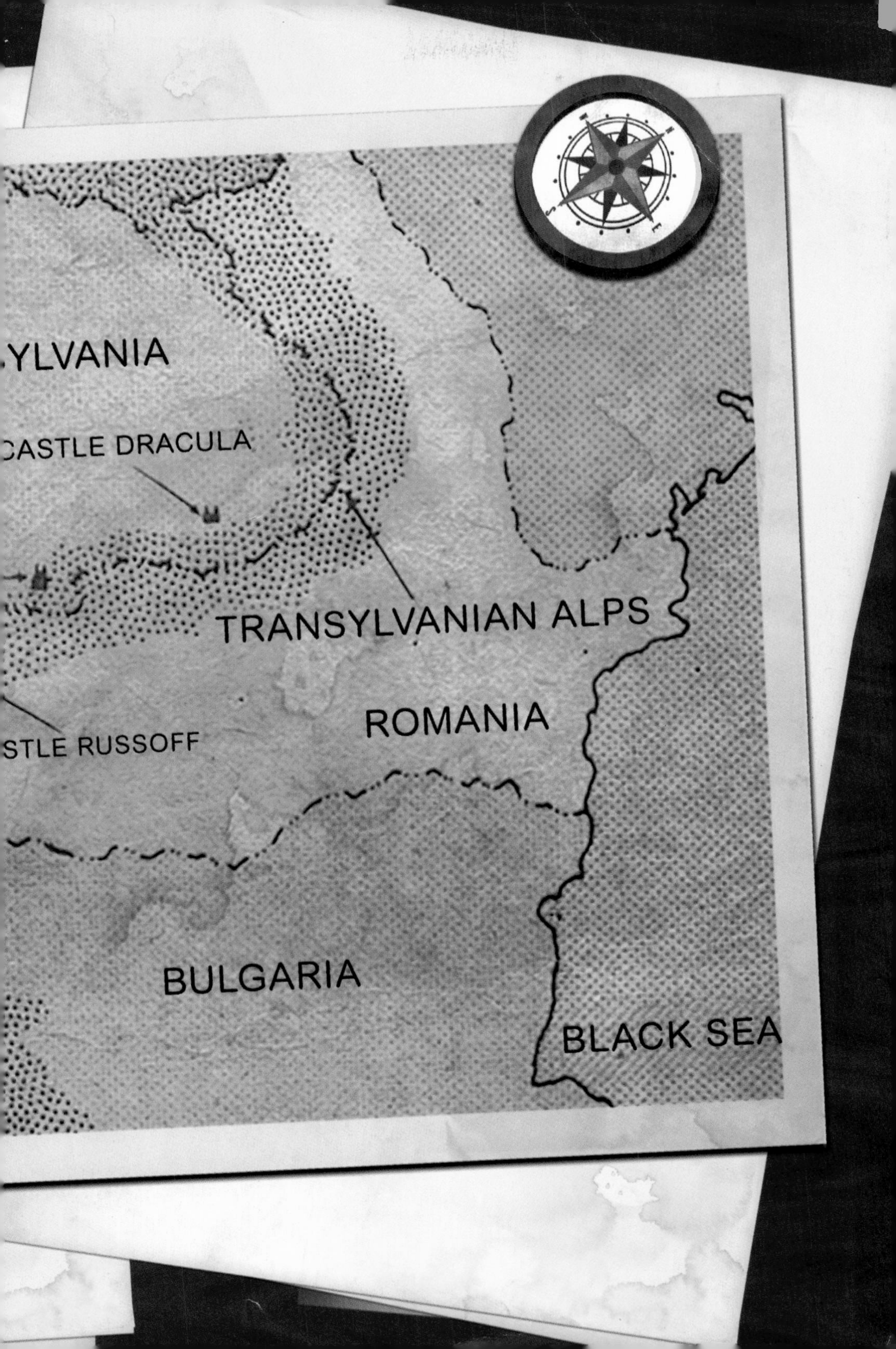
YLVANIA
CASTLE DRACULA
TRANSYLVANIAN ALPS
ROMANIA
STLE RUSSOFF
BULGARIA
BLACK SEA

CHAPTER ONE
SURROUNDED

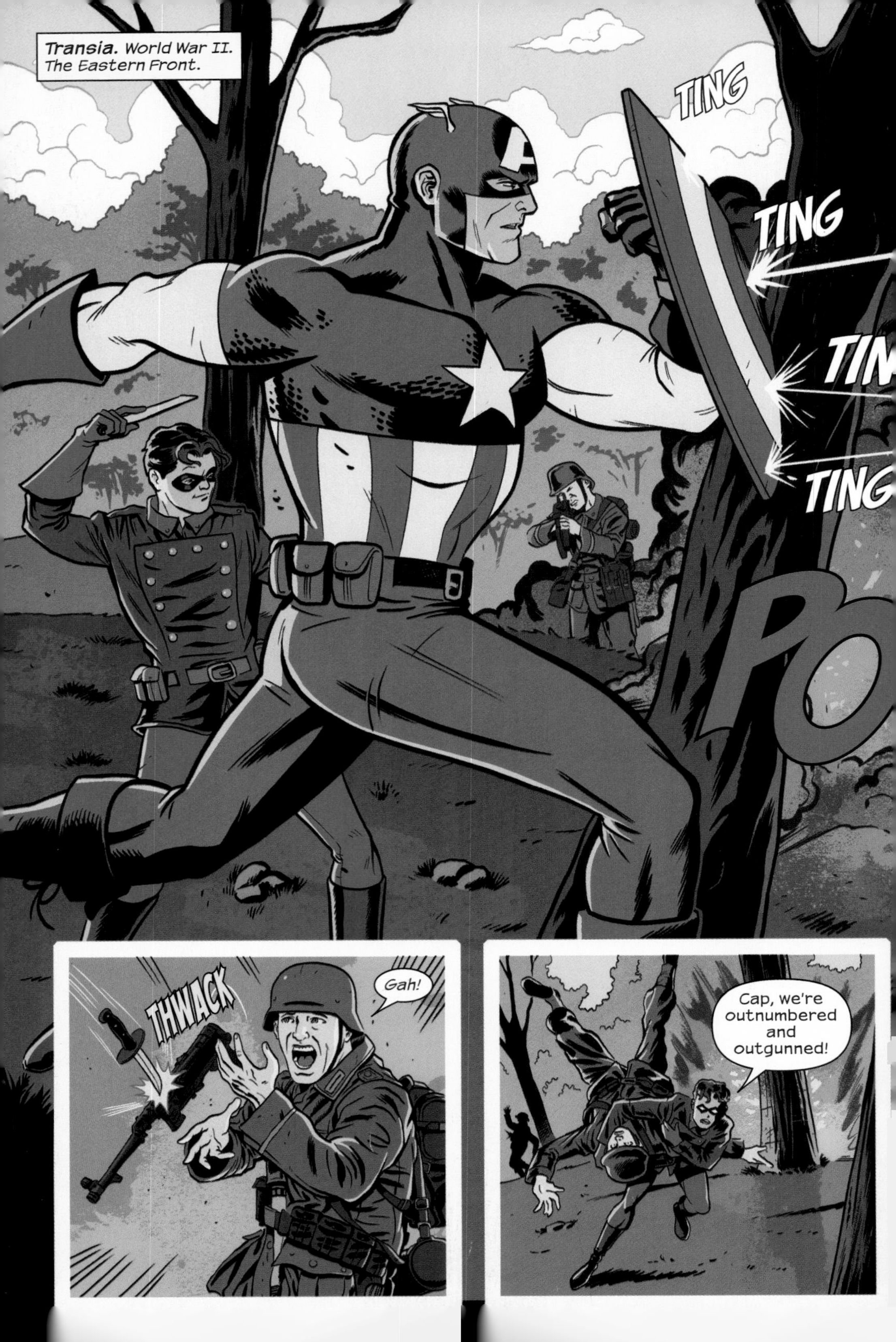
Transia. World War II. The Eastern Front.
TING
TING
TIN
TING
PO
THWACK
Gah!
Cap, we're outnumbered and outgunned!

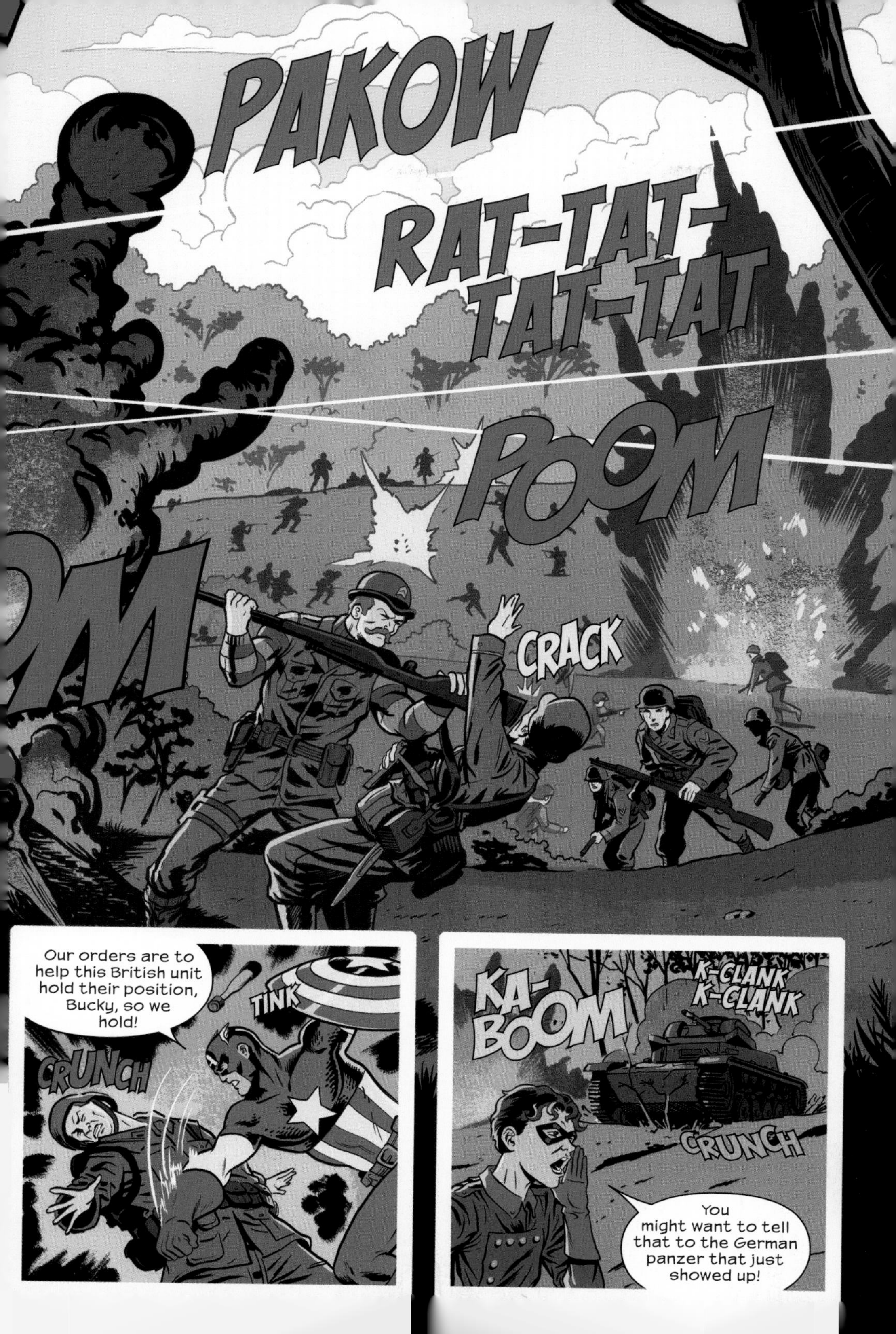
PAKOW
RAT-TAT-TAT-TAT
POOM
CRACK
Our orders are to help this British unit hold their position, Bucky, so we hold!
TINK
CRUNCH
KA-BOOM
K-CLANK K-CLANK
CRUNCH
You might want to tell that to the German panzer that just showed up!

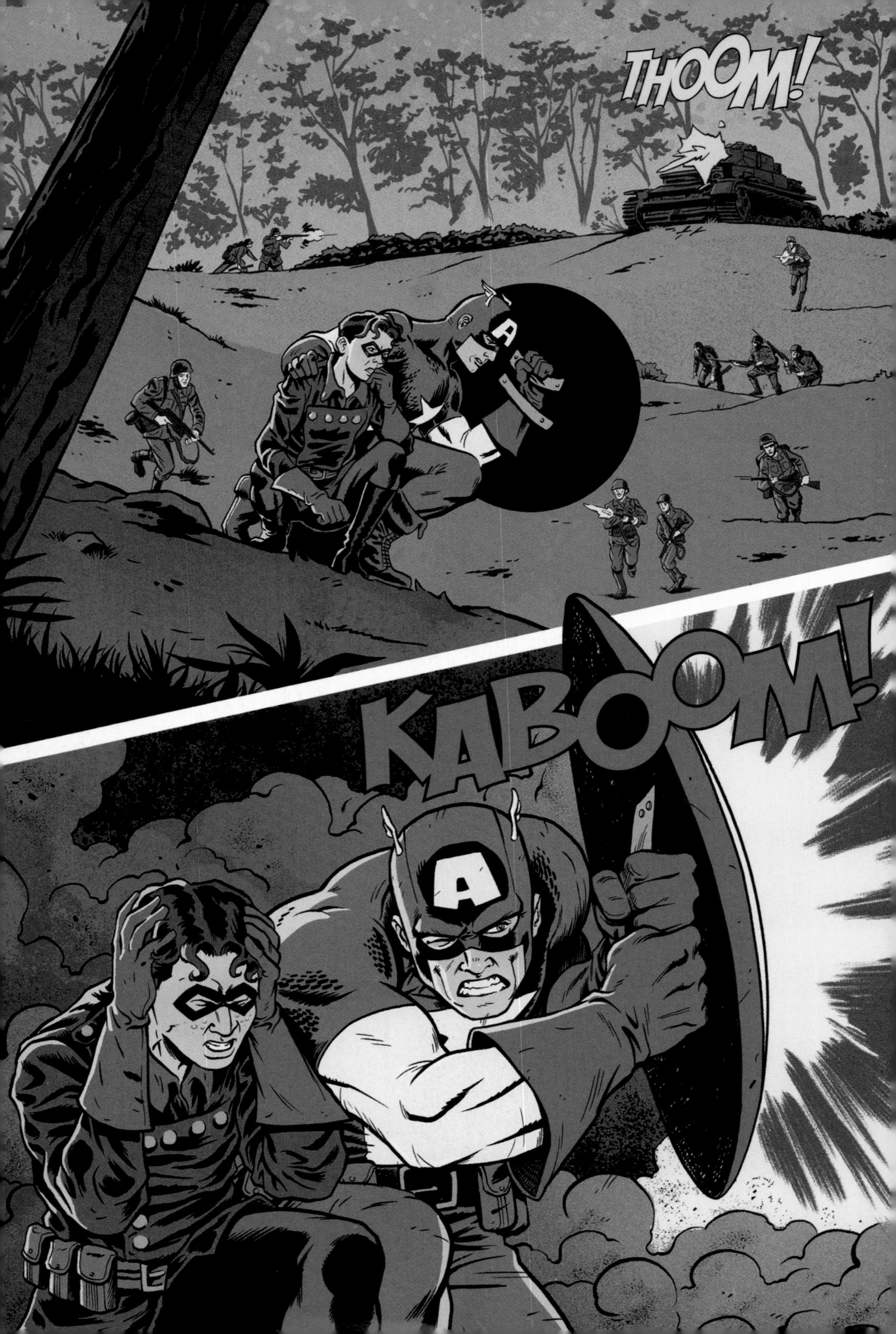

THOOM!
KABOOM!

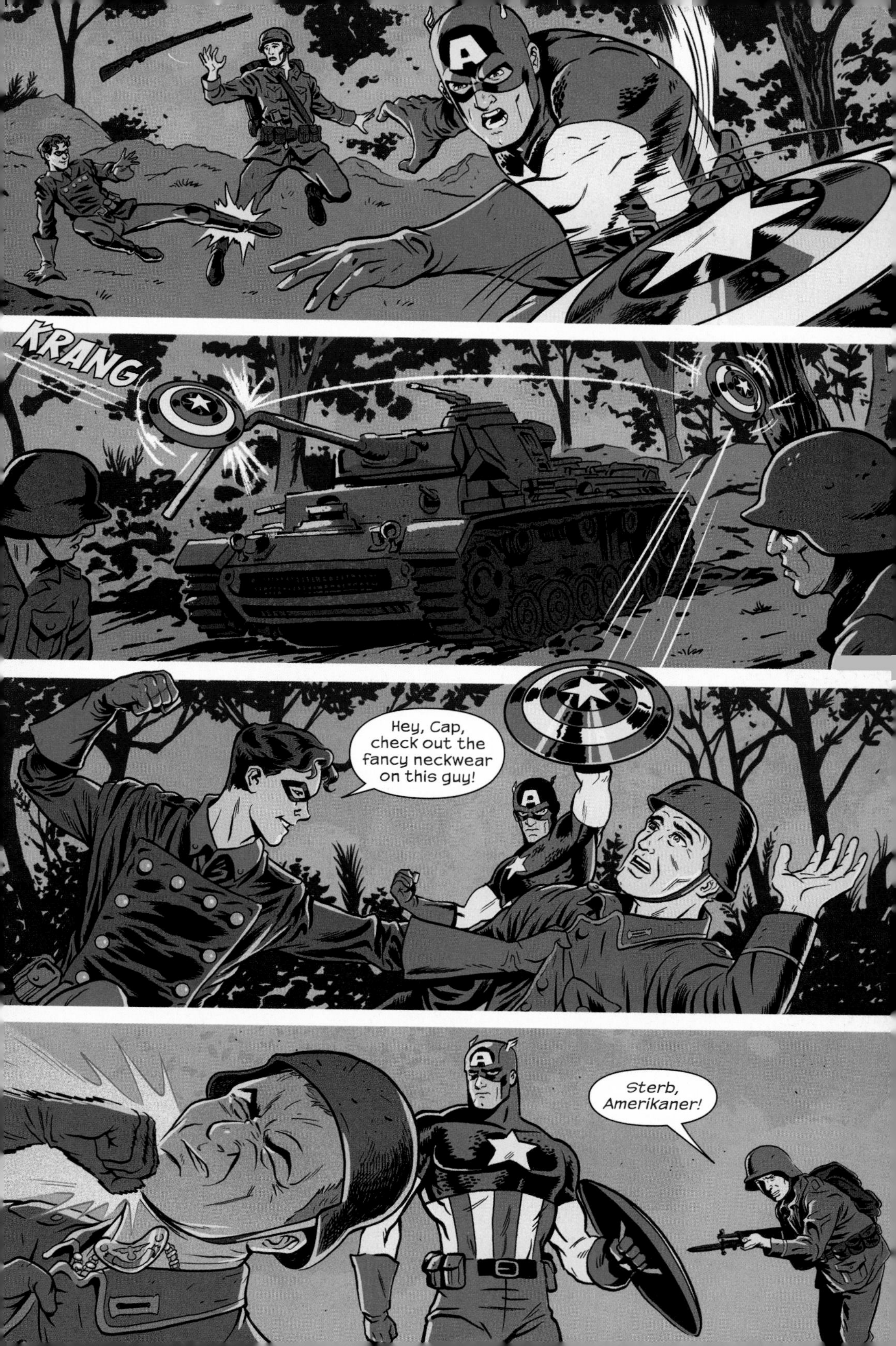
KRANG
Hey, Cap, check out the fancy neckwear on this guy!
Sterb, Amerikaner!

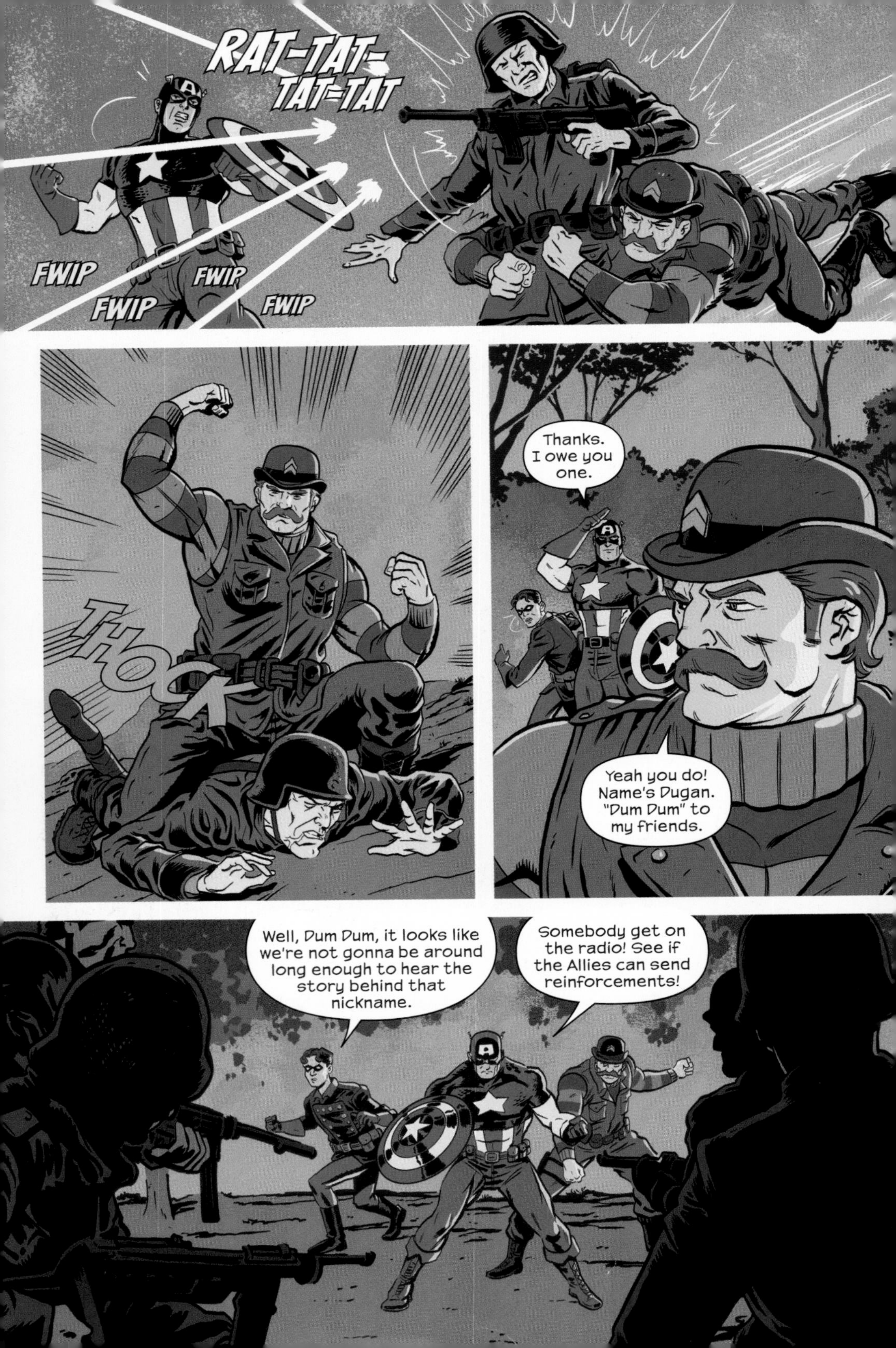
RAT-TAT-TAT-TAT
FWIP
FWIP
FWIP
FWIP
THOCK
Thanks. I owe you one.
Yeah you do! Name's Dugan. "Dum Dum" to my friends.
Well, Dum Dum, it looks like we're not gonna be around long enough to hear the story behind that nickname.
Somebody get on the radio! See if the Allies can send reinforcements!

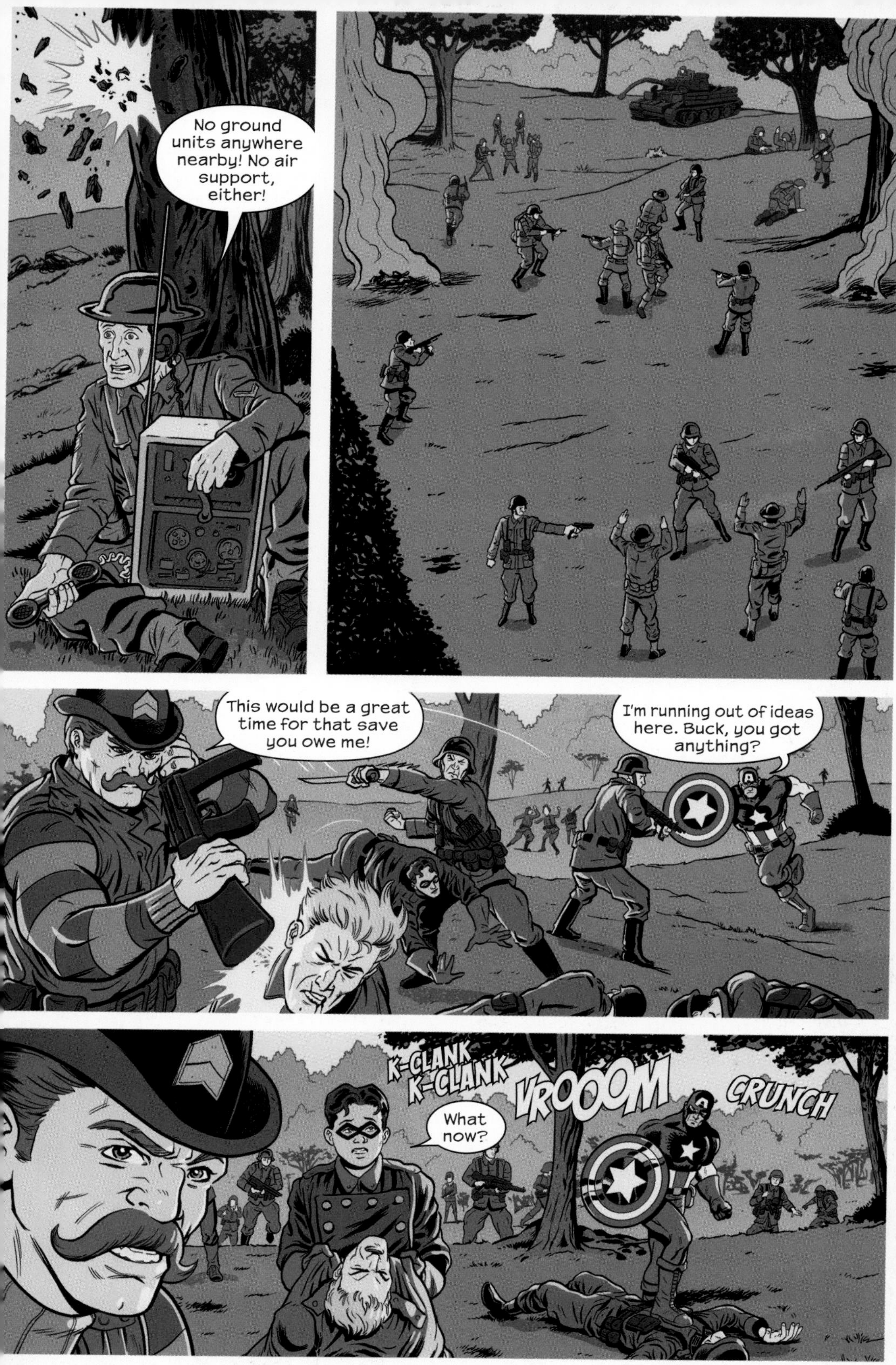
No ground units anywhere nearby! No air support, either!
This would be a great time for that save you owe me!
I'm running out of ideas here. Buck, you got anything?
K-CLANK
K-CLANK
VROOOM
CRUNCH
What now?

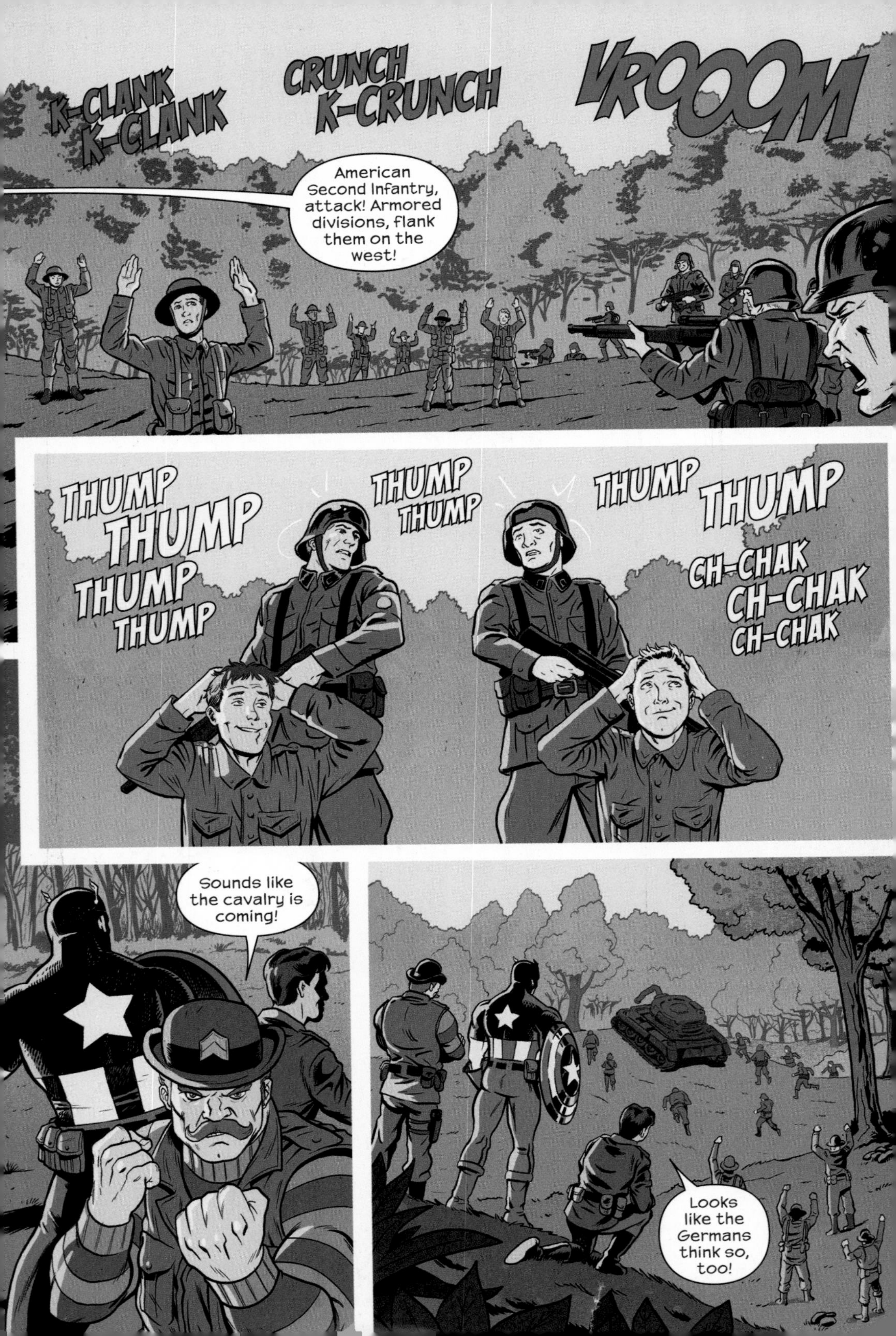
K-CLANK K-CLANK
CRUNCH K-CRUNCH
VROOOOM
American Second Infantry, attack! Armored divisions, flank them on the west!
THUMP THUMP THUMP THUMP
THUMP THUMP
THUMP THUMP
CH-CHAK CH-CHAK CH-CHAK
Sounds like the cavalry is coming!
Looks like the Germans think so, too!

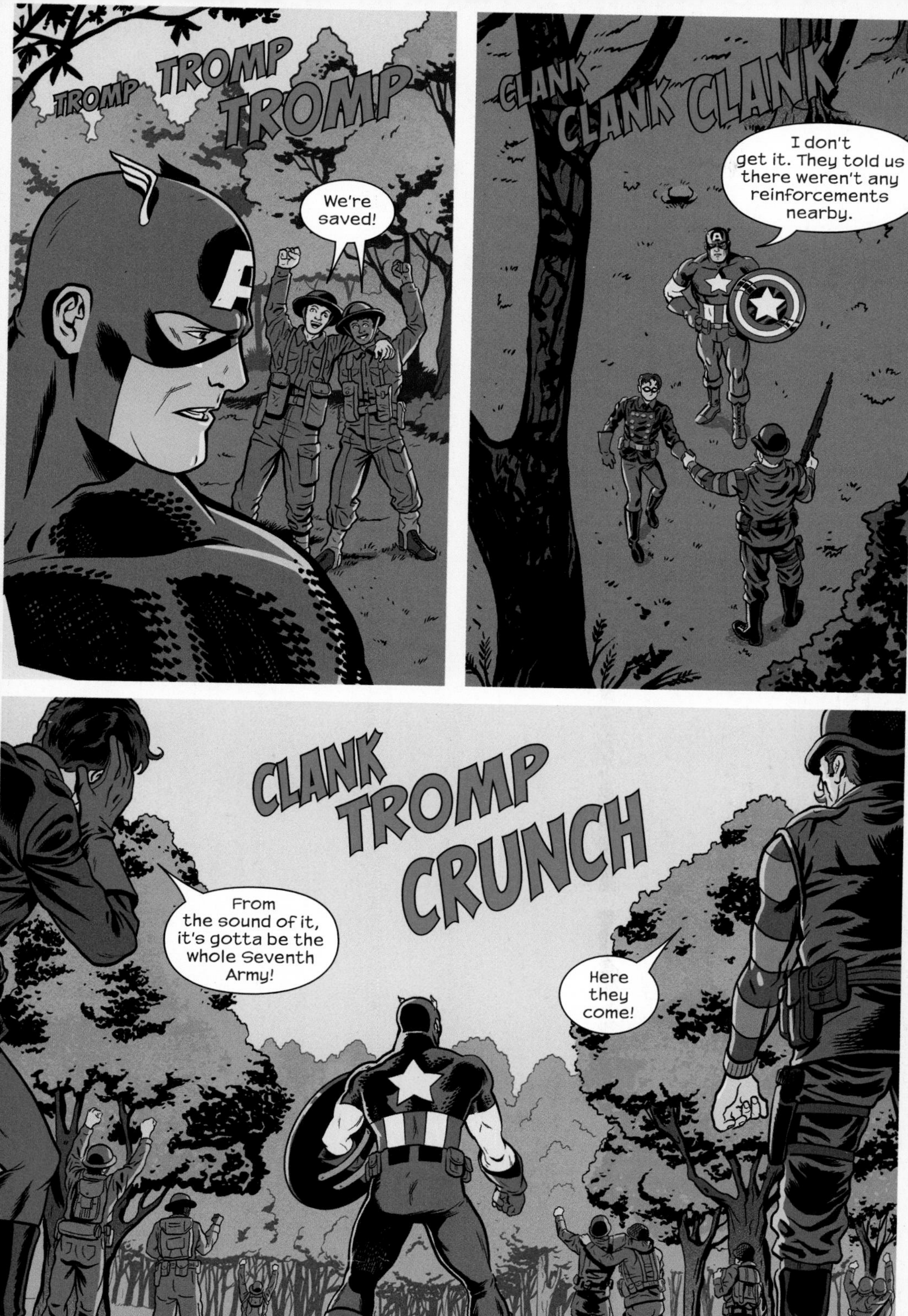
TROMP TROMP TROMP
We're saved!
CLANK CLANK CLANK
I don't get it. They told us there weren't any reinforcements nearby.
CLANK TROMP CRUNCH
From the sound of it, it's gotta be the whole Seventh Army!
Here they come!

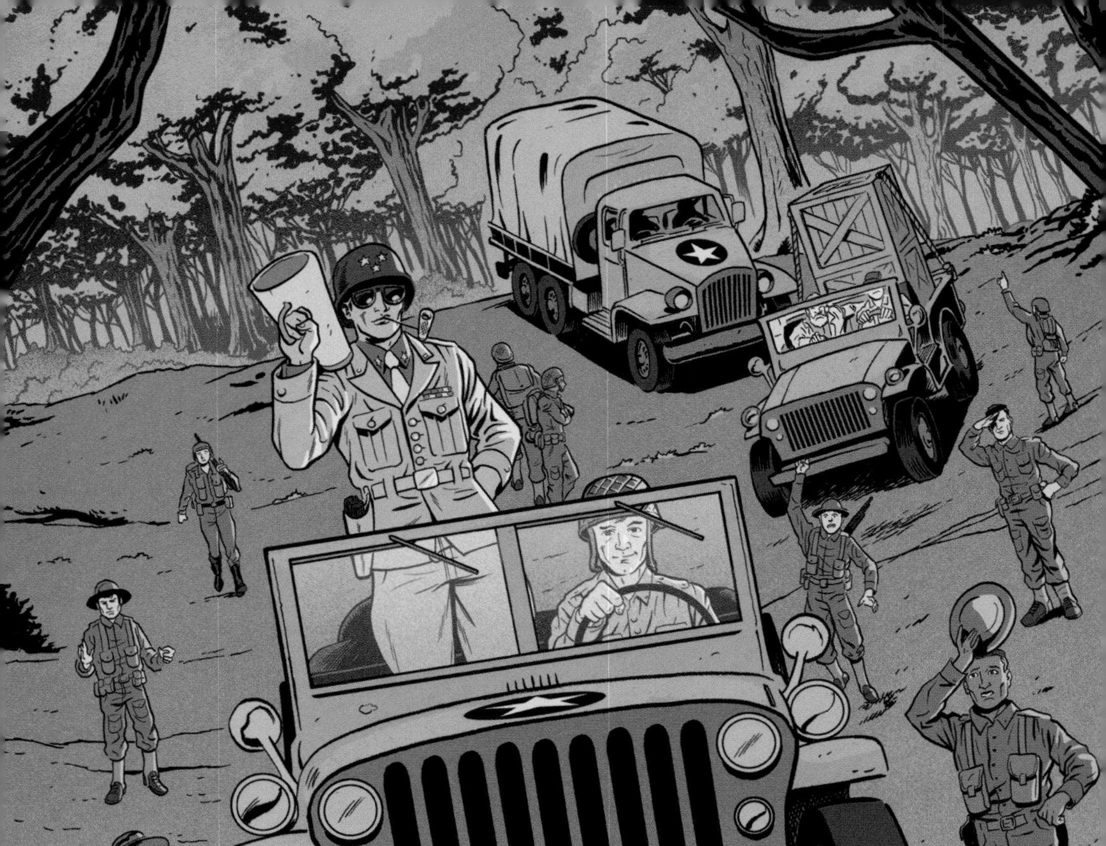
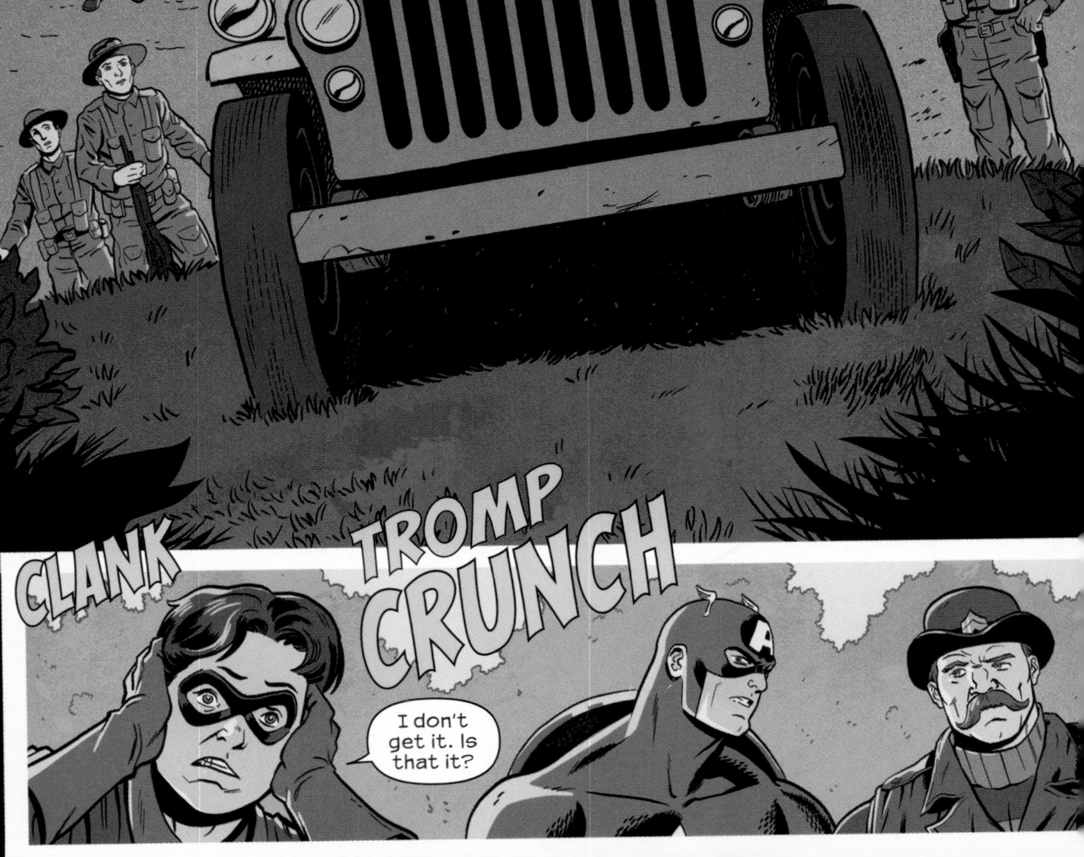
CLANK
TROMP
CRUNCH
I don't get it. Is that it?

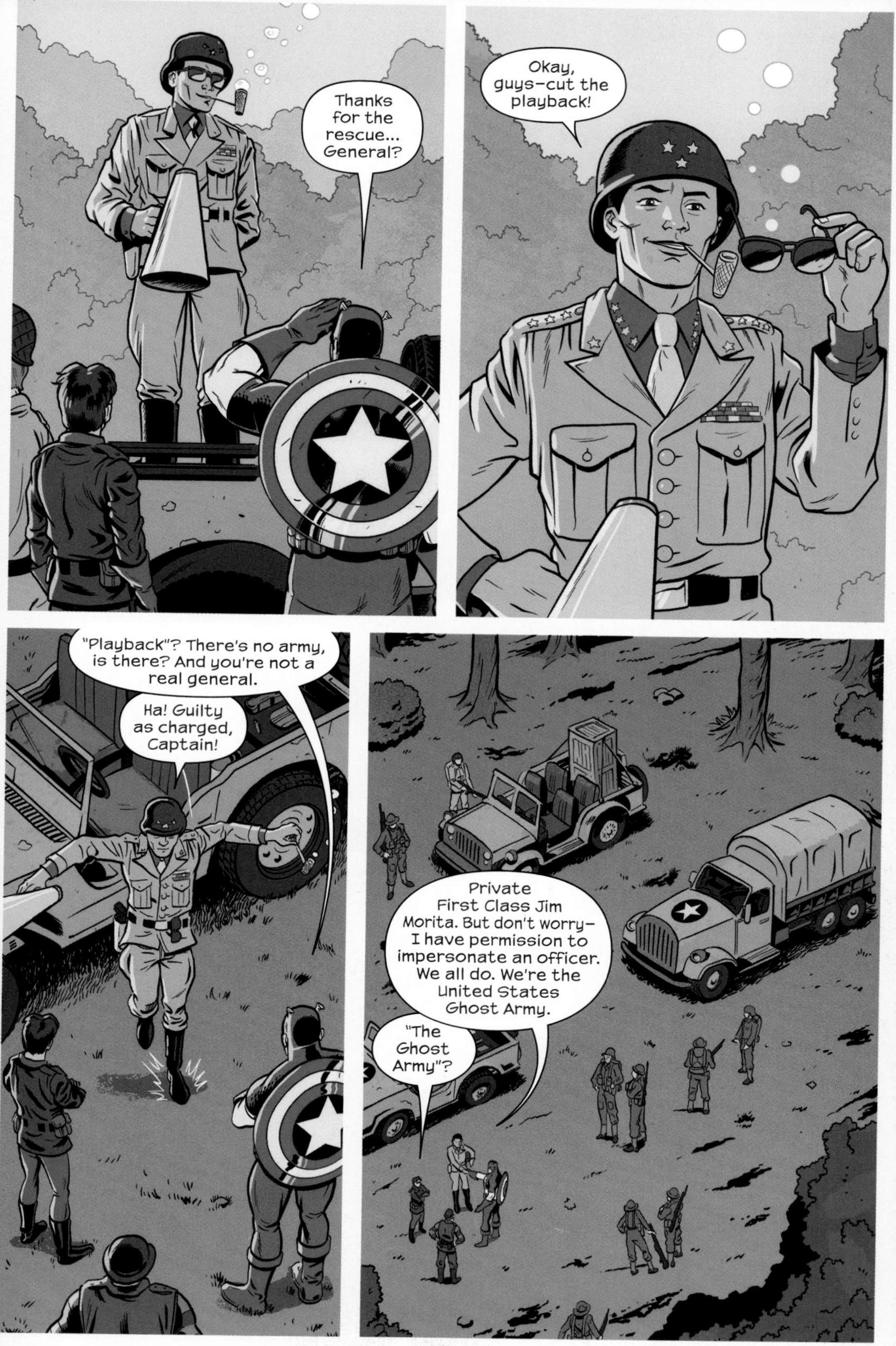
Thanks for the rescue... General?
Okay, guys—cut the playback!
"Playback"? There's no army, is there? And you're not a real general.
Ha! Guilty as charged, Captain!
Private First Class Jim Morita. But don't worry—I have permission to impersonate an officer. We all do. We're the United States Ghost Army.
"The Ghost Army"?

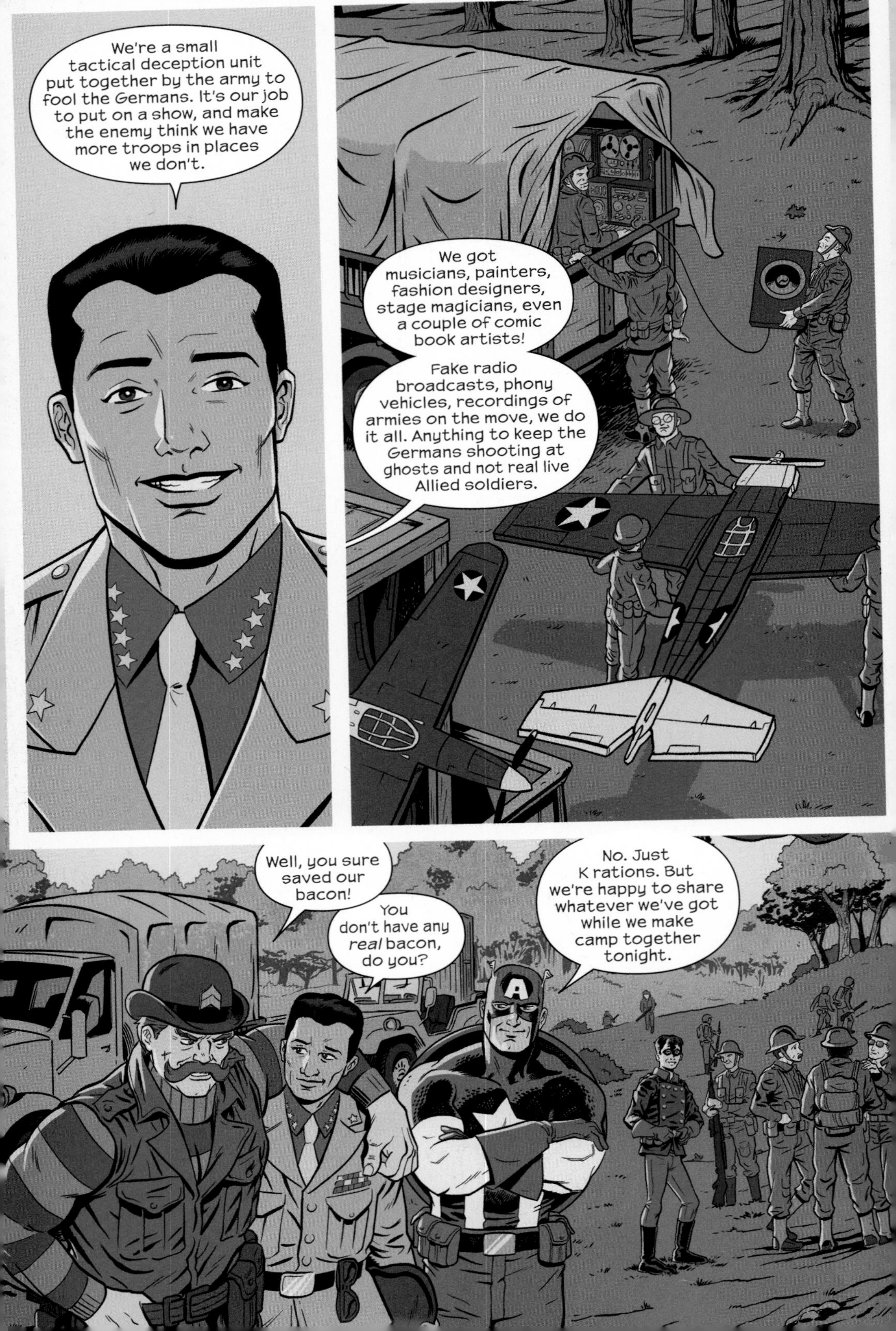
We're a small tactical deception unit put together by the army to fool the Germans. It's our job to put on a show, and make the enemy think we have more troops in places we don't.
We got musicians, painters, fashion designers, stage magicians, even a couple of comic book artists!
Fake radio broadcasts, phony vehicles, recordings of armies on the move, we do it all. Anything to keep the Germans shooting at ghosts and not real live Allied soldiers.
Well, you sure saved our bacon!
You don't have any *real* bacon, do you?
No. Just K rations. But we're happy to share whatever we've got while we make camp together tonight.

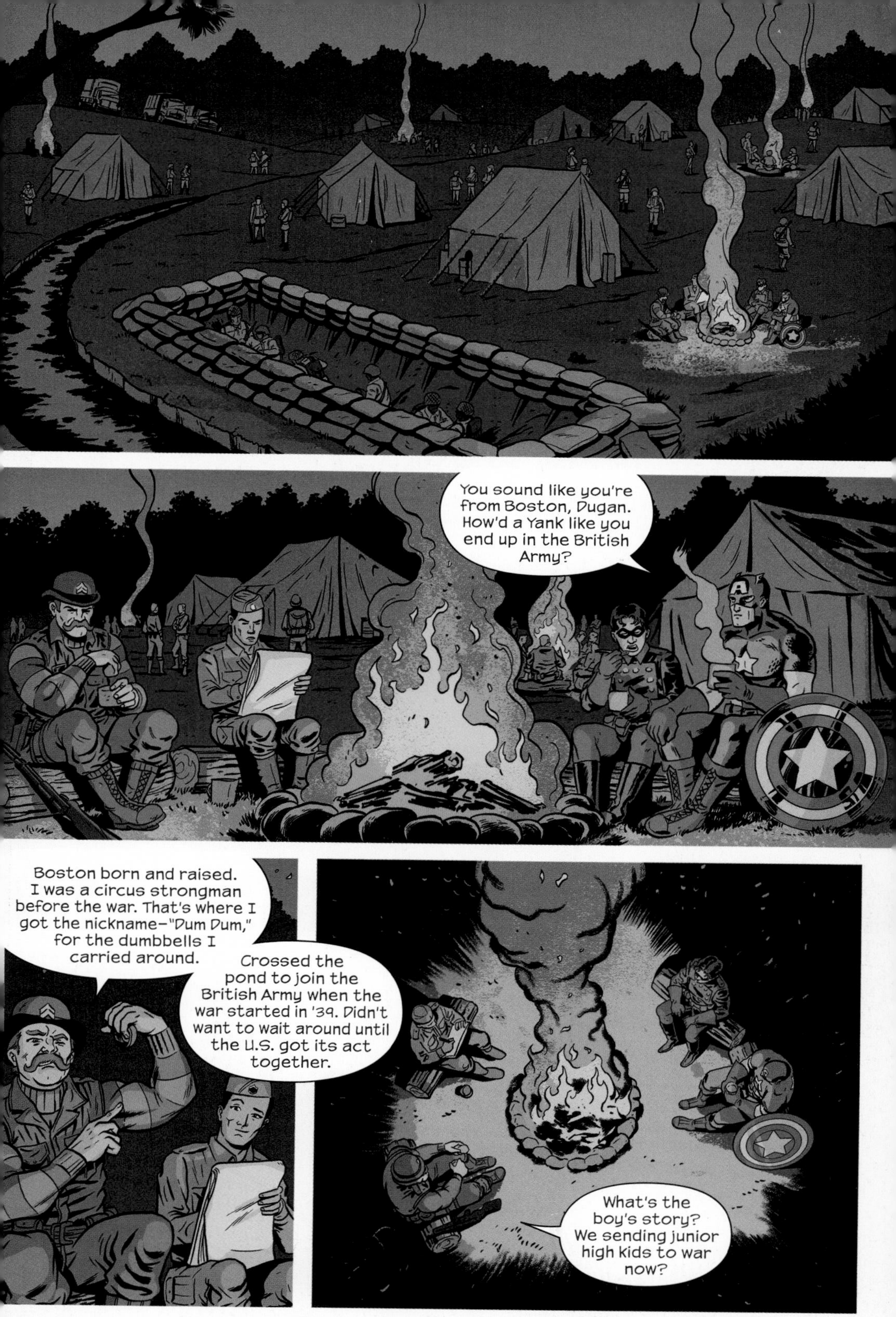
You sound like you're from Boston, Dugan. How'd a Yank like you end up in the British Army?
Boston born and raised. I was a circus strongman before the war. That's where I got the nickname—"Dum Dum," for the dumbbells I carried around.
Crossed the pond to join the British Army when the war started in '39. Didn't want to wait around until the U.S. got its act together.
What's the boy's story? We sending junior high kids to war now?

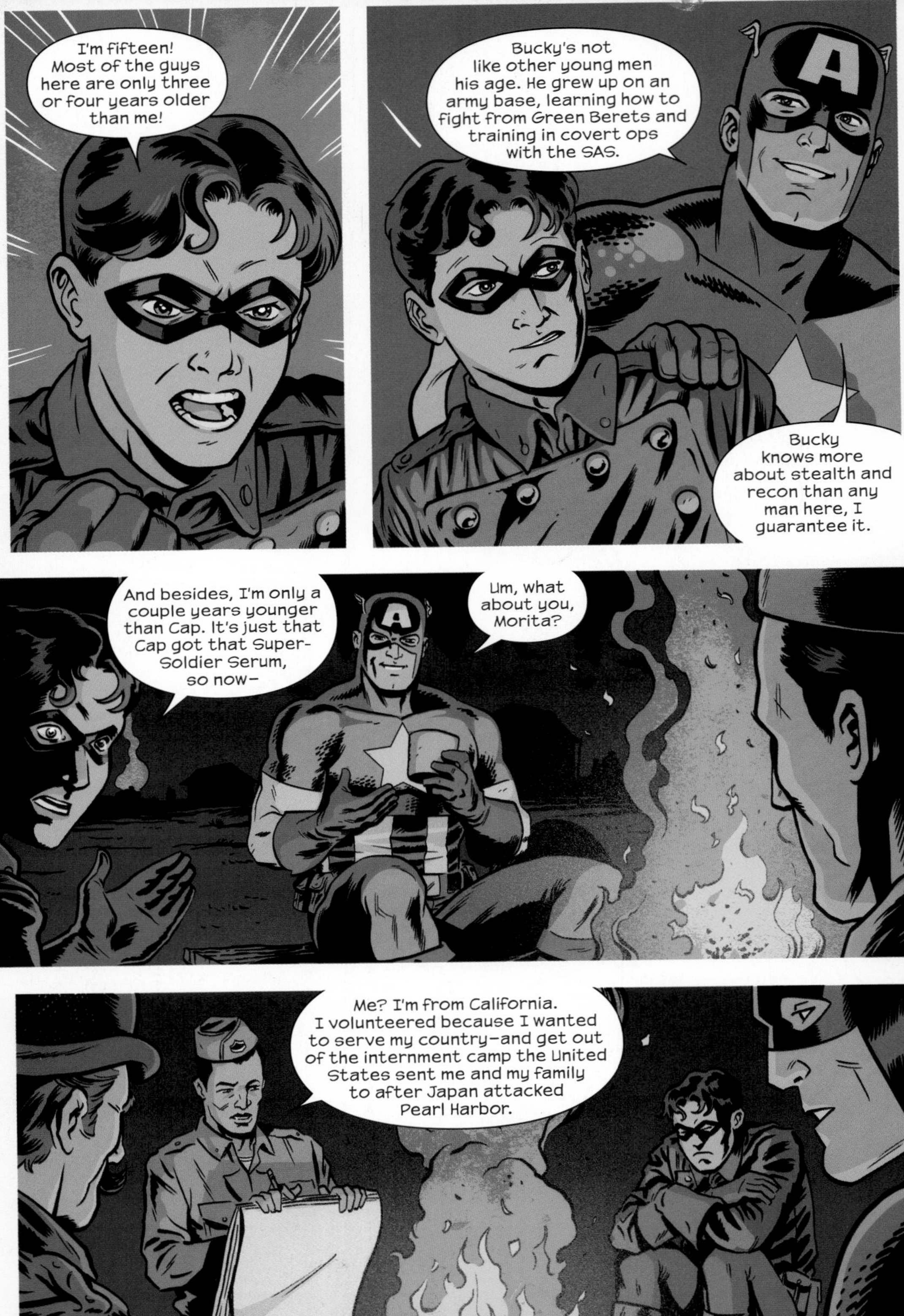
I'm fifteen! Most of the guys here are only three or four years older than me!
Bucky's not like other young men his age. He grew up on an army base, learning how to fight from Green Berets and training in covert ops with the SAS.
Bucky knows more about stealth and recon than any man here, I guarantee it.
And besides, I'm only a couple years younger than Cap. It's just that Cap got that Super-Soldier Serum, so now–
Um, what about you, Morita?
Me? I'm from California. I volunteered because I wanted to serve my country–and get out of the internment camp the United States sent me and my family to after Japan attacked Pearl Harbor.

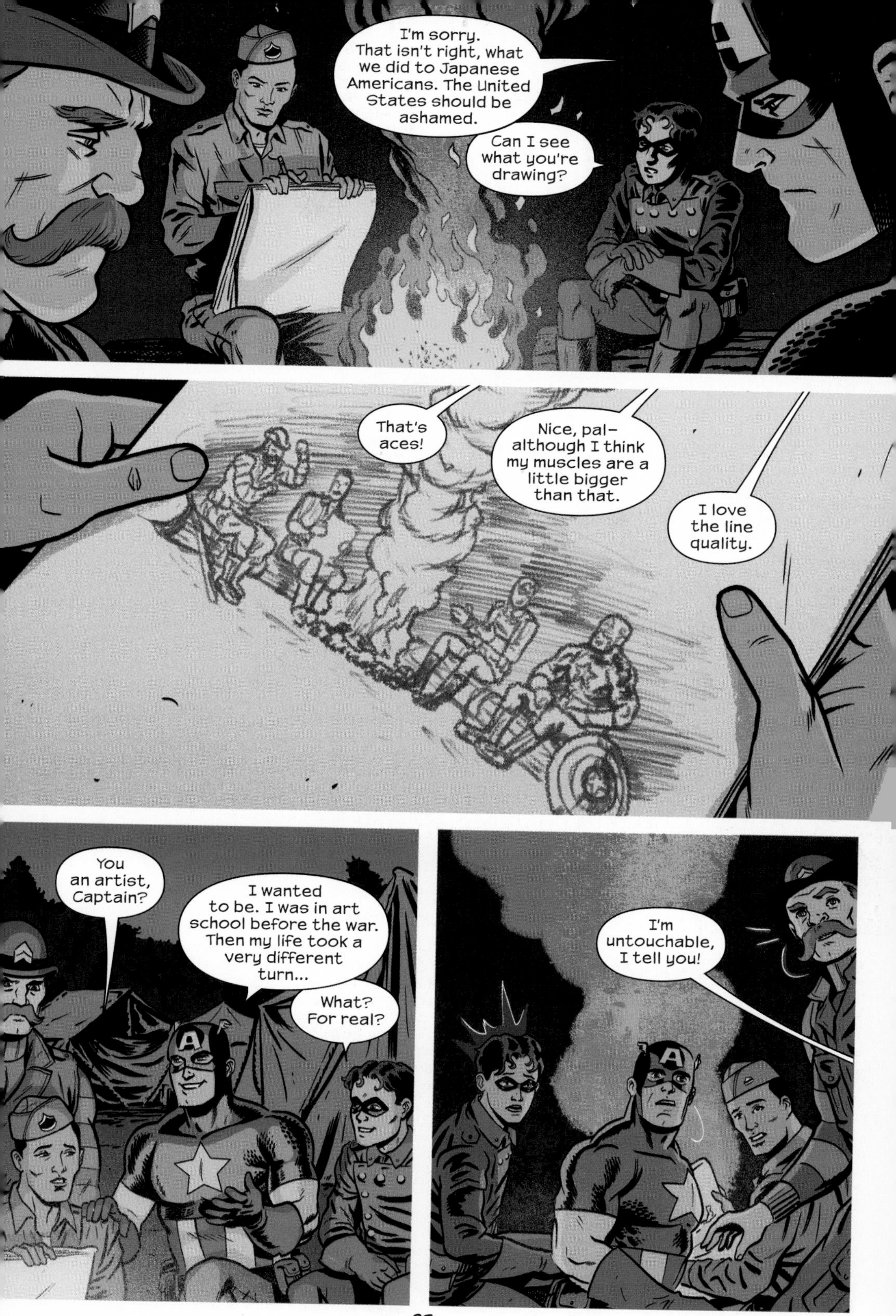
I'm sorry. That isn't right, what we did to Japanese Americans. The United States should be ashamed.
Can I see what you're drawing?
That's aces!
Nice, pal— although I think my muscles are a little bigger than that.
I love the line quality.
You an artist, Captain?
I wanted to be. I was in art school before the war. Then my life took a very different turn...
What? For real?
I'm untouchable, I tell you!

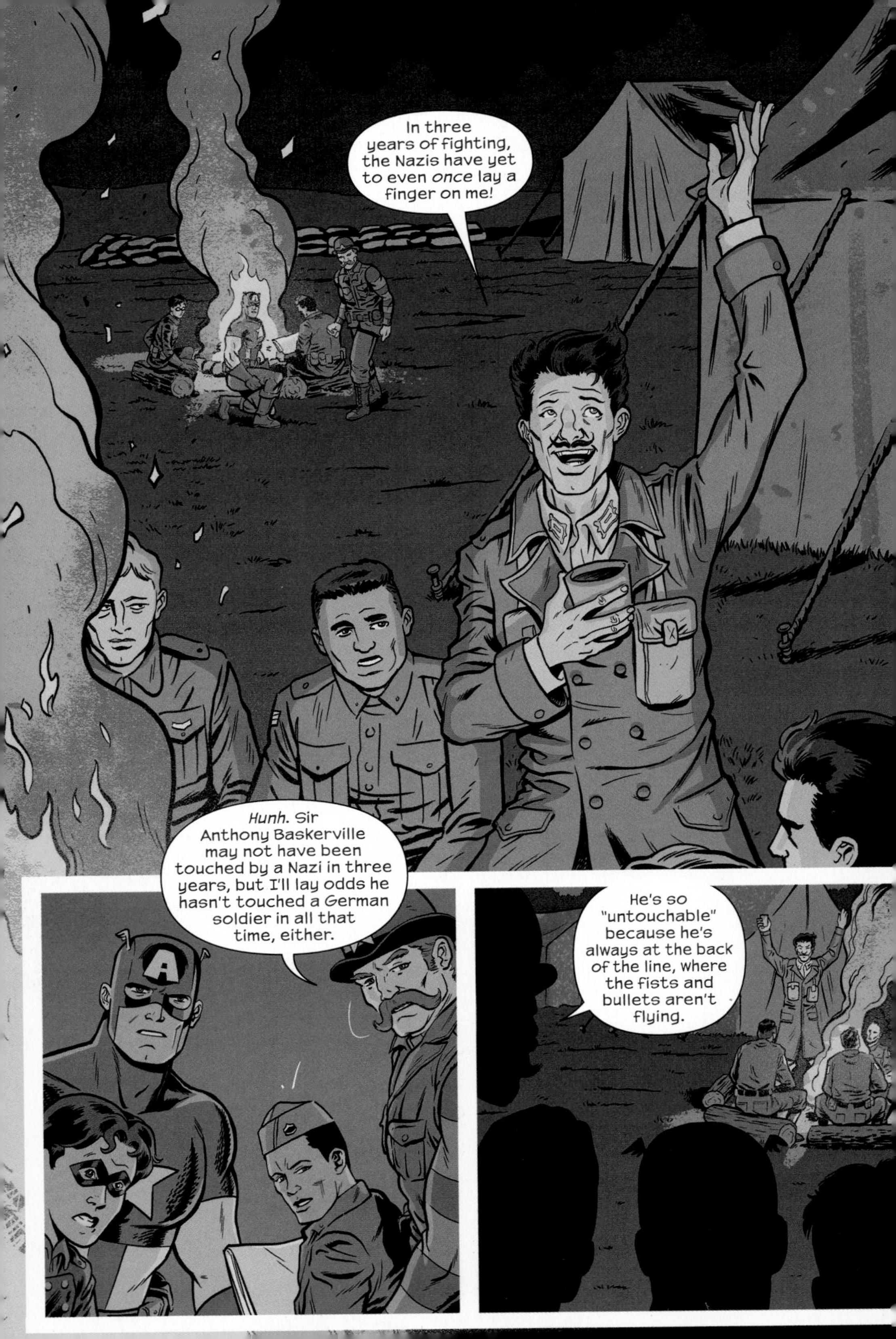
In three years of fighting, the Nazis have yet to even *once* lay a finger on me!
Hunh. Sir Anthony Baskerville may not have been touched by a Nazi in three years, but I'll lay odds he hasn't touched a German soldier in all that time, either.
He's so "untouchable" because he's always at the back of the line, where the fists and bullets aren't flying.

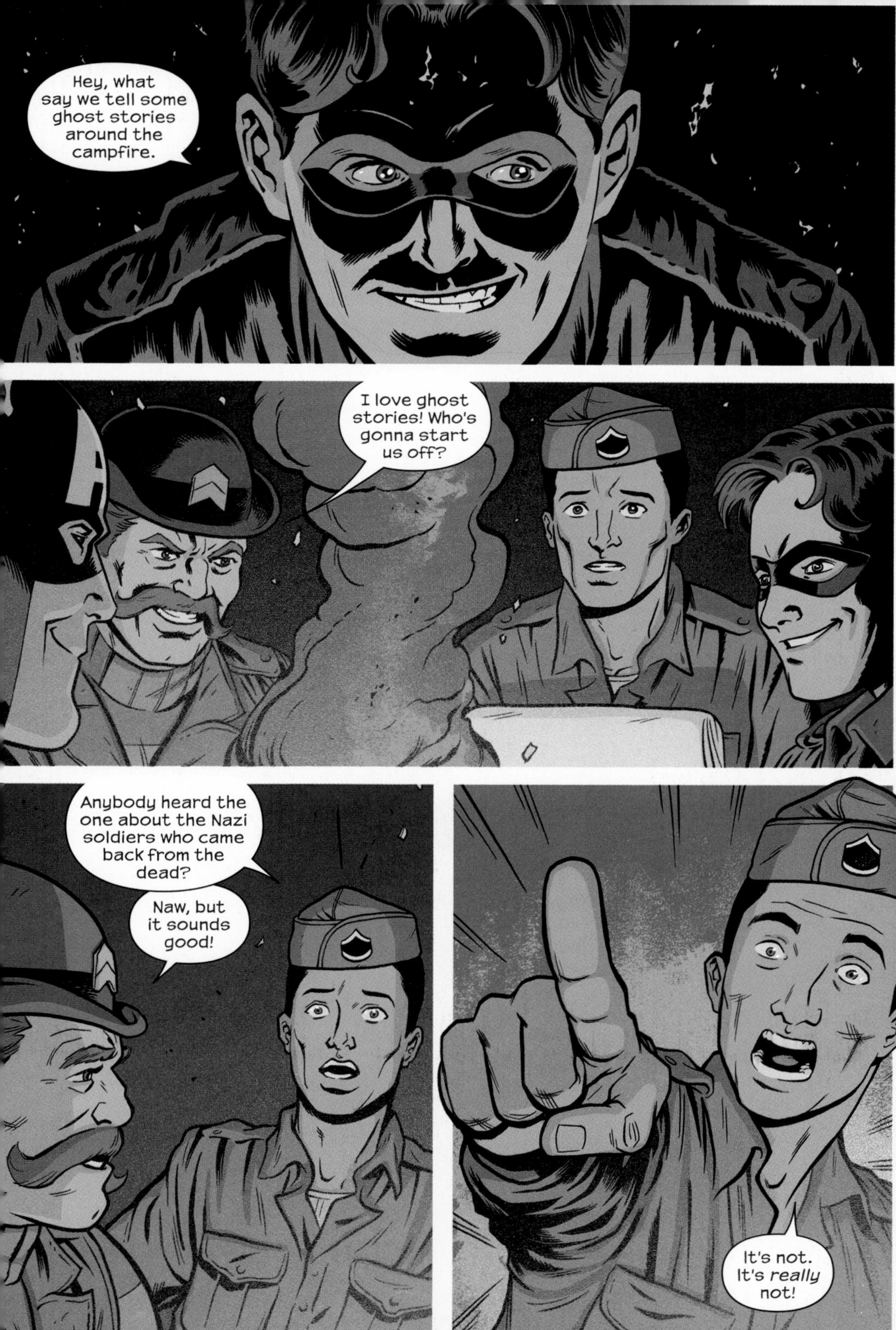
Hey, what say we tell some ghost stories around the campfire.
I love ghost stories! Who's gonna start us off?
Anybody heard the one about the Nazi soldiers who came back from the dead?
Naw, but it sounds good!
It's not. It's *really* not!

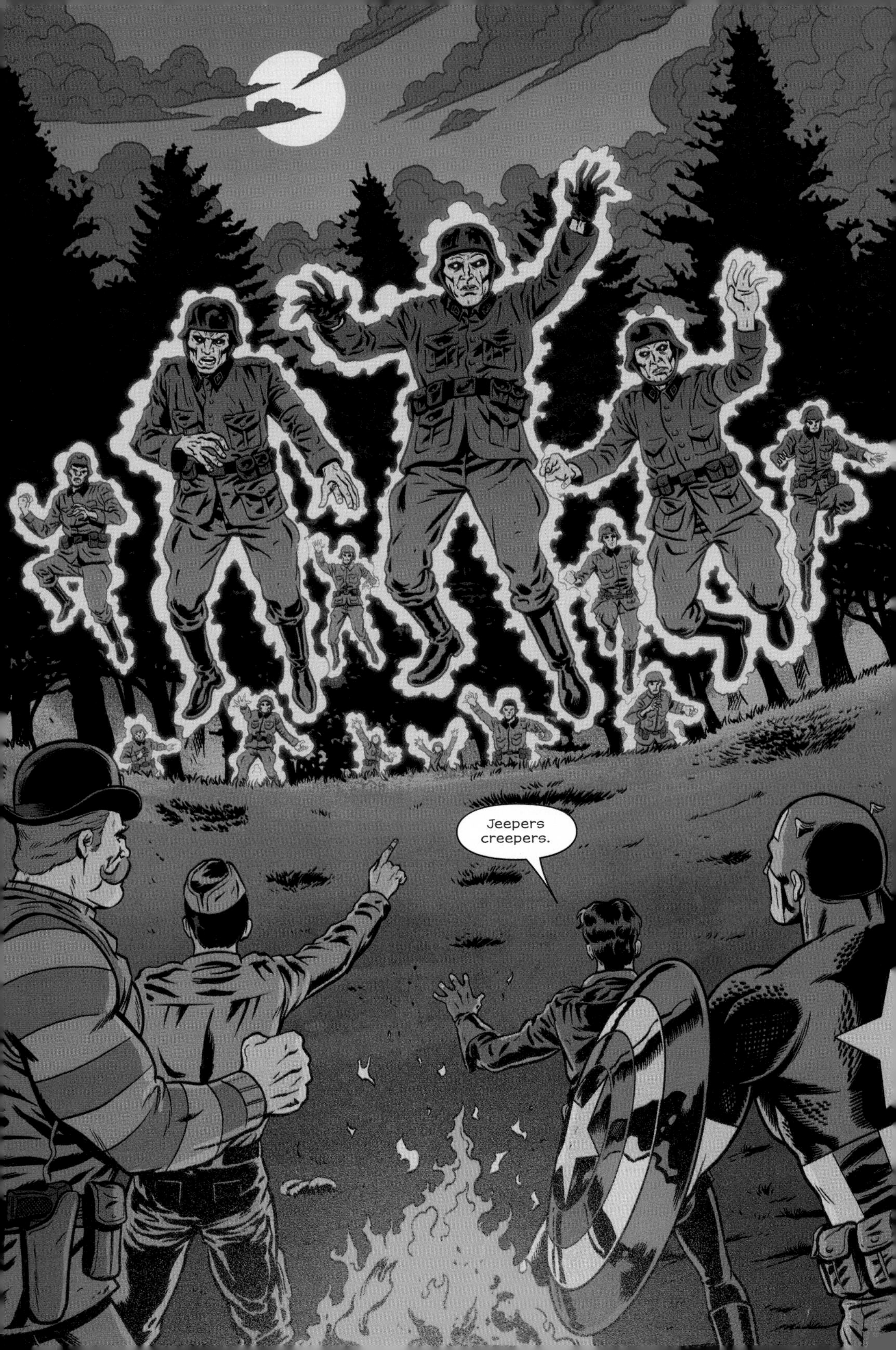
Jeepers
creepers.

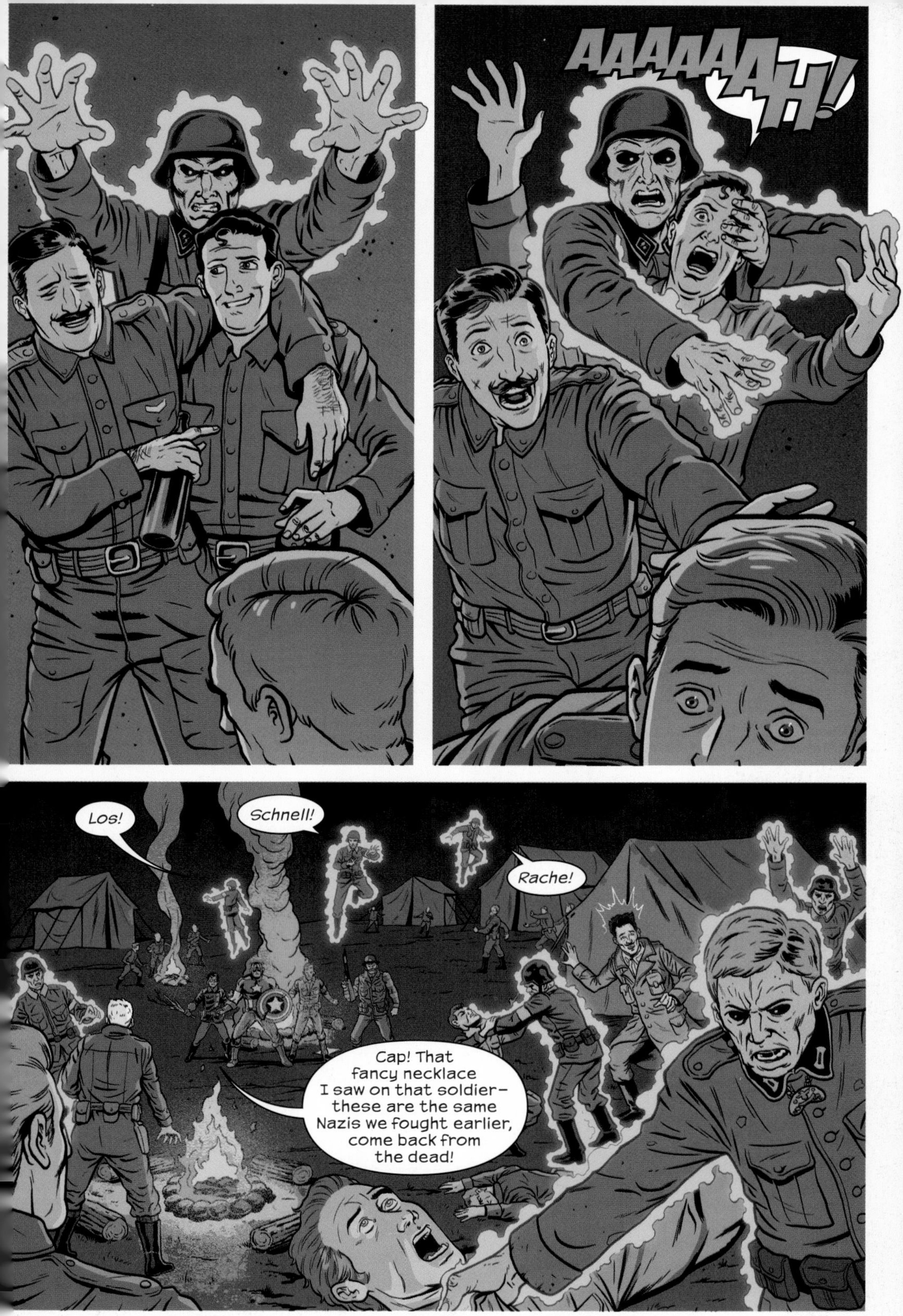
AAAAAAH!
Los!
Schnell!
Rache!
Cap! That fancy necklace I saw on that soldier– these are the same Nazis we fought earlier, come back from the dead!

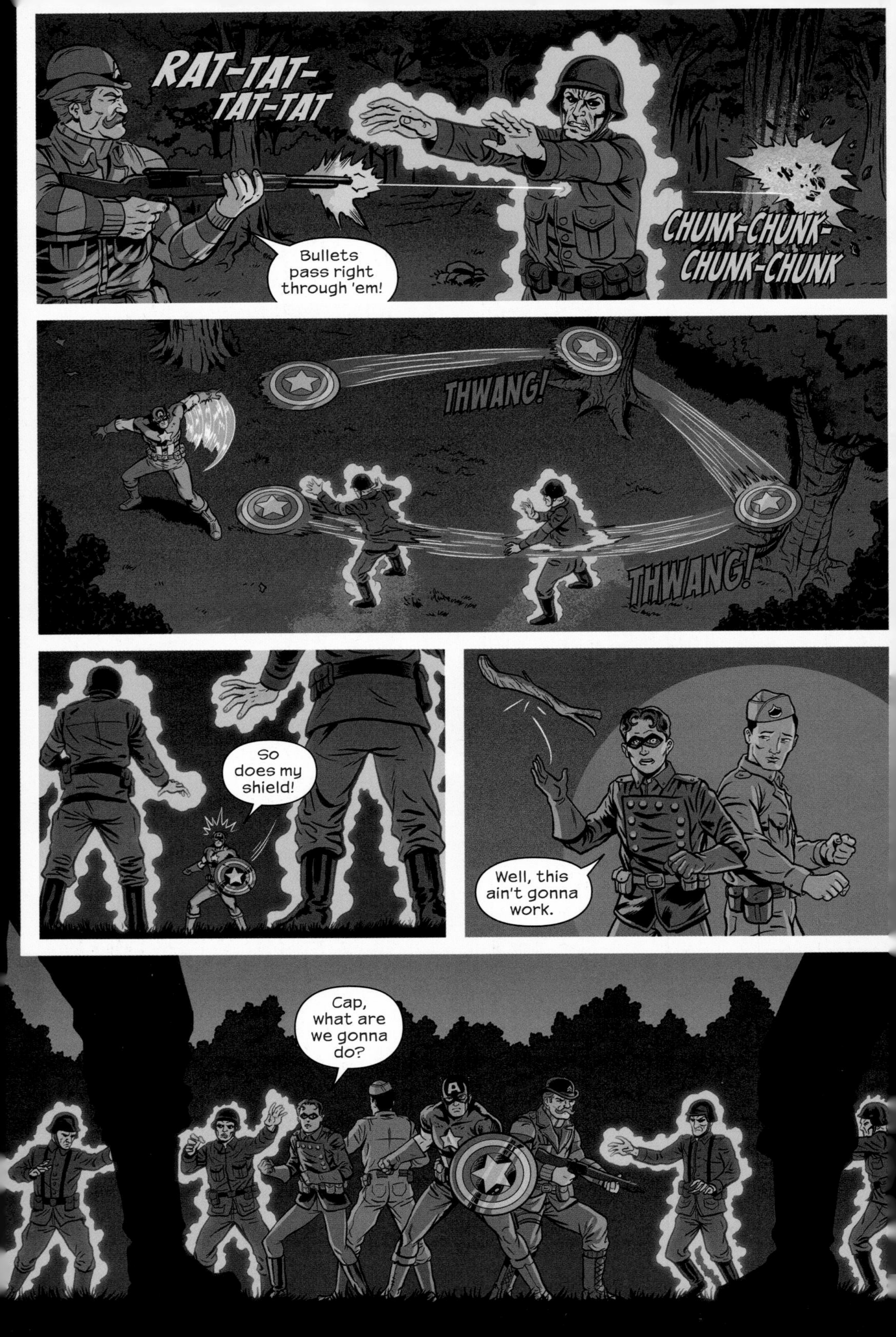
RAT-TAT-TAT-TAT
Bullets pass right through 'em!
CHUNK-CHUNK-CHUNK-CHUNK
THWANG!
THWANG!
So does my shield!
Well, this ain't gonna work.
Cap, what are we gonna do?

CHAPTER TWO
GHOSTS

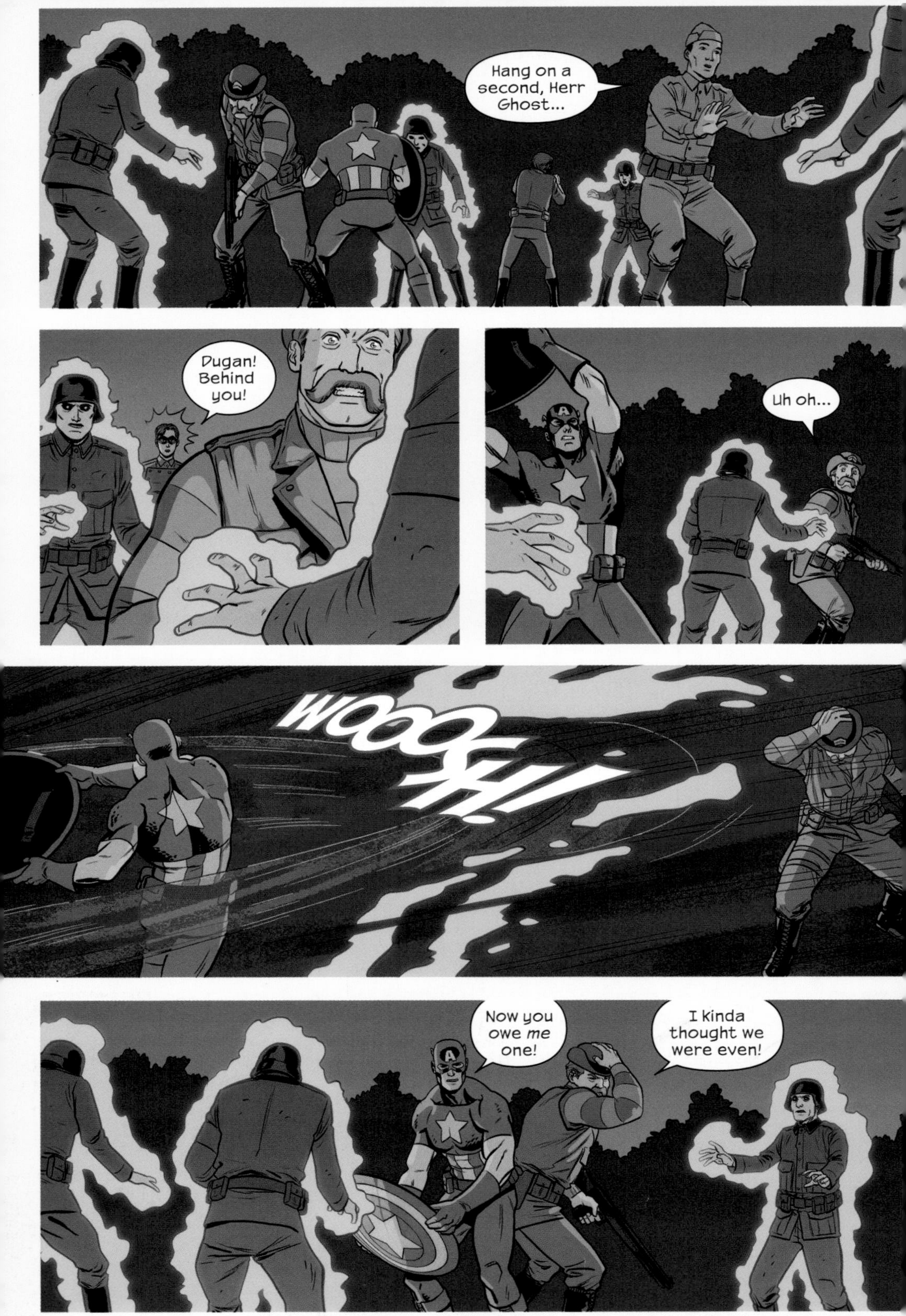

Hang on a second, Herr Ghost...
Dugan! Behind you!
Uh oh...
WOOOSH!!
Now you owe *me* one!
I kinda thought we were even!

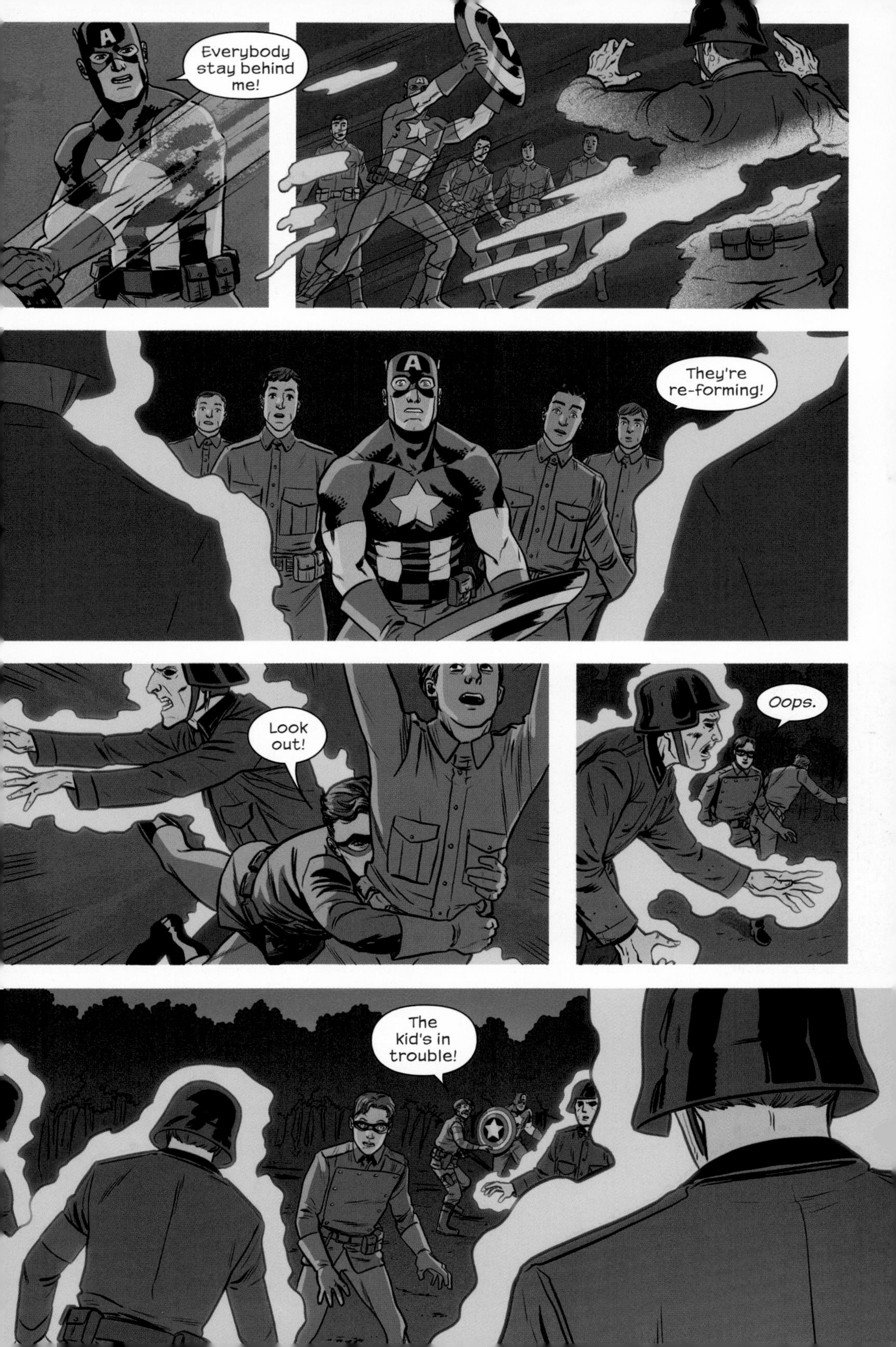
Everybody stay behind me!
They're re-forming!
Look out!
Oops.
The kid's in trouble!

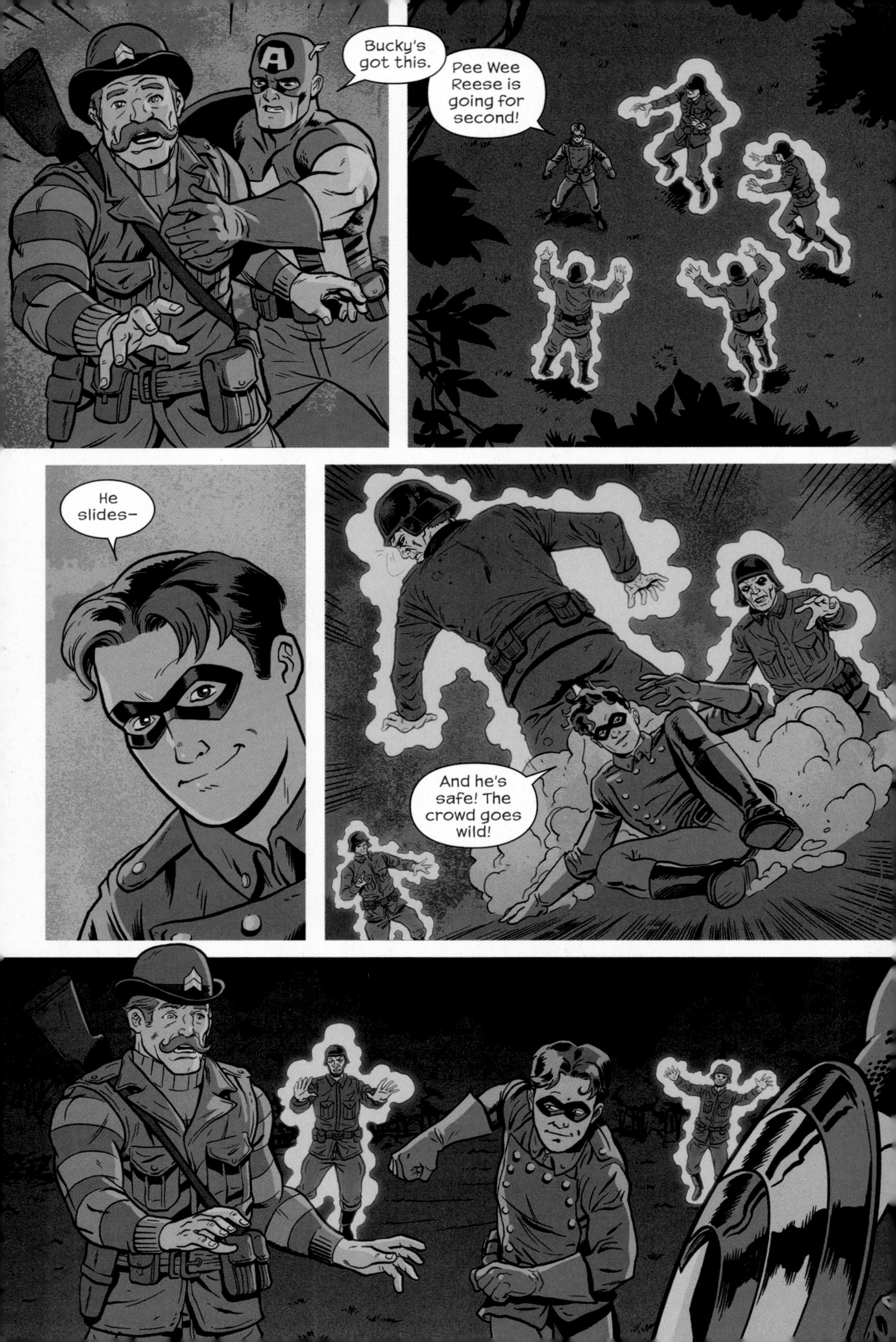
Bucky's got this.
Pee Wee Reese is going for second!
He slides–
And he's safe! The crowd goes wild!

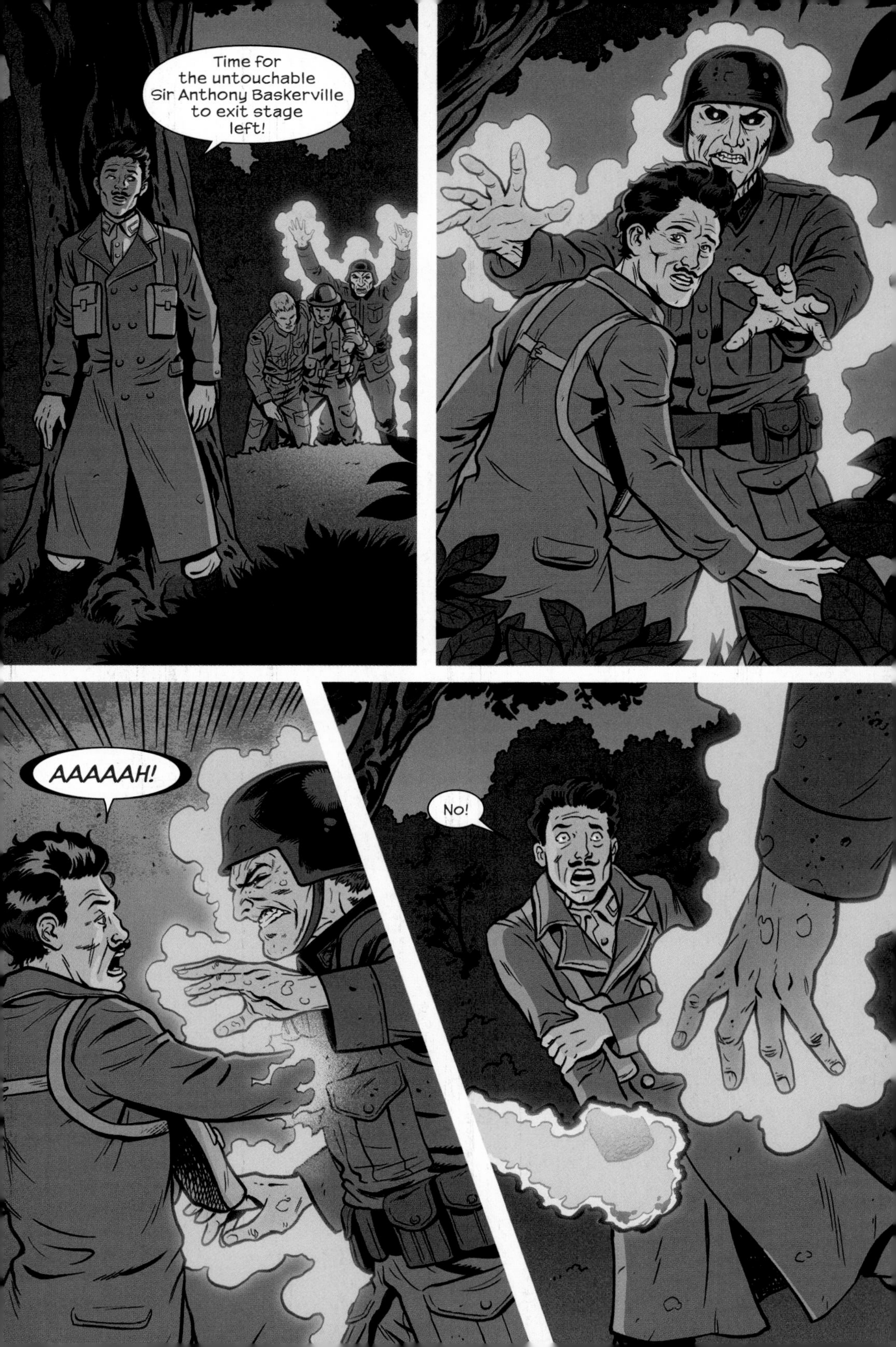
Time for the untouchable Sir Anthony Baskerville to exit stage left!
AAAAAH!
No!

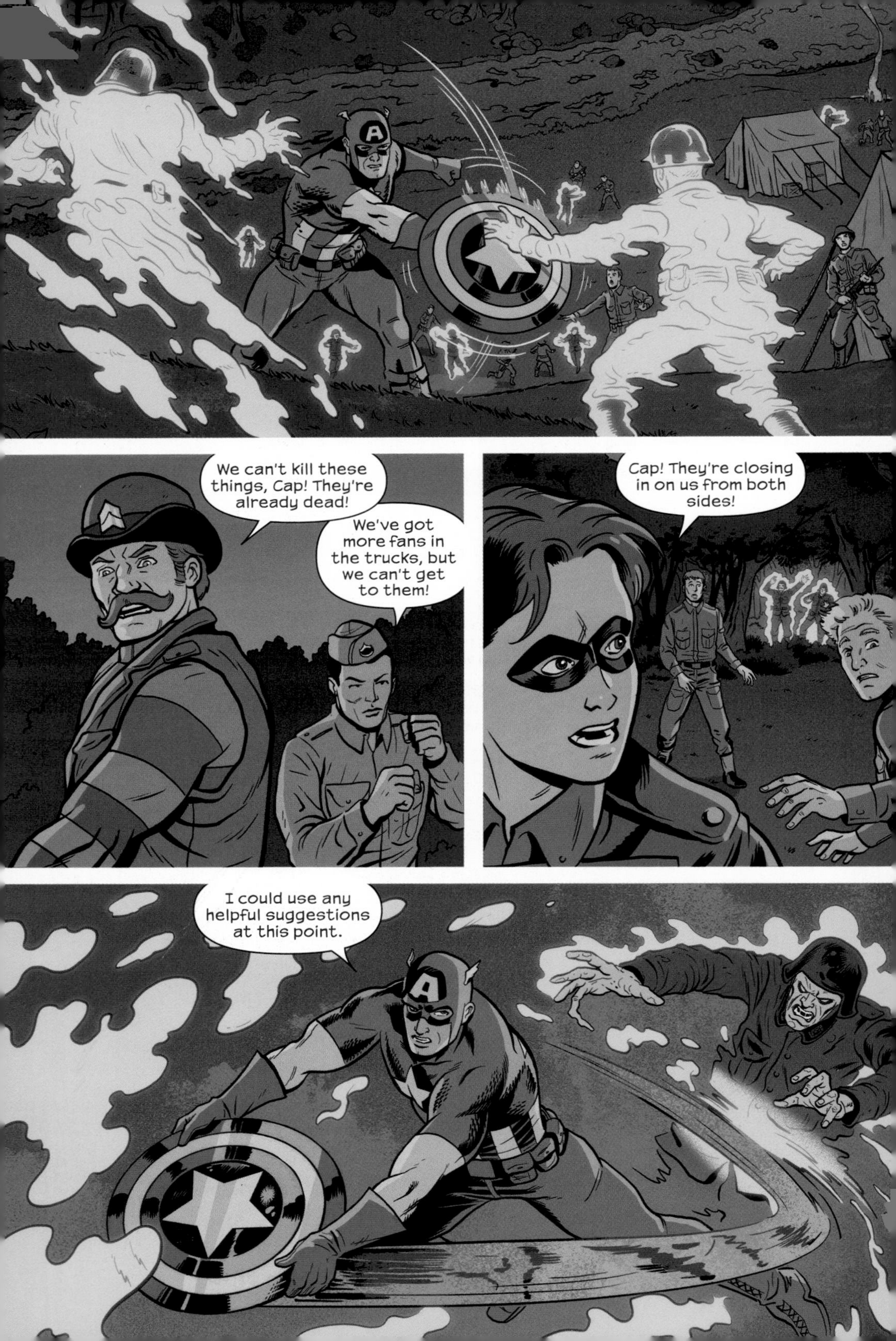
We can't kill these things, Cap! They're already dead!
We've got more fans in the trucks, but we can't get to them!
Cap! They're closing in on us from both sides!
I could use any helpful suggestions at this point.

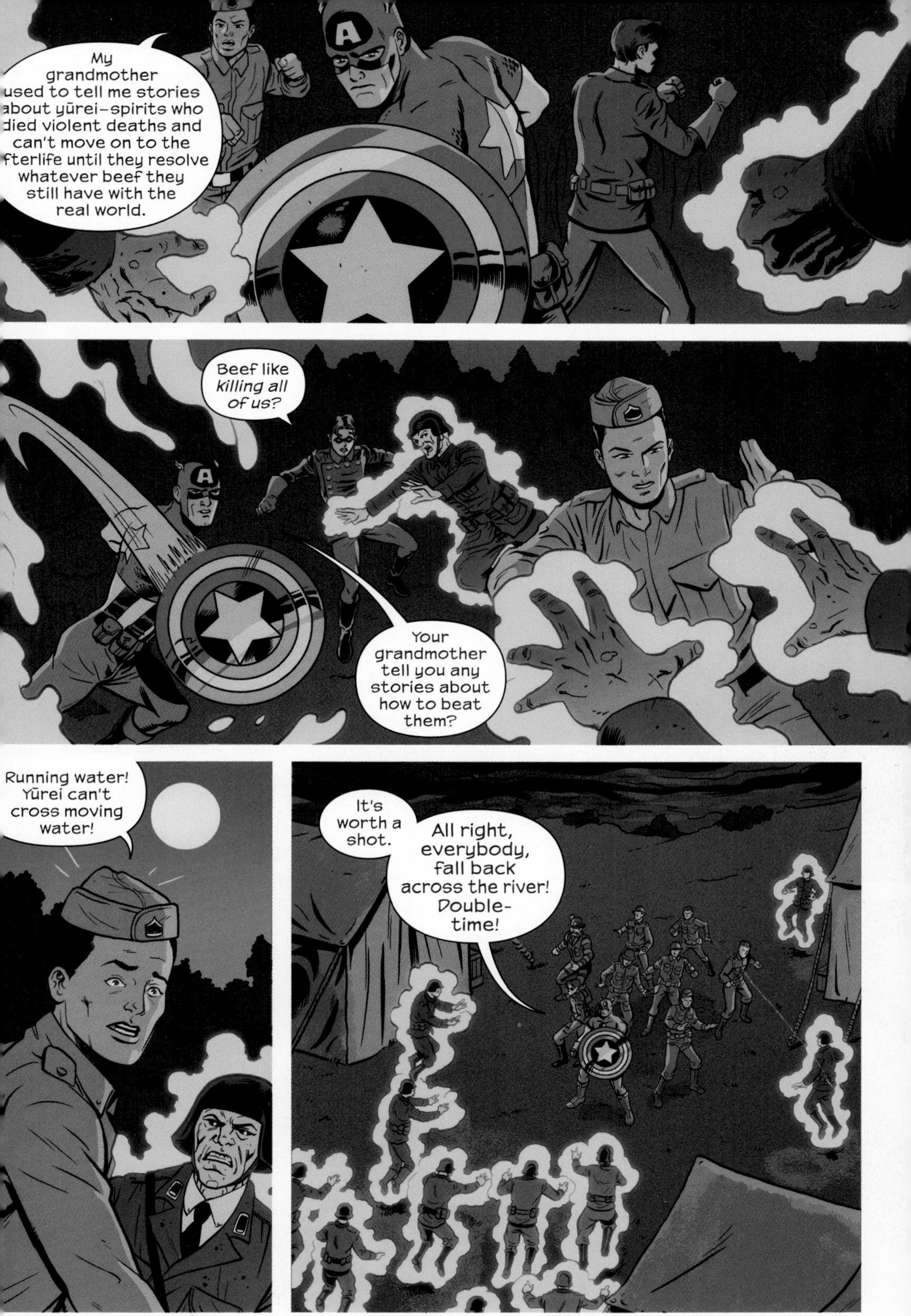
My grandmother used to tell me stories about yūrei–spirits who died violent deaths and can't move on to the fterlife until they resolve whatever beef they still have with the real world.
Beef like *killing all of us?*
Your grandmother tell you any stories about how to beat them?
Running water! Yūrei can't cross moving water!
It's worth a shot.
All right, everybody, fall back across the river! Double-time!

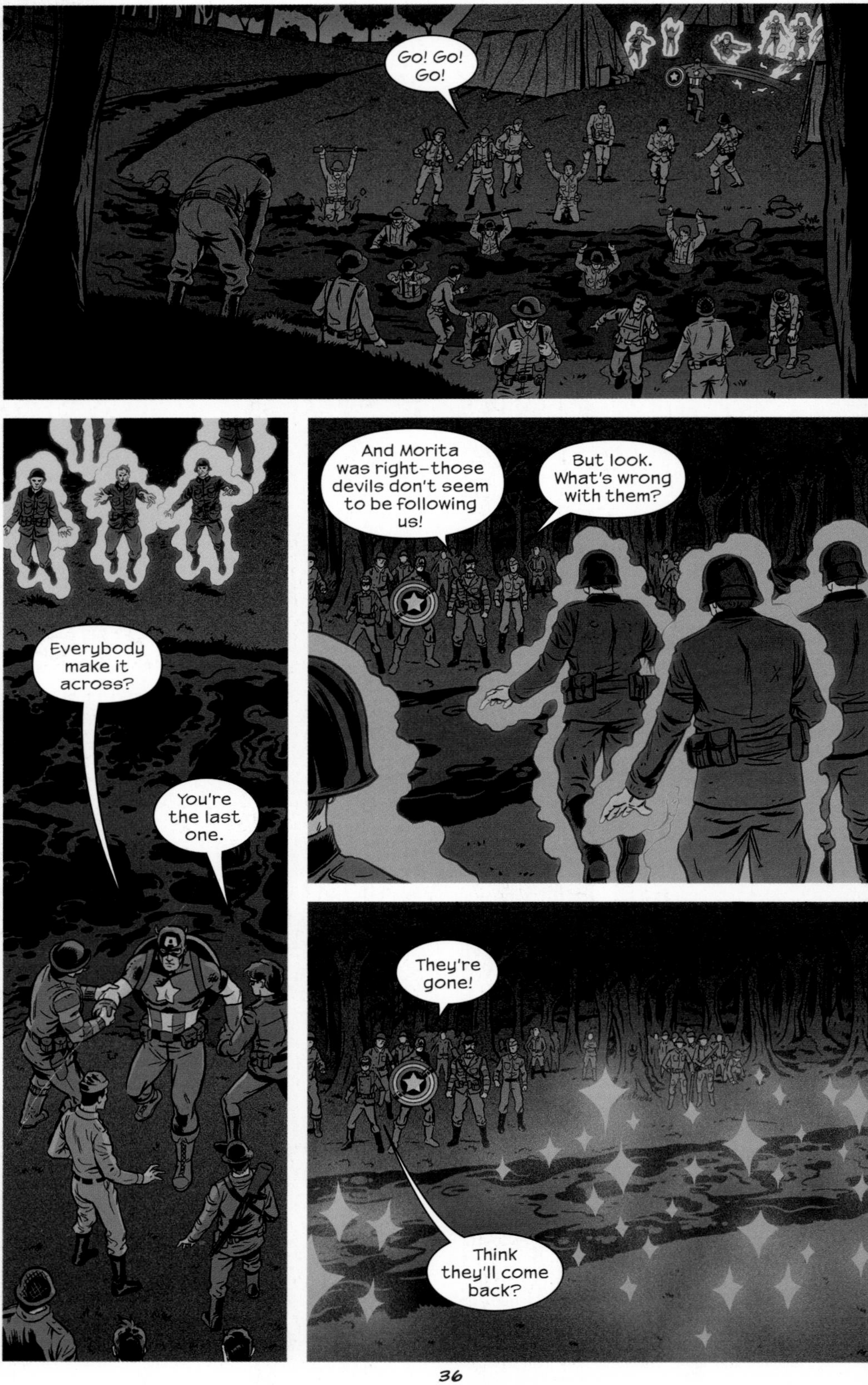
Go! Go! Go!
Everybody make it across?
You're the last one.
And Morita was right—those devils don't seem to be following us!
But look. What's wrong with them?
They're gone!
Think they'll come back?

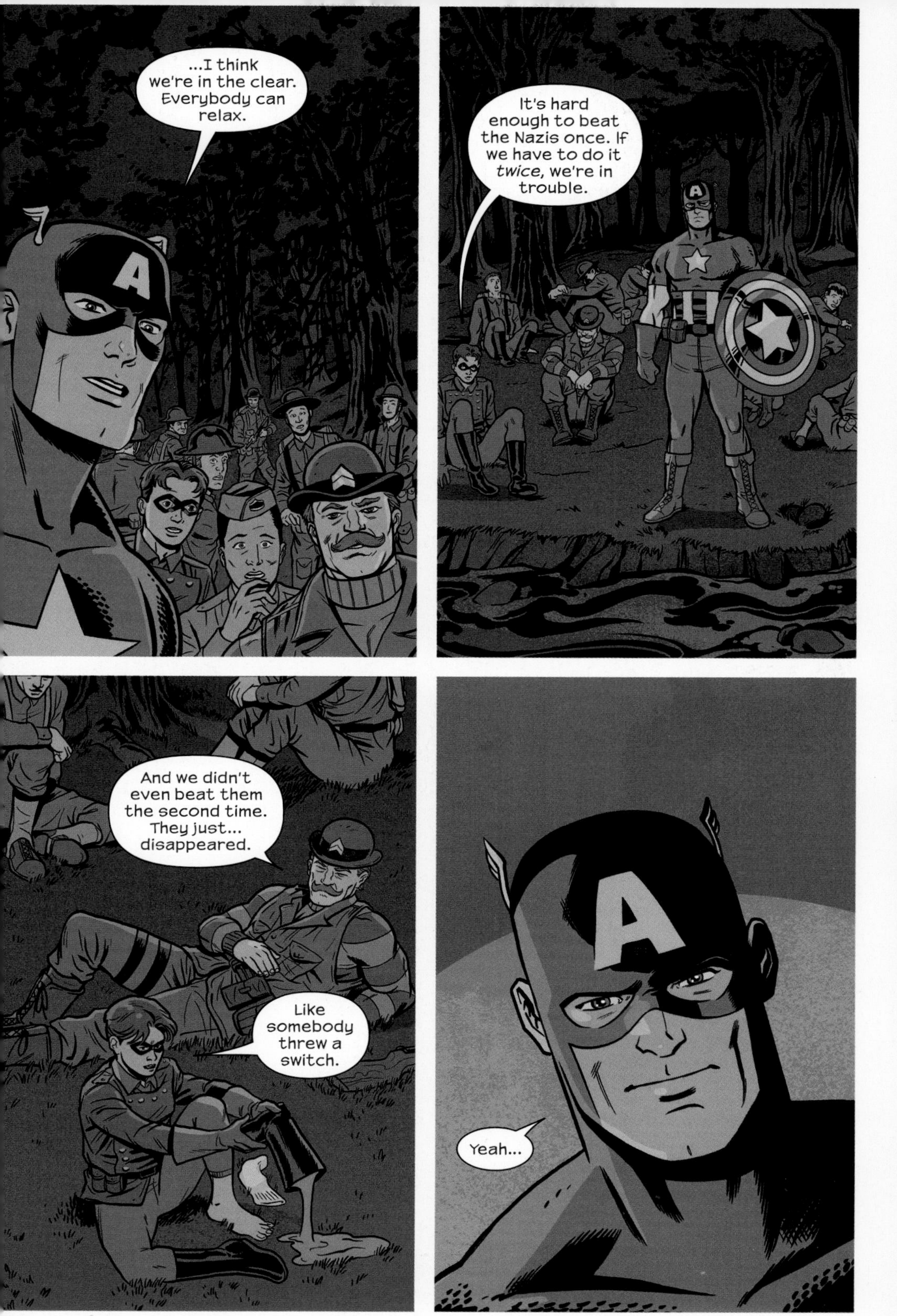
...I think we're in the clear. Everybody can relax.
It's hard enough to beat the Nazis once. If we have to do it *twice*, we're in trouble.
And we didn't even beat them the second time. They just... disappeared.
Like somebody threw a switch.
Yeah...

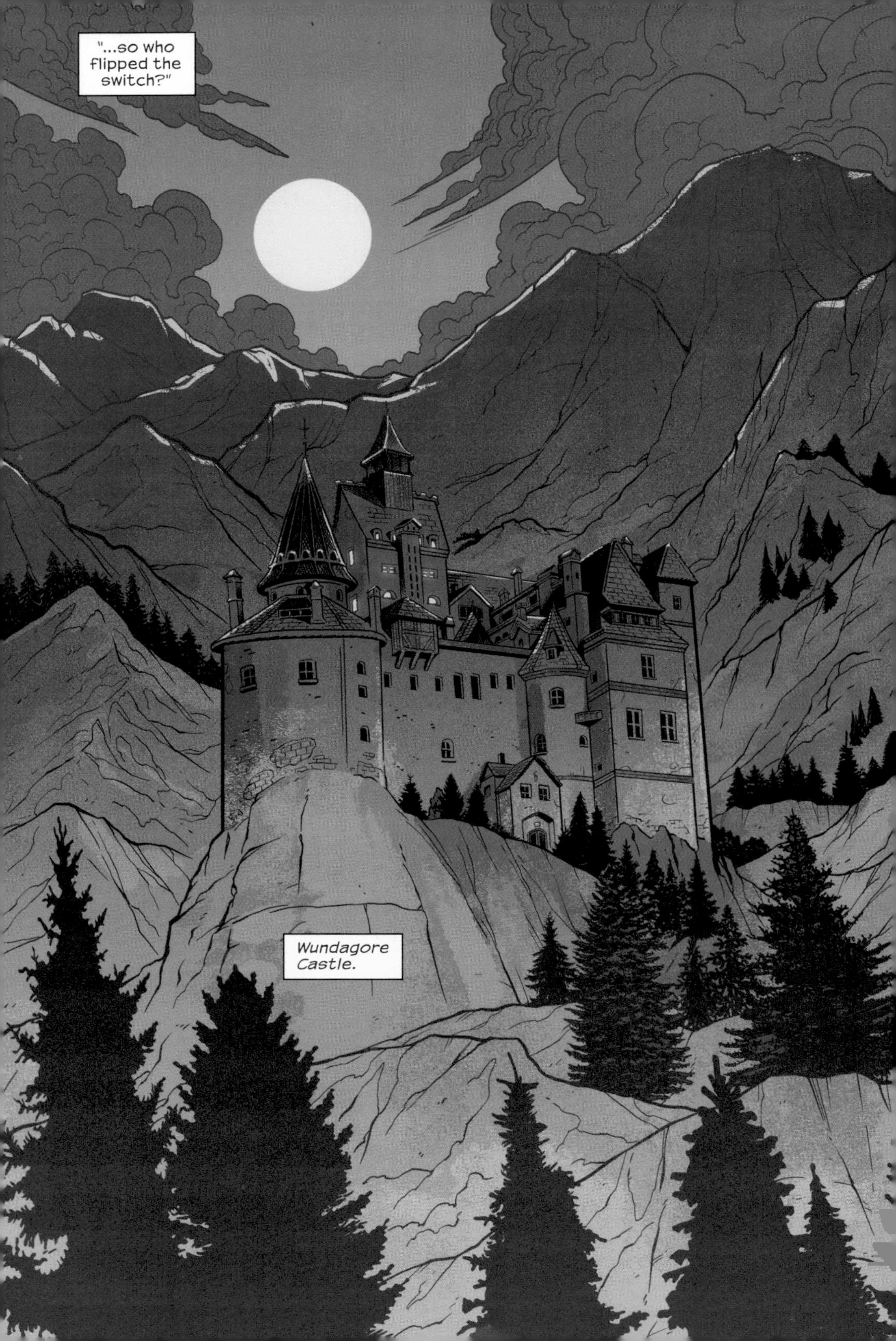
"...so who flipped the switch?"
Wundagore Castle.

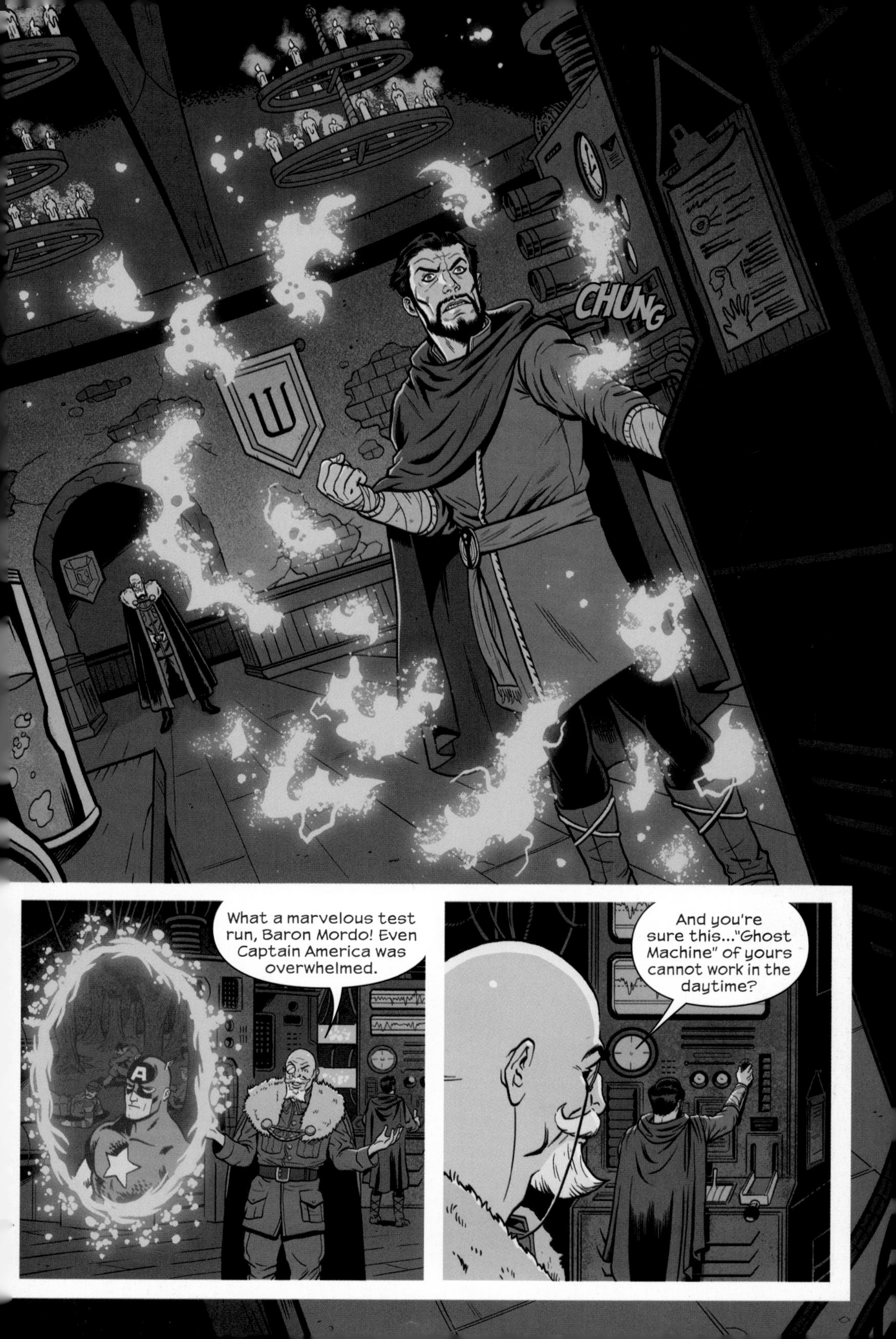
CHUNG
What a marvelous test run, Baron Mordo! Even Captain America was overwhelmed.
And you're sure this..."Ghost Machine" of yours cannot work in the daytime?

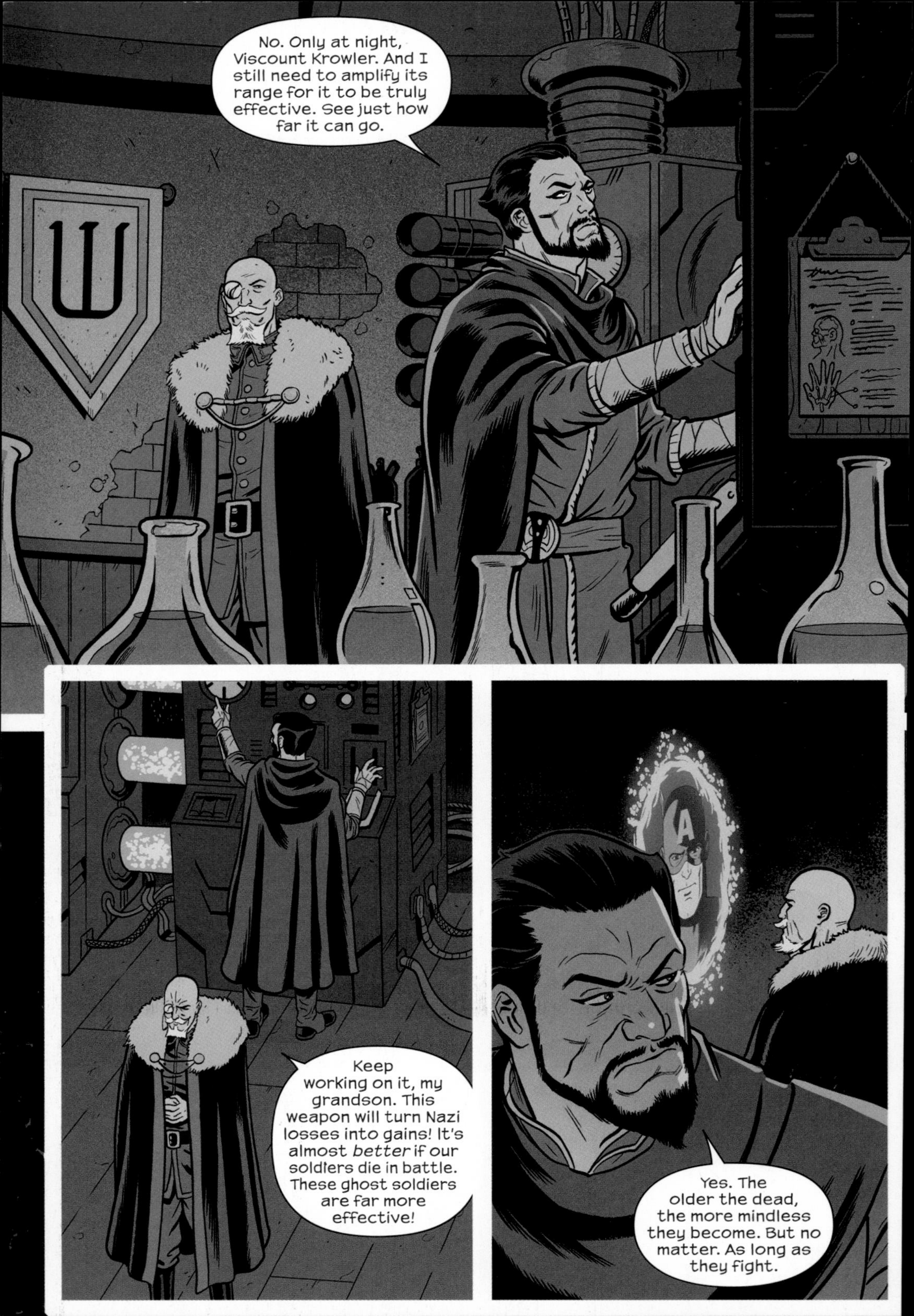
No. Only at night, Viscount Krowler. And I still need to amplify its range for it to be truly effective. See just how far it can go.
Keep working on it, my grandson. This weapon will turn Nazi losses into gains! It's almost *better* if our soldiers die in battle. These ghost soldiers are far more effective!
Yes. The older the dead, the more mindless they become. But no matter. As long as they fight.

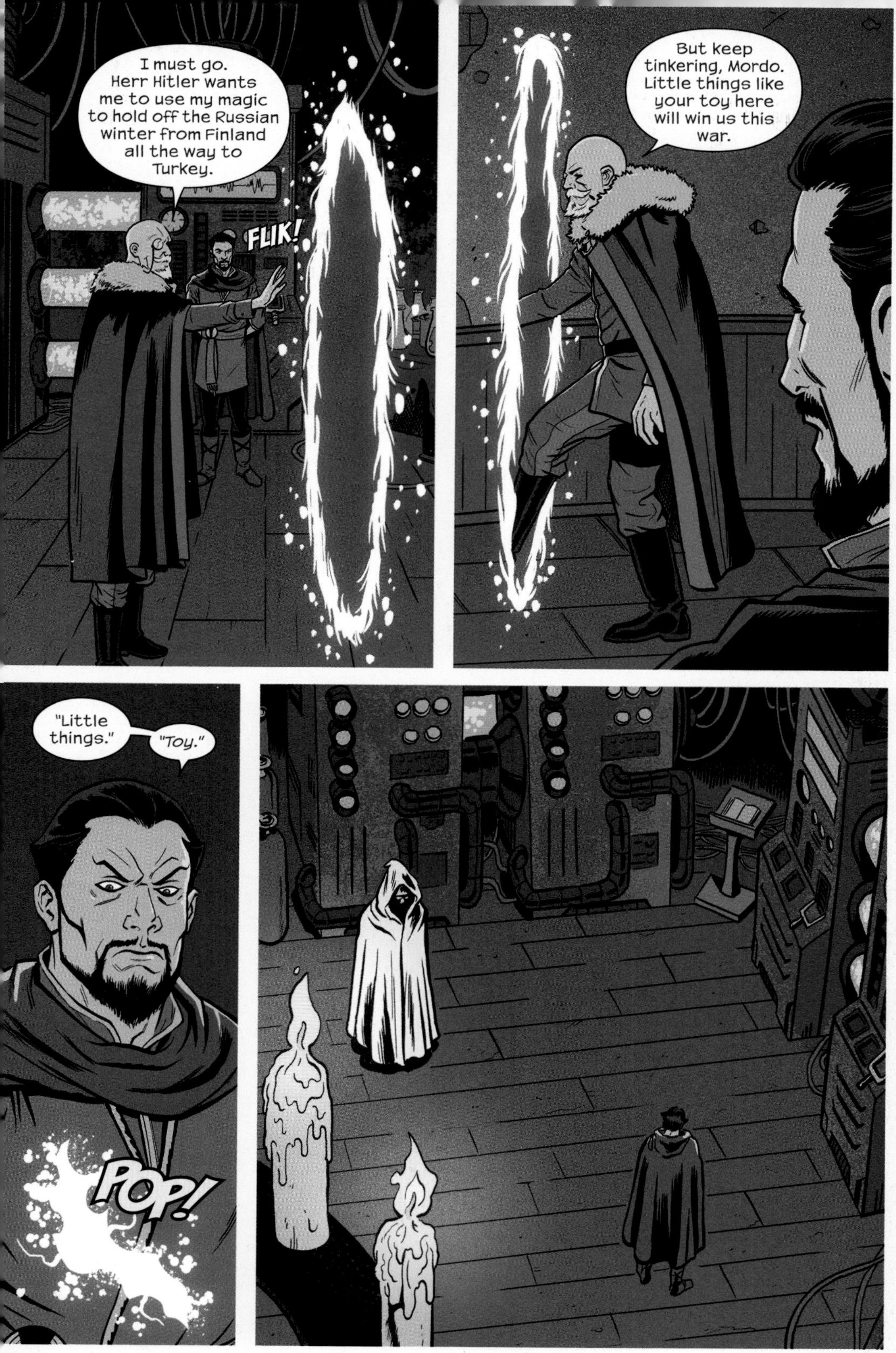

I must go. Herr Hitler wants me to use my magic to hold off the Russian winter from Finland all the way to Turkey.
FLIK!
But keep tinkering, Mordo. Little things like your toy here will win us this war.
"Little things."
"Toy."
POP!

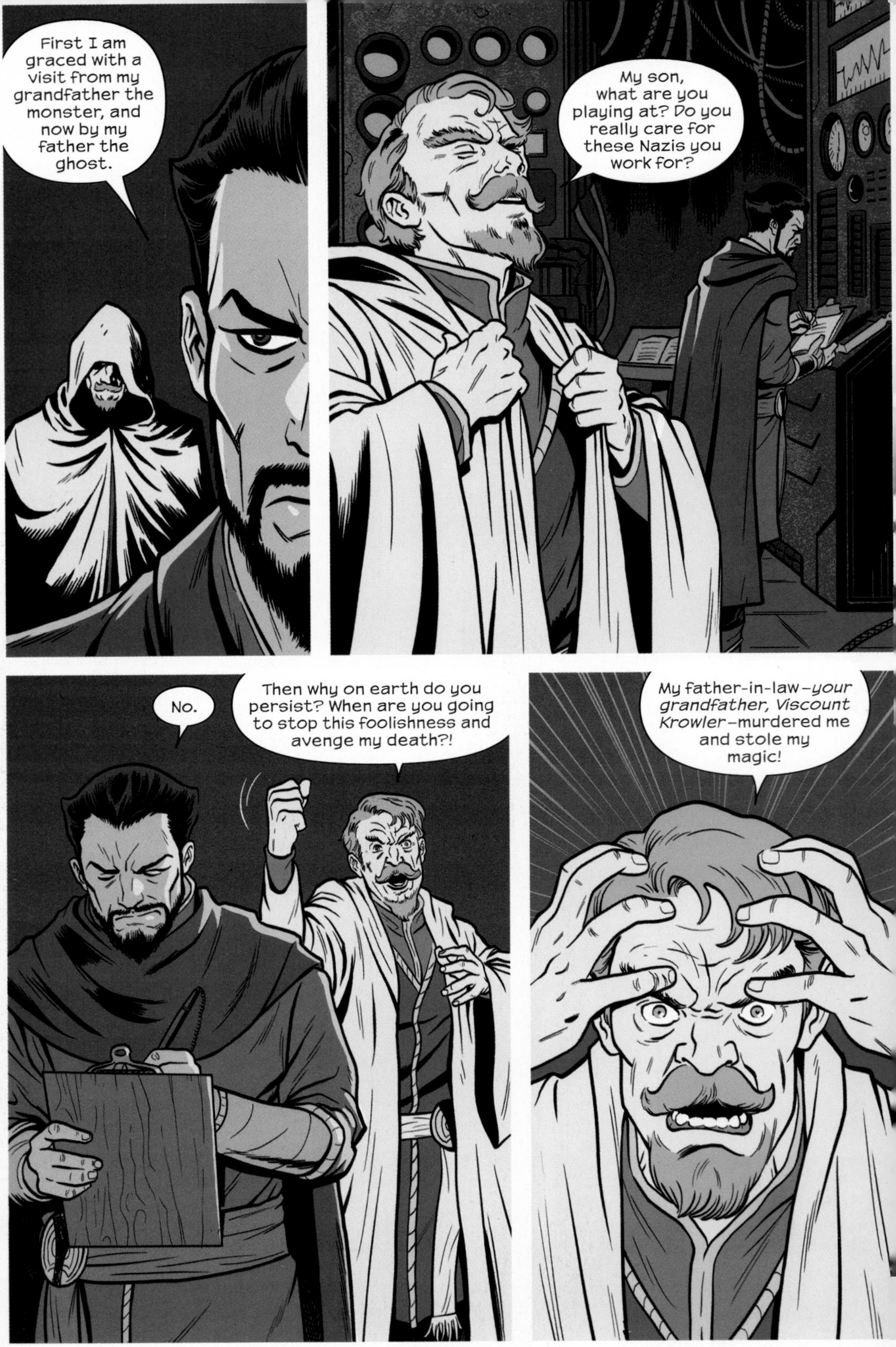
First I am graced with a visit from my grandfather the monster, and now by my father the ghost.
My son, what are you playing at? Do you really care for these Nazis you work for?
No.
Then why on earth do you persist? When are you going to stop this foolishness and avenge my death?!
My father-in-law–*your grandfather, Viscount Krowler*–murdered me and stole my magic!

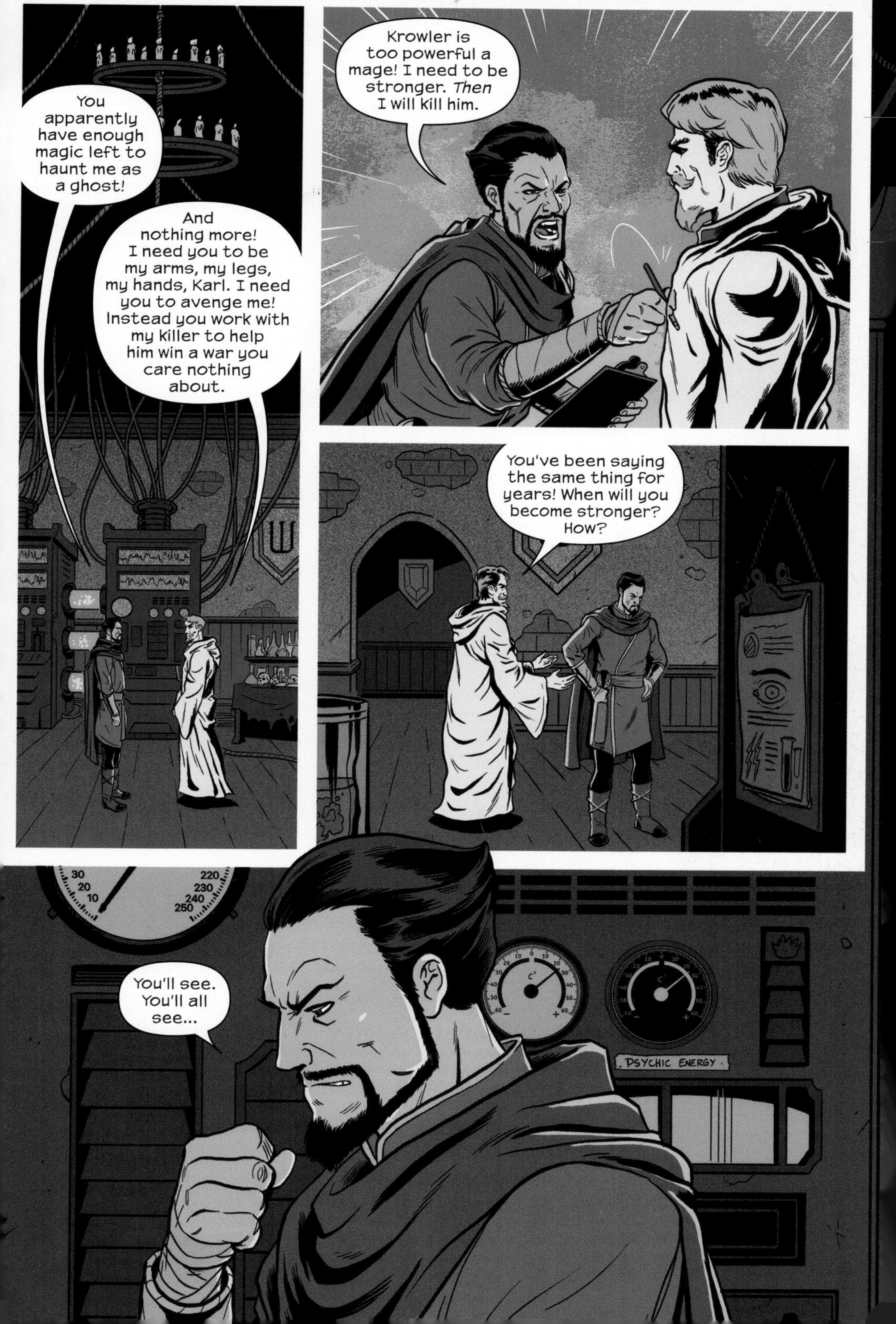
You apparently have enough magic left to haunt me as a ghost!
And nothing more! I need you to be my arms, my legs, my hands, Karl. I need you to avenge me! Instead you work with my killer to help him win a war you care nothing about.
Krowler is too powerful a mage! I need to be stronger. *Then* I will kill him.
You've been saying the same thing for years! When will you become stronger? How?
You'll see. You'll all see...
PSYCHIC ENERGY

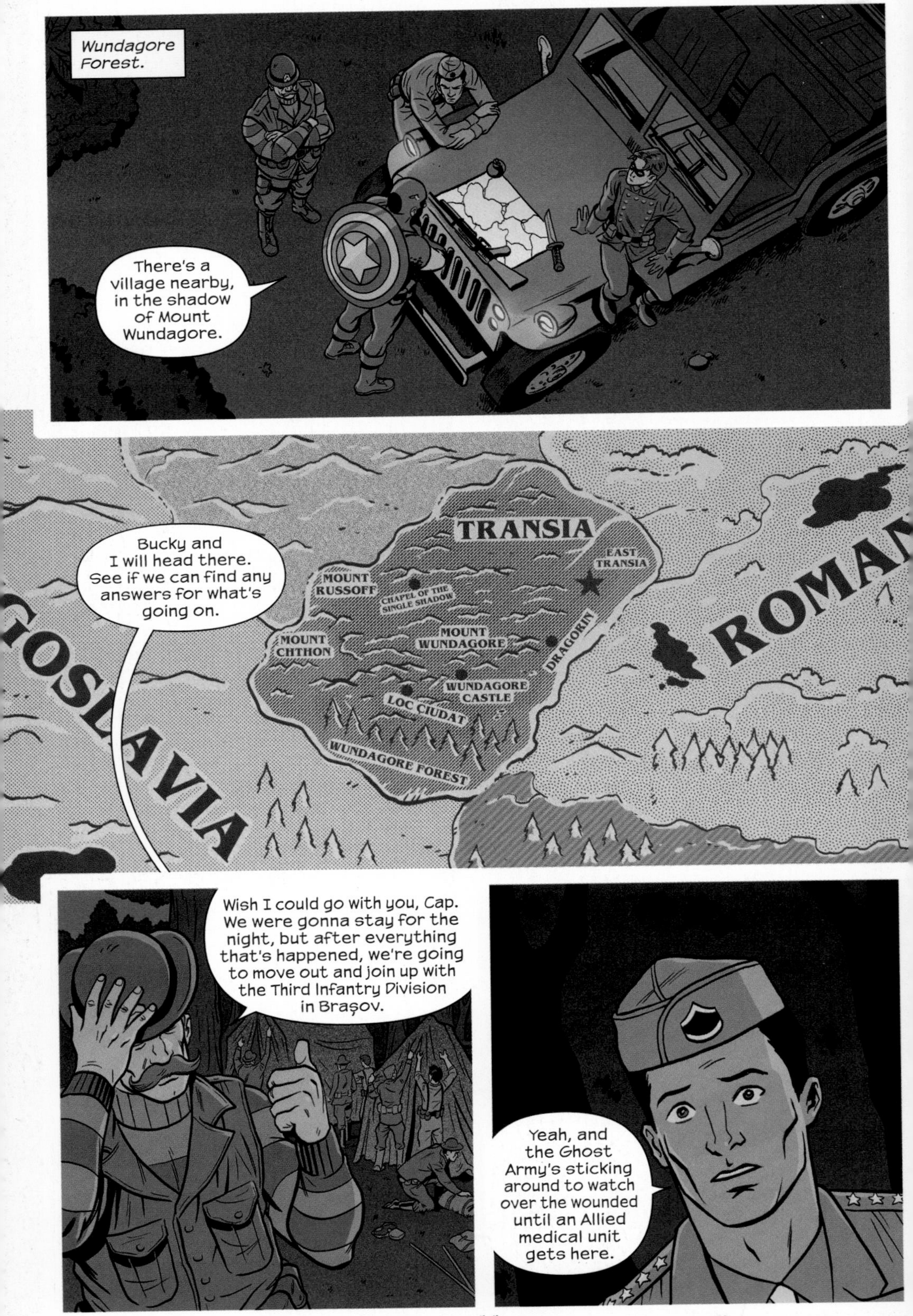
Wundagore Forest.
There's a village nearby, in the shadow of Mount Wundagore.
Bucky and I will head there. See if we can find any answers for what's going on.
TRANSIA
EAST TRANSIA
MOUNT RUSSOFF
CHAPEL OF THE SINGLE SHADOW
MOUNT WUNDAGORE
MOUNT CHTHON
DRAGORIN
WUNDAGORE CASTLE
LOC CIUDAT
WUNDAGORE FOREST
GOSLAVIA
ROMAN
Wish I could go with you, Cap. We were gonna stay for the night, but after everything that's happened, we're going to move out and join up with the Third Infantry Division in Brașov.
Yeah, and the Ghost Army's sticking around to watch over the wounded until an Allied medical unit gets here.

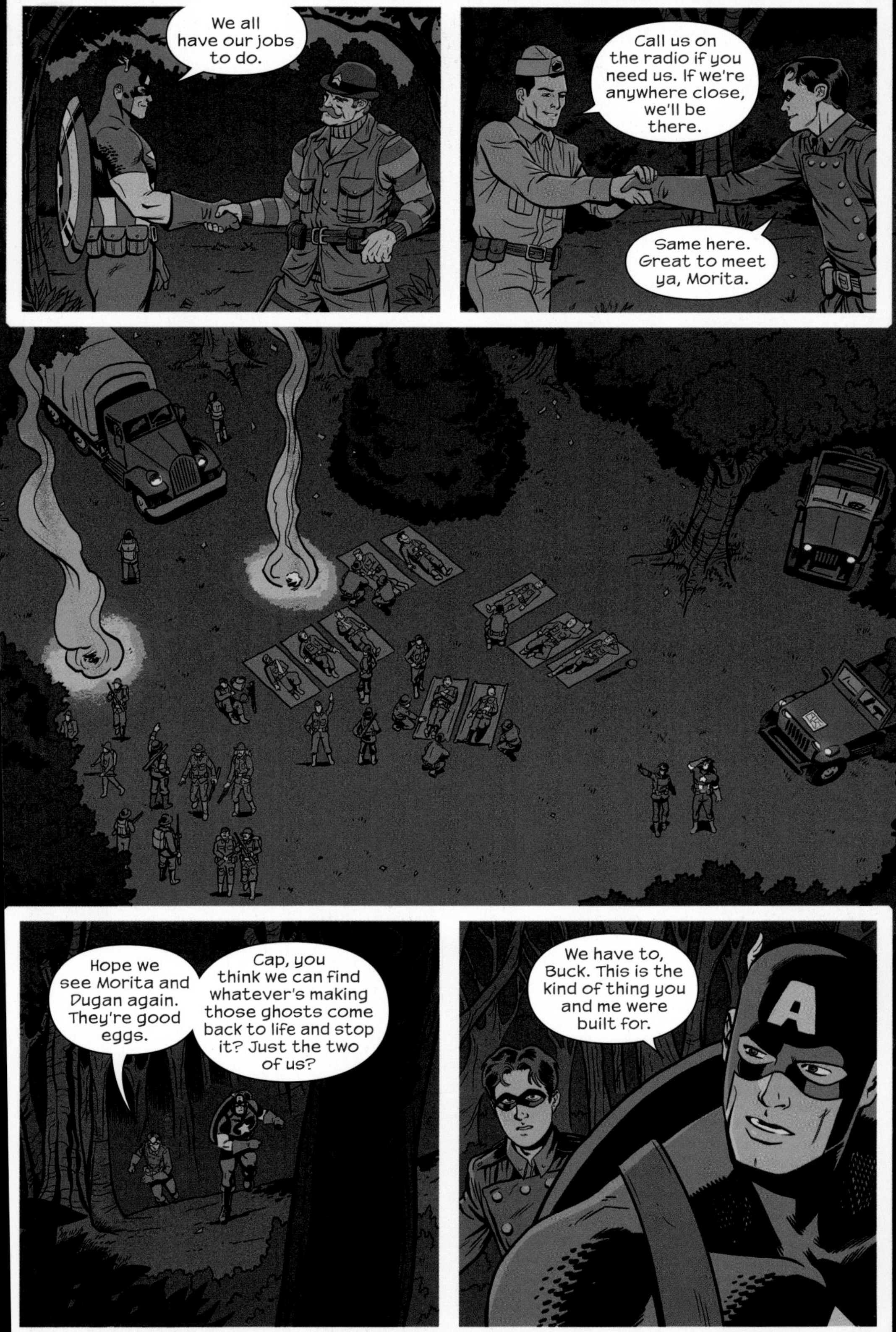
We all have our jobs to do.
Call us on the radio if you need us. If we're anywhere close, we'll be there.
Same here. Great to meet ya, Morita.
Hope we see Morita and Dugan again. They're good eggs.
Cap, you think we can find whatever's making those ghosts come back to life and stop it? Just the two of us?
We have to, Buck. This is the kind of thing you and me were built for.

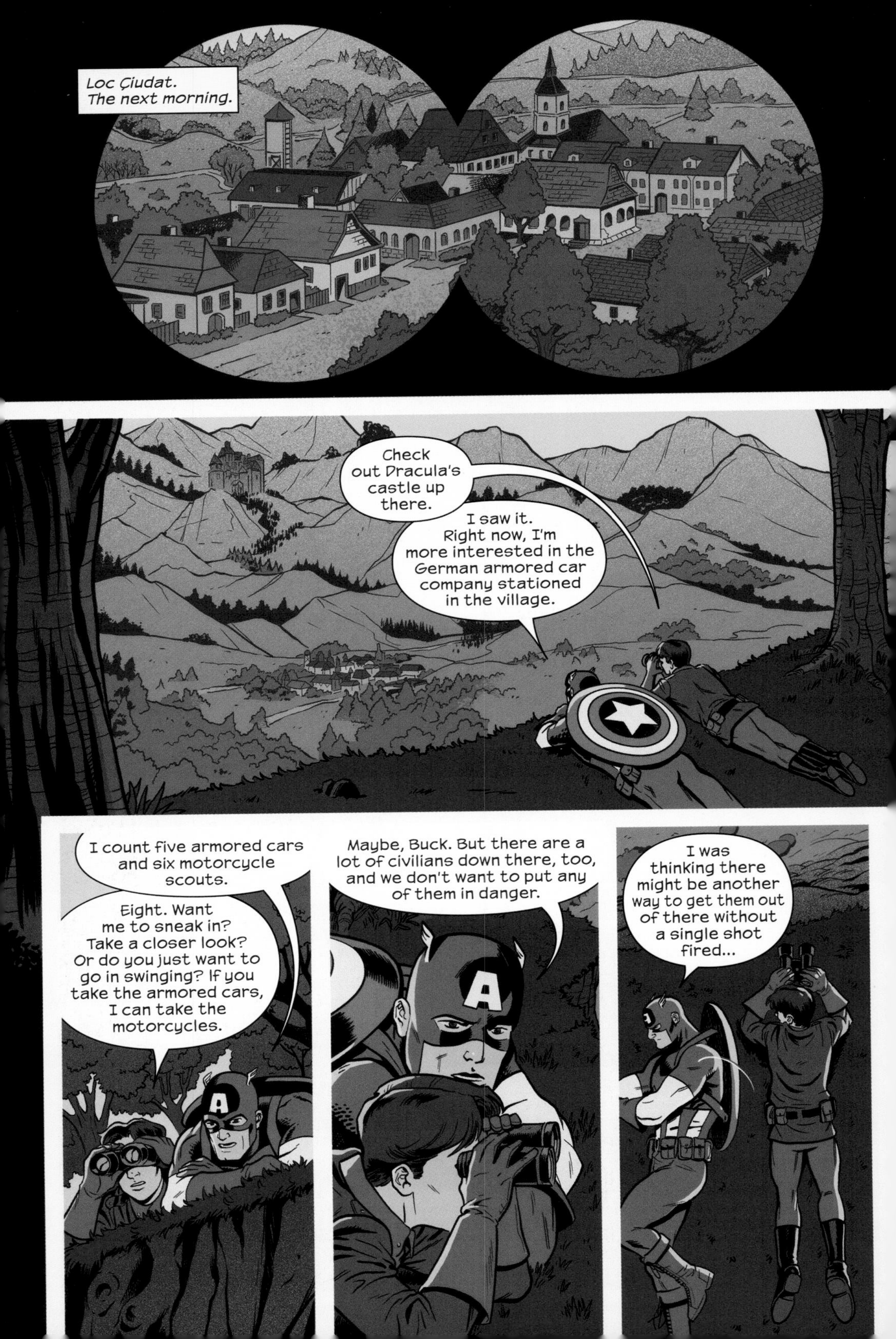
Loc Çiudat. The next morning.
Check out Dracula's castle up there.
I saw it. Right now, I'm more interested in the German armored car company stationed in the village.
I count five armored cars and six motorcycle scouts.
Eight. Want me to sneak in? Take a closer look? Or do you just want to go in swinging? If you take the armored cars, I can take the motorcycles.
Maybe, Buck. But there are a lot of civilians down there, too, and we don't want to put any of them in danger.
I was thinking there might be another way to get them out of there without a single shot fired...

CHAPTER THREE
MAGIC

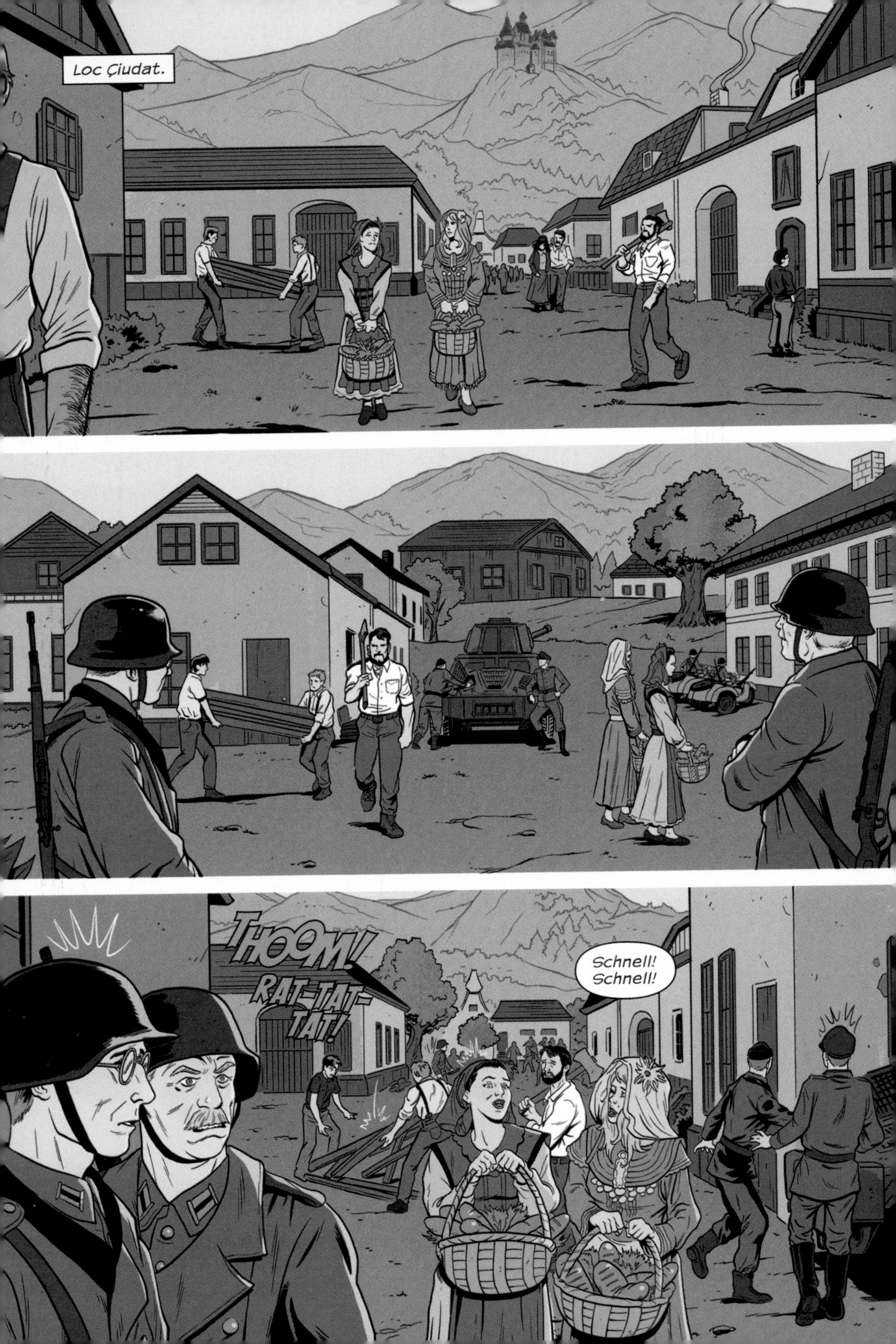
Loc Çiudat.
THOOM!
RAT-TAT-TAT!
Schnell! Schnell!

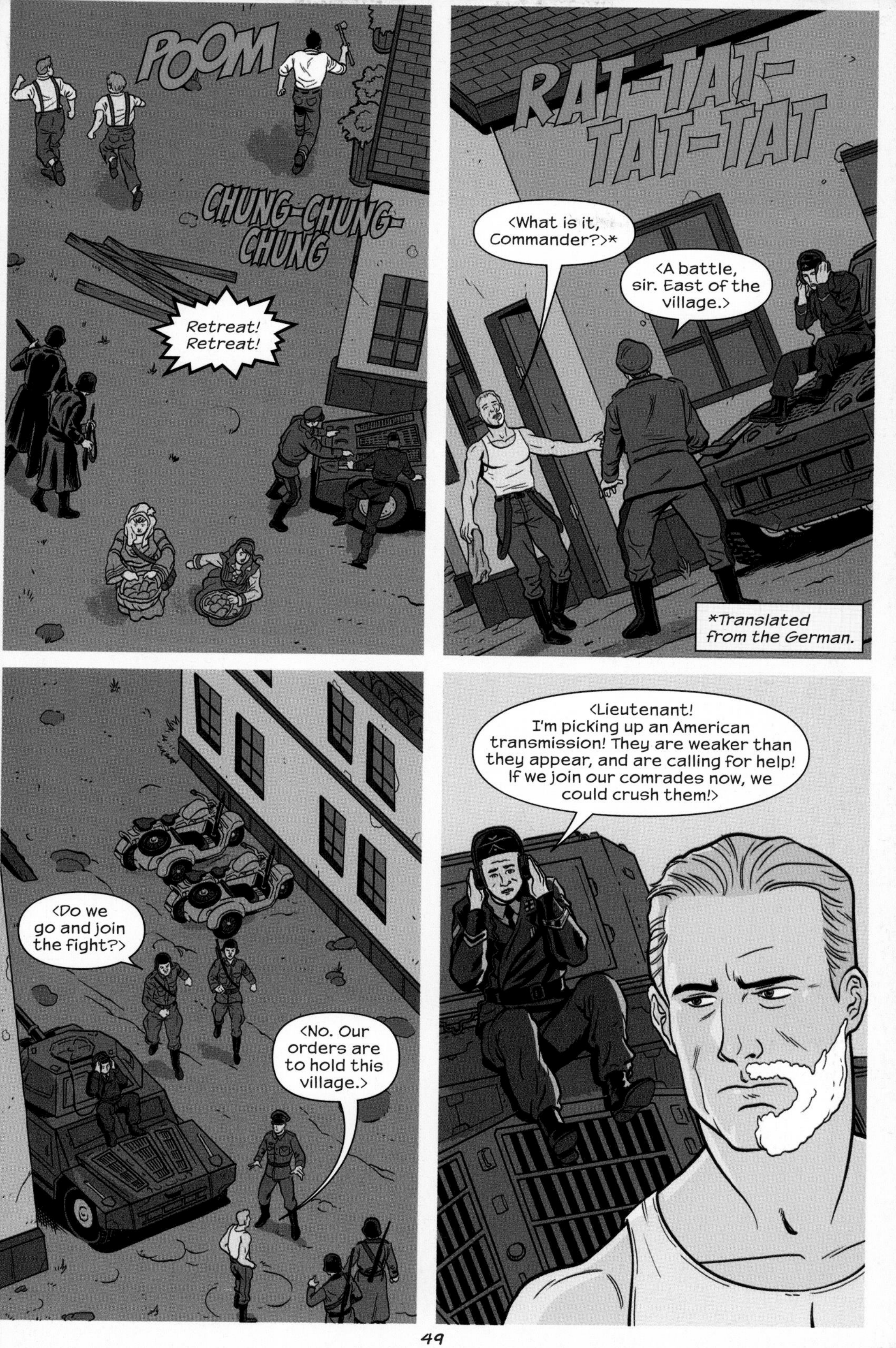
POOM
CHUNG-CHUNG-CHUNG
Retreat! Retreat!
RAT-TAT-TAT-TAT
<What is it, Commander?>*
<A battle, sir. East of the village.>
*Translated from the German.
<Do we go and join the fight?>
<No. Our orders are to hold this village.>
<Lieutenant! I'm picking up an American transmission! They are weaker than they appear, and are calling for help! If we join our comrades now, we could crush them!>

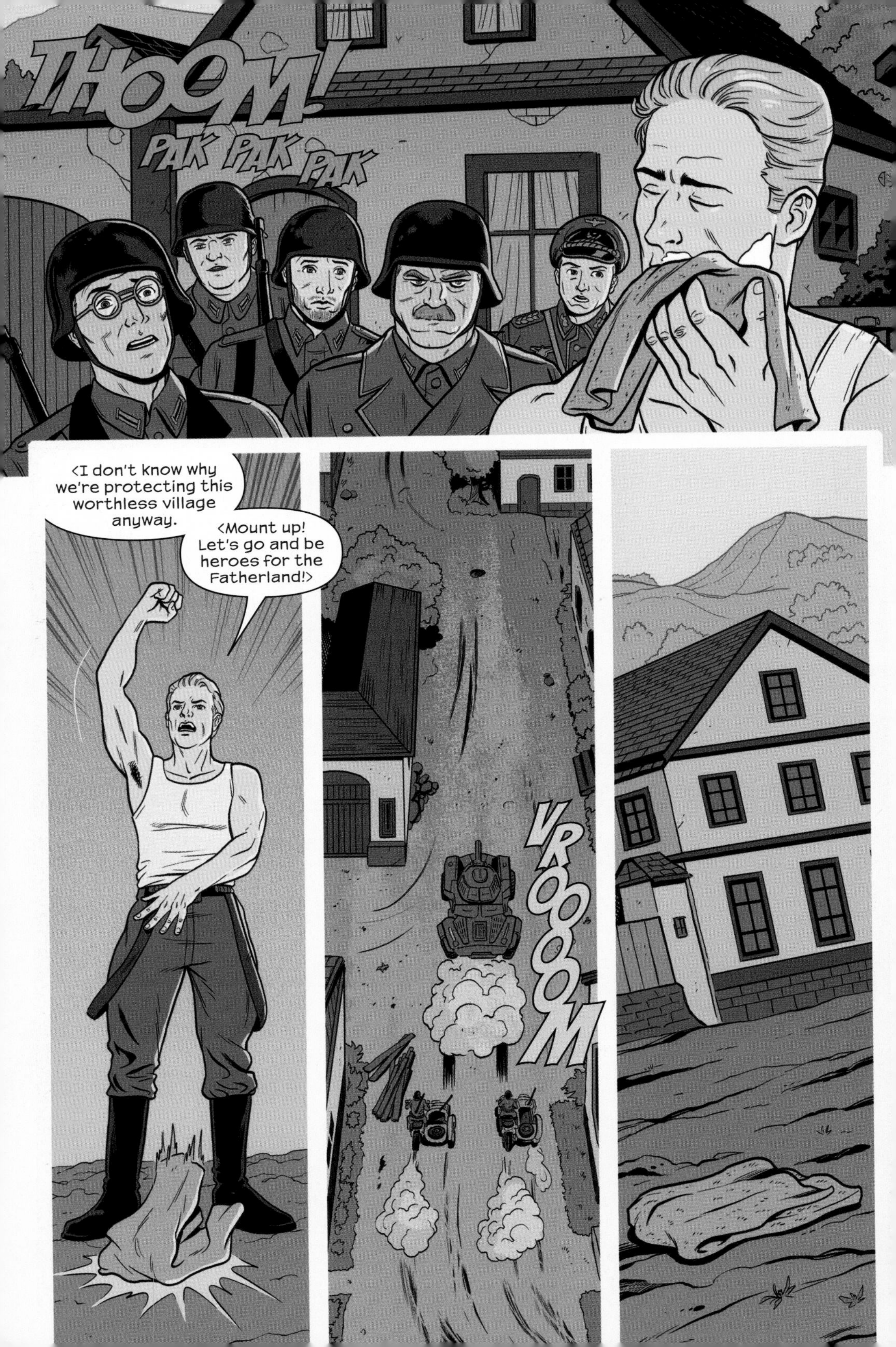
THOOM!
PAK PAK PAK
<I don't know why we're protecting this worthless village anyway.
<Mount up! Let's go and be heroes for the Fatherland!>
VROOOOOM

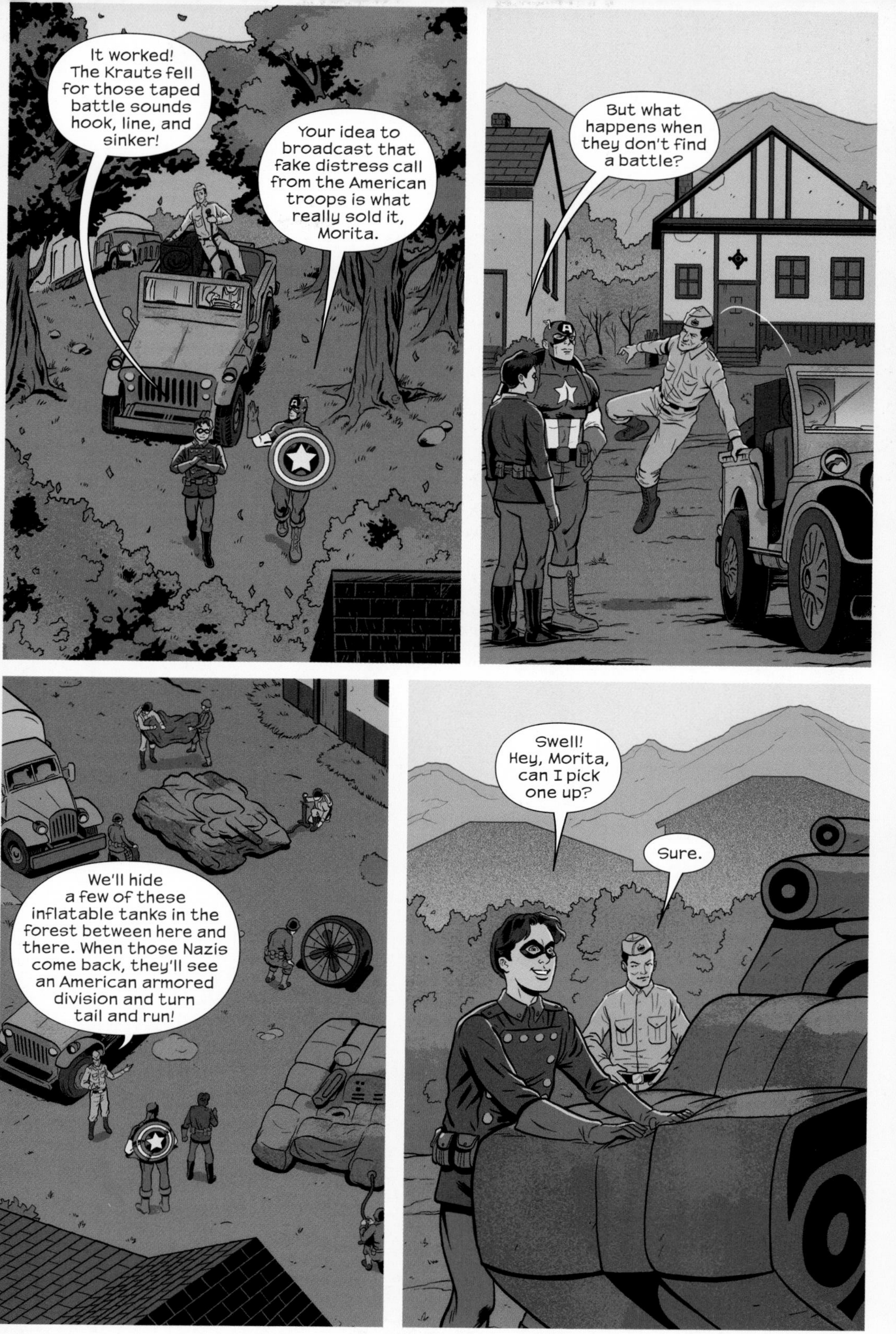
It worked! The Krauts fell for those taped battle sounds hook, line, and sinker!
Your idea to broadcast that fake distress call from the American troops is what really sold it, Morita.
But what happens when they don't find a battle?
We'll hide a few of these inflatable tanks in the forest between here and there. When those Nazis come back, they'll see an American armored division and turn tail and run!
Swell! Hey, Morita, can I pick one up?
Sure.

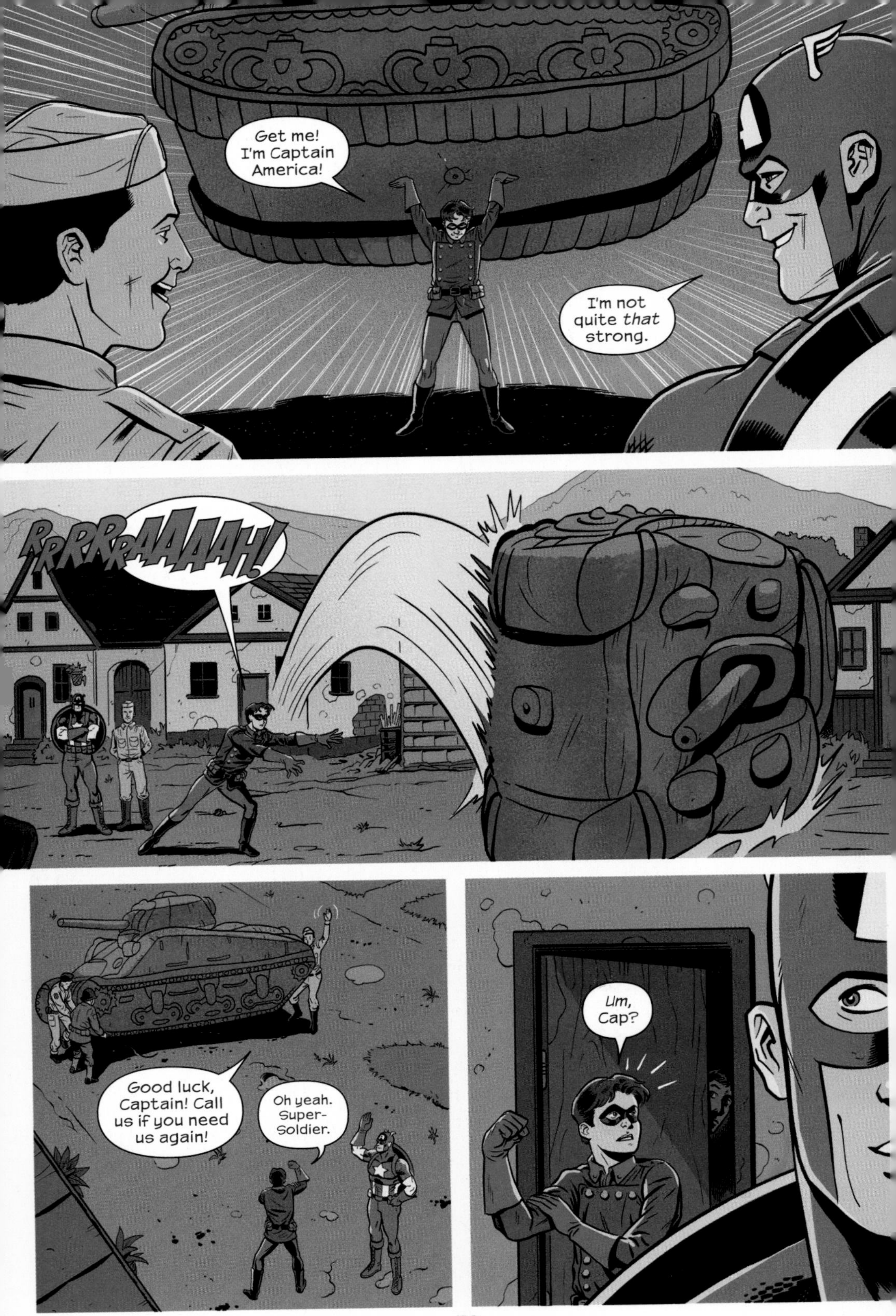
Get me! I'm Captain America!
I'm not quite *that* strong.
RRRRRAAAAAH!
Good luck, Captain! Call us if you need us again!
Oh yeah. Super-Soldier.
Um, Cap?

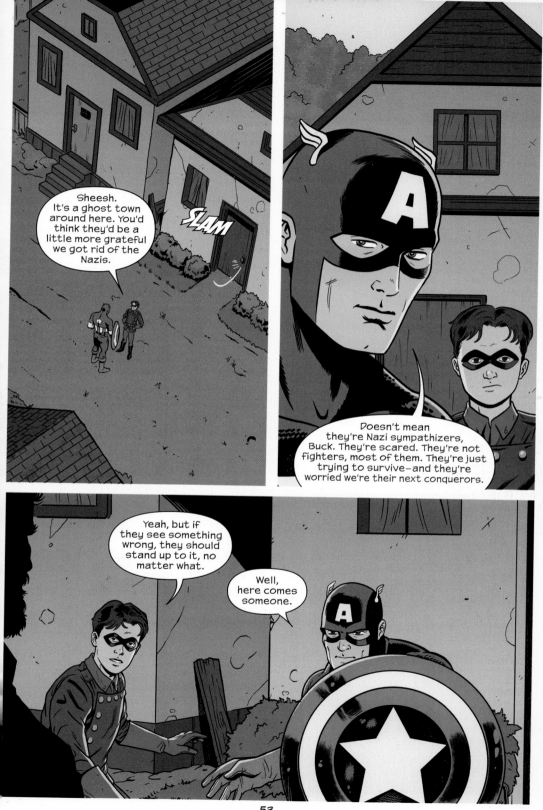

Sheesh. It's a ghost town around here. You'd think they'd be a little more grateful we got rid of the Nazis.

SLAM

Doesn't mean they're Nazi sympathizers, Buck. They're scared. They're not fighters, most of them. They're just trying to survive—and they're worried we're their next conquerors.

Yeah, but if they see something wrong, they should stand up to it, no matter what.

Well, here comes someone.

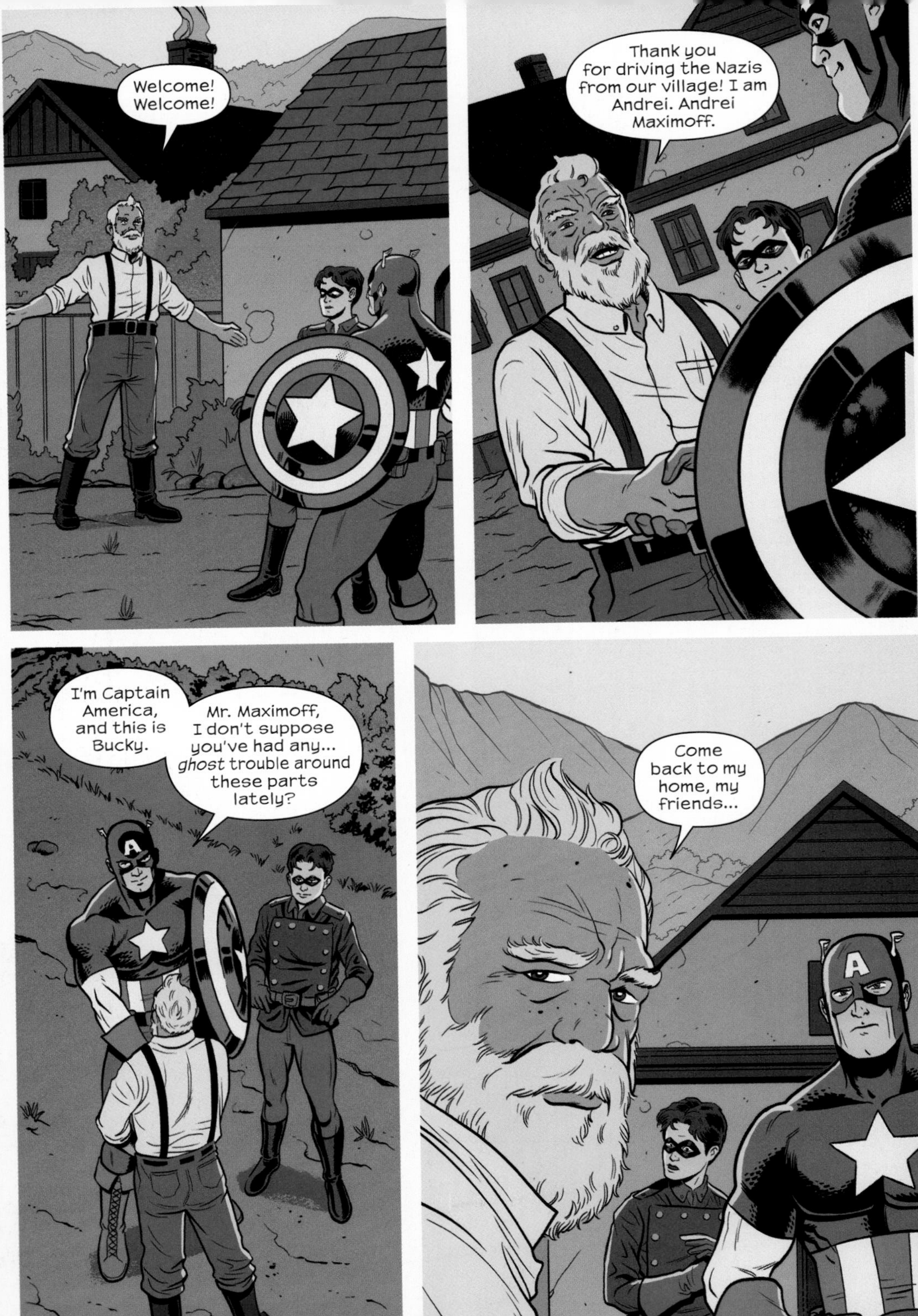
Welcome! Welcome!
Thank you for driving the Nazis from our village! I am Andrei. Andrei Maximoff.
I'm Captain America, and this is Bucky.
Mr. Maximoff, I don't suppose you've had any... *ghost* trouble around these parts lately?
Come back to my home, my friends...

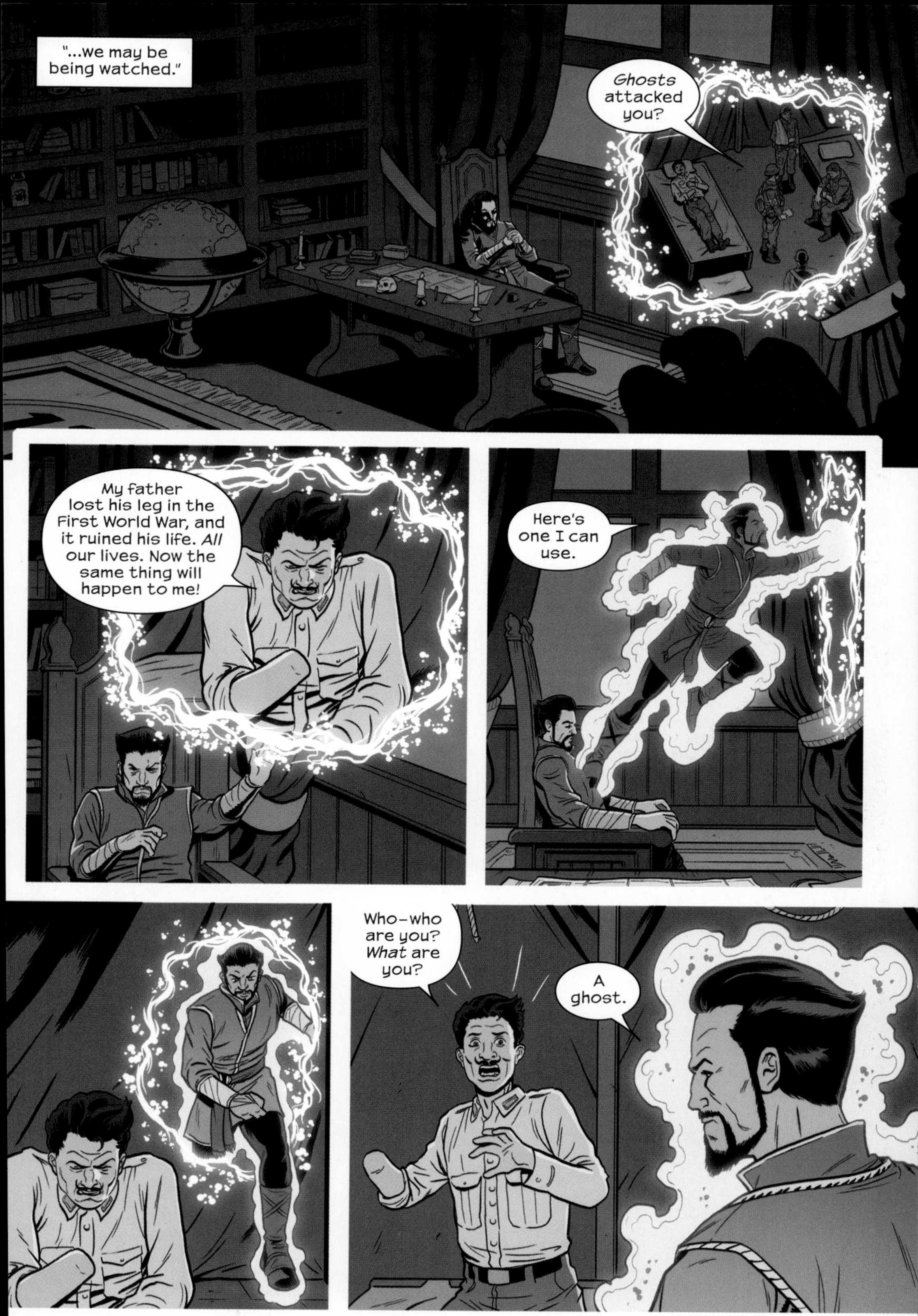
"...we may be being watched."
Ghosts attacked you?
My father lost his leg in the First World War, and it ruined his life. All our lives. Now the same thing will happen to me!
Here's one I can use.
Who-who are you? What are you?
A ghost.

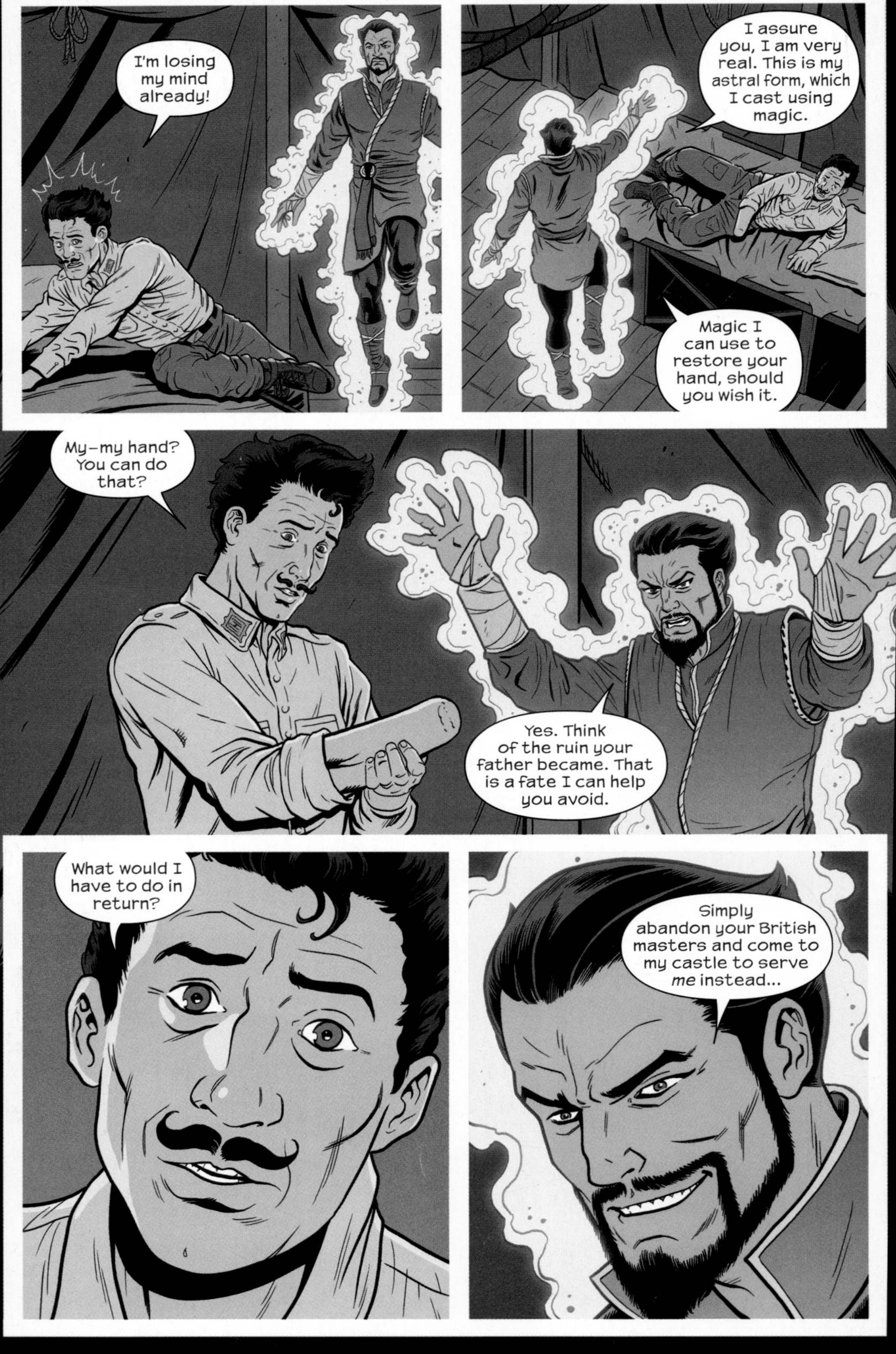
I'm losing my mind already!
I assure you, I am very real. This is my astral form, which I cast using magic.
Magic I can use to restore your hand, should you wish it.
My—my hand? You can do that?
Yes. Think of the ruin your father became. That is a fate I can help you avoid.
What would I have to do in return?
Simply abandon your British masters and come to my castle to serve *me* instead...

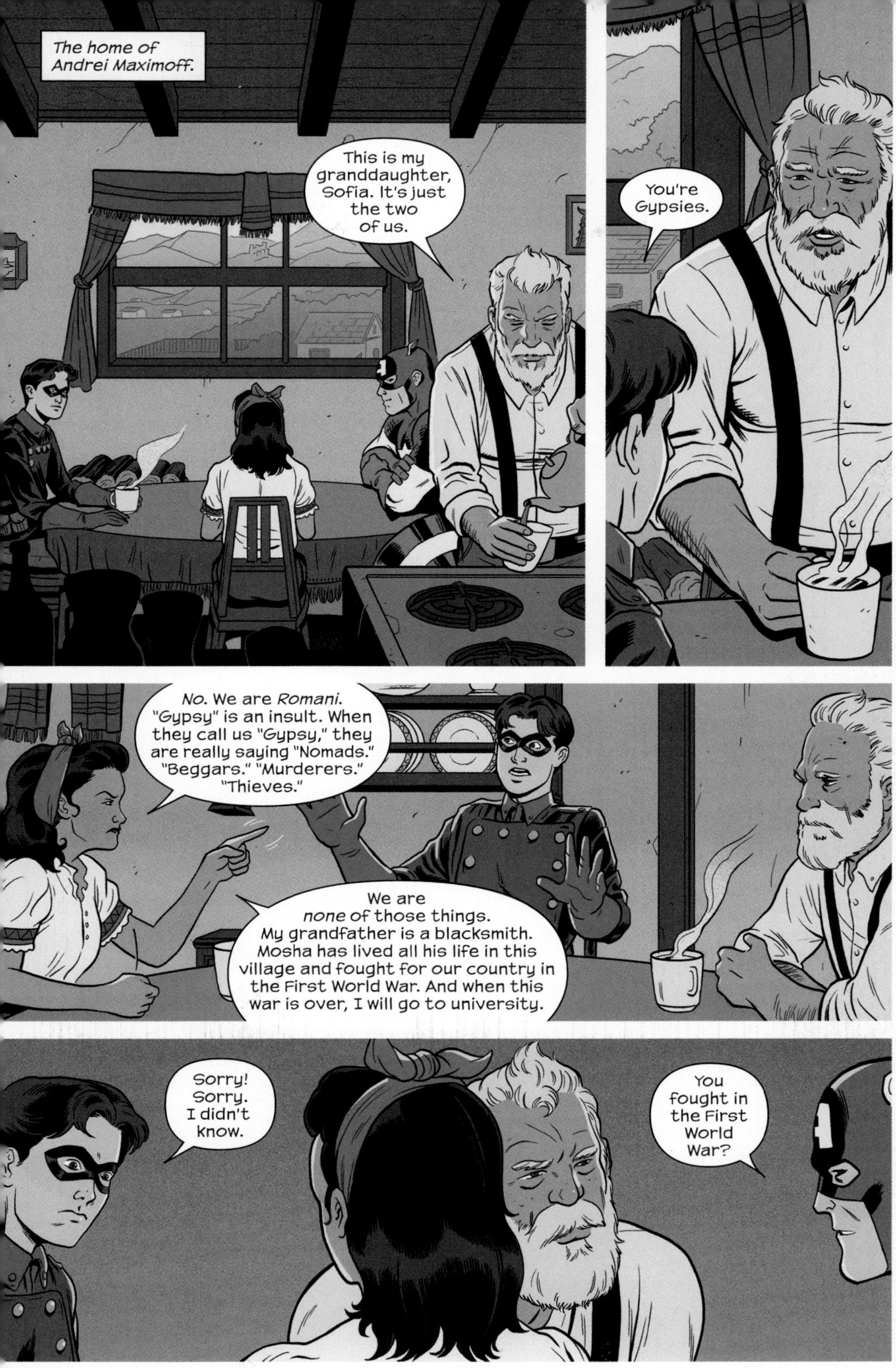
The home of Andrei Maximoff.
This is my granddaughter, Sofia. It's just the two of us.
You're Gypsies.
No. We are *Romani*. "Gypsy" is an insult. When they call us "Gypsy," they are really saying "Nomads." "Beggars." "Murderers." "Thieves."
We are *none* of those things. My grandfather is a blacksmith. Mosha has lived all his life in this village and fought for our country in the First World War. And when this war is over, I will go to university.
Sorry! Sorry. I didn't know.
You fought in the First World War?

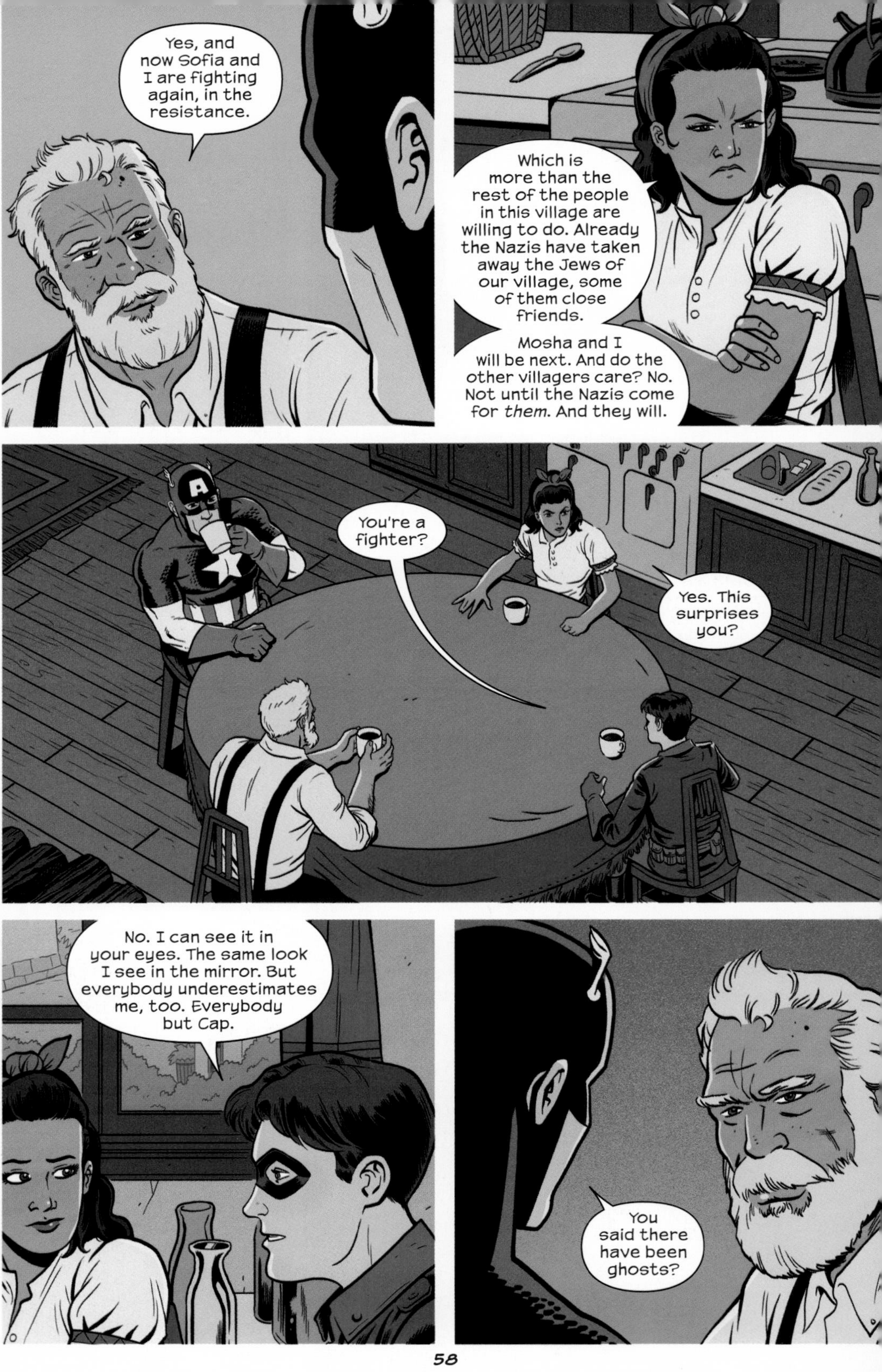
Yes, and now Sofia and I are fighting again, in the resistance.
Which is more than the rest of the people in this village are willing to do. Already the Nazis have taken away the Jews of our village, some of them close friends.
Mosha and I will be next. And do the other villagers care? No. Not until the Nazis come for *them*. And they will.
You're a fighter?
Yes. This surprises you?
No. I can see it in your eyes. The same look I see in the mirror. But everybody underestimates me, too. Everybody but Cap.
You said there have been ghosts?

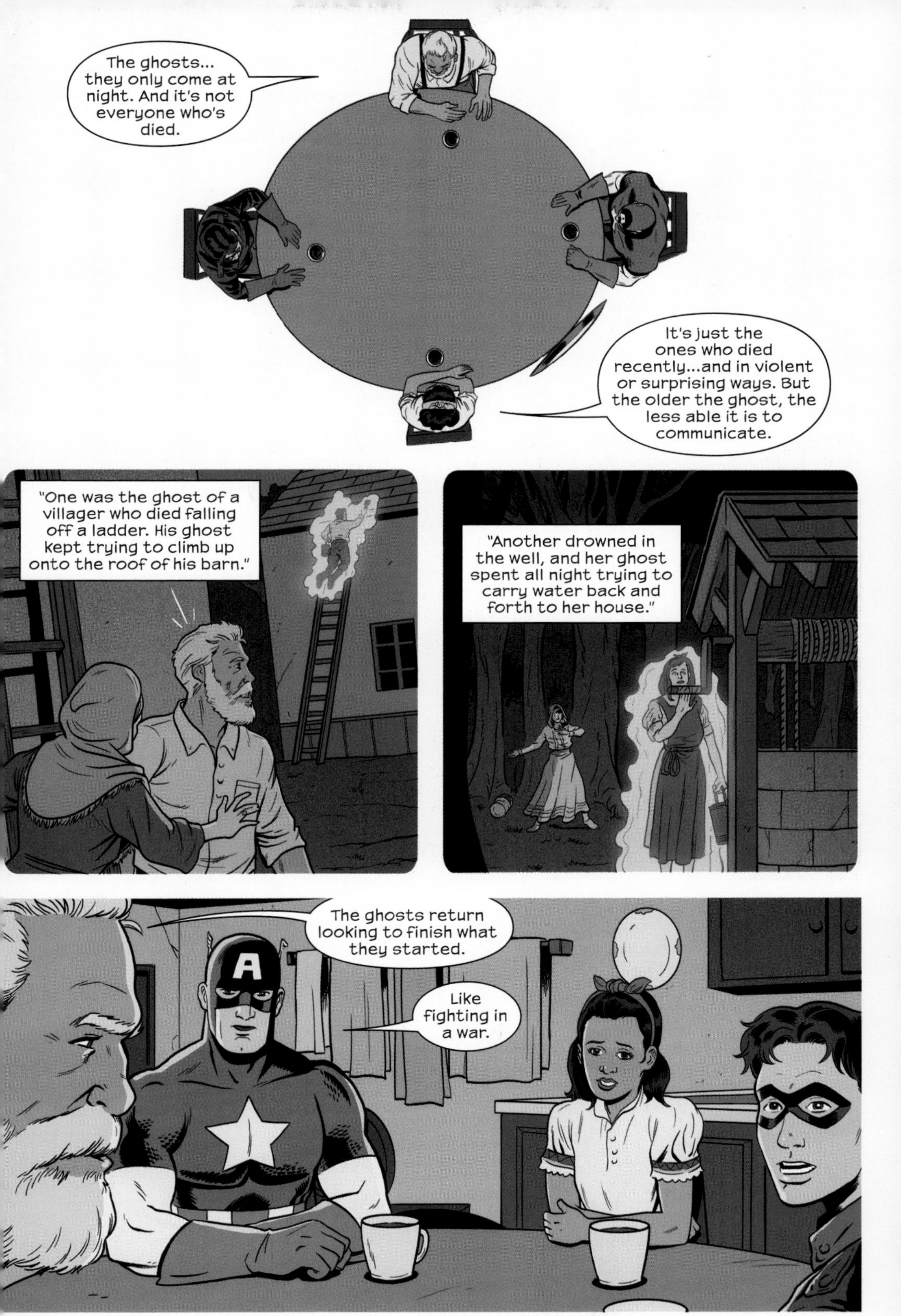
The ghosts... they only come at night. And it's not everyone who's died.
It's just the ones who died recently...and in violent or surprising ways. But the older the ghost, the less able it is to communicate.
"One was the ghost of a villager who died falling off a ladder. His ghost kept trying to climb up onto the roof of his barn."
"Another drowned in the well, and her ghost spent all night trying to carry water back and forth to her house."
The ghosts return looking to finish what they started.
Like fighting in a war.

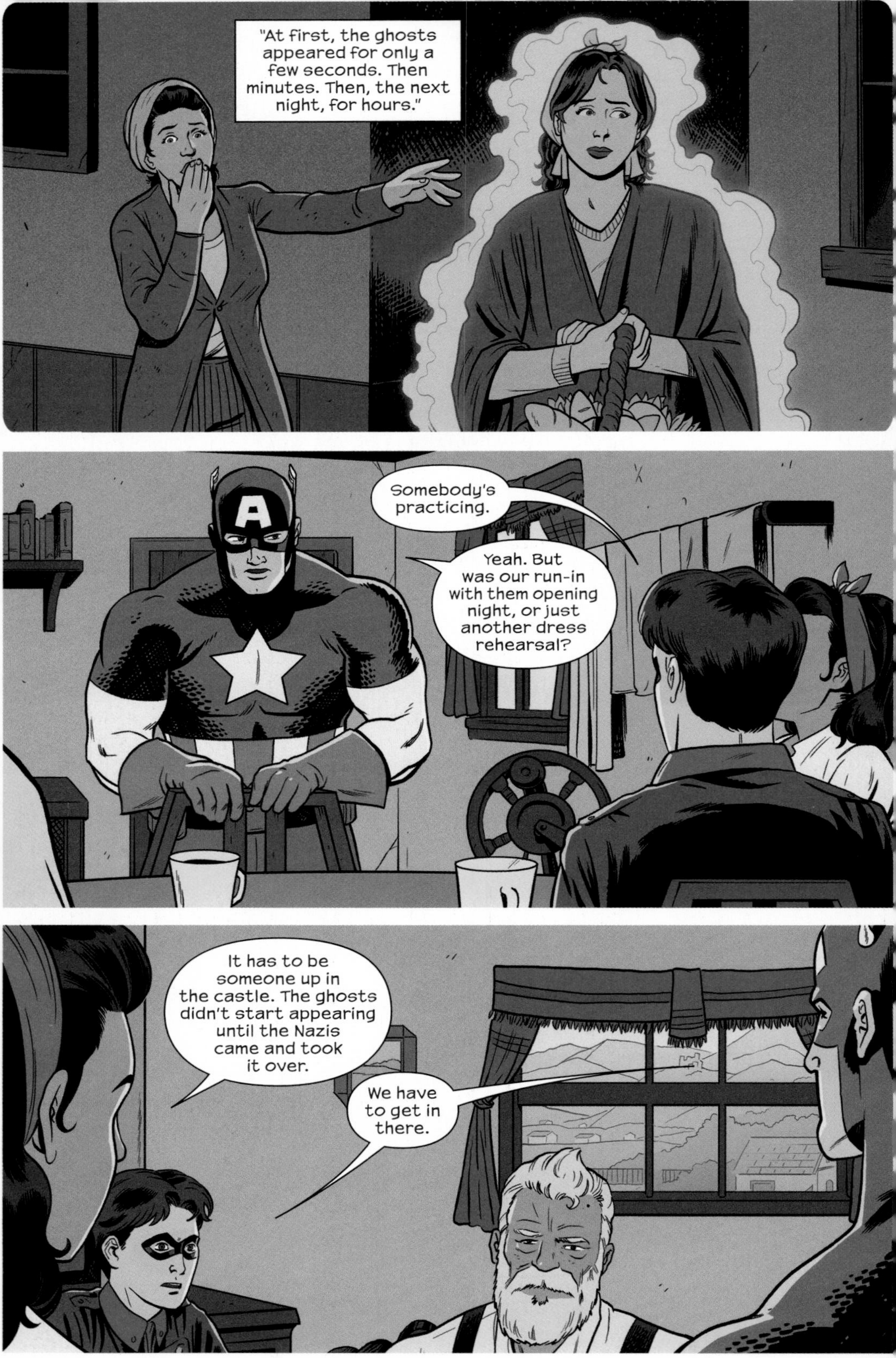
"At first, the ghosts appeared for only a few seconds. Then minutes. Then, the next night, for hours."
Somebody's practicing.
Yeah. But was our run-in with them opening night, or just another dress rehearsal?
It has to be someone up in the castle. The ghosts didn't start appearing until the Nazis came and took it over.
We have to get in there.

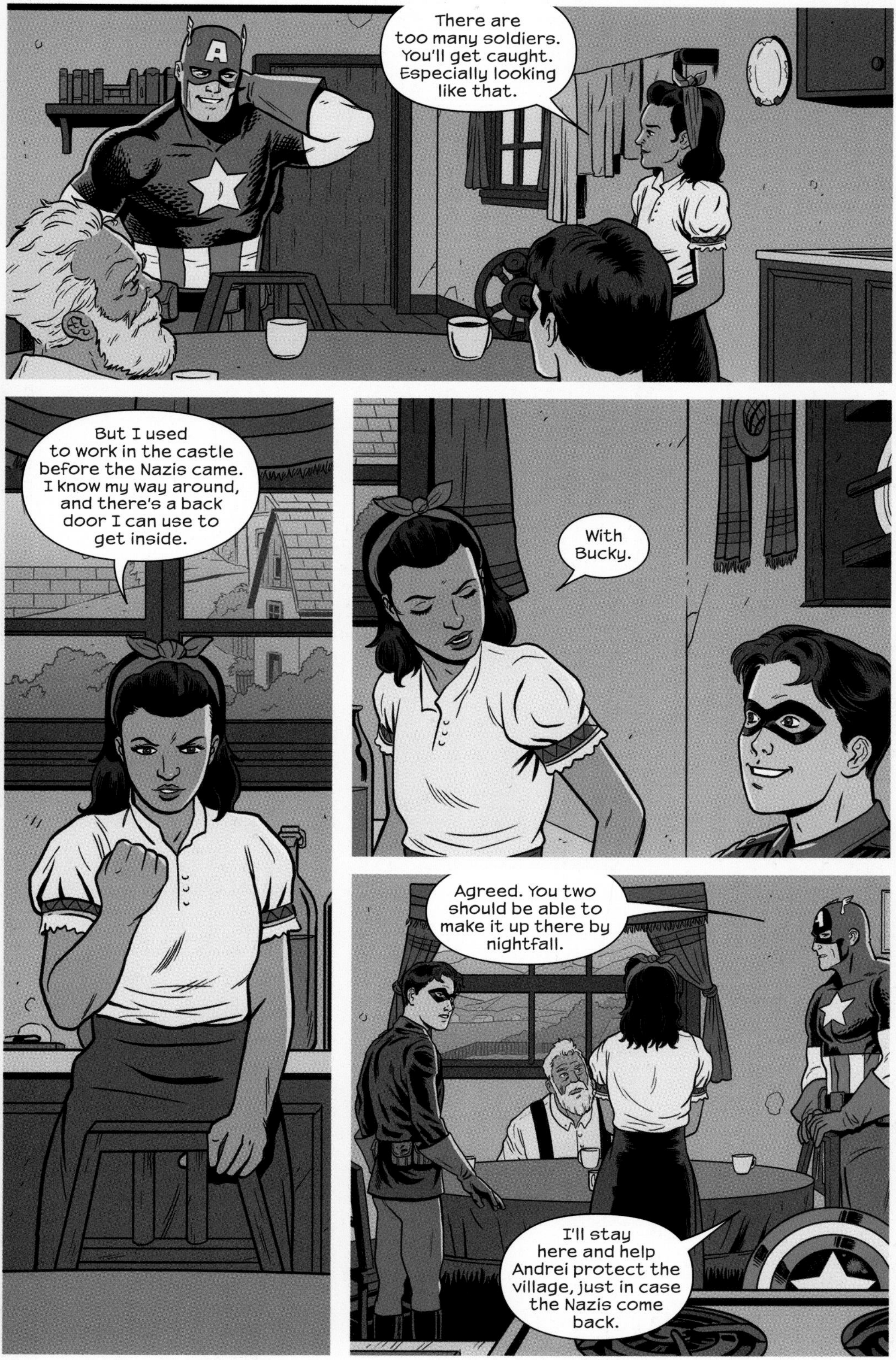
There are too many soldiers. You'll get caught. Especially looking like that.
But I used to work in the castle before the Nazis came. I know my way around, and there's a back door I can use to get inside.
With Bucky.
Agreed. You two should be able to make it up there by nightfall.
I'll stay here and help Andrei protect the village, just in case the Nazis come back.

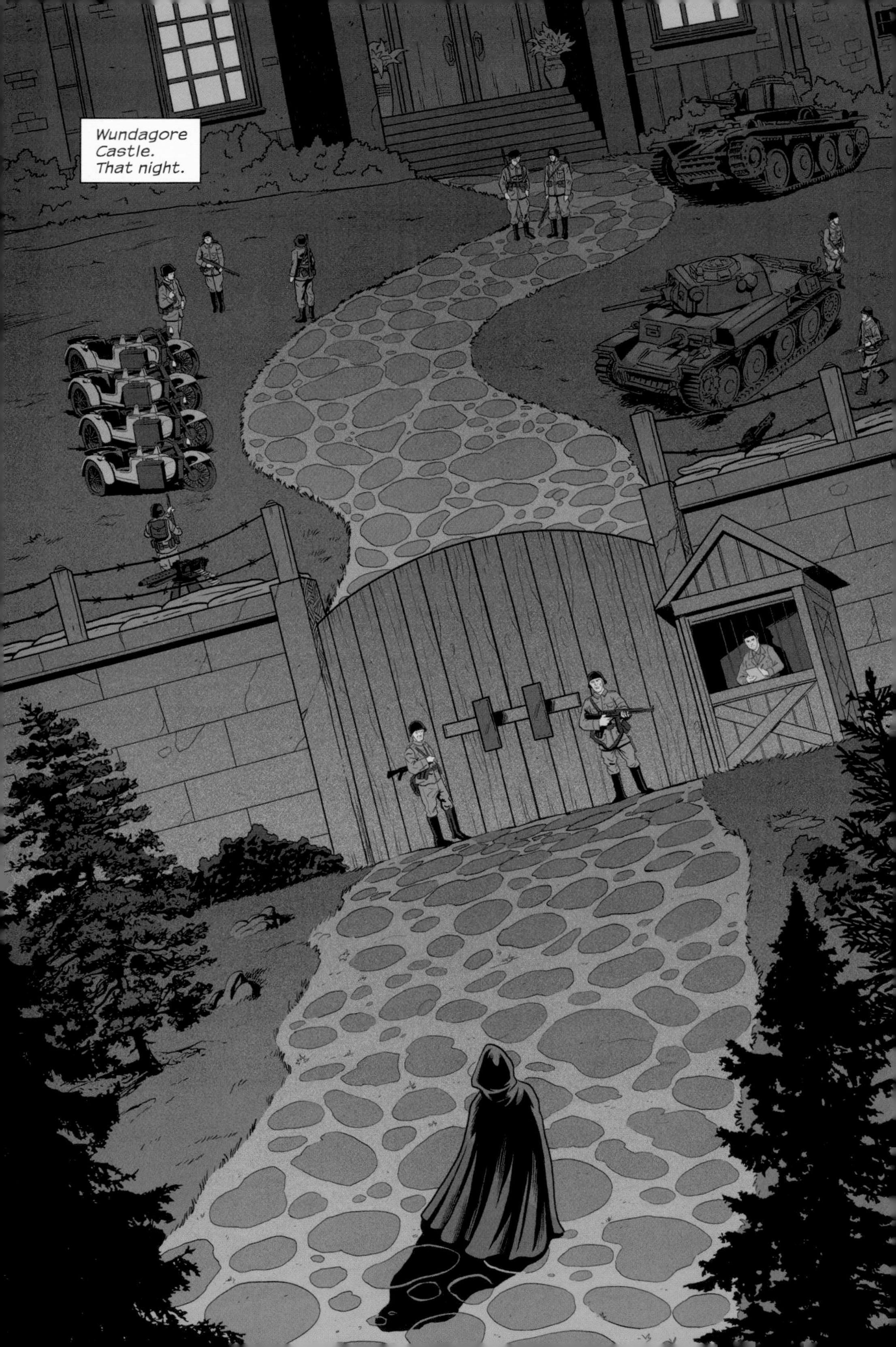
Wundagore Castle. That night.

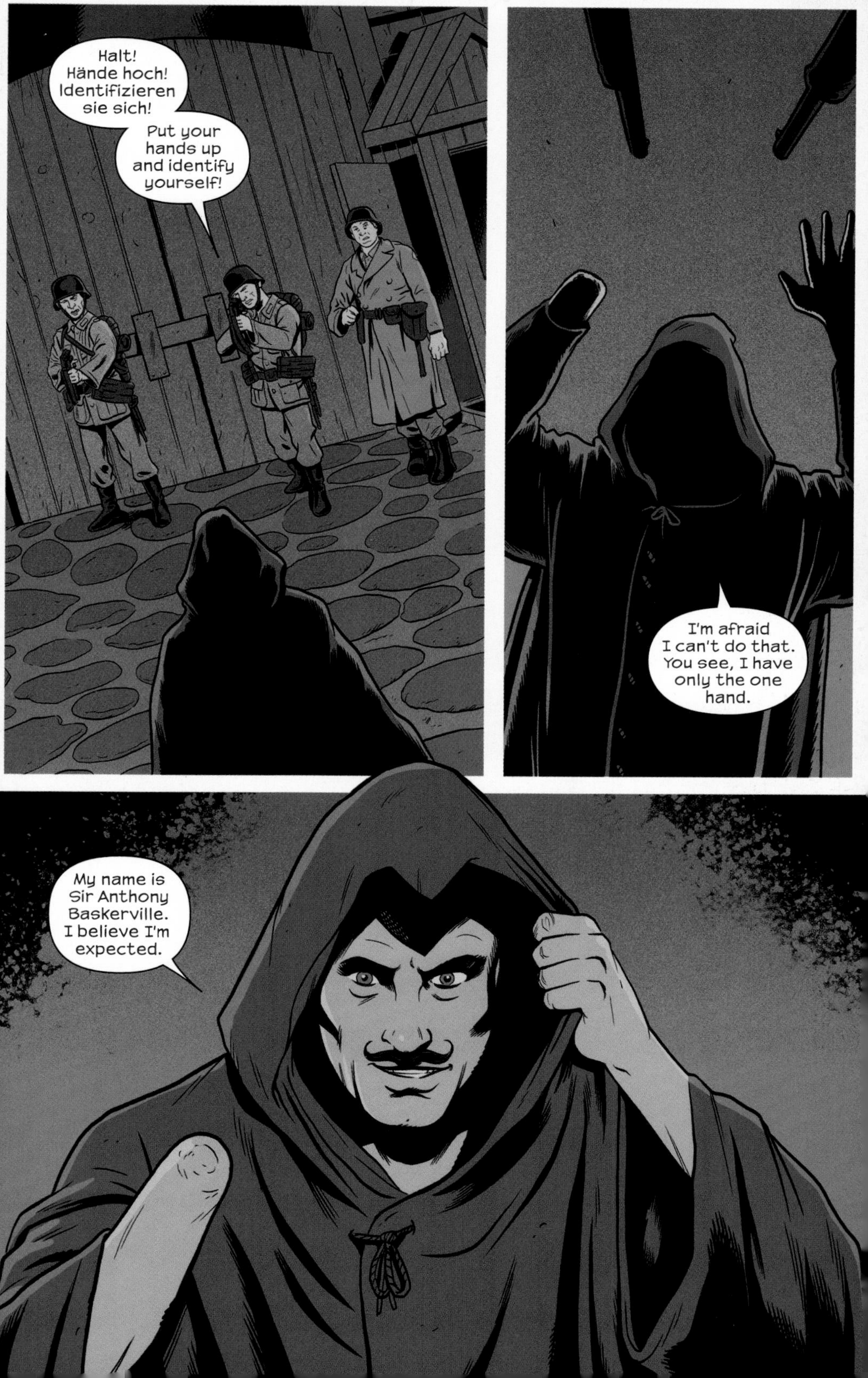
Halt! Hände hoch! Identifizieren sie sich!
Put your hands up and identify yourself!
I'm afraid I can't do that. You see, I have only the one hand.
My name is Sir Anthony Baskerville. I believe I'm expected.

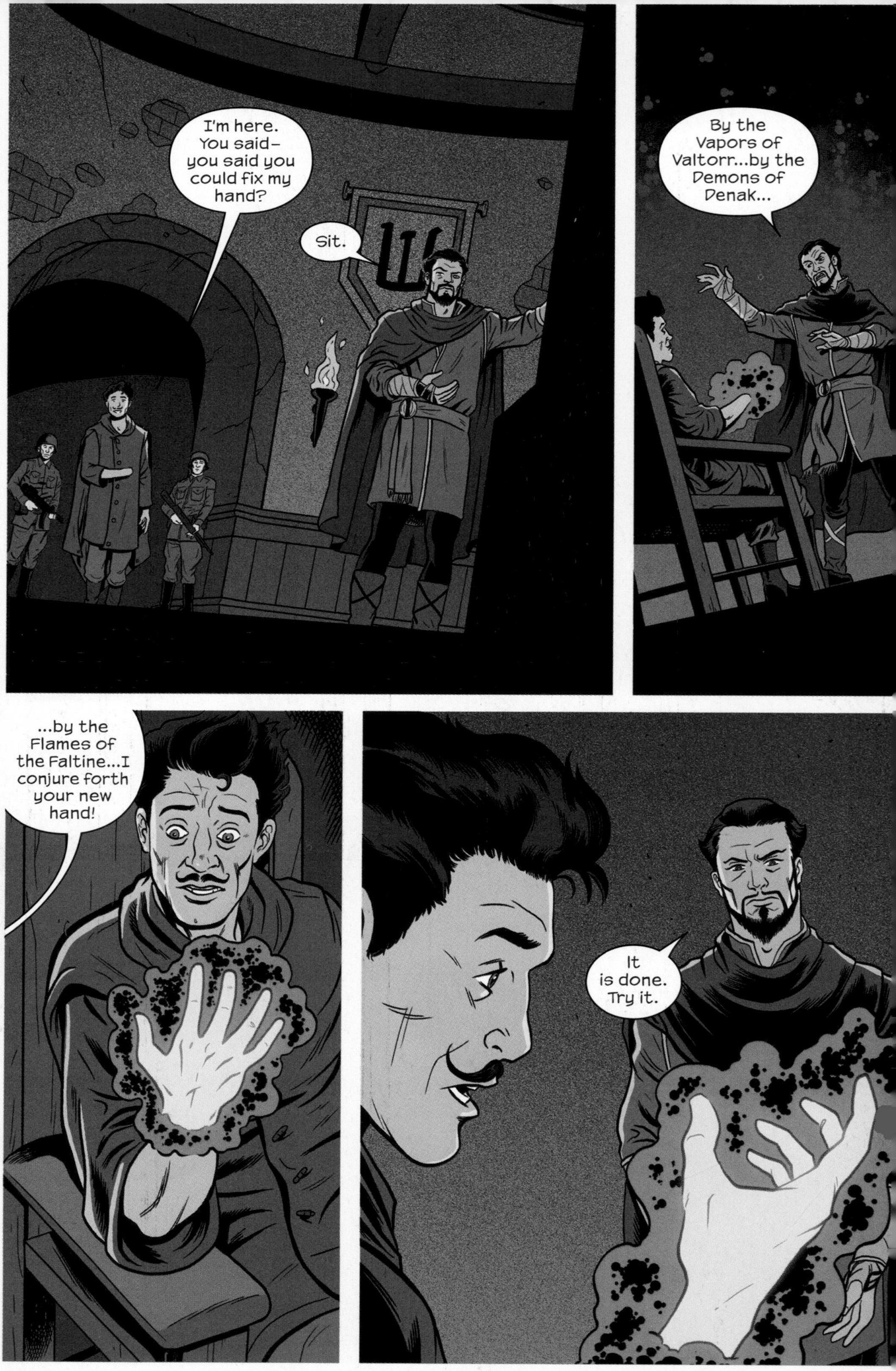
I'm here. You said– you said you could fix my hand?
Sit.
By the Vapors of Valtorr...by the Demons of Denak...
...by the Flames of the Faltine...I conjure forth your new hand!
It is done. Try it.

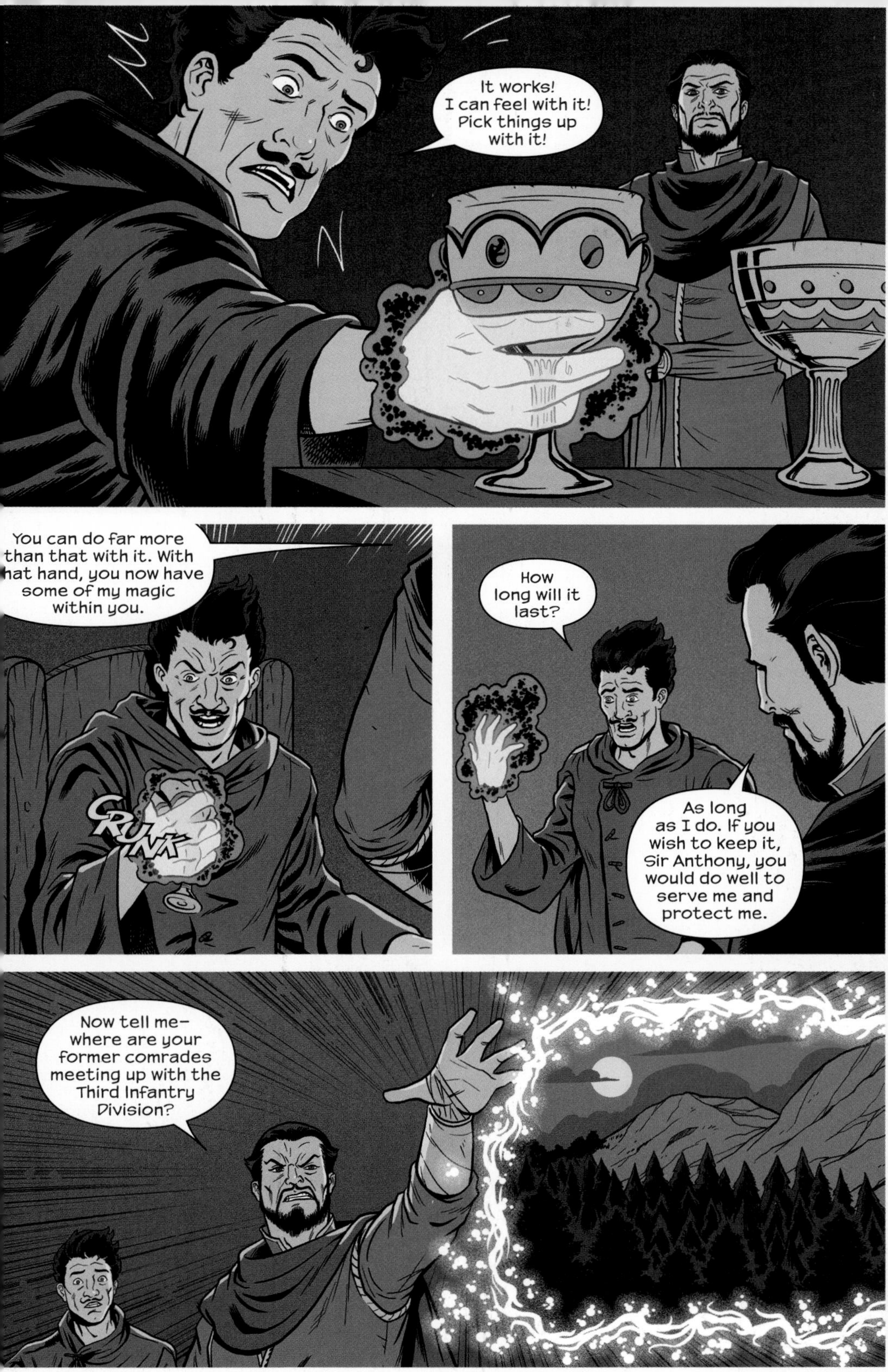

It works! I can feel with it! Pick things up with it!
You can do far more than that with it. With hat hand, you now have some of my magic within you.
CRUNK
How long will it last?
As long as I do. If you wish to keep it, Sir Anthony, you would do well to serve me and protect me.
Now tell me— where are your former comrades meeting up with the Third Infantry Division?

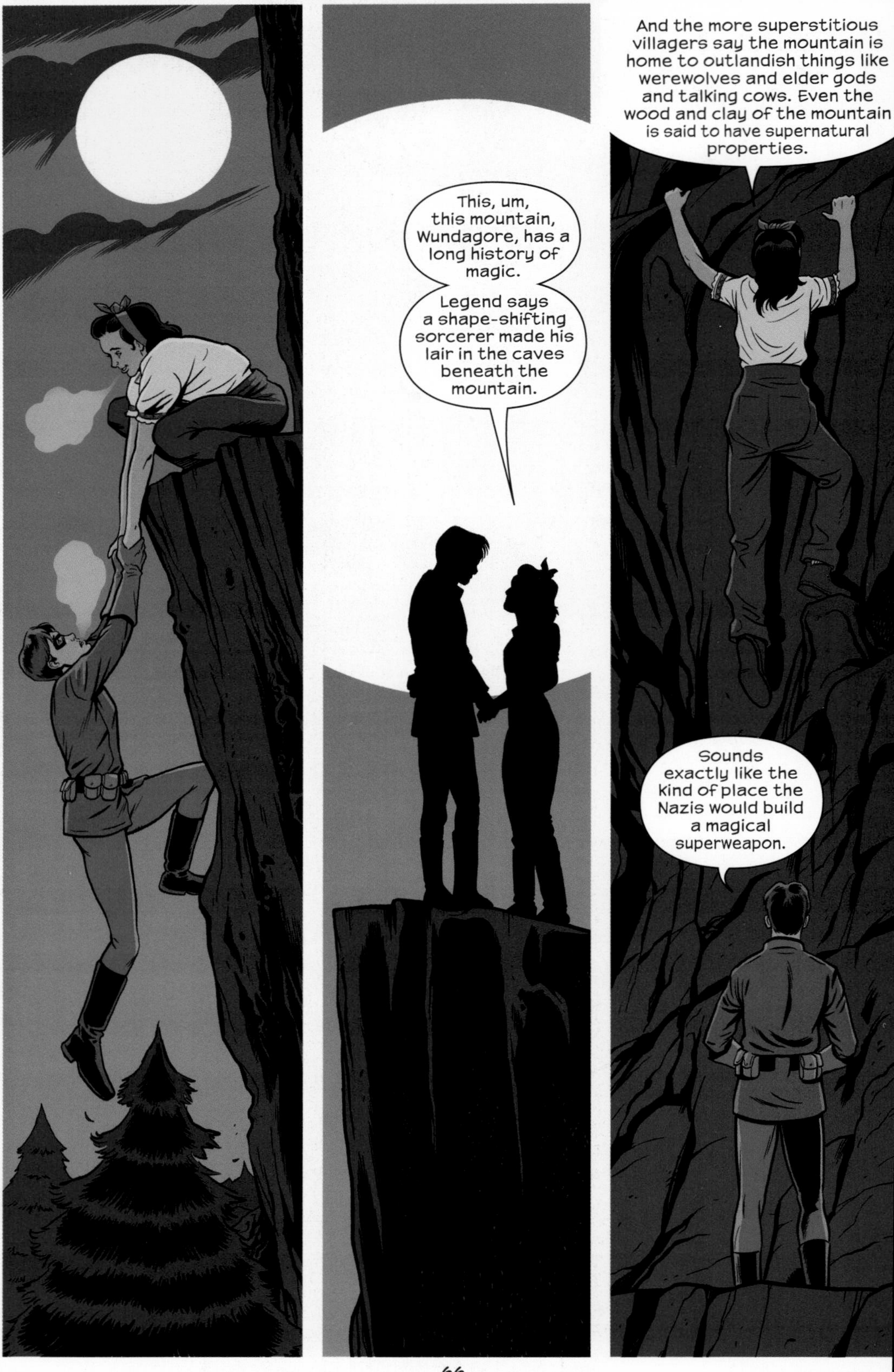
This, um, this mountain, Wundagore, has a long history of magic.
Legend says a shape-shifting sorcerer made his lair in the caves beneath the mountain.
And the more superstitious villagers say the mountain is home to outlandish things like werewolves and elder gods and talking cows. Even the wood and clay of the mountain is said to have supernatural properties.
Sounds exactly like the kind of place the Nazis would build a magical superweapon.

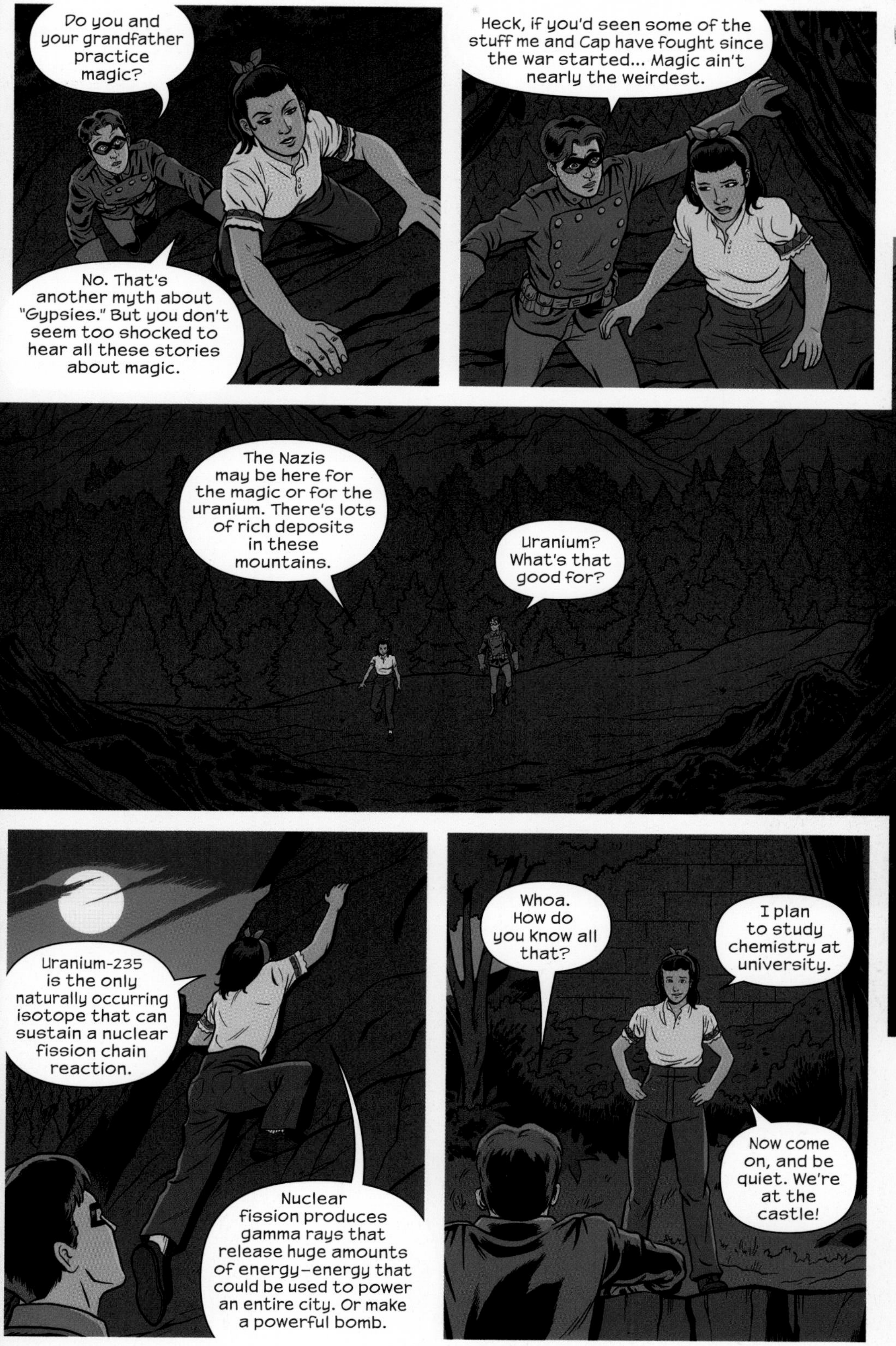
Do you and your grandfather practice magic?
No. That's another myth about "Gypsies." But you don't seem too shocked to hear all these stories about magic.
Heck, if you'd seen some of the stuff me and Cap have fought since the war started... Magic ain't nearly the weirdest.
The Nazis may be here for the magic or for the uranium. There's lots of rich deposits in these mountains.
Uranium? What's that good for?
Uranium-235 is the only naturally occurring isotope that can sustain a nuclear fission chain reaction.
Nuclear fission produces gamma rays that release huge amounts of energy—energy that could be used to power an entire city. Or make a powerful bomb.
Whoa. How do you know all that?
I plan to study chemistry at university.
Now come on, and be quiet. We're at the castle!

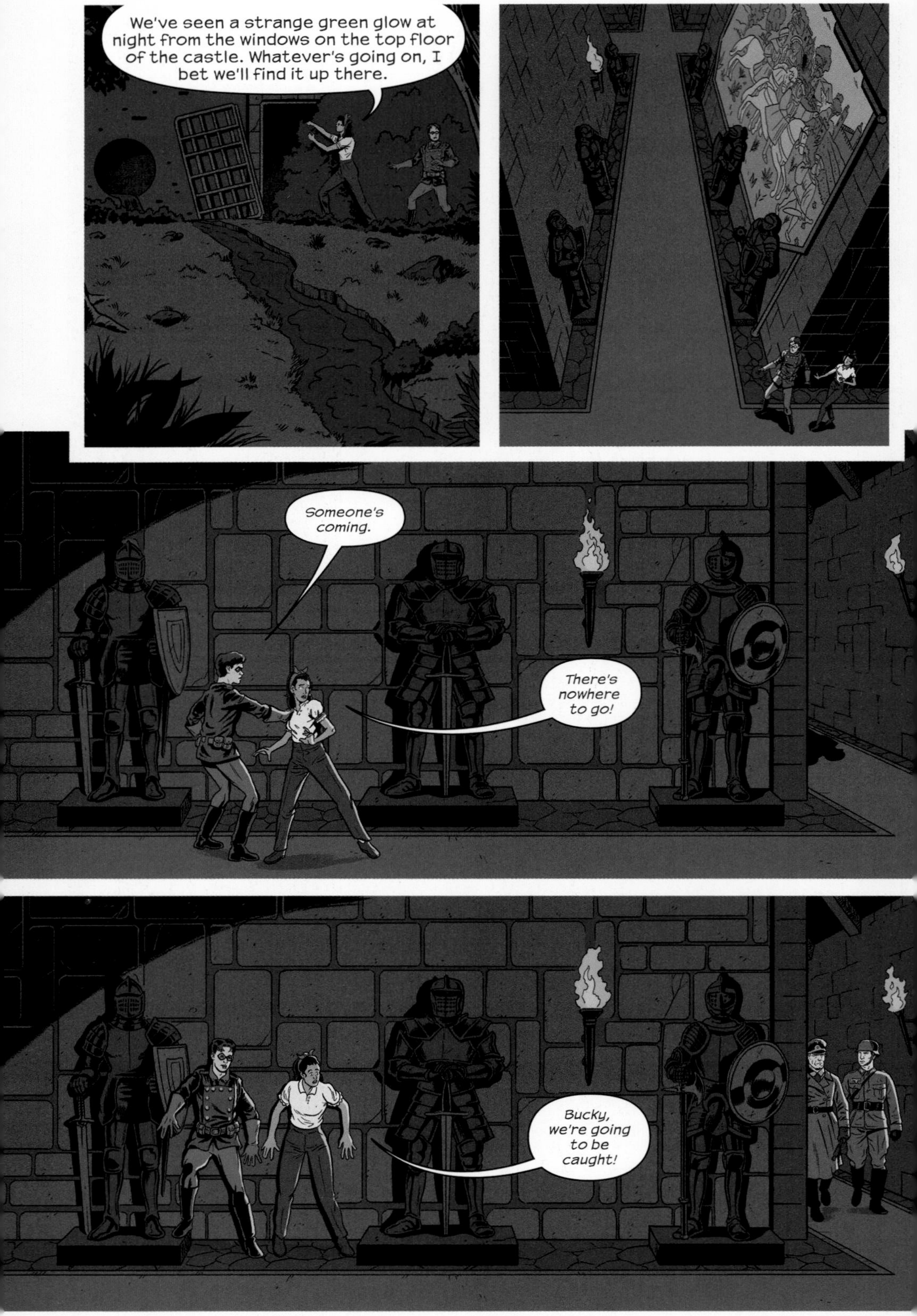
We've seen a strange green glow at night from the windows on the top floor of the castle. Whatever's going on, I bet we'll find it up there.
Someone's coming.
There's nowhere to go!
Bucky, we're going to be caught!

CHAPTER FOUR
BUCKY

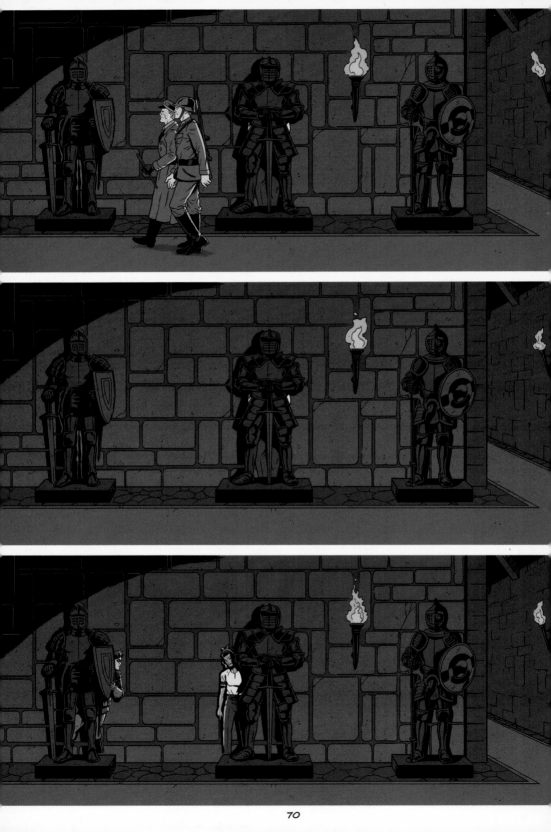

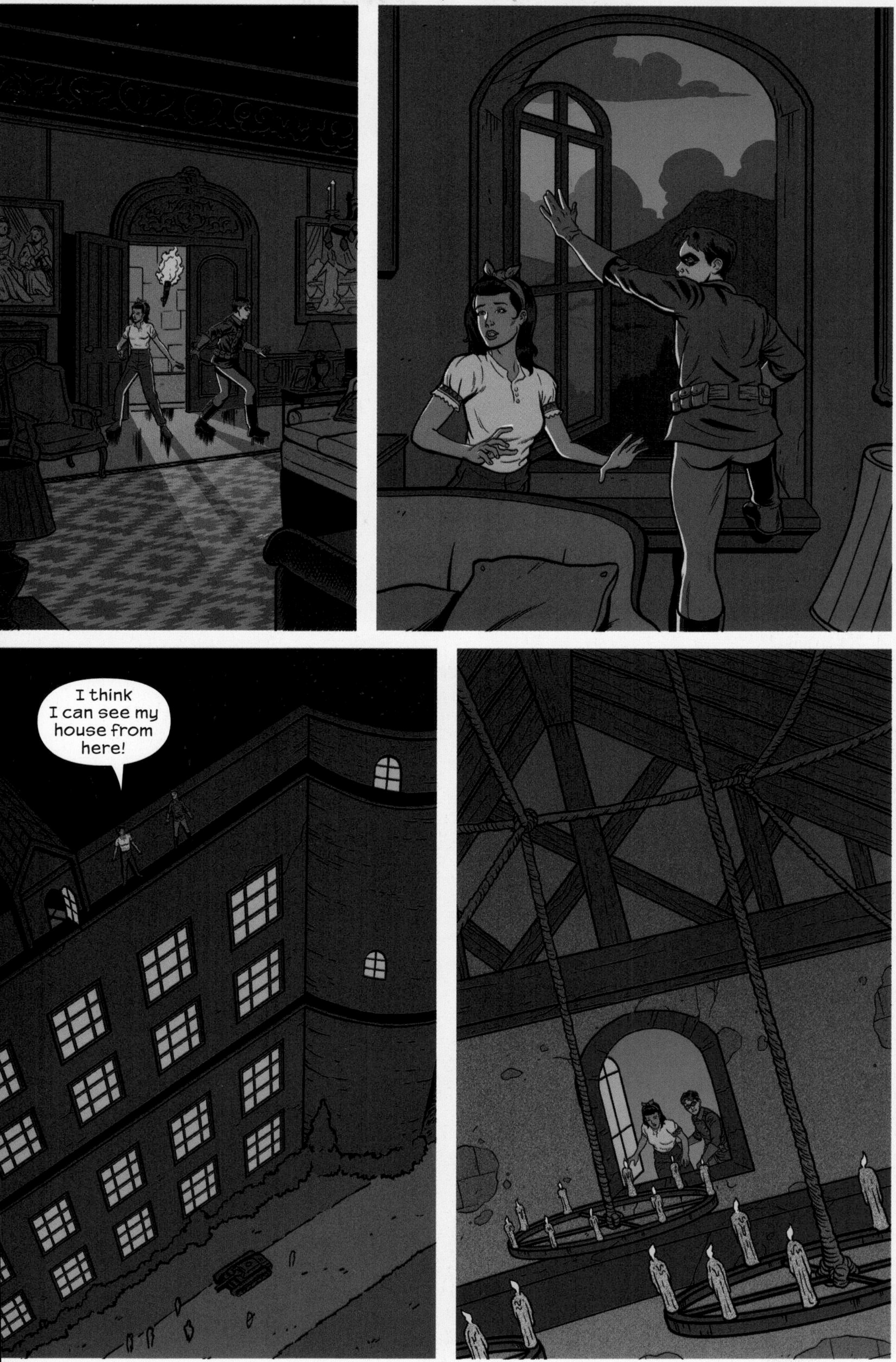
I think I can see my house from here!

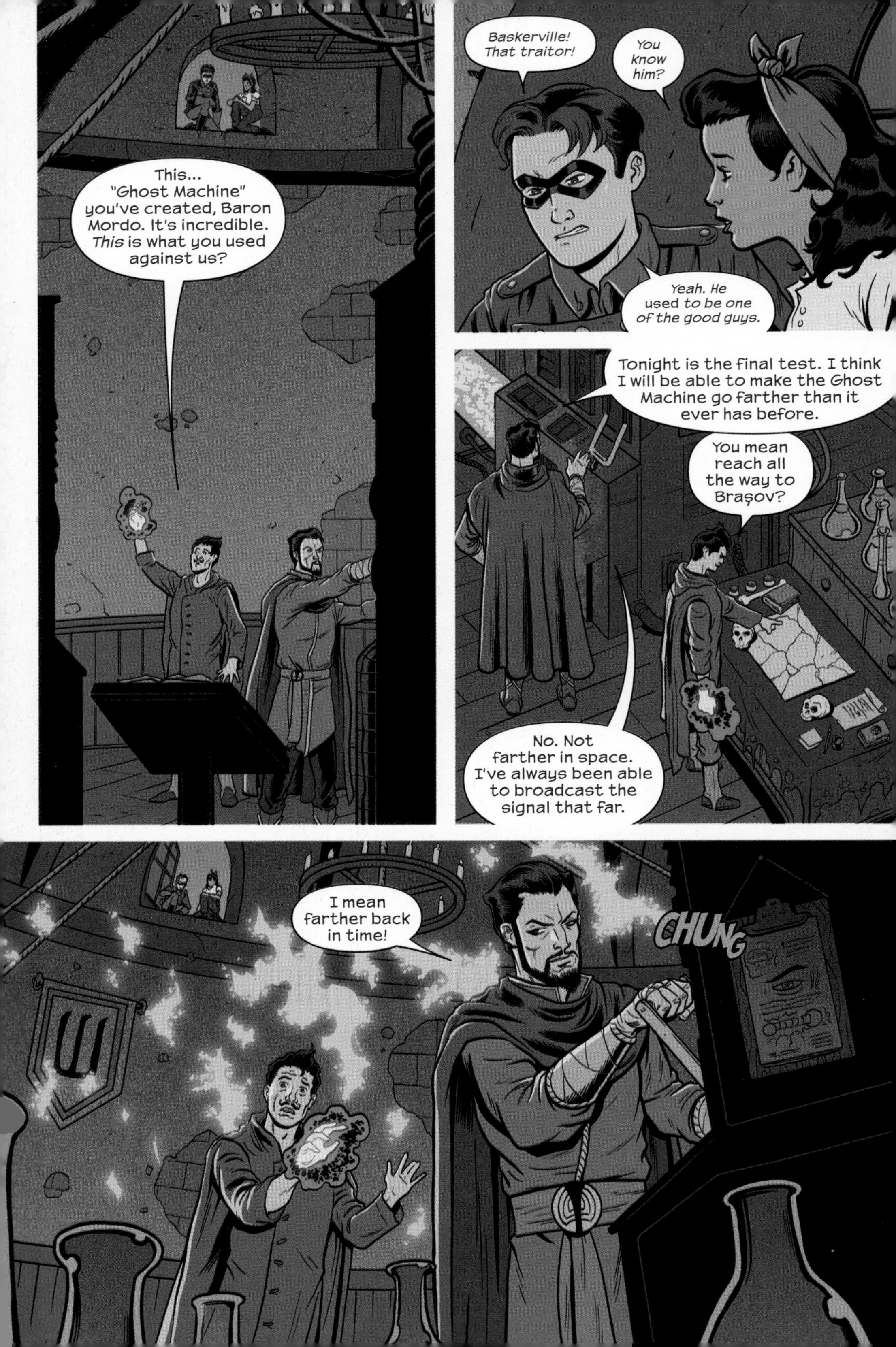
This... "Ghost Machine" you've created, Baron Mordo. It's incredible. *This* is what you used against us?
Baskerville! That traitor!
You know him?
Yeah. He used to be one of the good guys.
Tonight is the final test. I think I will be able to make the Ghost Machine go farther than it ever has before.
You mean reach all the way to Braşov?
No. Not farther in space. I've always been able to broadcast the signal that far.
I mean farther back in time!
CHUNG

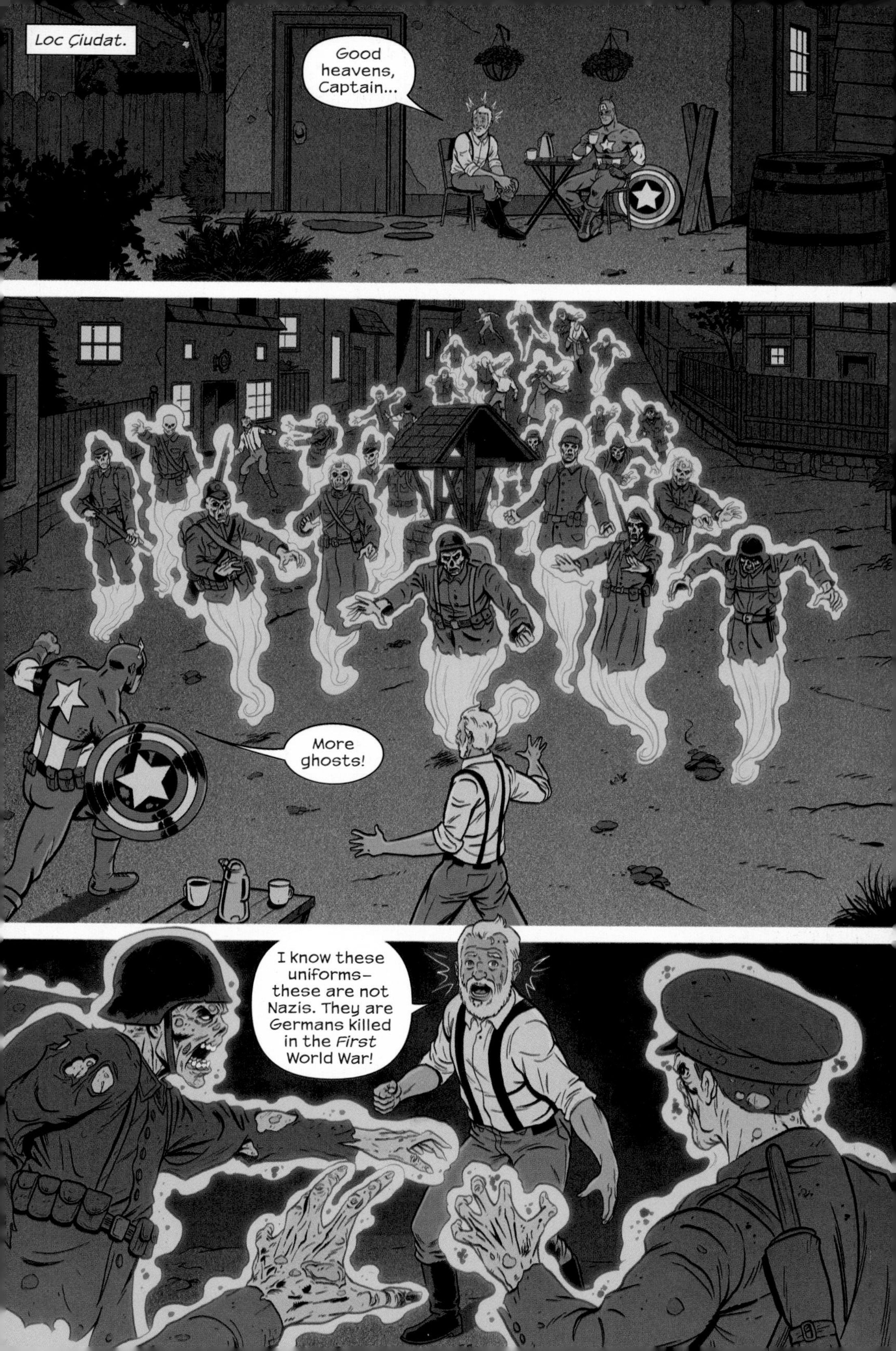
Loc Çiudat.
Good heavens, Captain...
More ghosts!
I know these uniforms– these are not Nazis. They are Germans killed in the *First* World War!

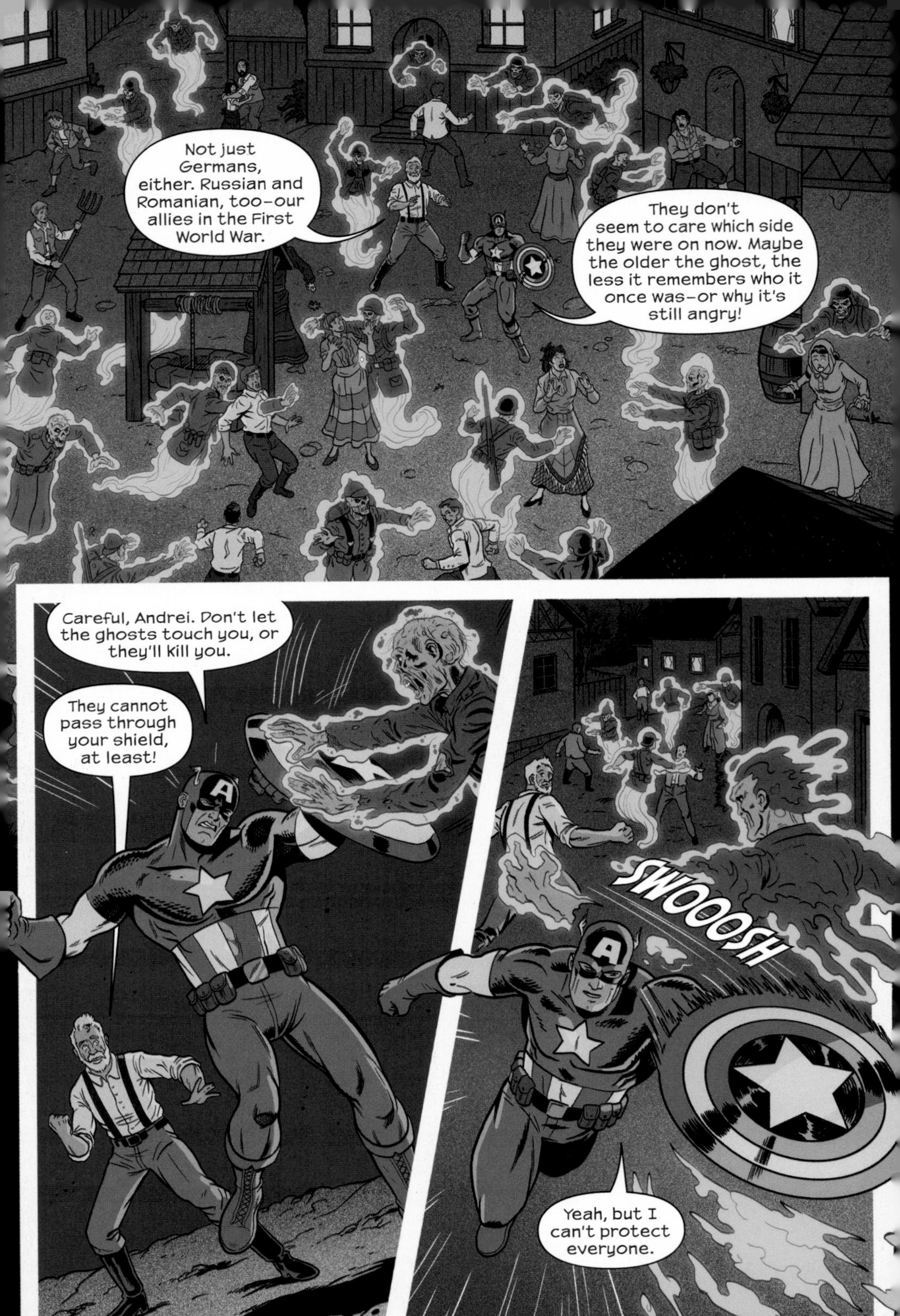
Not just Germans, either. Russian and Romanian, too—our allies in the First World War.
They don't seem to care which side they were on now. Maybe the older the ghost, the less it remembers who it once was—or why it's still angry!
Careful, Andrei. Don't let the ghosts touch you, or they'll kill you.
They cannot pass through your shield, at least!
SWOOOSH
Yeah, but I can't protect everyone.

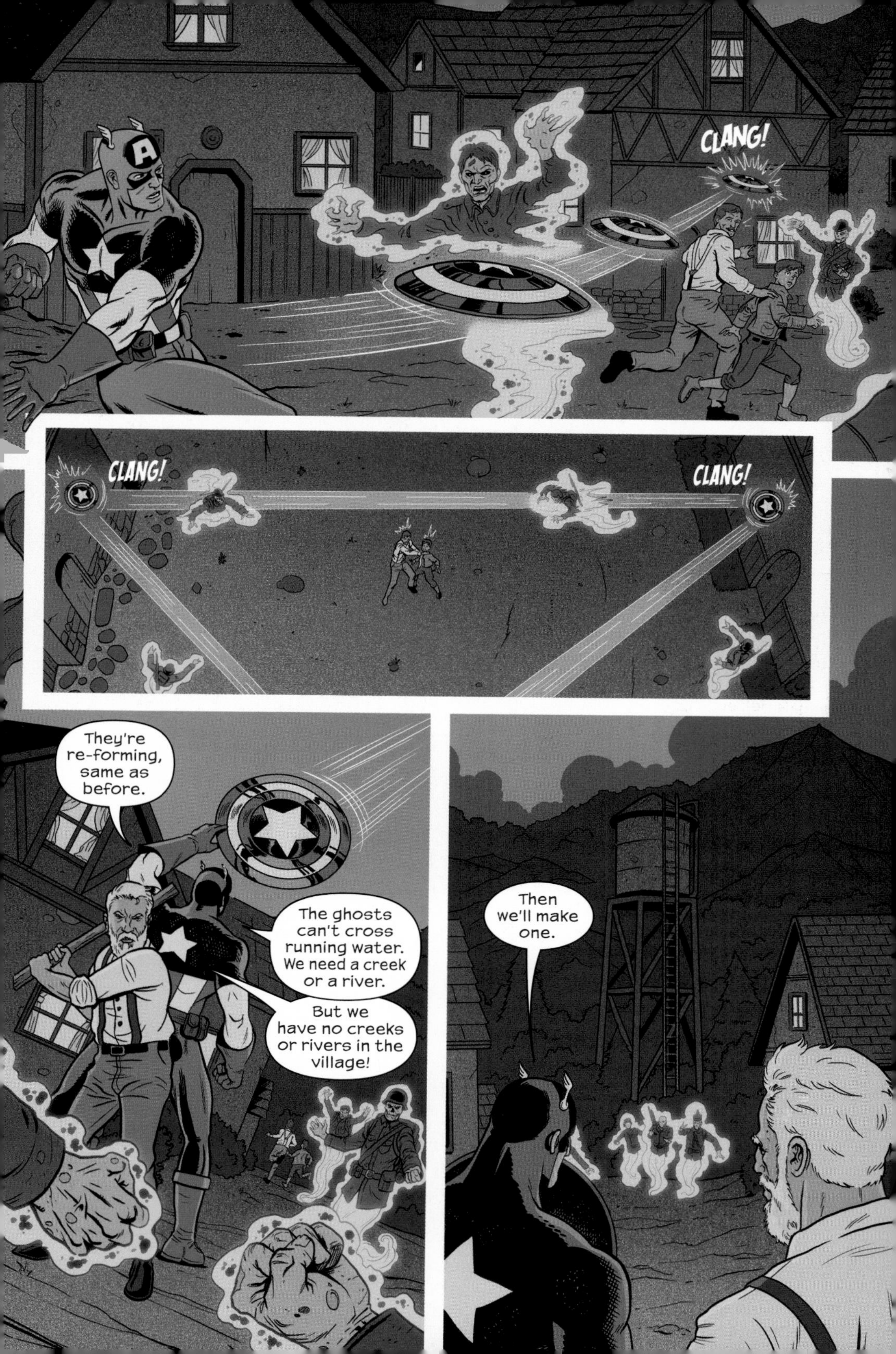
CLANG!
CLANG!
CLANG!
They're re-forming, same as before.
The ghosts can't cross running water. We need a creek or a river.
But we have no creeks or rivers in the village!
Then we'll make one.

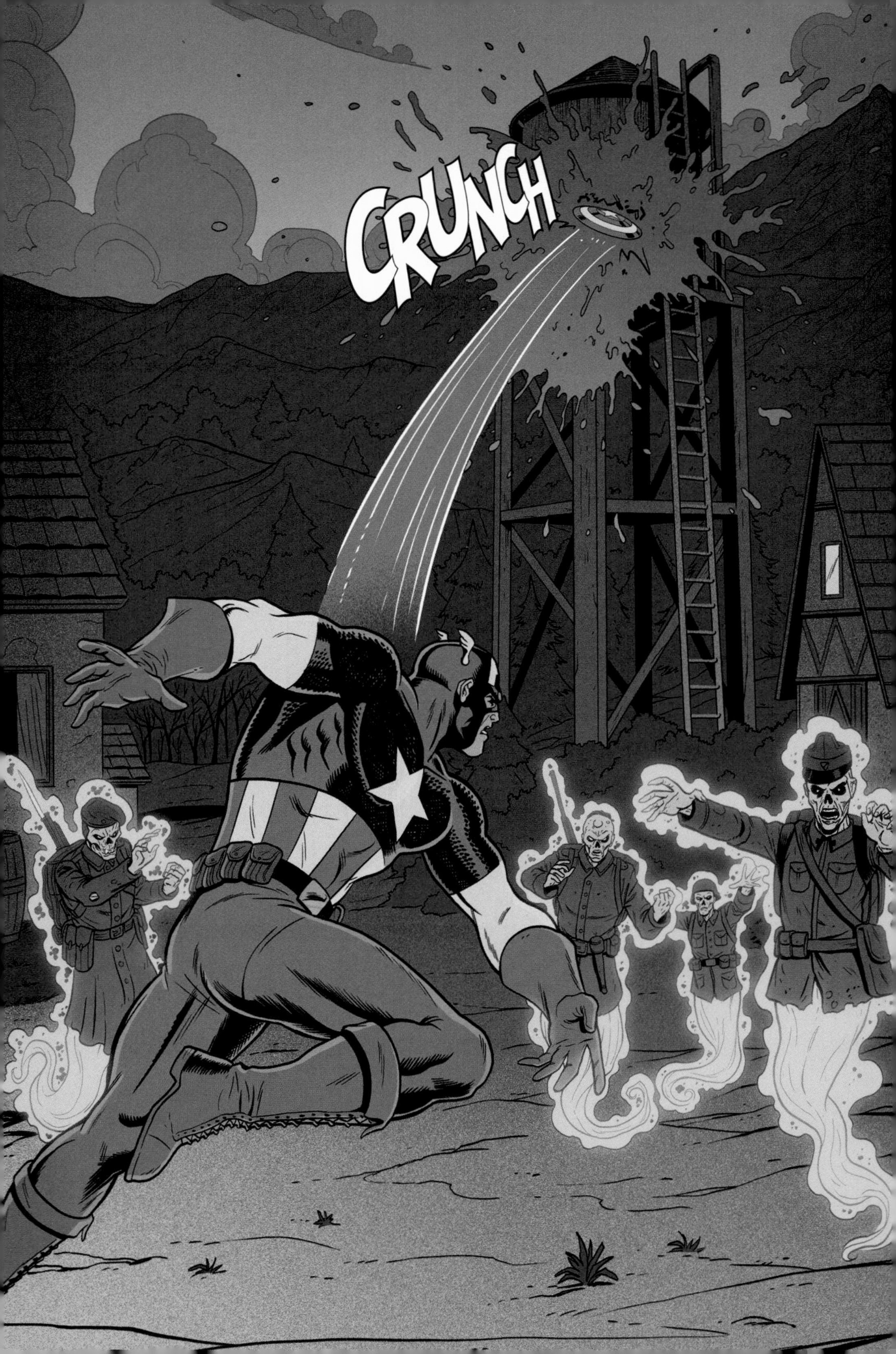
CRUNCH

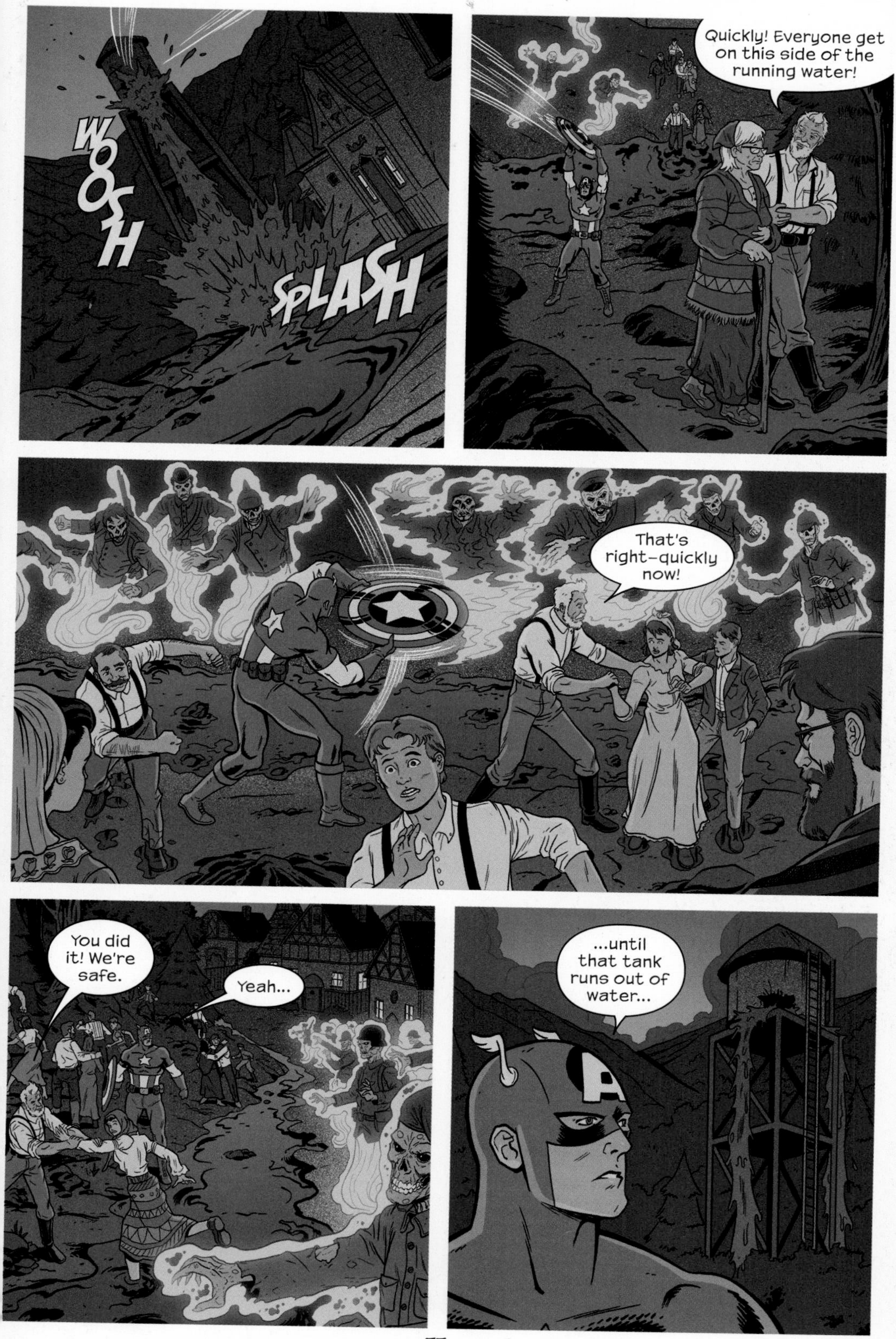
WOOSH
SPLASH
Quickly! Everyone get on this side of the running water!
That's right—quickly now!
You did it! We're safe.
Yeah...
...until that tank runs out of water...

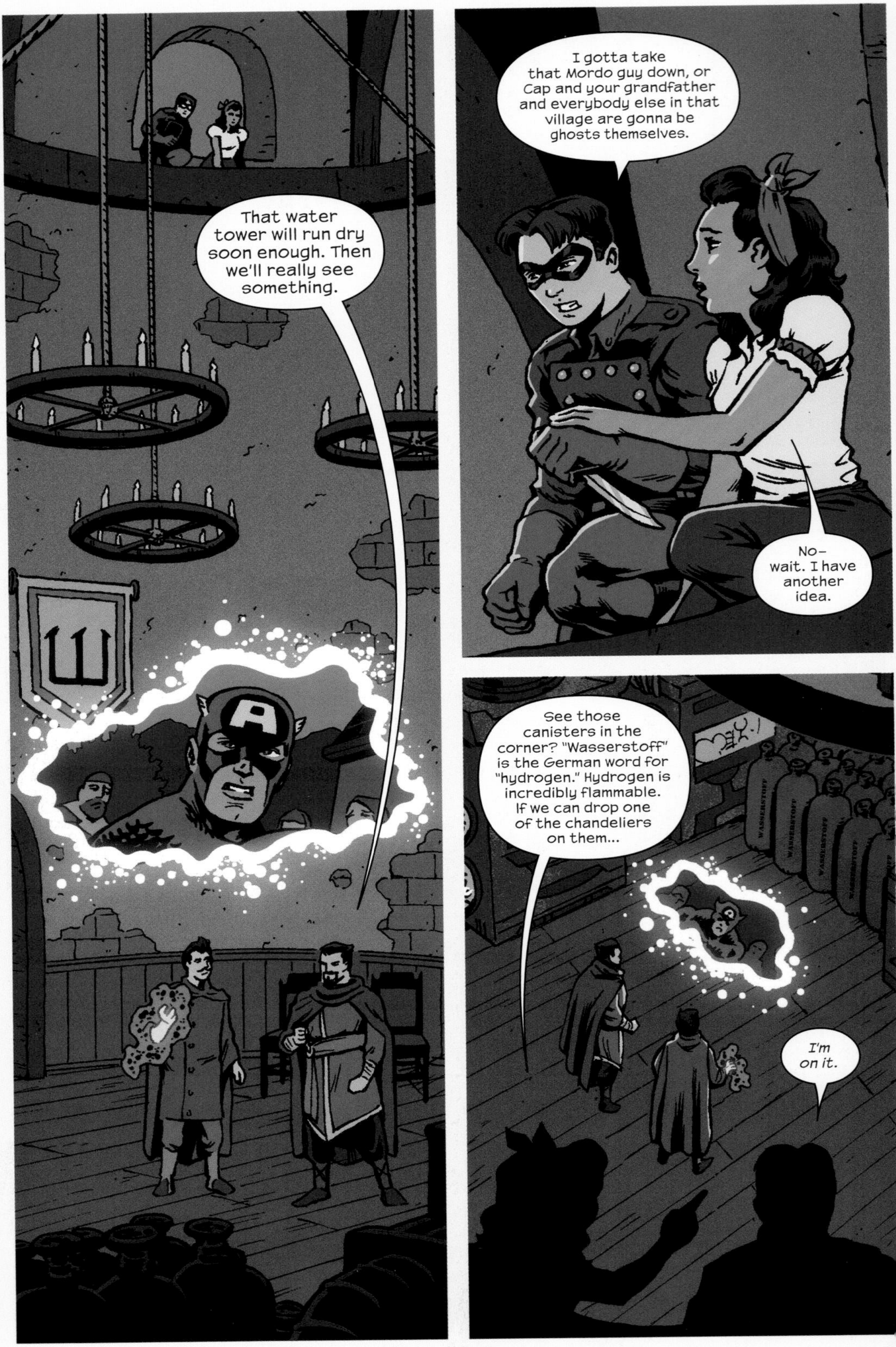
That water tower will run dry soon enough. Then we'll really see something.
I gotta take that Mordo guy down, or Cap and your grandfather and everybody else in that village are gonna be ghosts themselves.
No— wait. I have another idea.
See those canisters in the corner? "Wasserstoff" is the German word for "hydrogen." Hydrogen is incredibly flammable. If we can drop one of the chandeliers on them...
I'm on it.

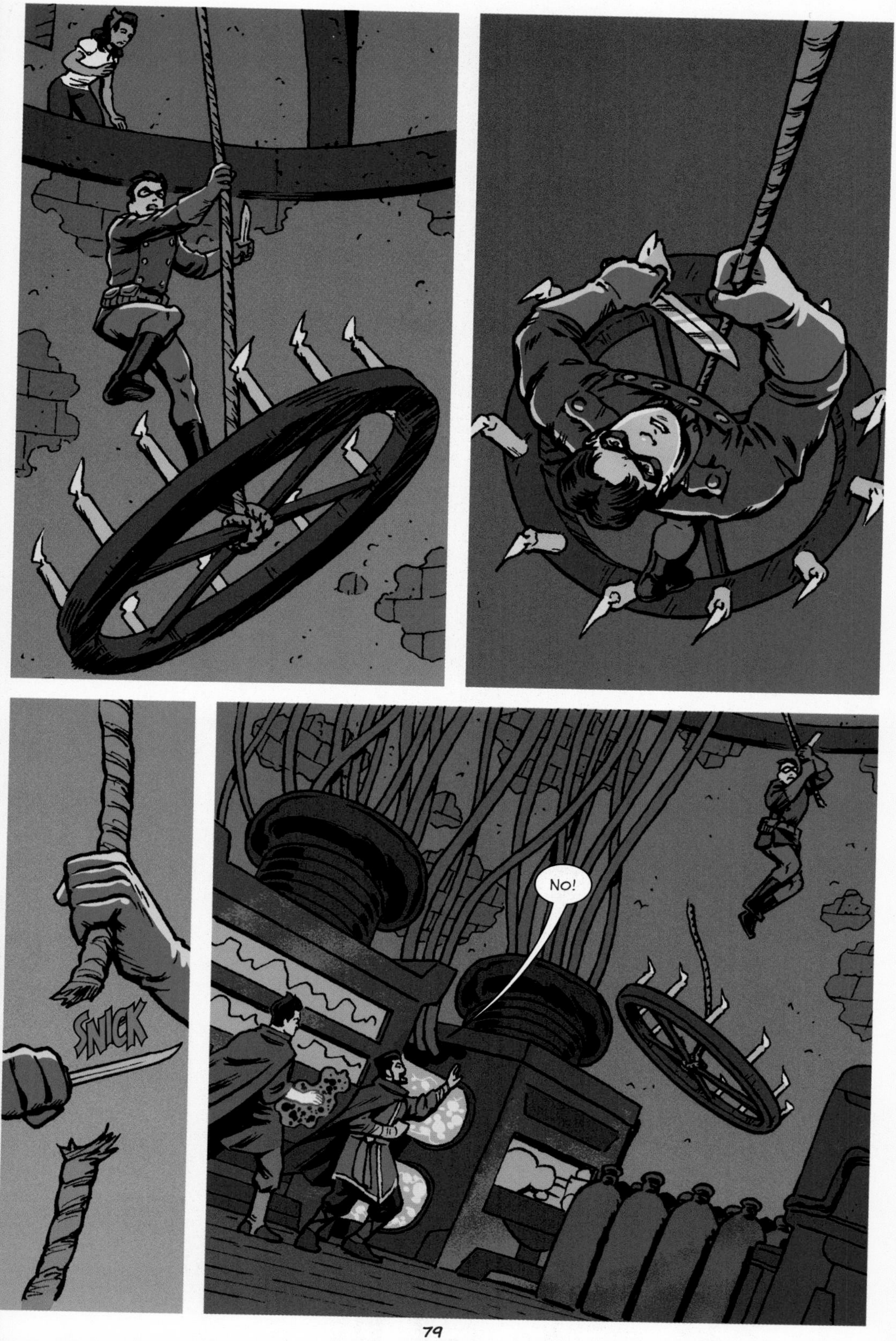
SNICK
NO!

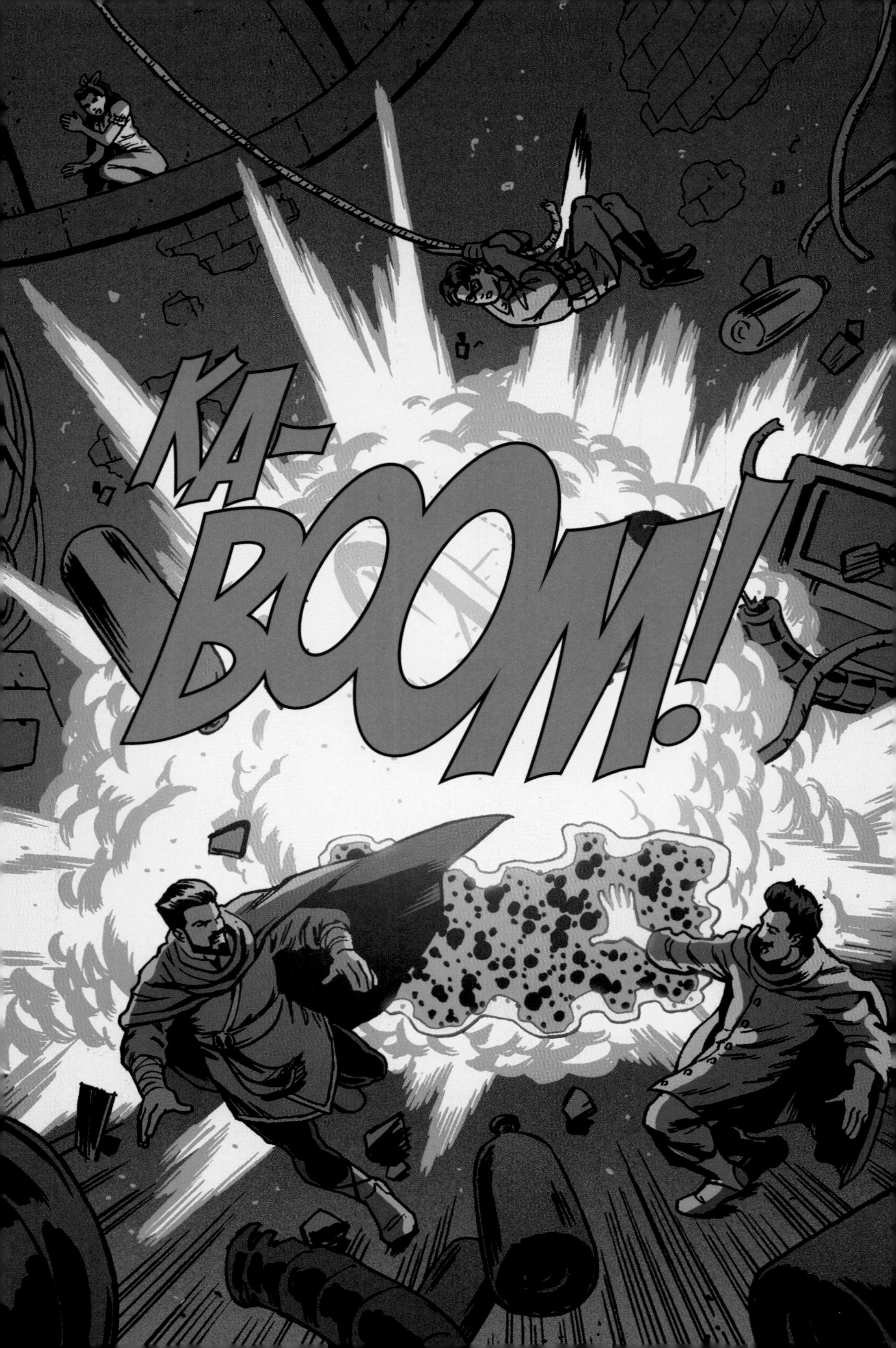
KA-BOOM!

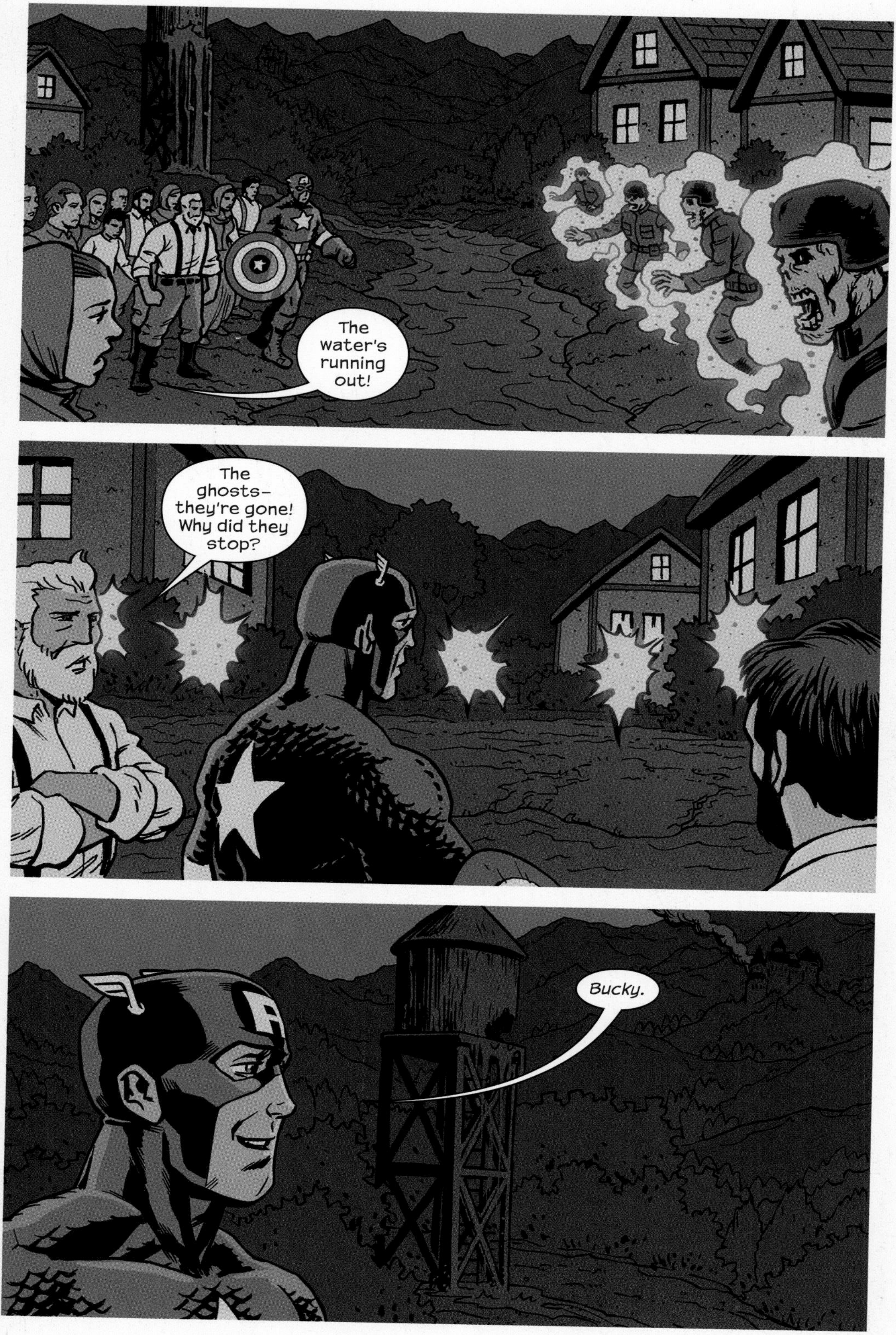
The water's running out!
The ghosts–they're gone! Why did they stop?
Bucky.

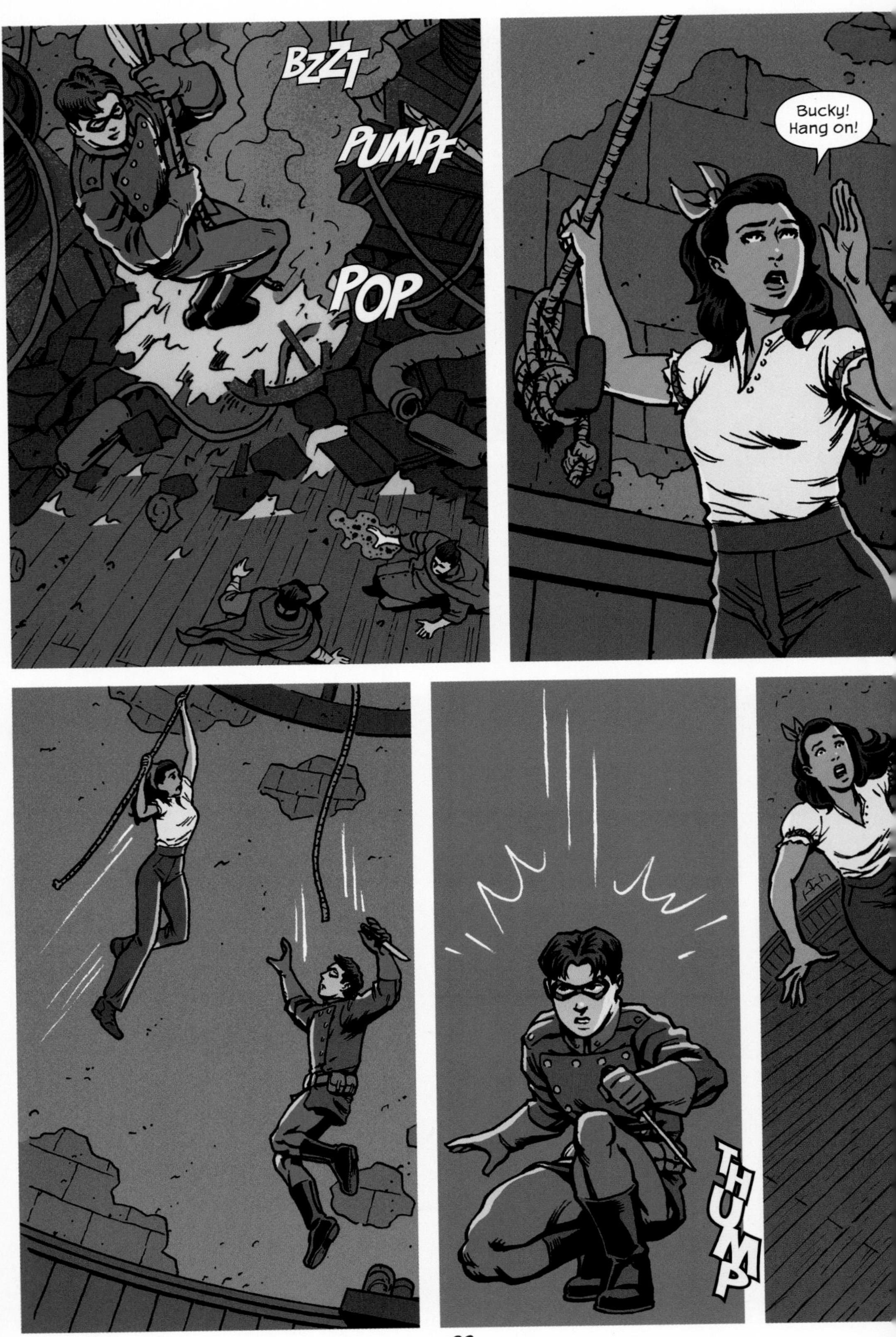
BZZT
PUMPF
POP
Bucky! Hang on!
THUMP

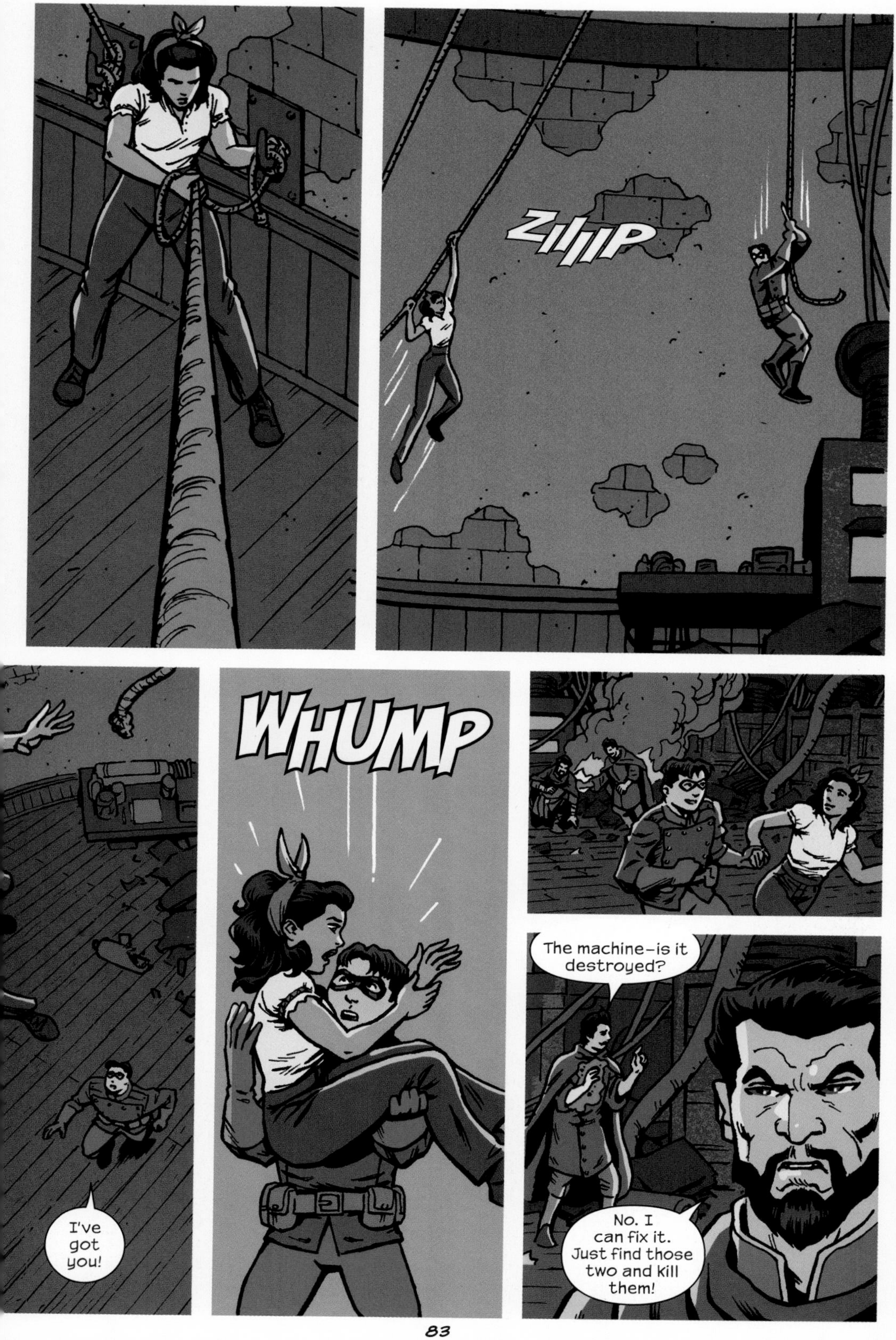
ZIIIIP
WHUMP
I've got you!
The machine—is it destroyed?
No. I can fix it. Just find those two and kill them!

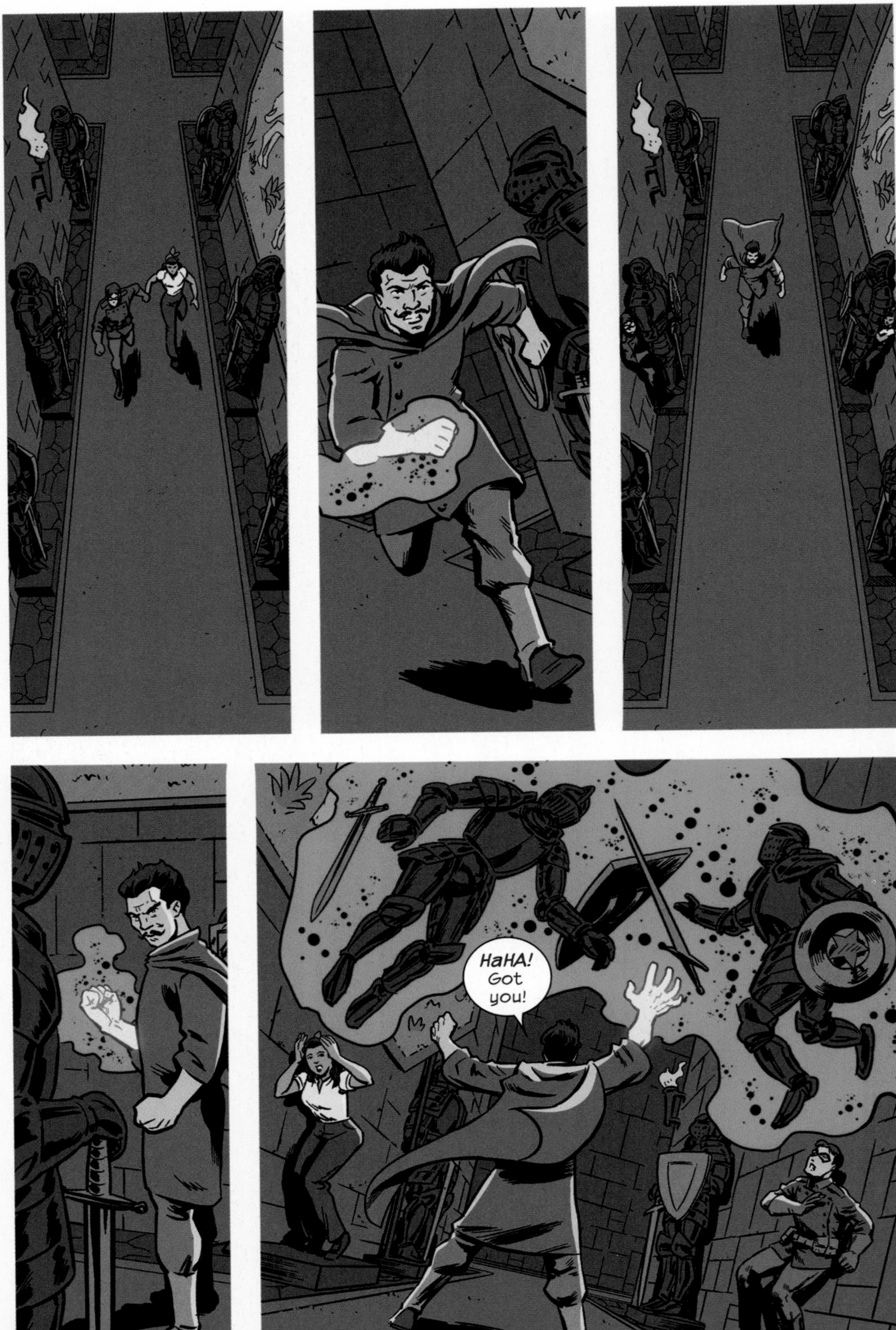
HaHA! Got you!

CHAPTER FIVE
POWER

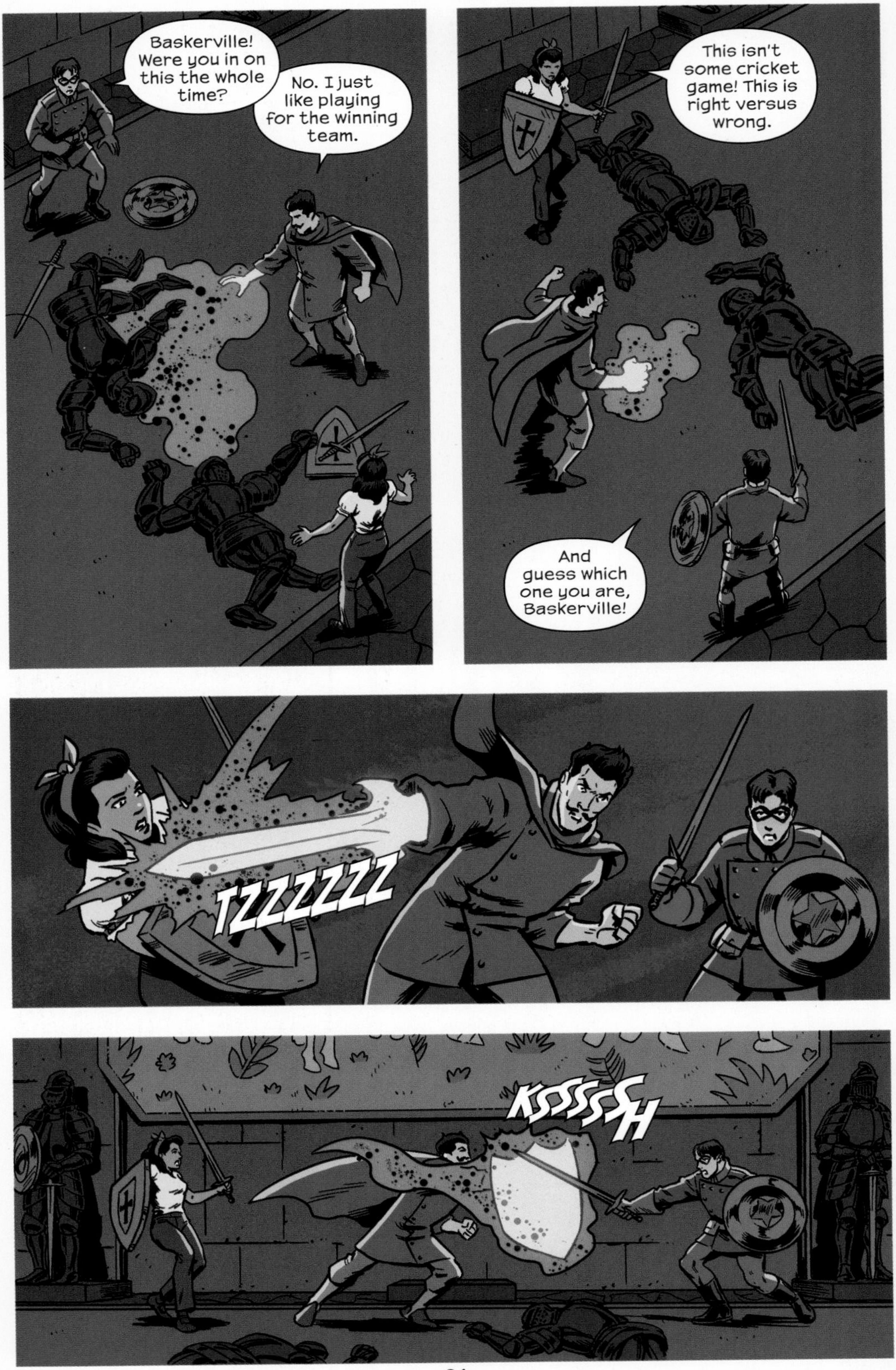
Baskerville! Were you in on this the whole time?
No. I just like playing for the winning team.
This isn't some cricket game! This is right versus wrong.
And guess which one you are, Baskerville!
TZZZZZZ
KSSSSH

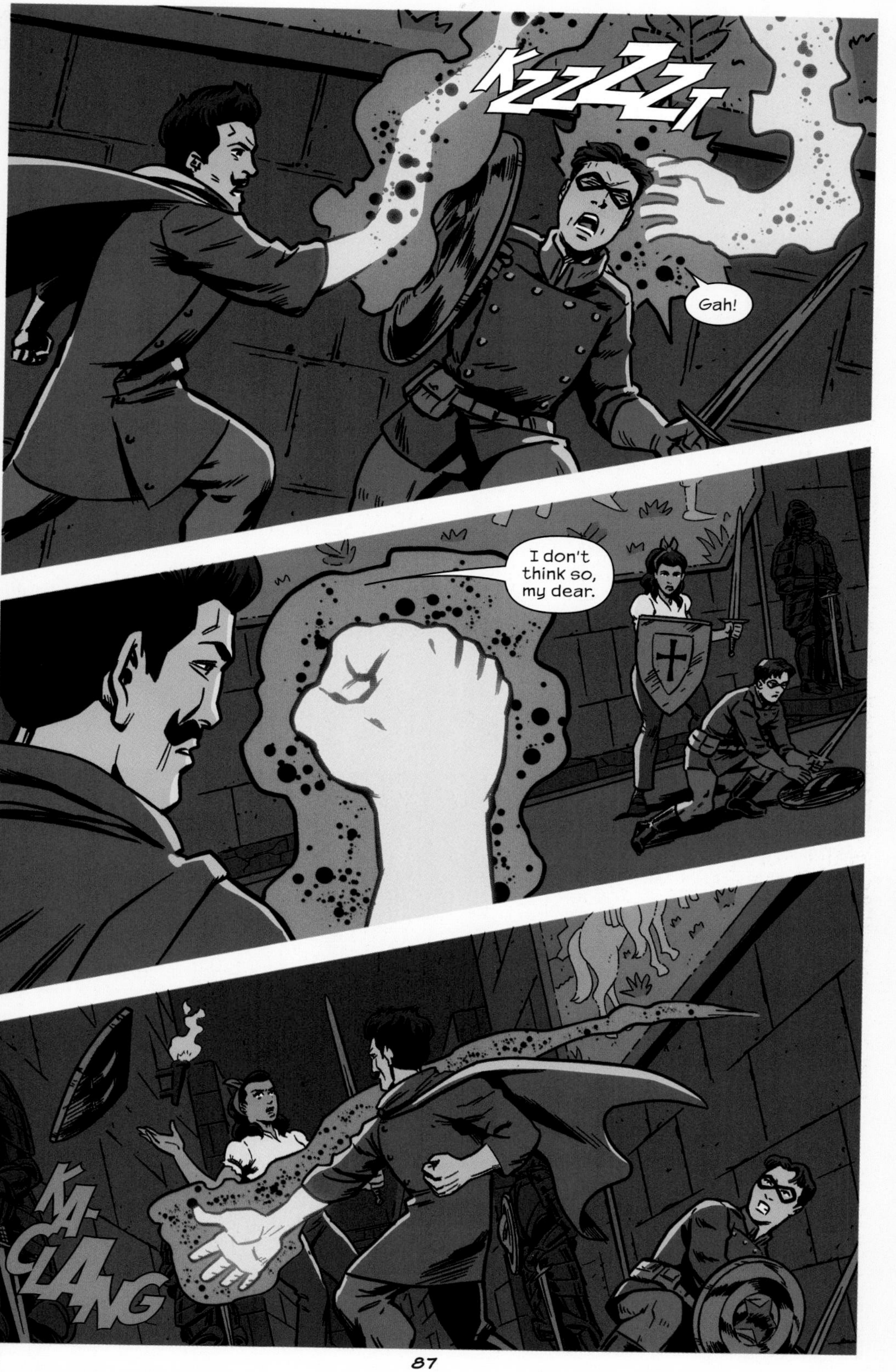
KZZZZT
Gah!
I don't think so, my dear.
KA-CLANG

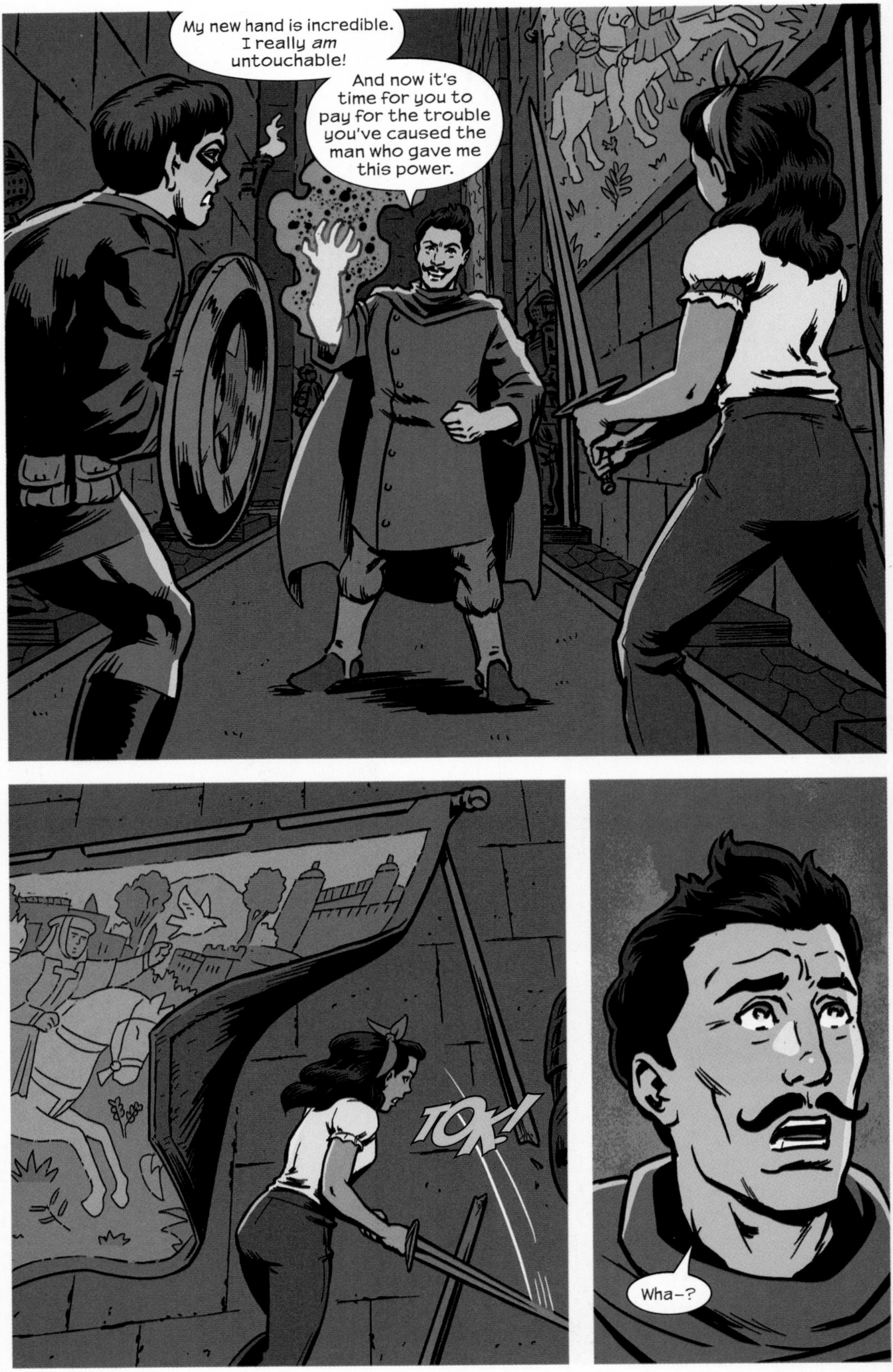
My new hand is incredible. I really *am* untouchable!
And now it's time for you to pay for the trouble you've caused the man who gave me this power.
TOK!
Wha-?

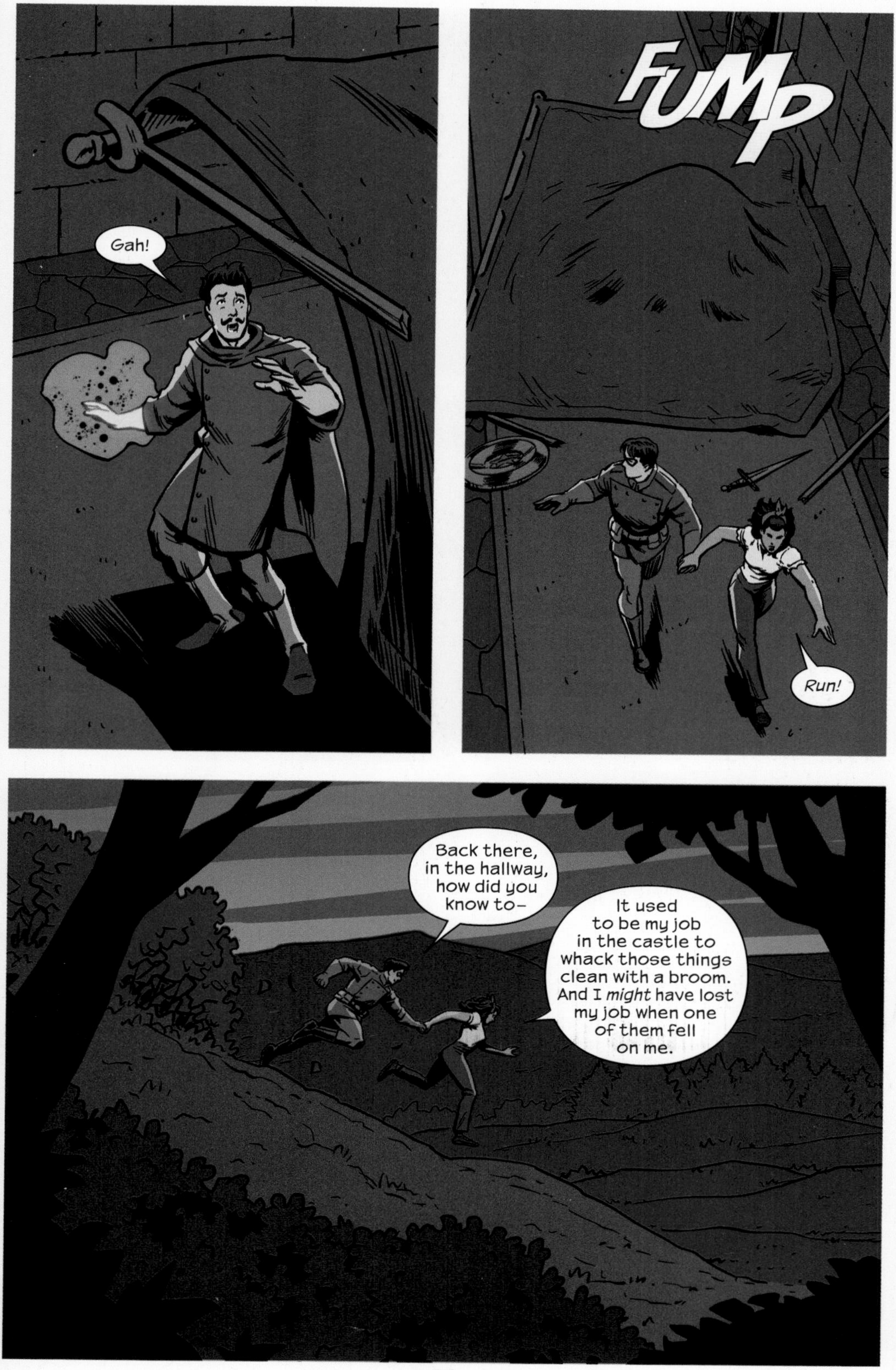
Gah!
FUMP
Run!
Back there, in the hallway, how did you know to–
It used to be my job in the castle to whack those things clean with a broom. And I *might* have lost my job when one of them fell on me.

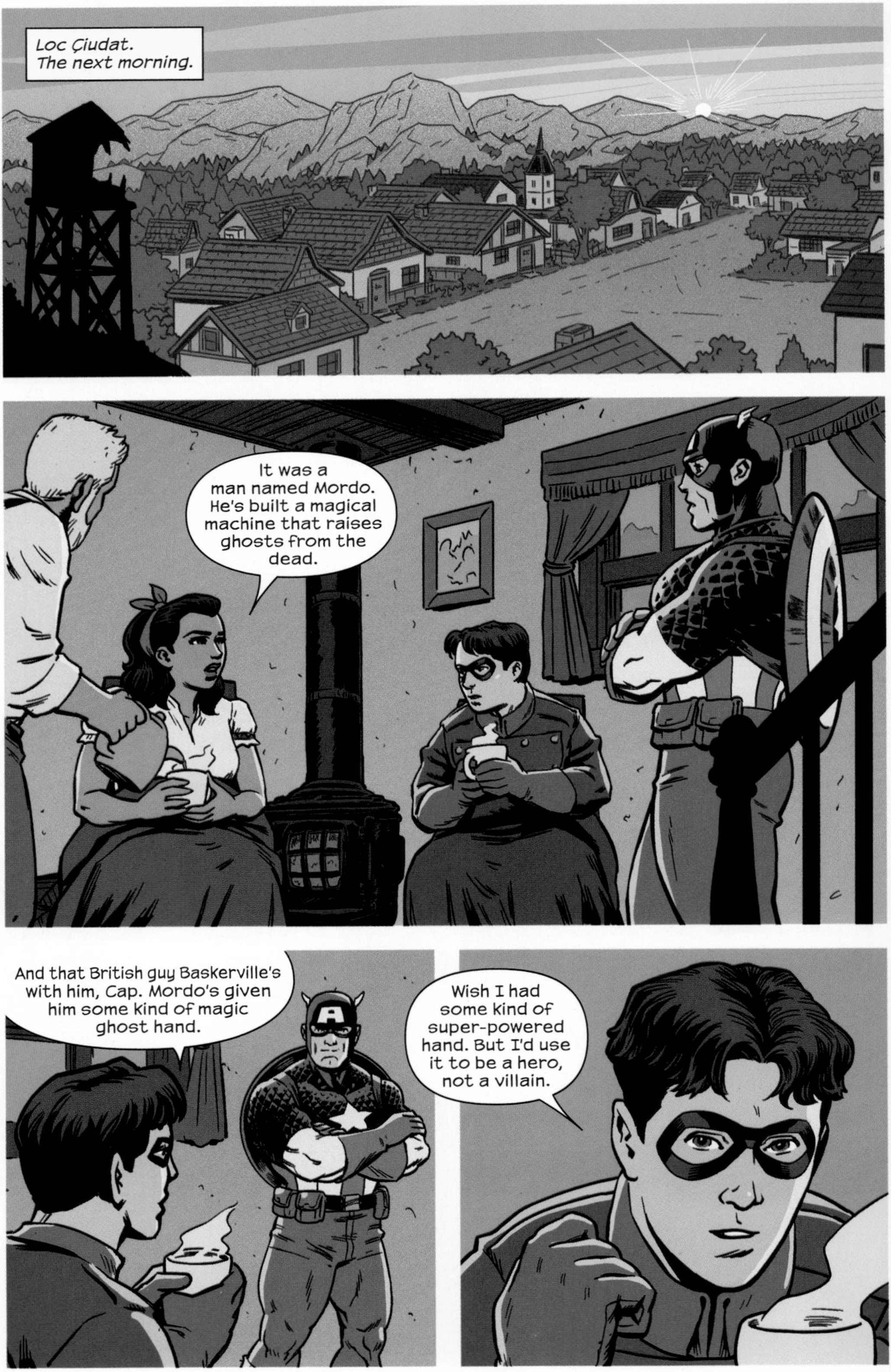
Loc Çiudat. The next morning.
It was a man named Mordo. He's built a magical machine that raises ghosts from the dead.
And that British guy Baskerville's with him, Cap. Mordo's given him some kind of magic ghost hand.
Wish I had some kind of super-powered hand. But I'd use it to be a hero, not a villain.

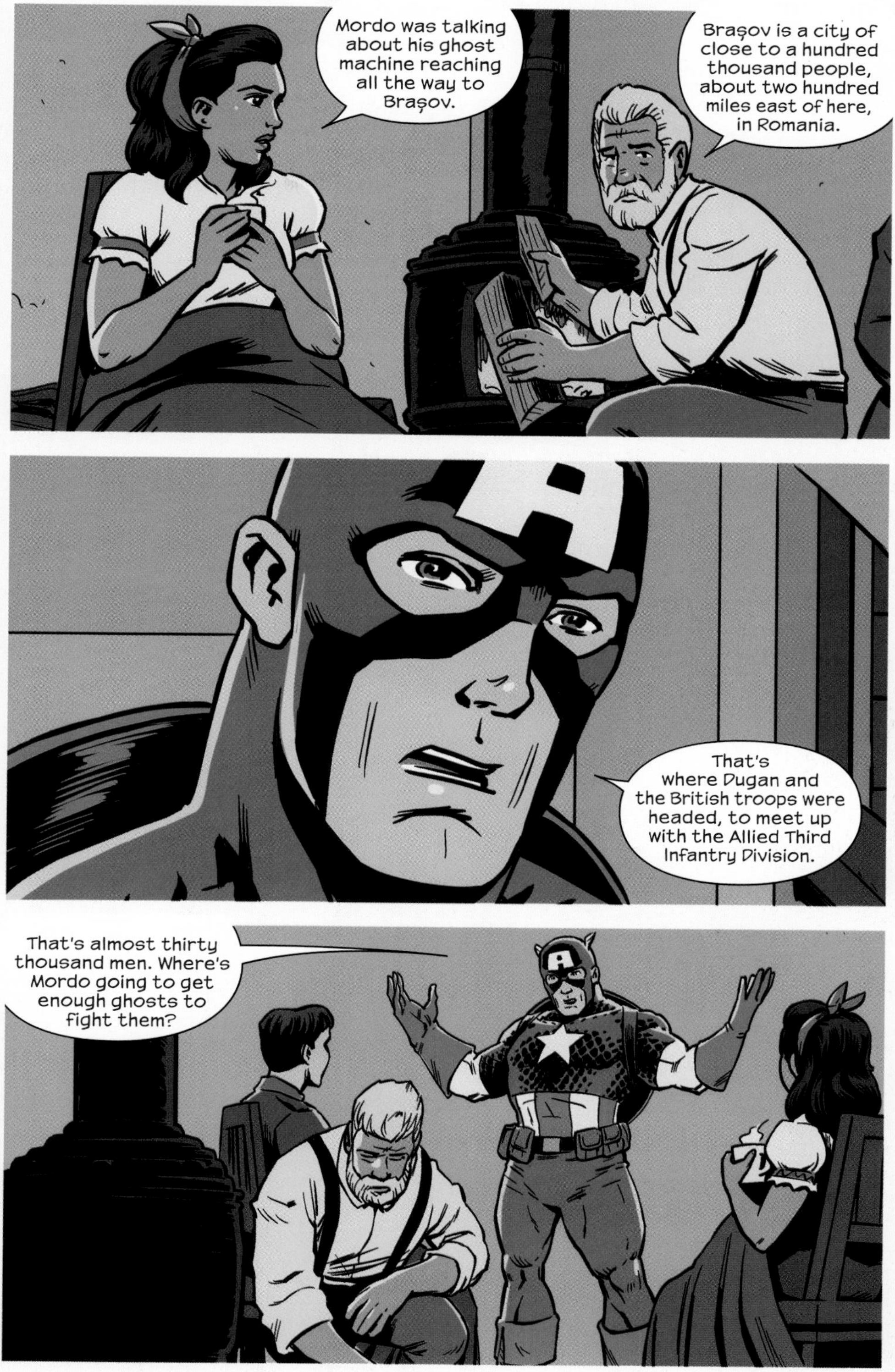
Mordo was talking about his ghost machine reaching all the way to Brașov.
Brașov is a city of close to a hundred thousand people, about two hundred miles east of here, in Romania.
That's where Dugan and the British troops were headed, to meet up with the Allied Third Infantry Division.
That's almost thirty thousand men. Where's Mordo going to get enough ghosts to fight them?

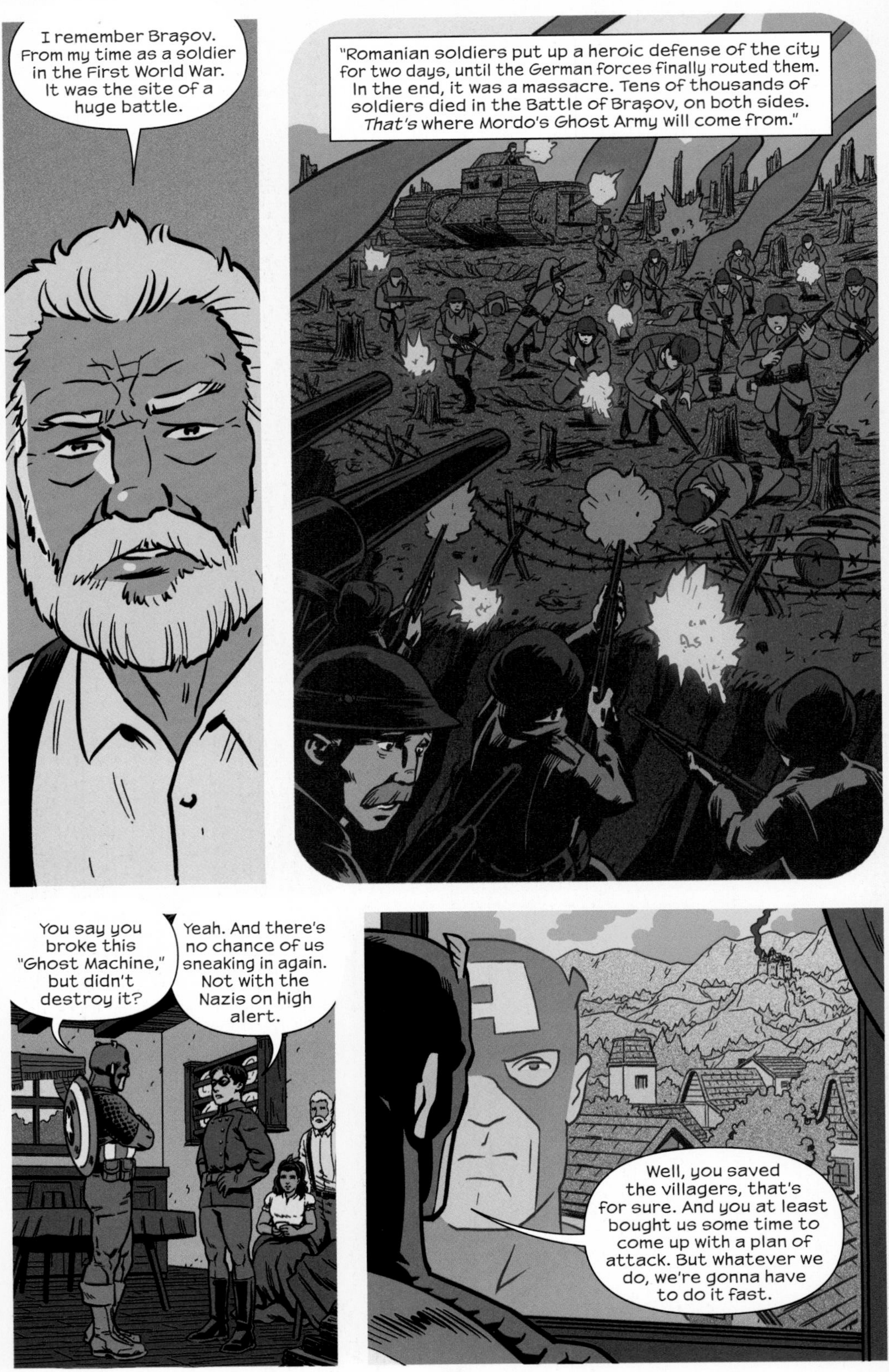
I remember Brașov. From my time as a soldier in the First World War. It was the site of a huge battle.
"Romanian soldiers put up a heroic defense of the city for two days, until the German forces finally routed them. In the end, it was a massacre. Tens of thousands of soldiers died in the Battle of Brașov, on both sides. *That's* where Mordo's Ghost Army will come from."
You say you broke this "Ghost Machine," but didn't destroy it?
Yeah. And there's no chance of us sneaking in again. Not with the Nazis on high alert.
Well, you saved the villagers, that's for sure. And you at least bought us some time to come up with a plan of attack. But whatever we do, we're gonna have to do it fast.

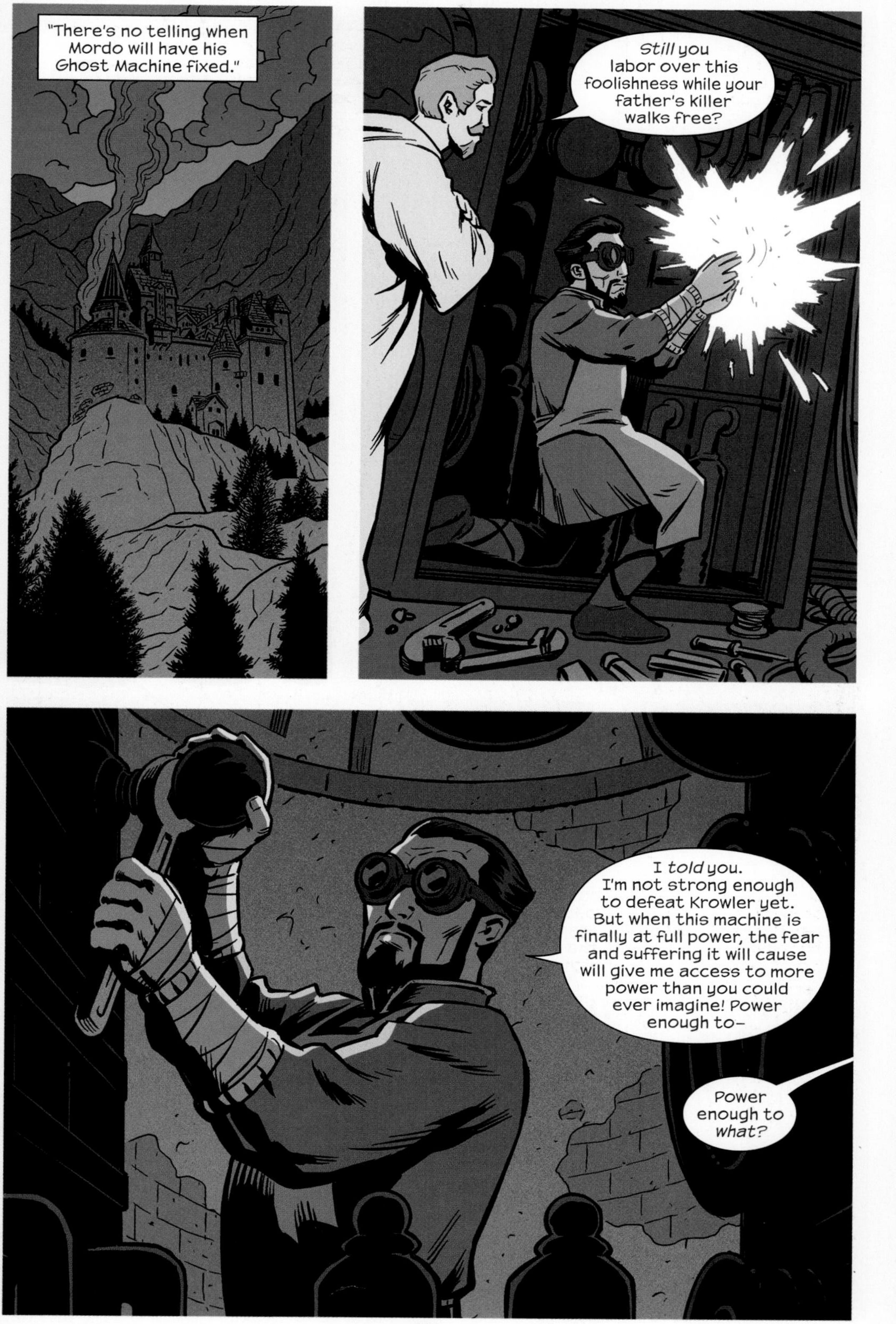
"There's no telling when Mordo will have his Ghost Machine fixed."
Still you labor over this foolishness while your father's killer walks free?
I *told* you. I'm not strong enough to defeat Krowler yet. But when this machine is finally at full power, the fear and suffering it will cause will give me access to more power than you could ever imagine! Power enough to–
Power enough to *what?*

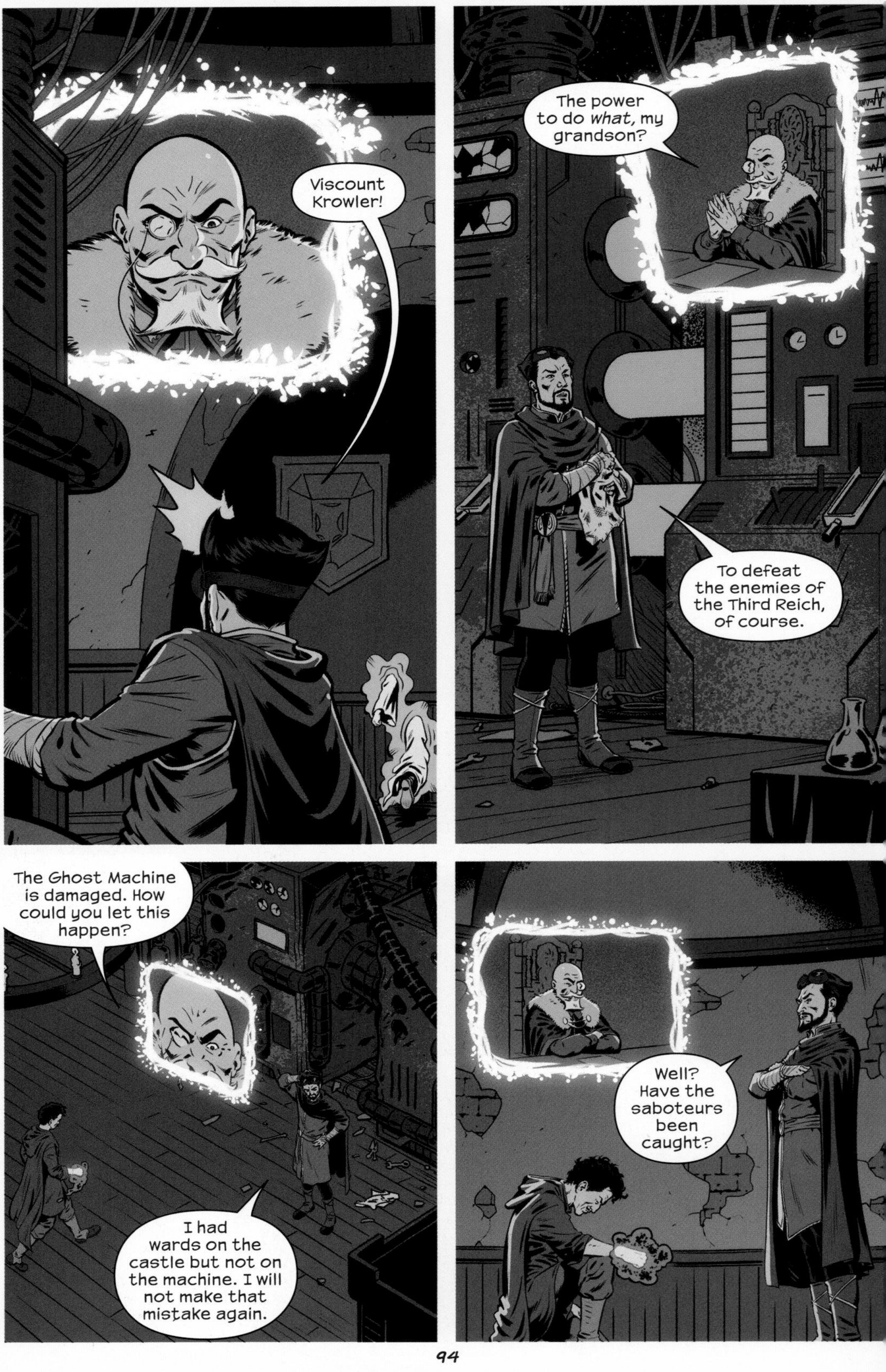
Viscount Krowler!
The power to do *what,* my grandson?
To defeat the enemies of the Third Reich, of course.
The Ghost Machine is damaged. How could you let this happen?
I had wards on the castle but not on the machine. I will not make that mistake again.
Well? Have the saboteurs been caught?

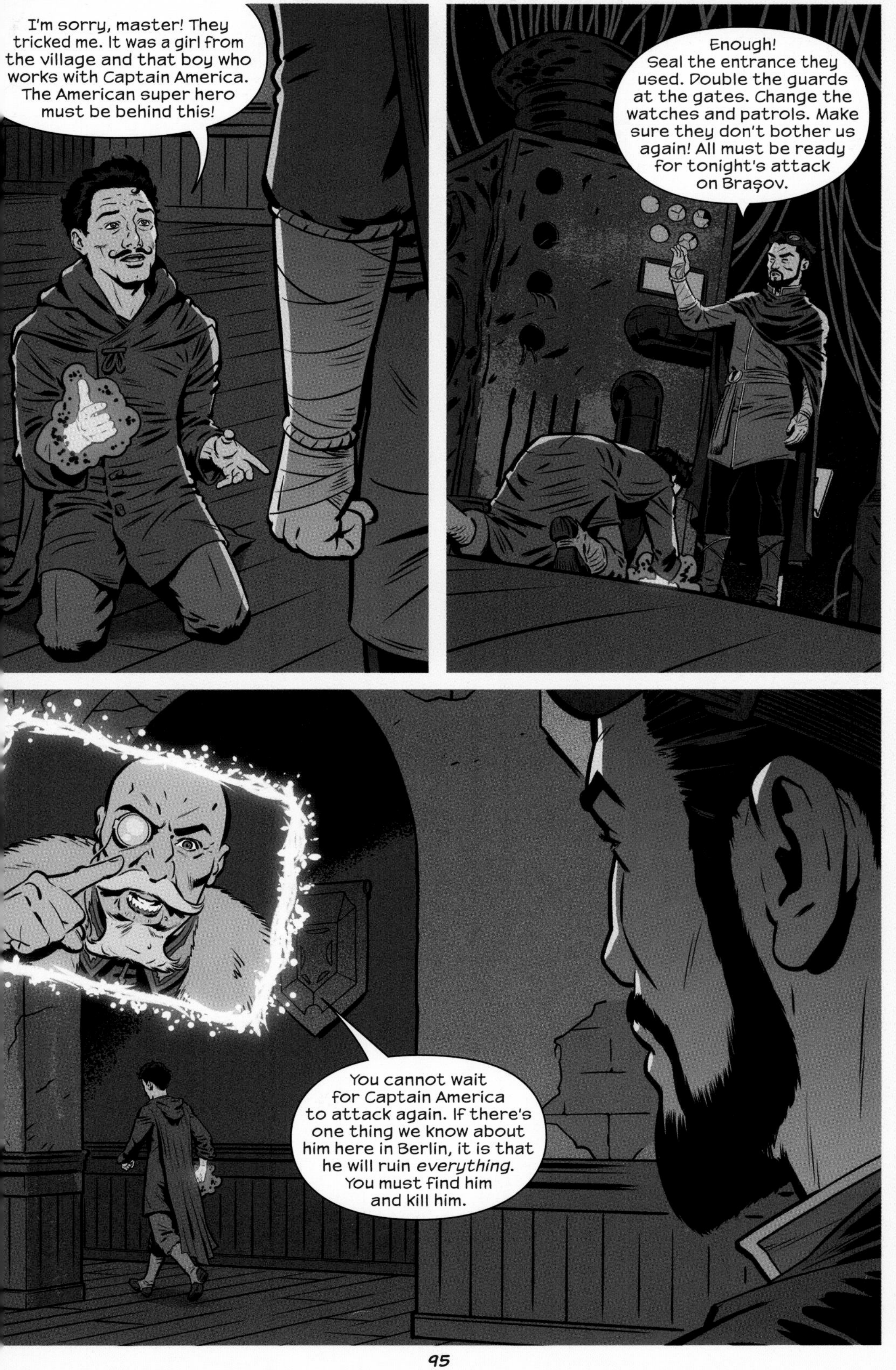
I'm sorry, master! They tricked me. It was a girl from the village and that boy who works with Captain America. The American super hero must be behind this!
Enough! Seal the entrance they used. Double the guards at the gates. Change the watches and patrols. Make sure they don't bother us again! All must be ready for tonight's attack on Brașov.
You cannot wait for Captain America to attack again. If there's one thing we know about him here in Berlin, it is that he will ruin *everything*. You must find him and kill him.

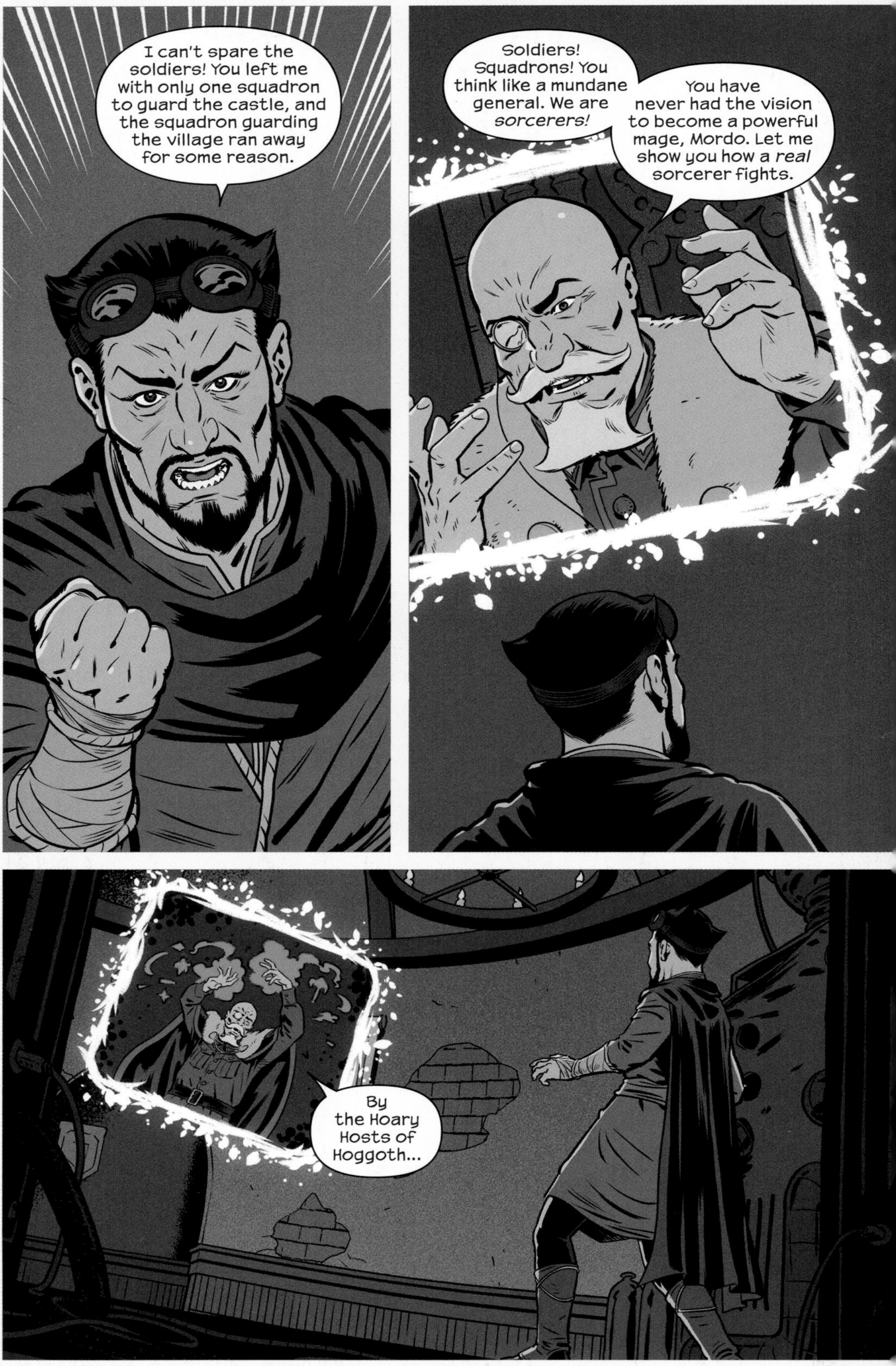
I can't spare the soldiers! You left me with only one squadron to guard the castle, and the squadron guarding the village ran away for some reason.
Soldiers! Squadrons! You think like a mundane general. We are *sorcerers!*
You have never had the vision to become a powerful mage, Mordo. Let me show you how a *real* sorcerer fights.
By the Hoary Hosts of Hoggoth...

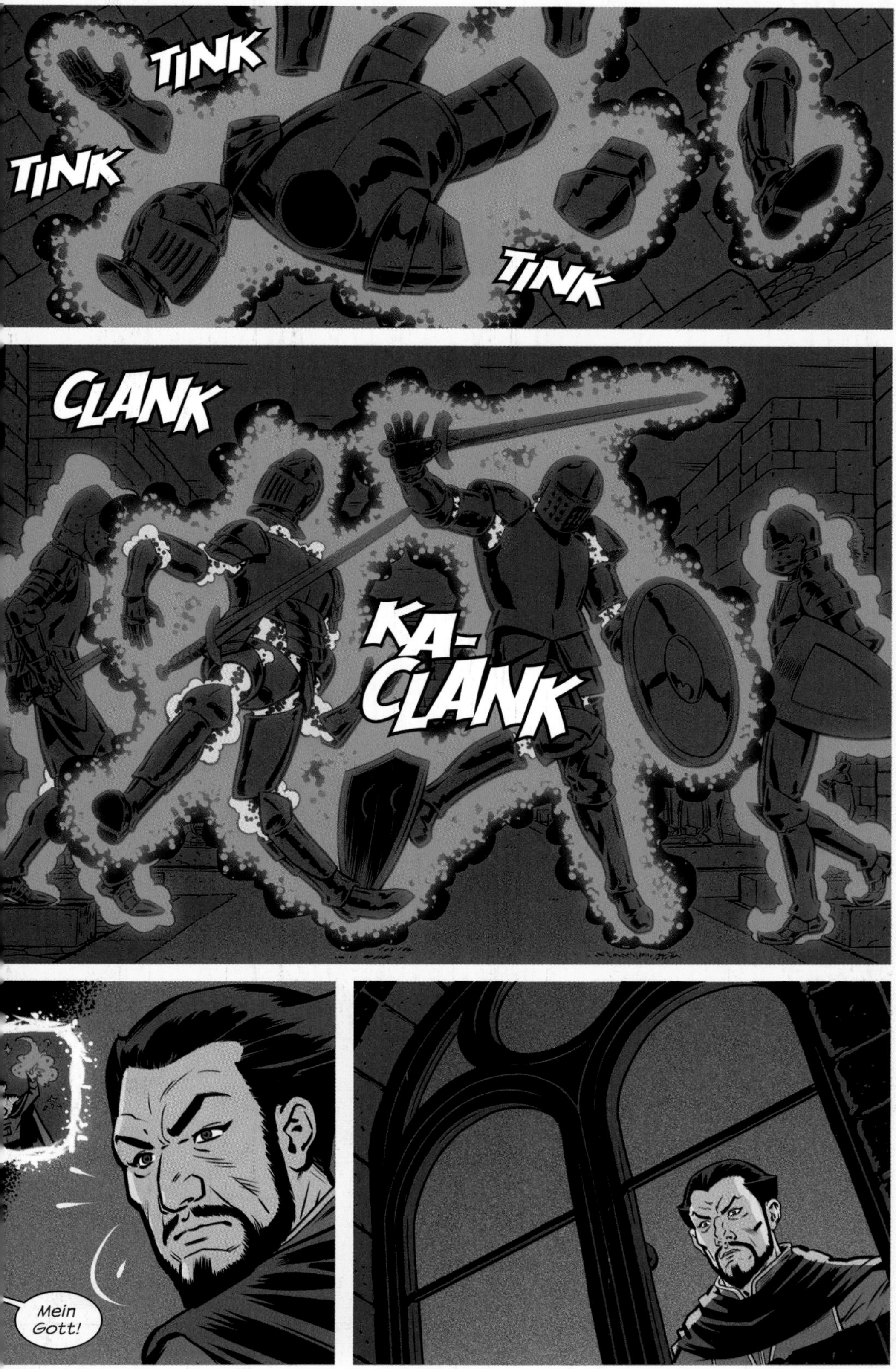
TINK
TINK
TINK
CLANK
KA-CLANK
Mein Gott!

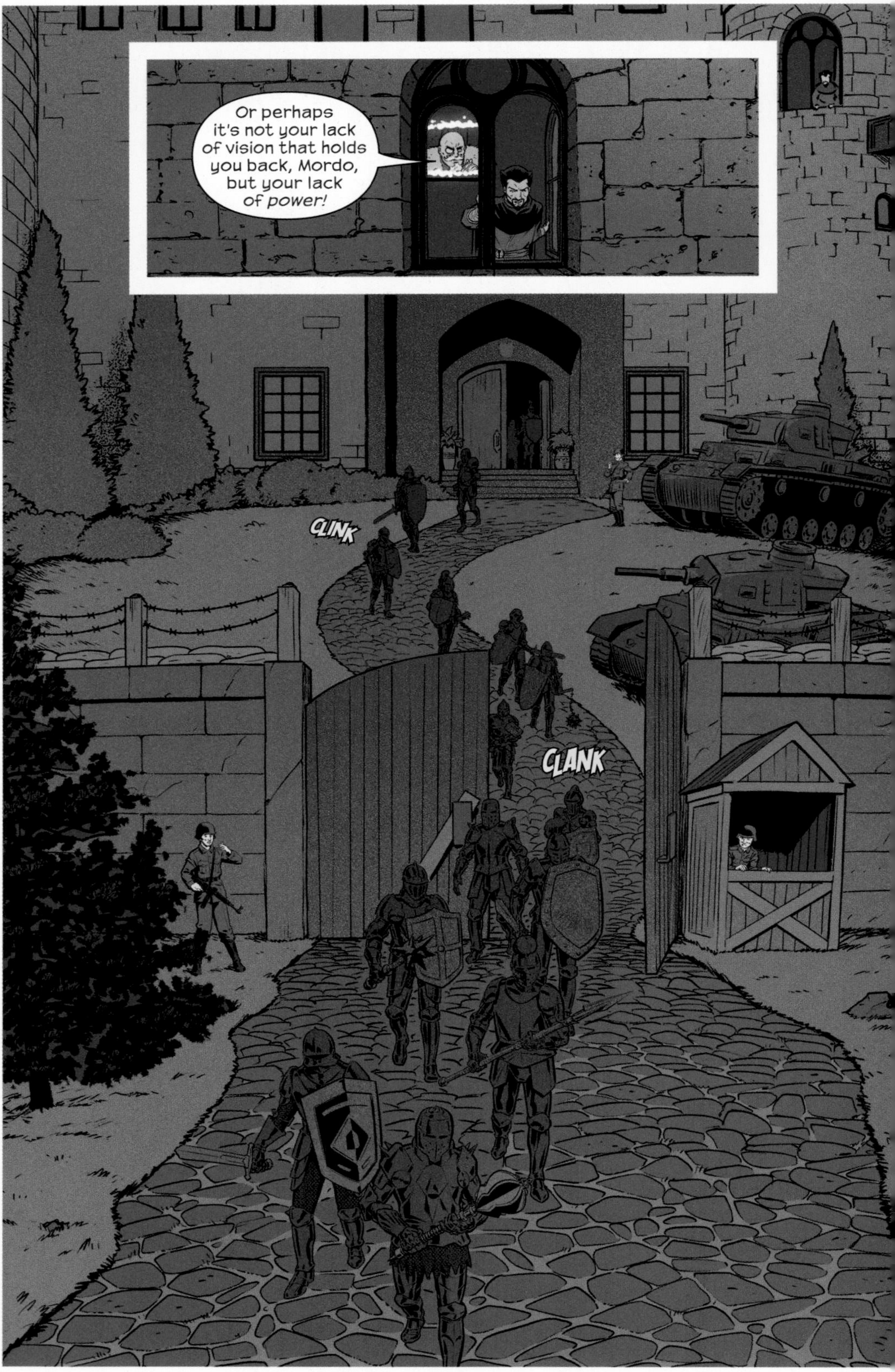
Or perhaps it's not your lack of vision that holds you back, Mordo, but your lack of *power*!
CLINK
CLANK

CHAPTER SIX
CLASH

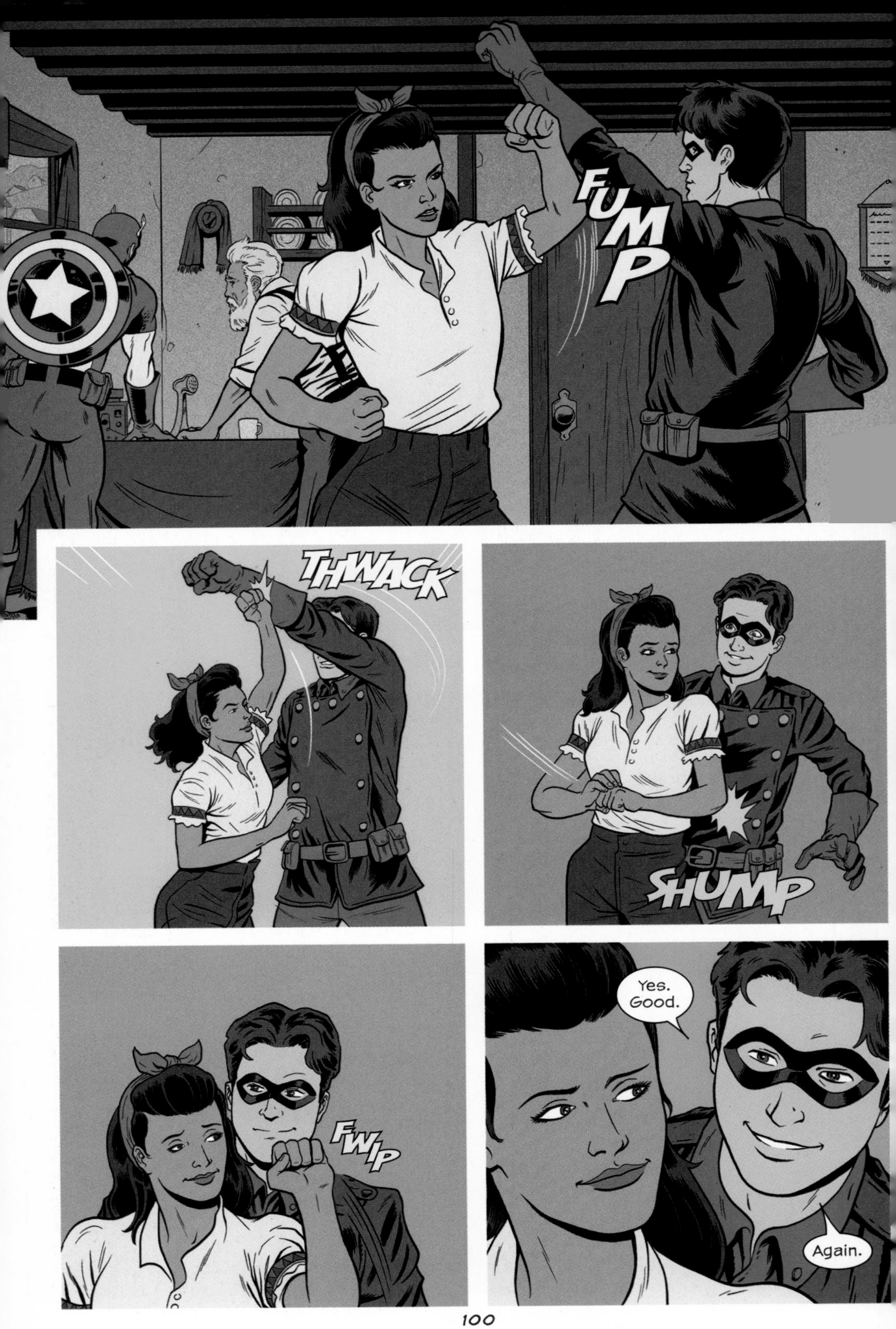
FUMP
THWACK
SHUMP
FWIP
Yes. Good.
Again.

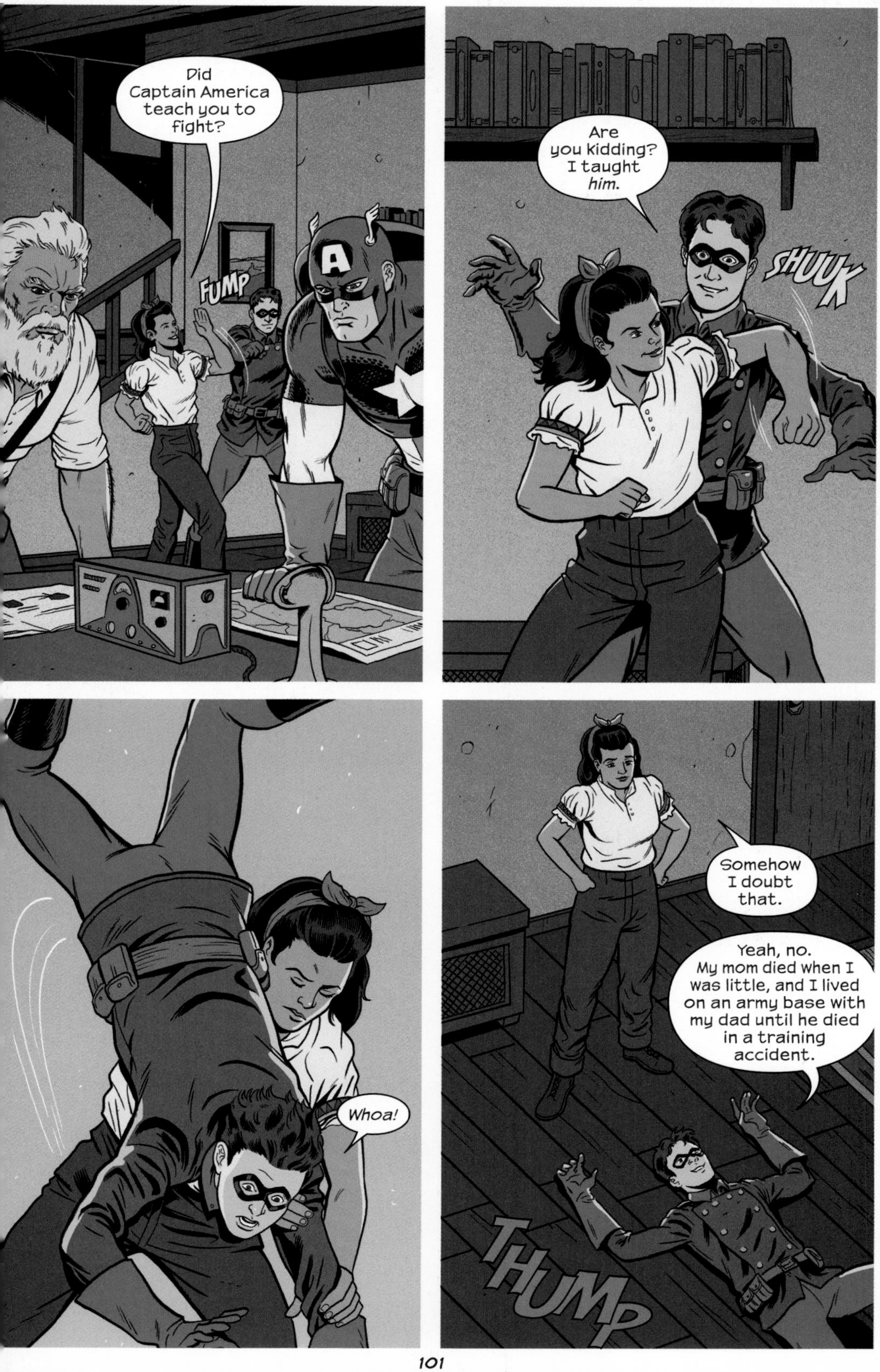
Did Captain America teach you to fight?
FUMP
Are you kidding? I taught *him*.
SHUUK
Whoa!
Somehow I doubt that.
Yeah, no. My mom died when I was little, and I lived on an army base with my dad until he died in a training accident.
THUMP

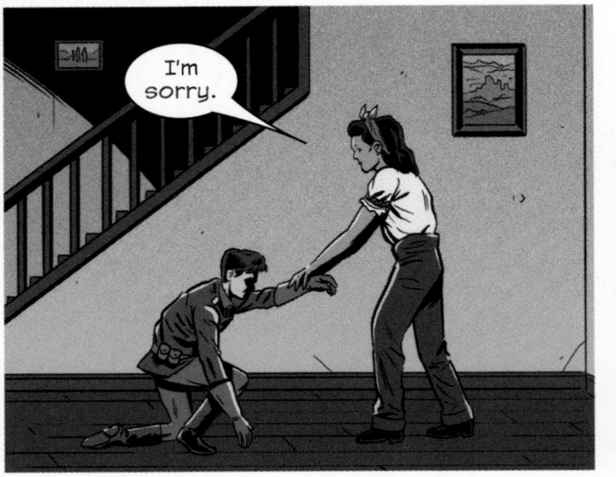
I'm sorry.

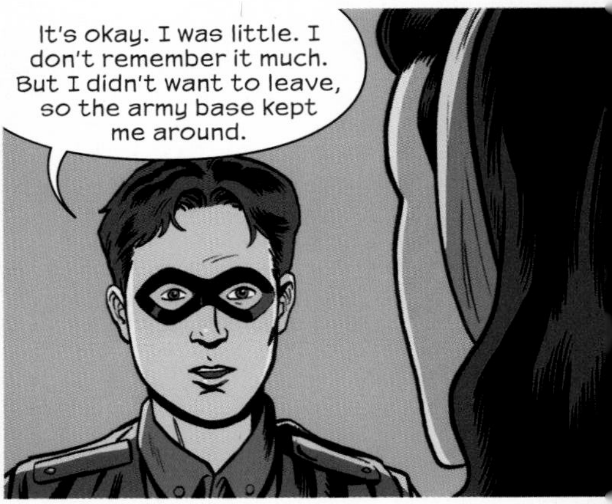
It's okay. I was little. I don't remember it much. But I didn't want to leave, so the army base kept me around.

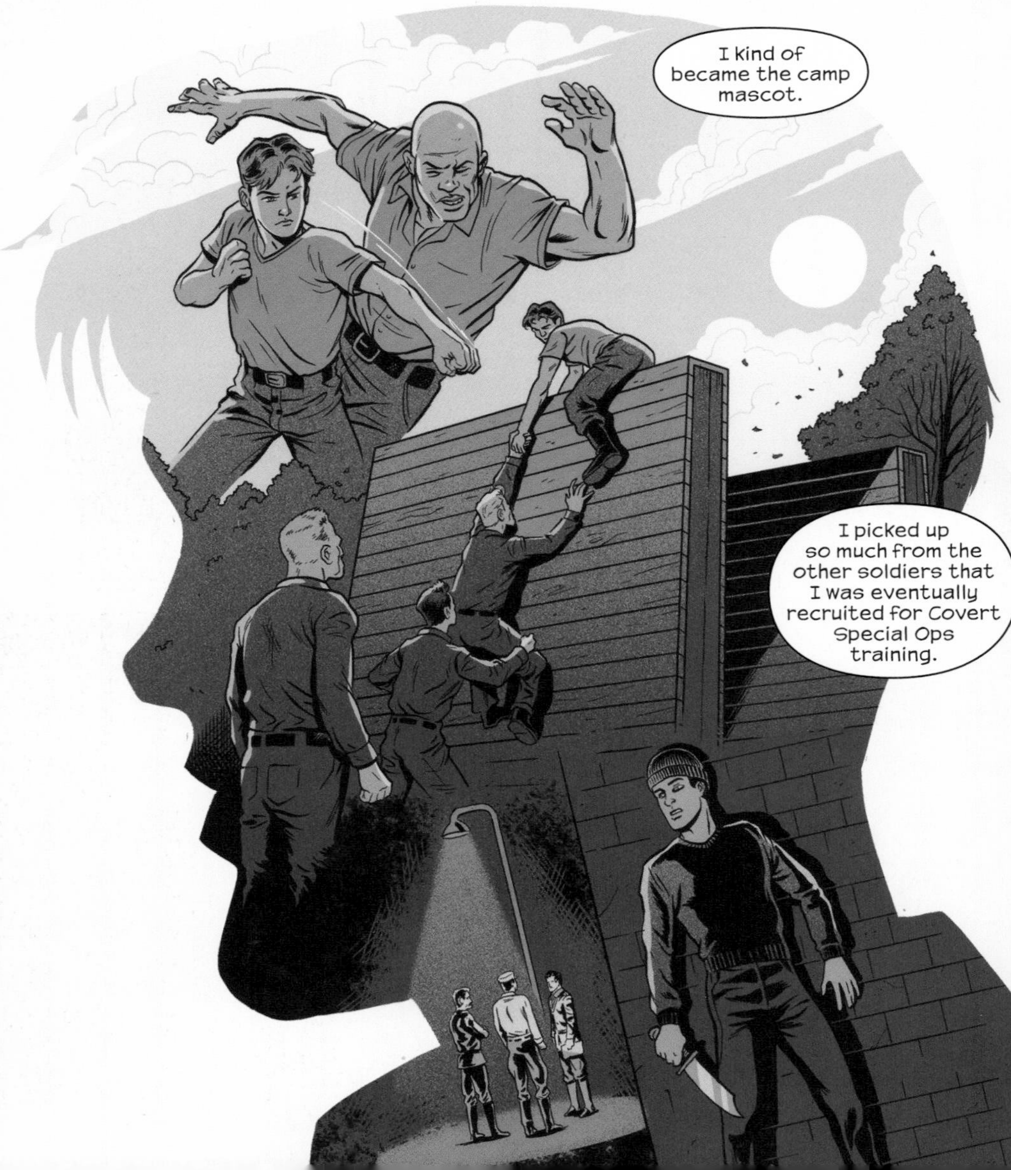
I kind of became the camp mascot.
I picked up so much from the other soldiers that I was eventually recruited for Covert Special Ops training.

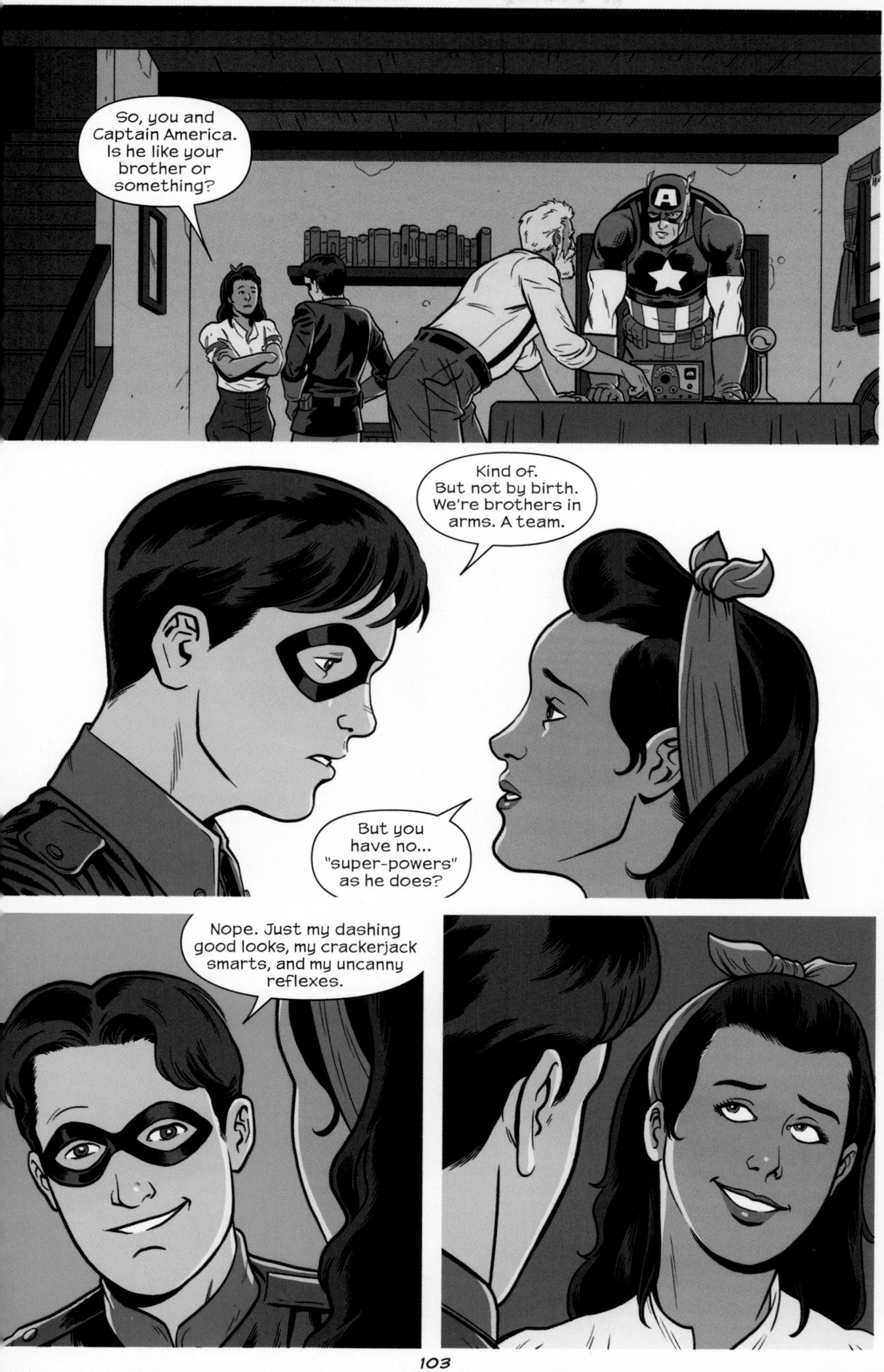

So, you and Captain America. Is he like your brother or something?
Kind of. But not by birth. We're brothers in arms. A team.
But you have no... "super-powers" as he does?
Nope. Just my dashing good looks, my crackerjack smarts, and my uncanny reflexes.

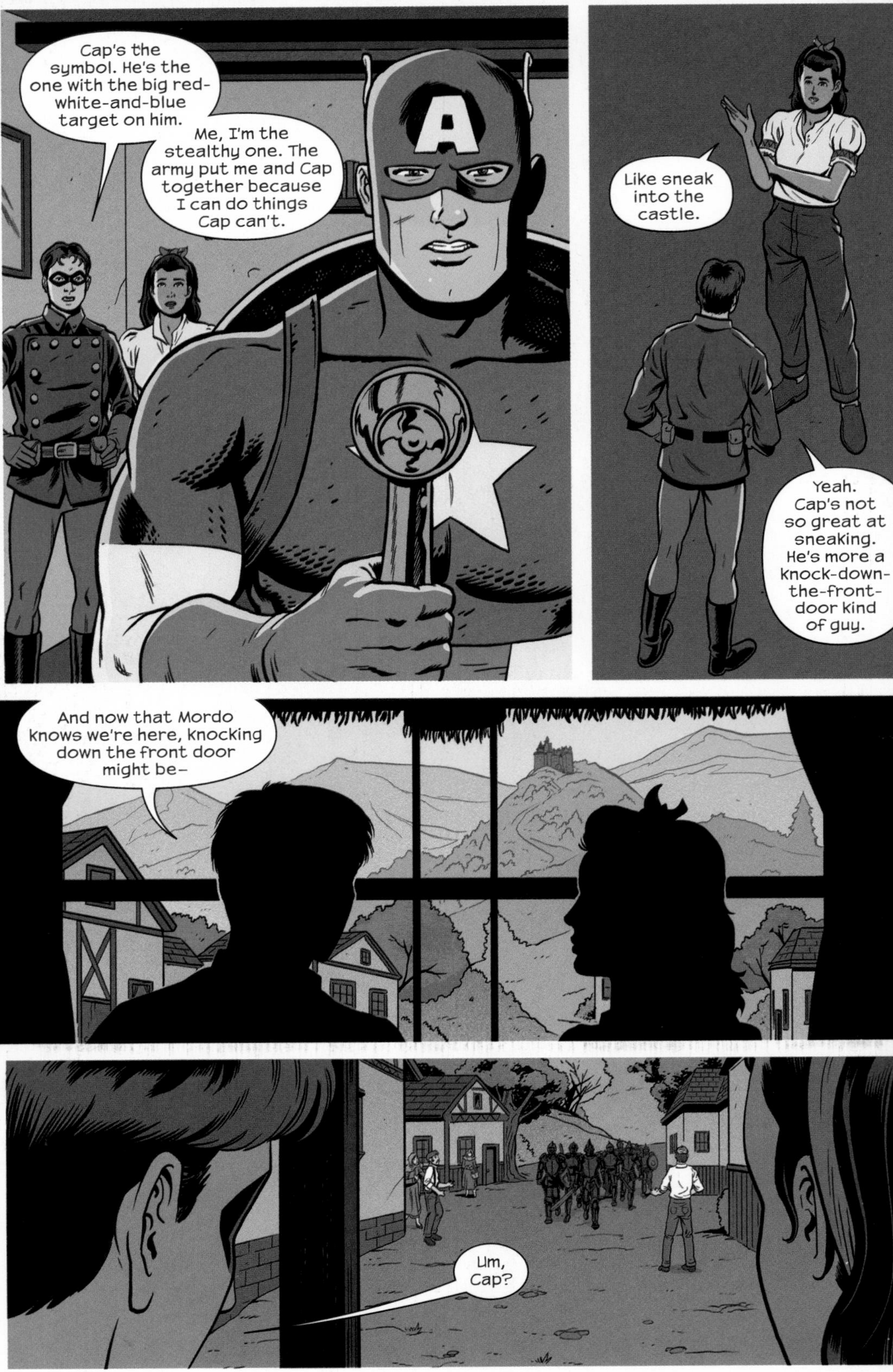

Cap's the symbol. He's the one with the big red-white-and-blue target on him.
Me, I'm the stealthy one. The army put me and Cap together because I can do things Cap can't.
Like sneak into the castle.
Yeah. Cap's not so great at sneaking. He's more a knock-down-the-front-door kind of guy.
And now that Mordo knows we're here, knocking down the front door might be–
Um, Cap?

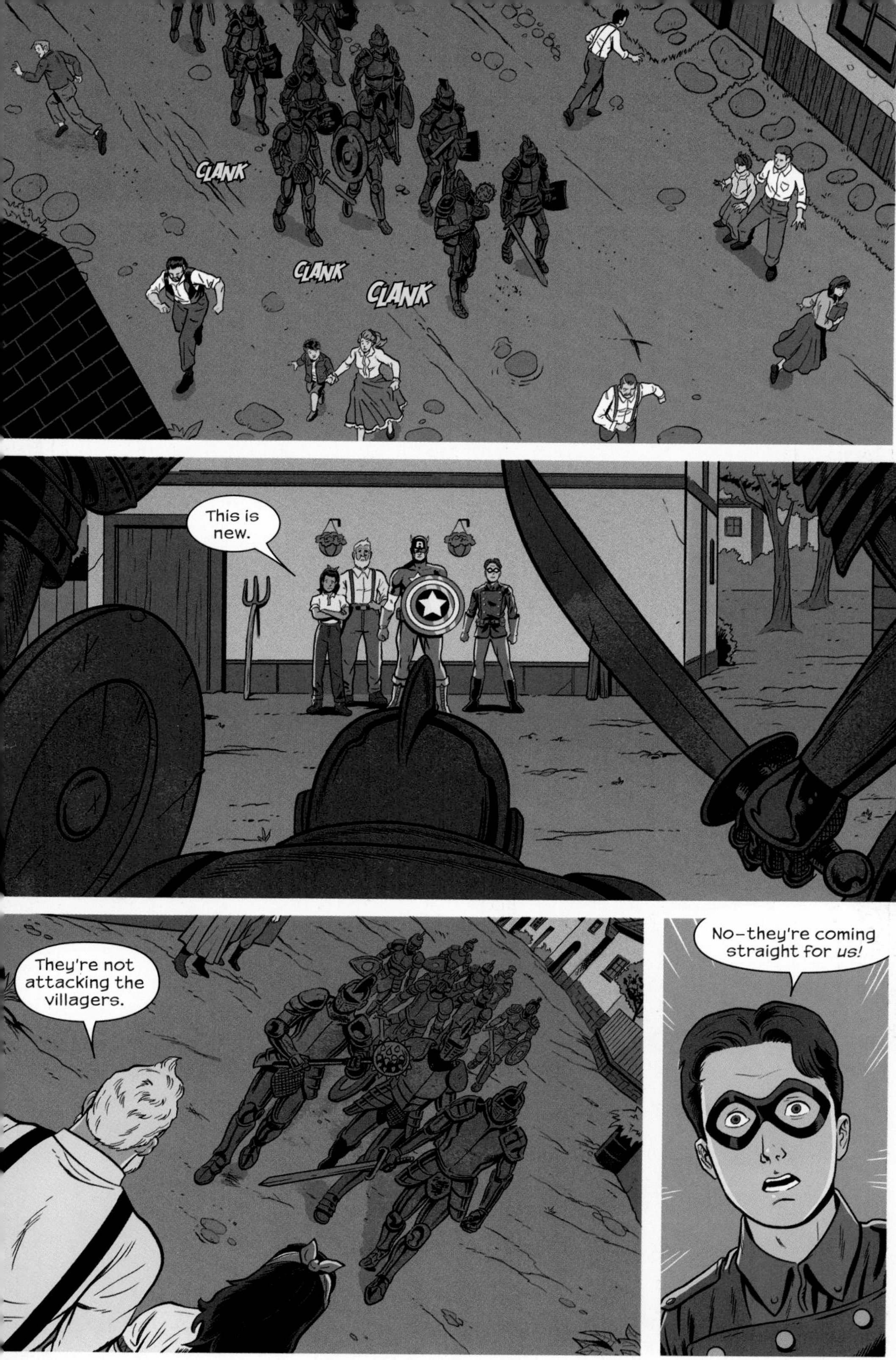
CLANK
CLANK
CLANK
This is new.
They're not attacking the villagers.
No–they're coming straight for *us!*

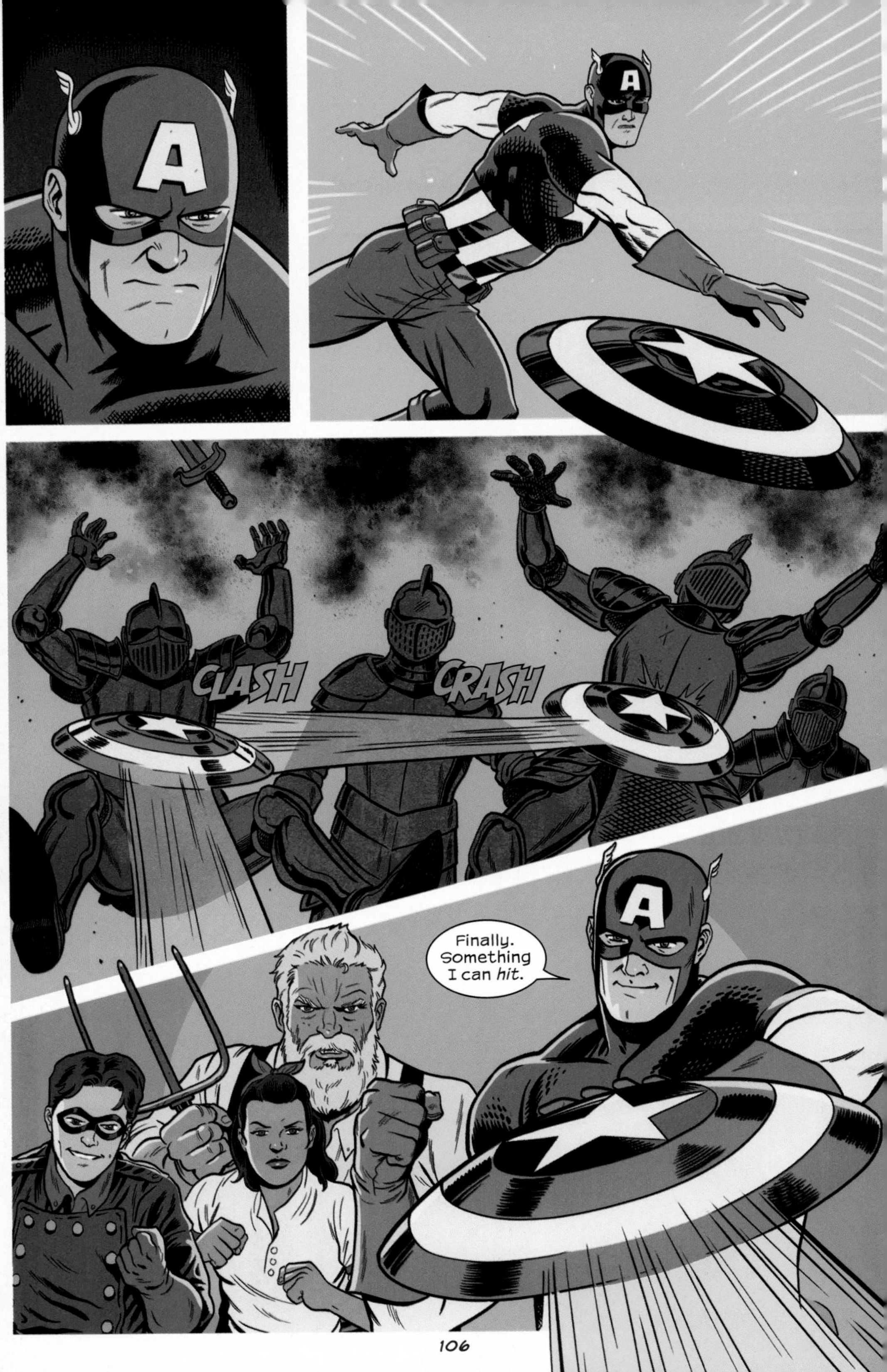
CLASH
CRASH
Finally. Something I can *hit*.

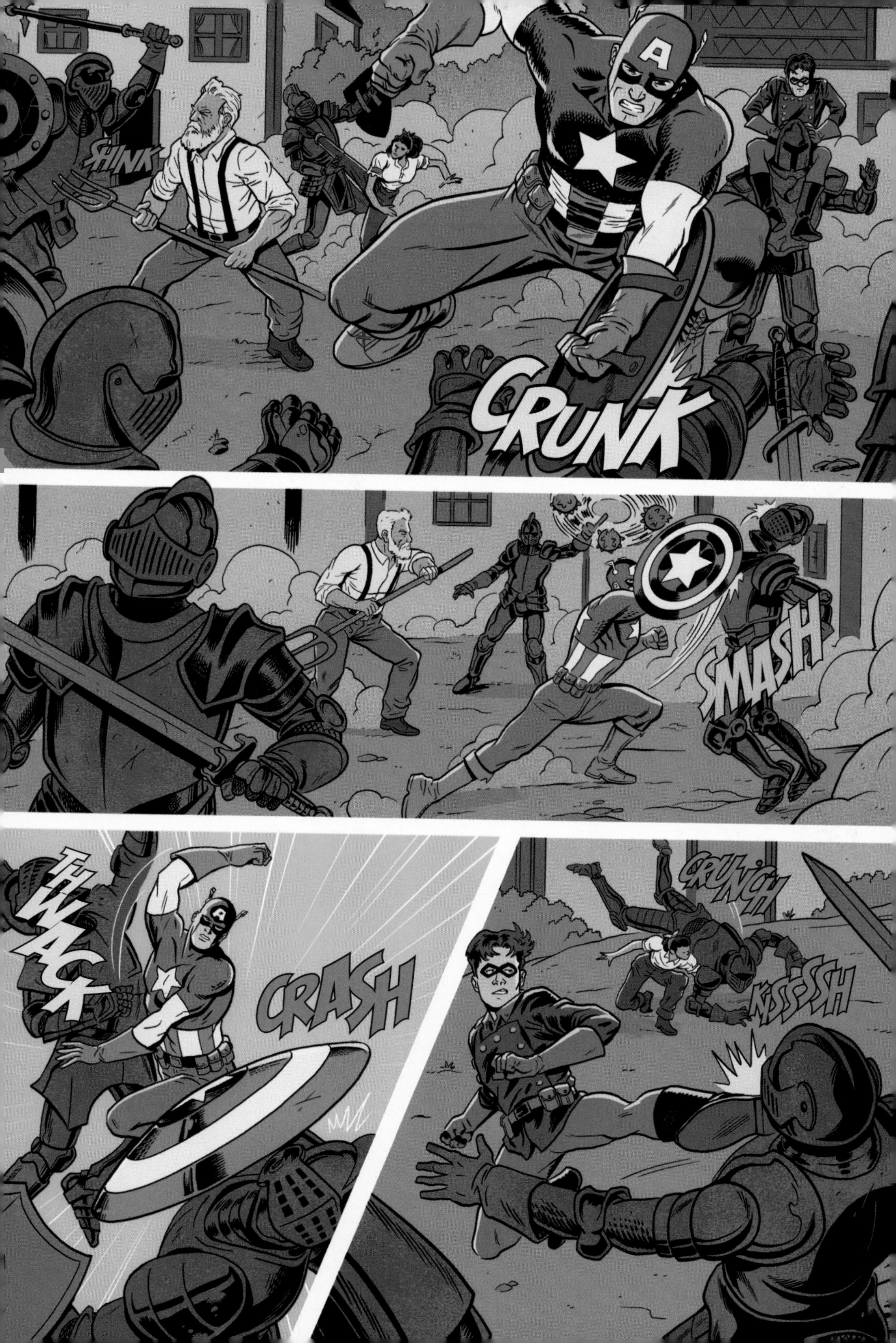

SHINK
CRUNK
SMASH
THWACK
CRASH
CRUNCH
KSSSSH

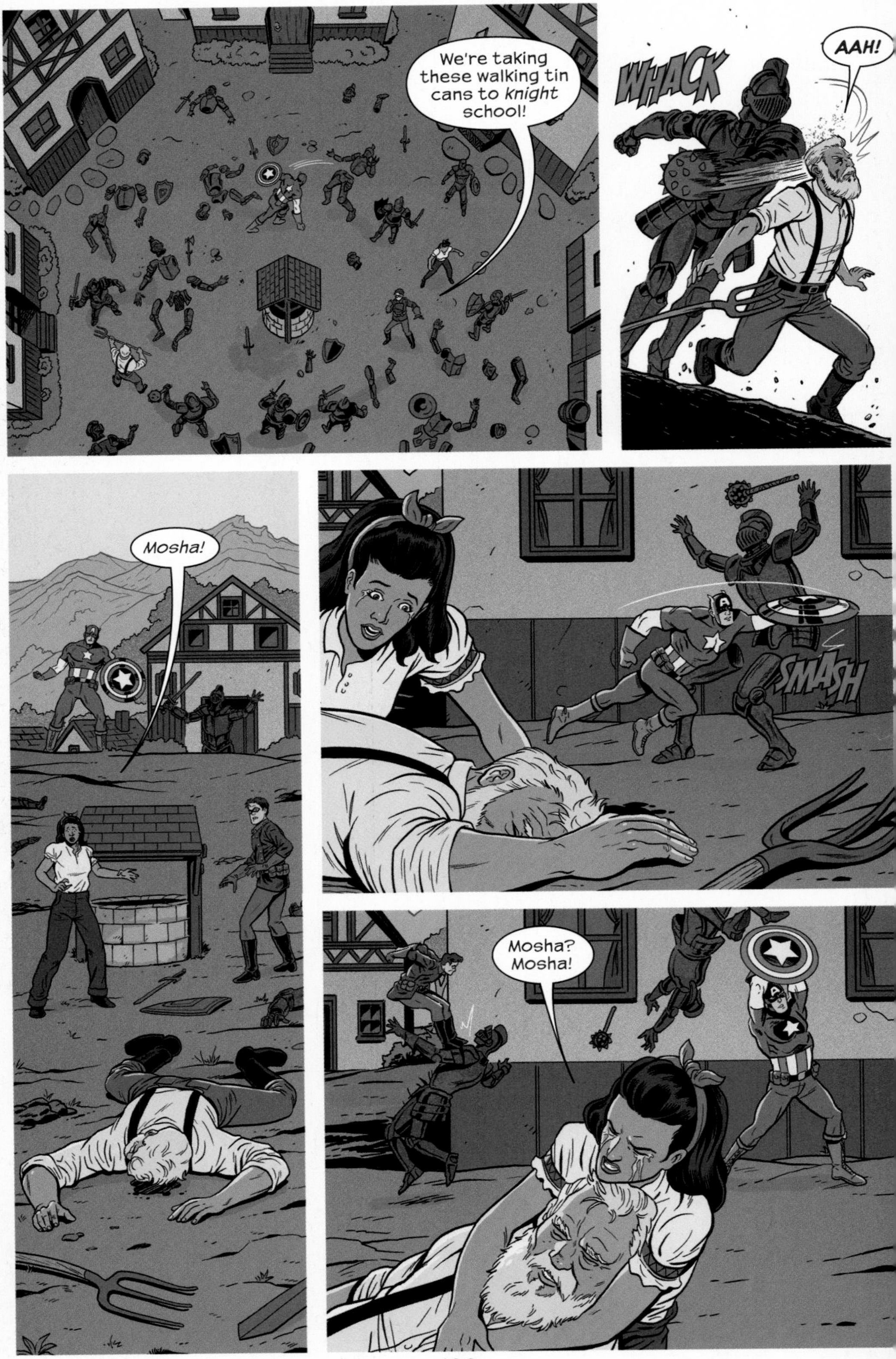
We're taking these walking tin cans to *knight* school!
WHACK
AAH!
Mosha!
SMASH
Mosha? Mosha!

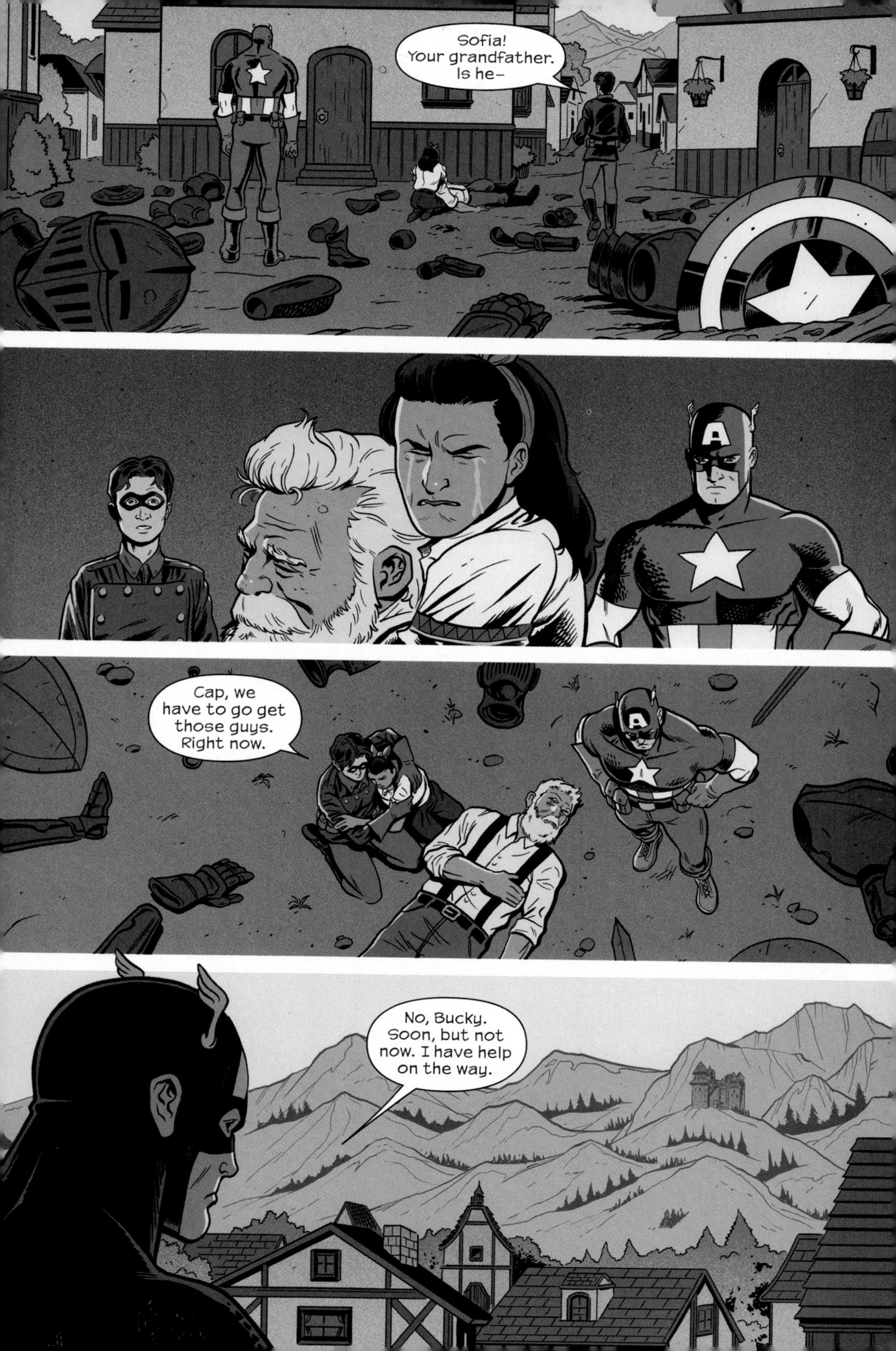
Sofia! Your grandfather. Is he–
Cap, we have to go get those guys. Right now.
No, Bucky. Soon, but not now. I have help on the way.

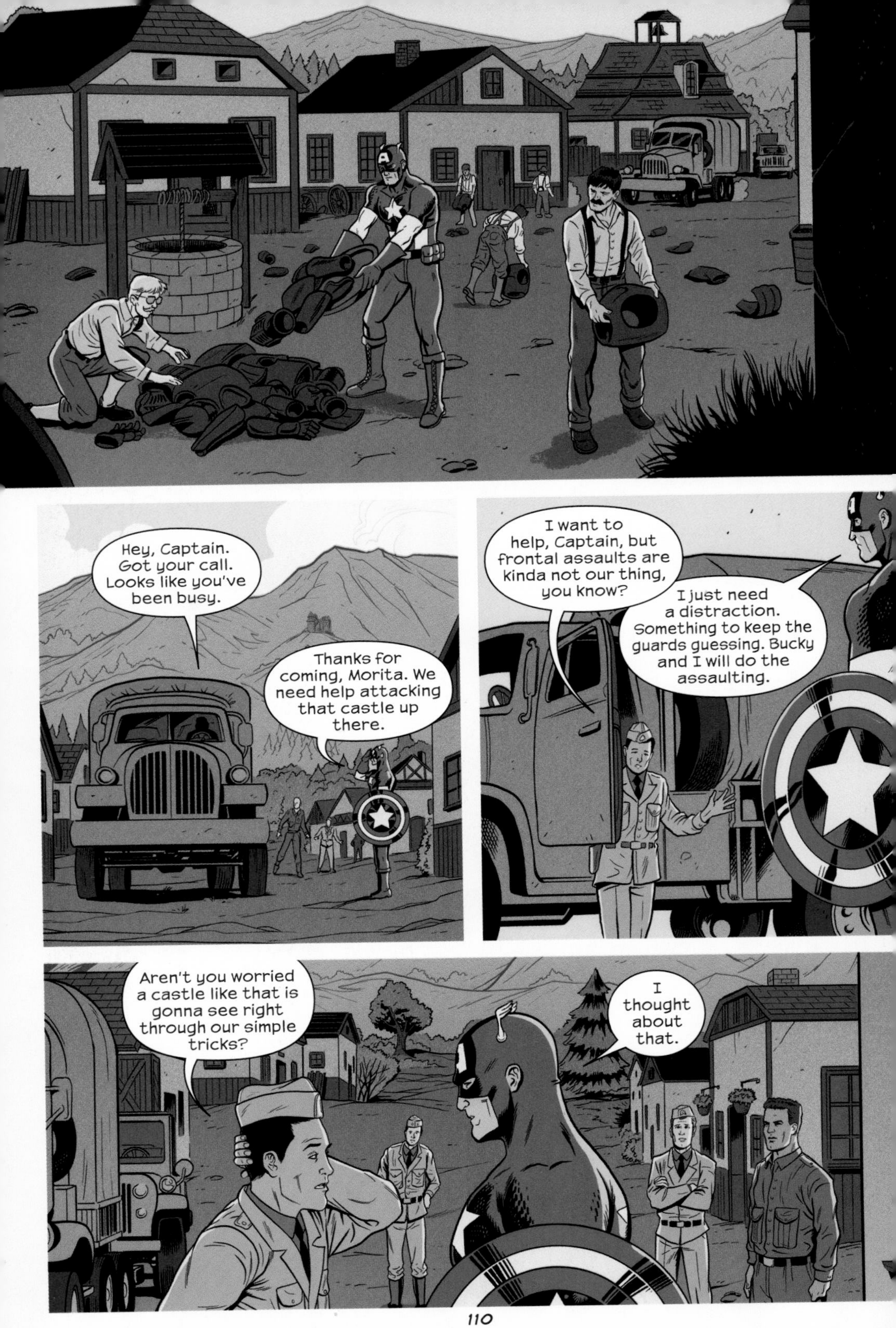
Hey, Captain. Got your call. Looks like you've been busy.
Thanks for coming, Morita. We need help attacking that castle up there.
I want to help, Captain, but frontal assaults are kinda not our thing, you know?
I just need a distraction. Something to keep the guards guessing. Bucky and I will do the assaulting.
Aren't you worried a castle like that is gonna see right through our simple tricks?
I thought about that.

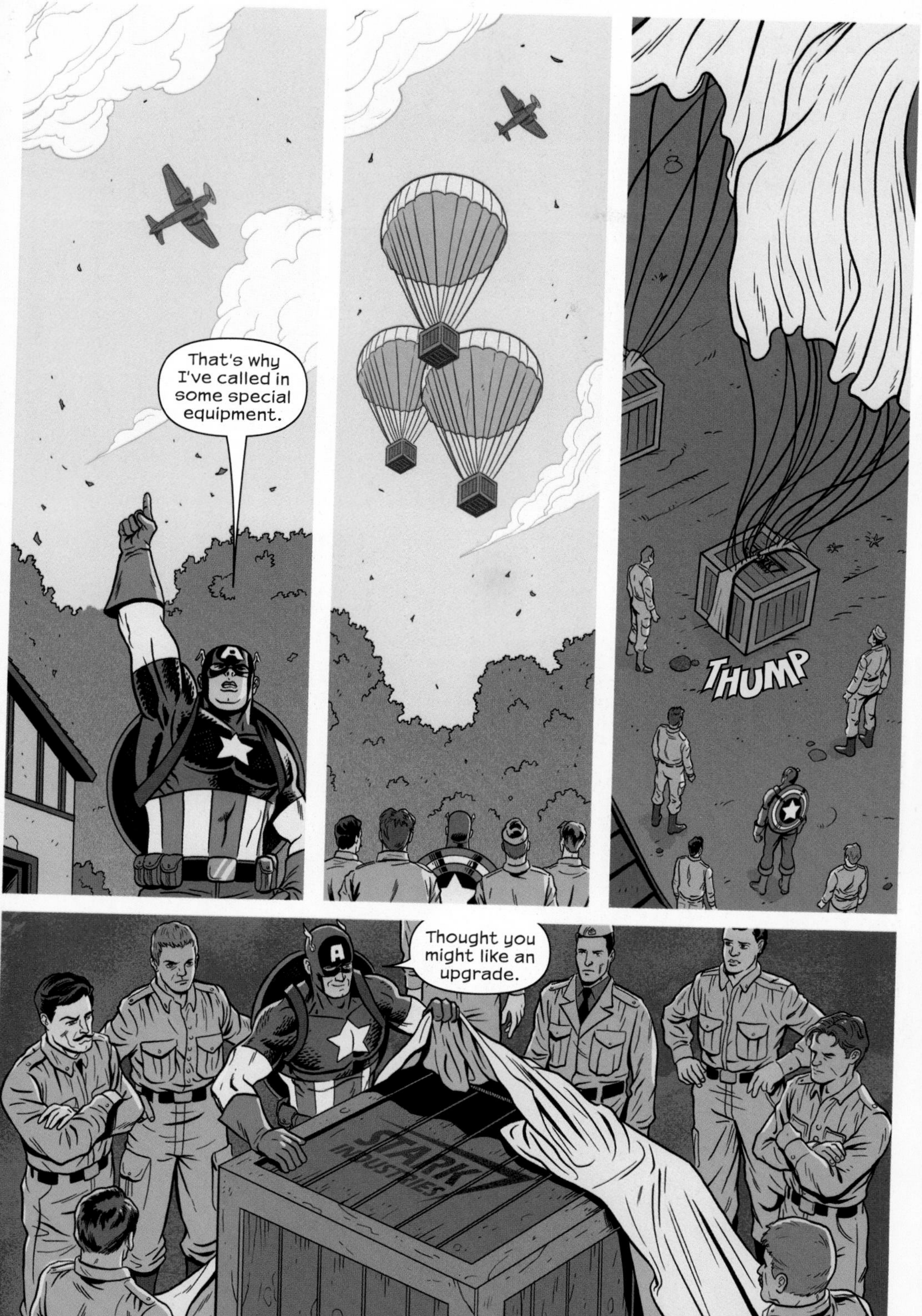
That's why I've called in some special equipment.
THUMP
Thought you might like an upgrade.
STARK INDUSTRIES

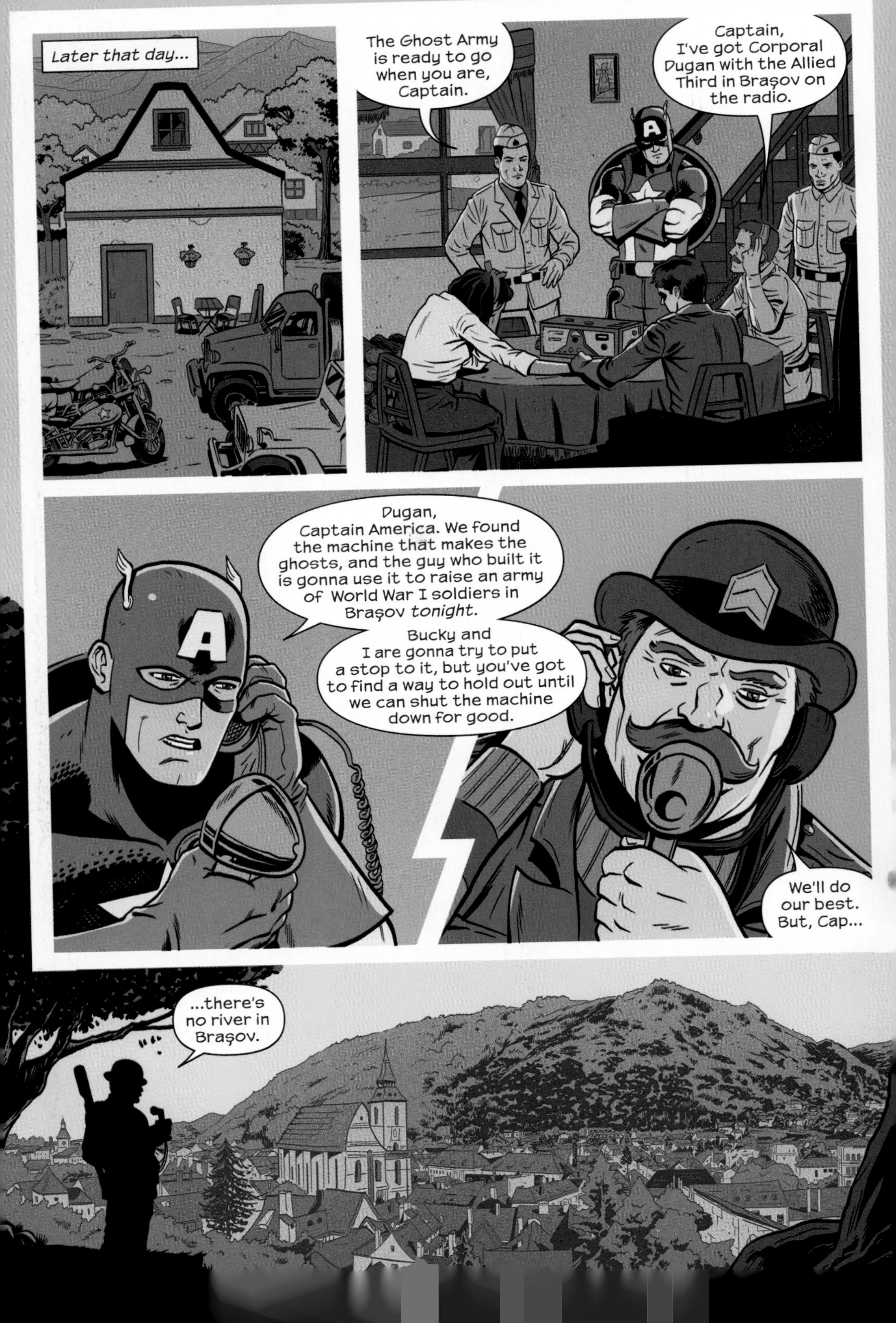
Later that day...
The Ghost Army is ready to go when you are, Captain.
Captain, I've got Corporal Dugan with the Allied Third in Braşov on the radio.
Dugan, Captain America. We found the machine that makes the ghosts, and the guy who built it is gonna use it to raise an army of World War I soldiers in Braşov *tonight*.
Bucky and I are gonna try to put a stop to it, but you've got to find a way to hold out until we can shut the machine down for good.
We'll do our best. But, Cap...
...there's no river in Braşov.

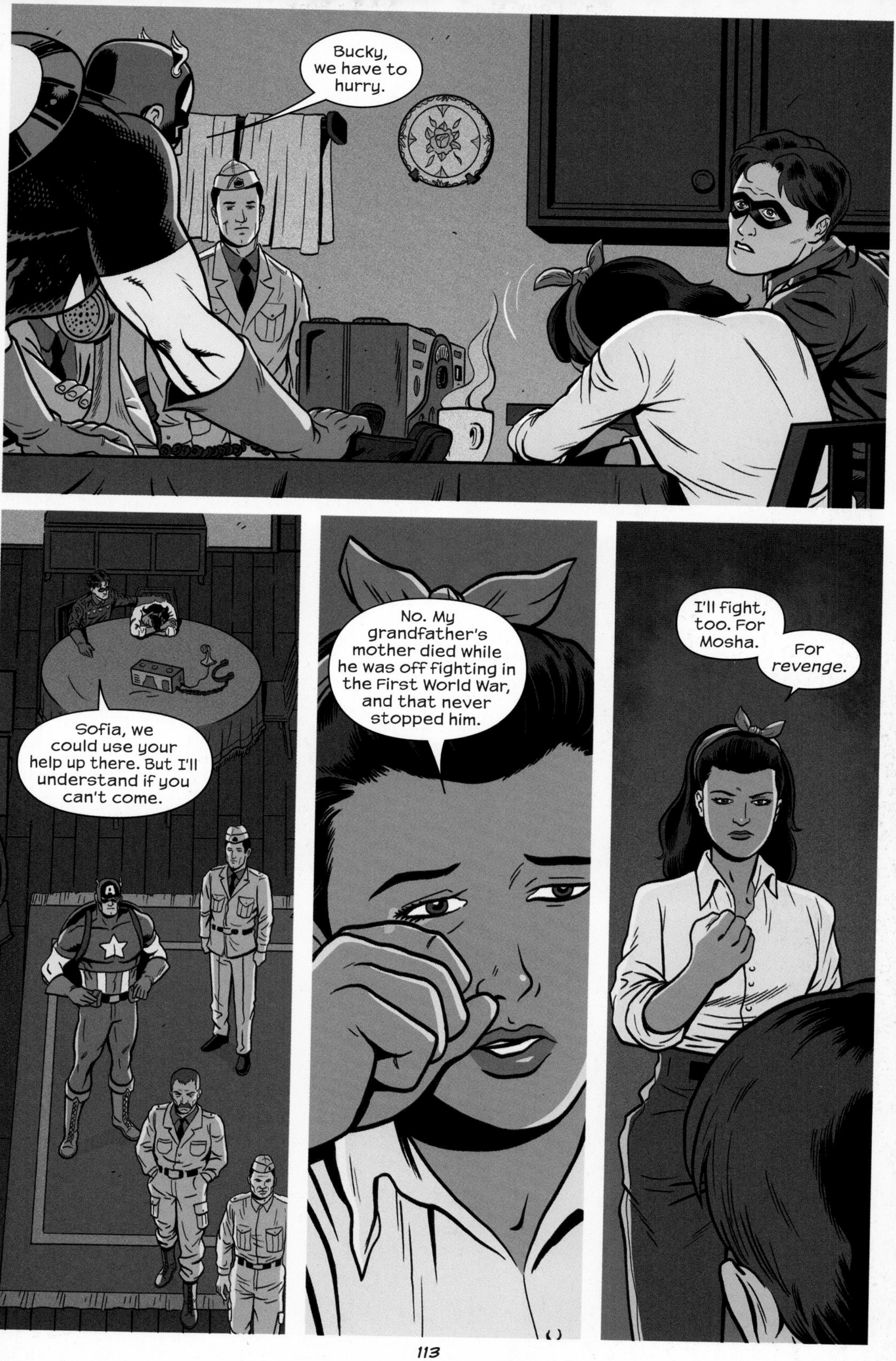
Bucky, we have to hurry.
Sofia, we could use your help up there. But I'll understand if you can't come.
No. My grandfather's mother died while he was off fighting in the First World War, and that never stopped him.
I'll fight, too. For Mosha.
For *revenge*.

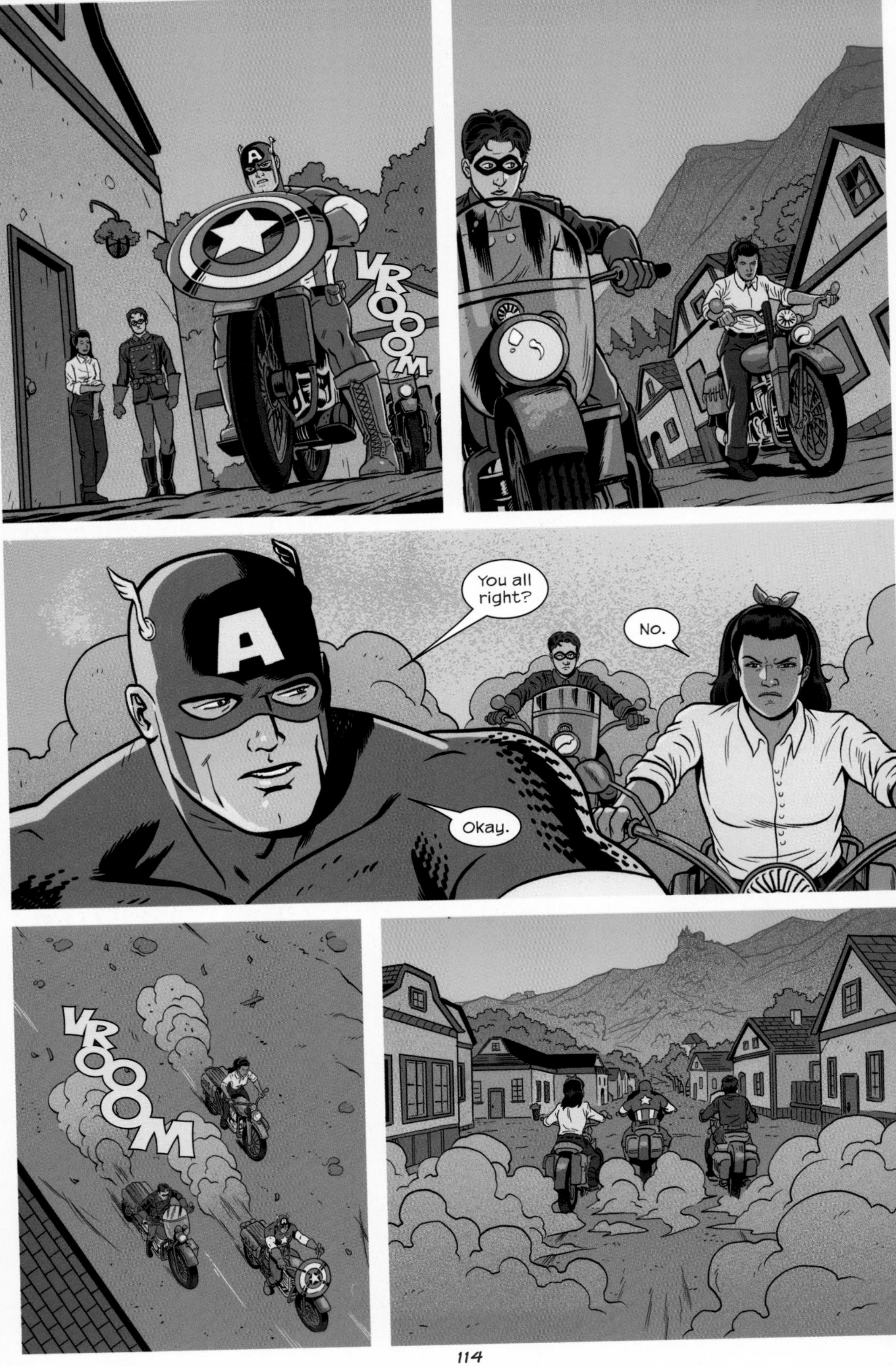
VROOOM
You all right?
No.
Okay.
VROOOM

CHAPTER SEVEN
ENTRANCES

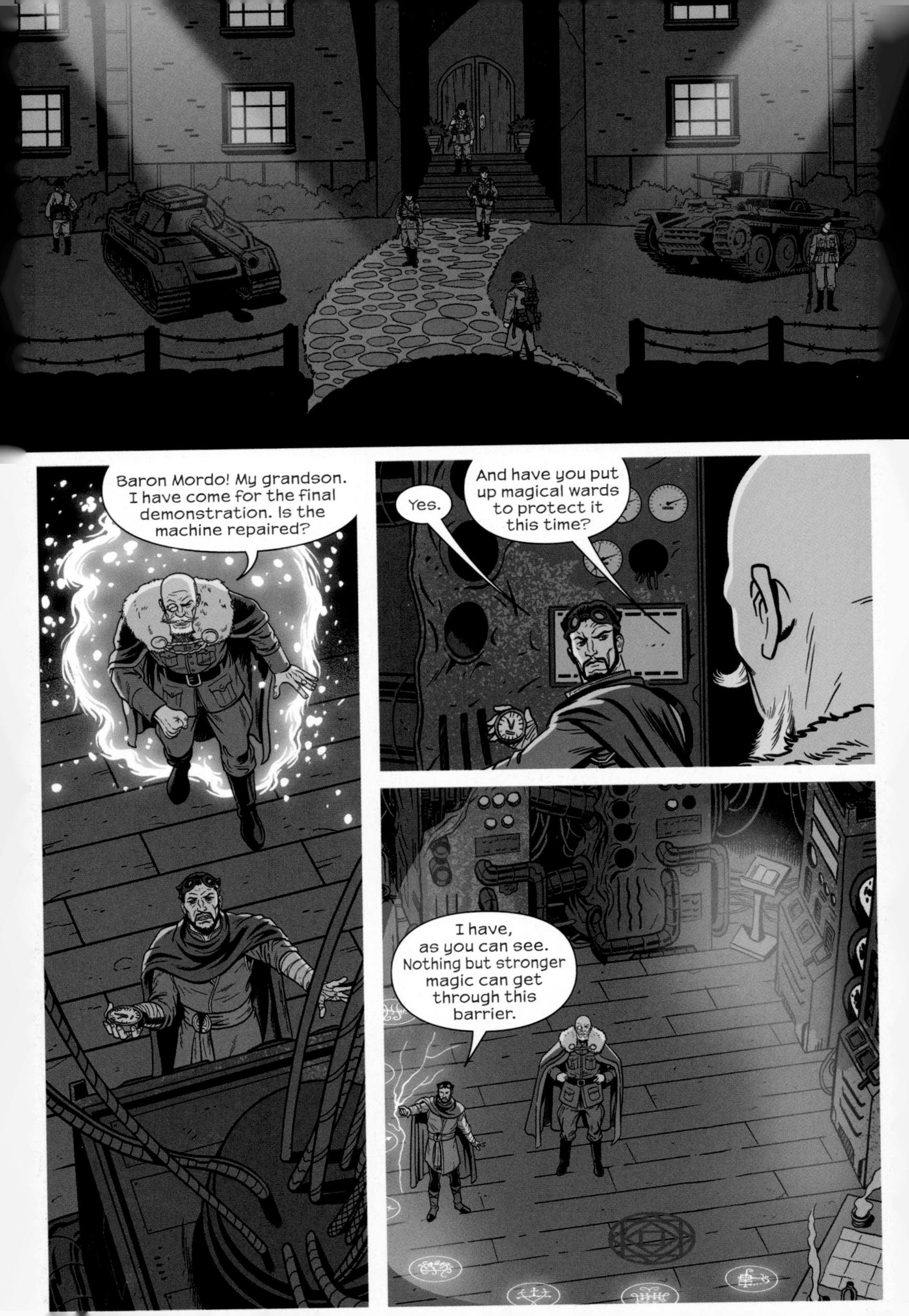
Baron Mordo! My grandson. I have come for the final demonstration. Is the machine repaired?
Yes.
And have you put up magical wards to protect it this time?
I have, as you can see. Nothing but stronger magic can get through this barrier.

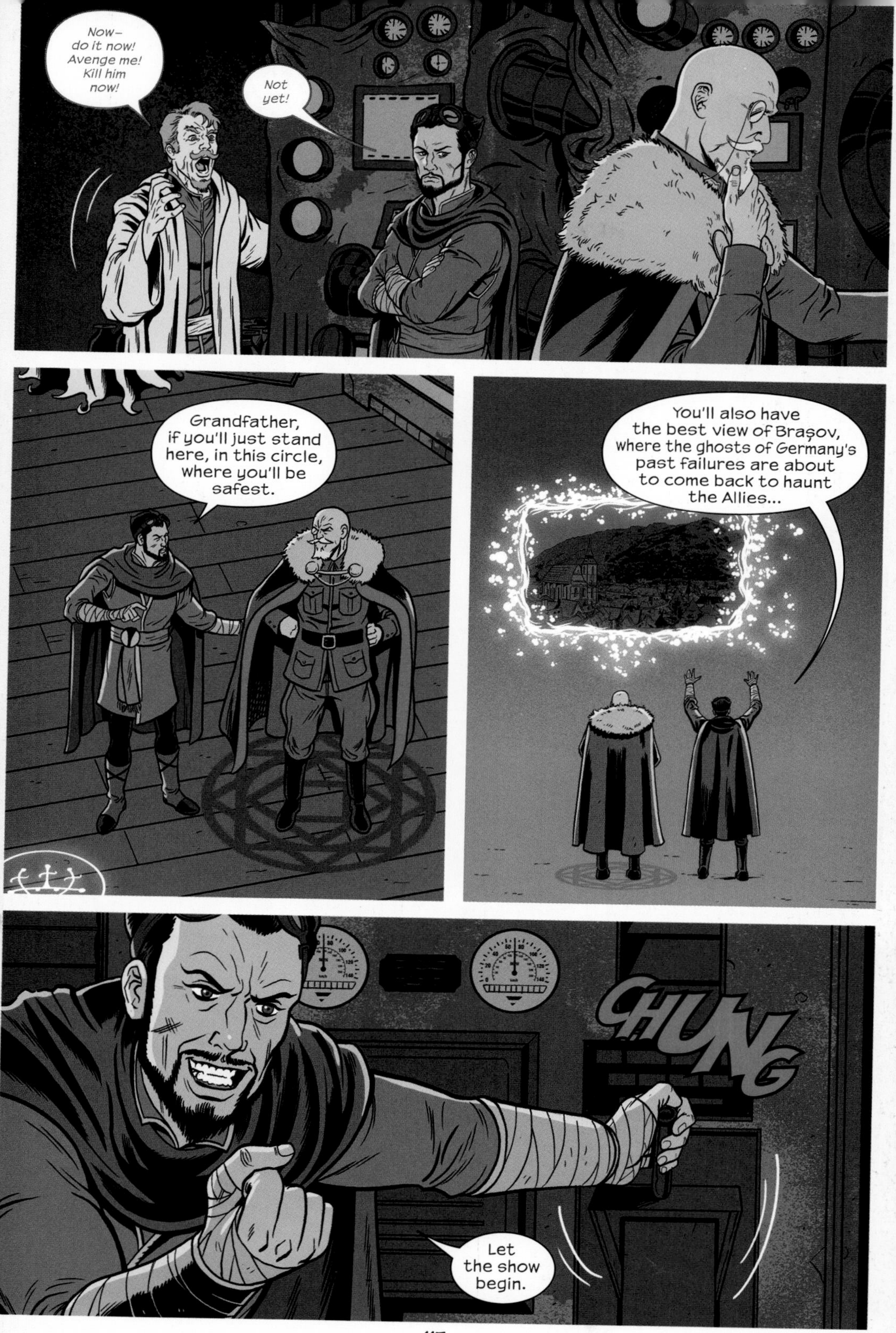
Now– do it now! Avenge me! Kill him now!
Not yet!
Grandfather, if you'll just stand here, in this circle, where you'll be safest.
You'll also have the best view of Brașov, where the ghosts of Germany's past failures are about to come back to haunt the Allies...
CHUNG
Let the show begin.

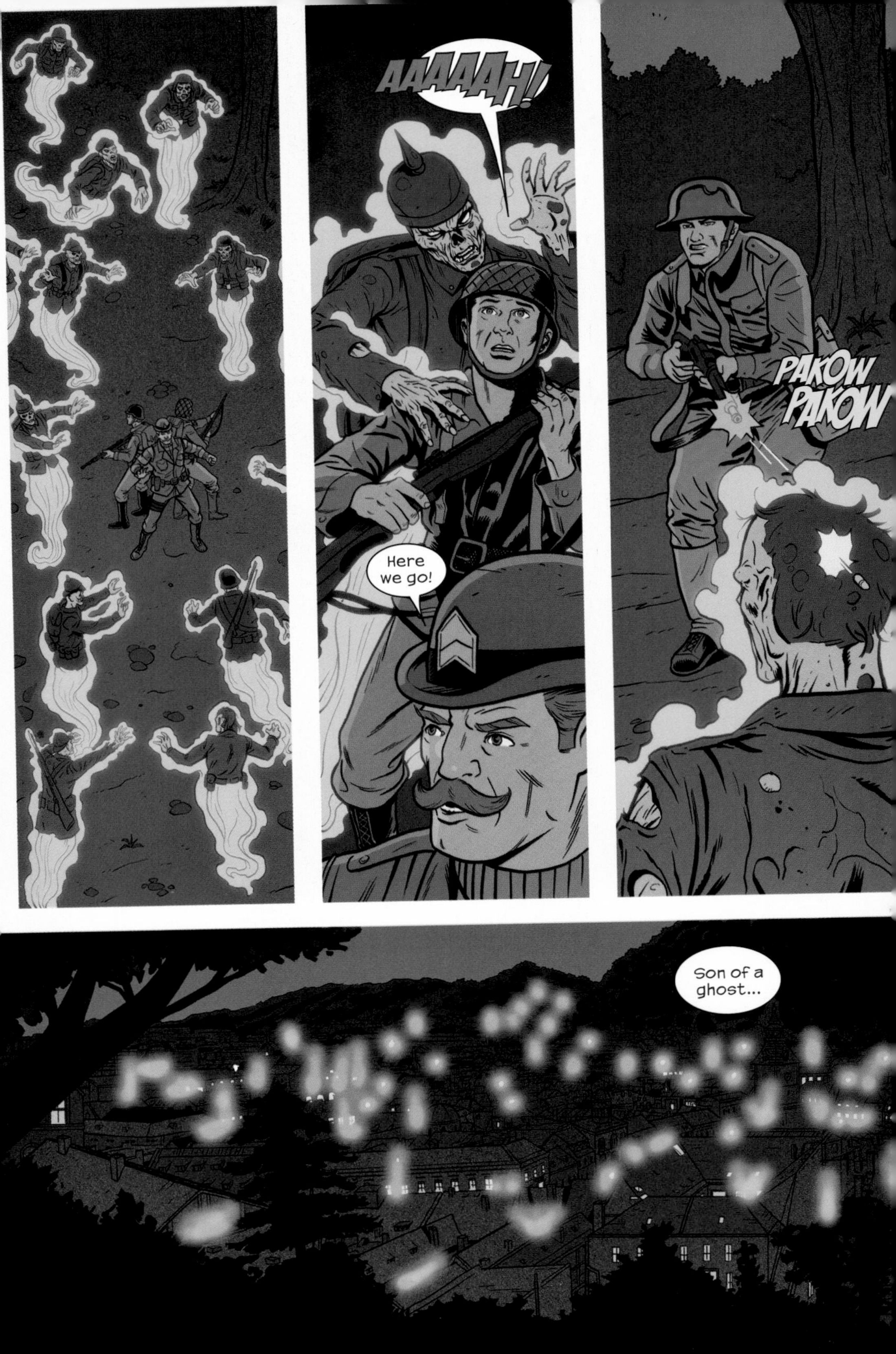
AAAAAH!
Here we go!
PAKOW PAKOW
Son of a ghost...

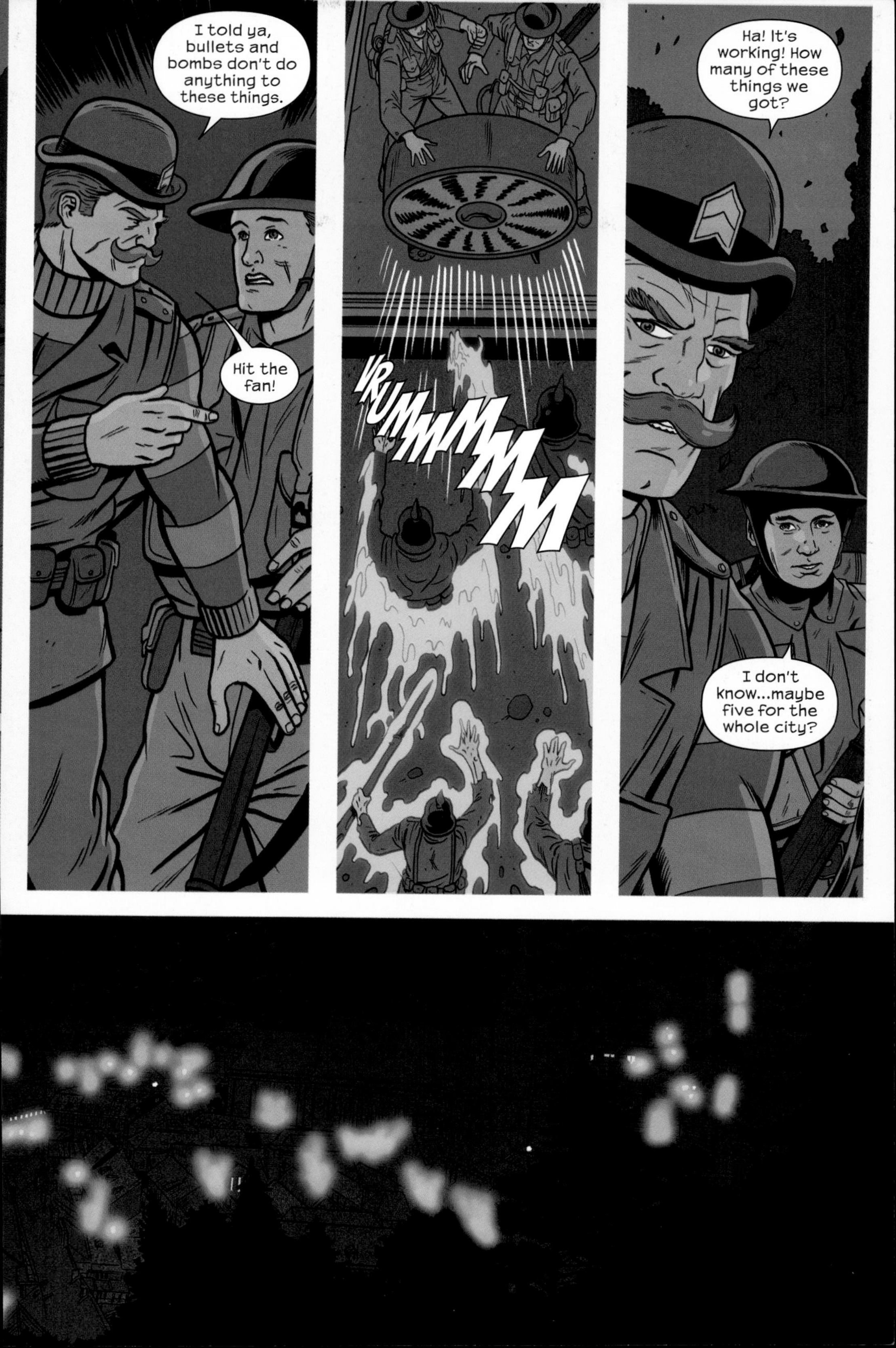
I told ya, bullets and bombs don't do anything to these things.
Hit the fan!
VRUMMMMMM
Ha! It's working! How many of these things we got?
I don't know...maybe five for the whole city?

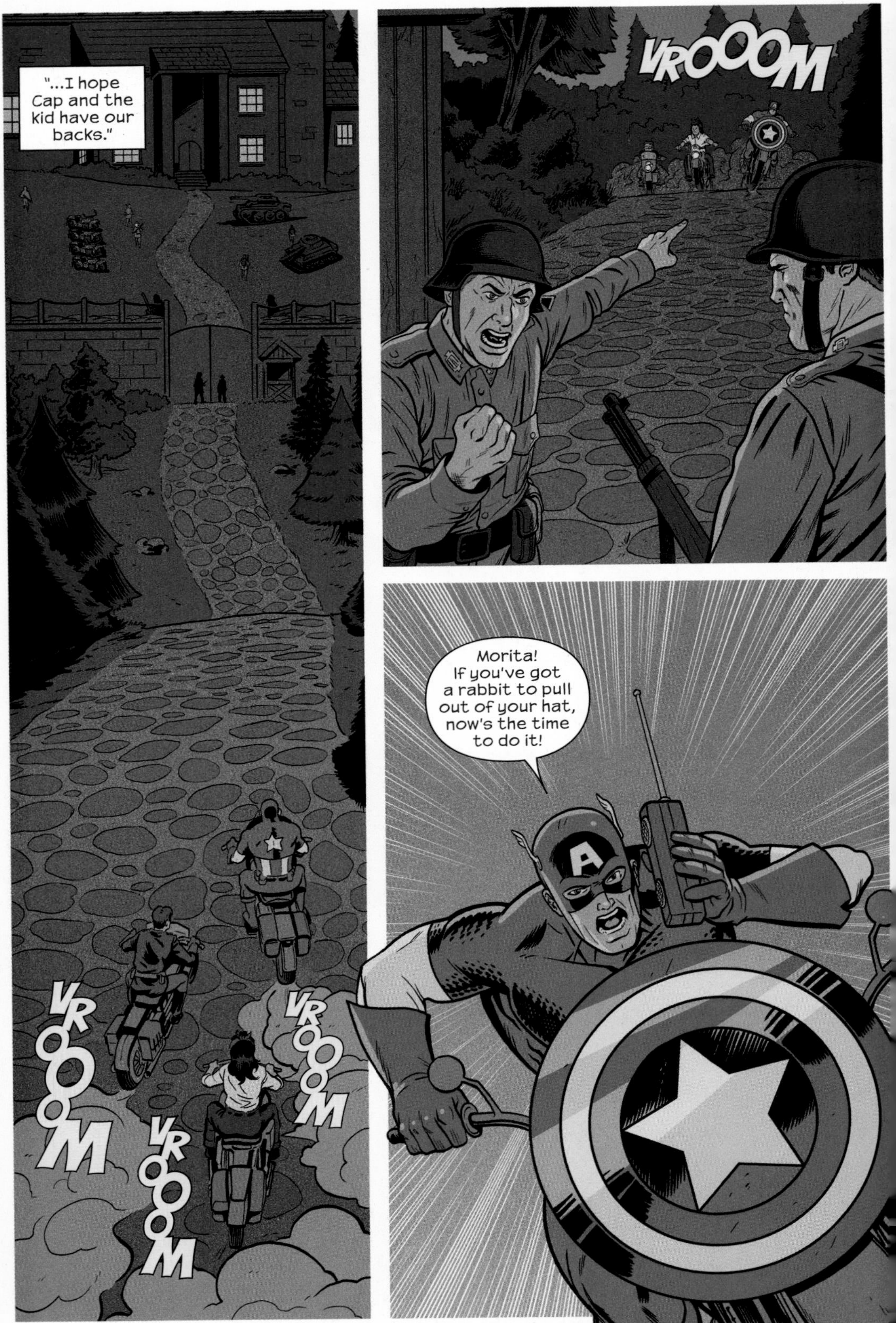
"...I hope Cap and the kid have our backs."
VROOOM
VROOOM
VROOOM
VROOOM
Morita! If you've got a rabbit to pull out of your hat, now's the time to do it!

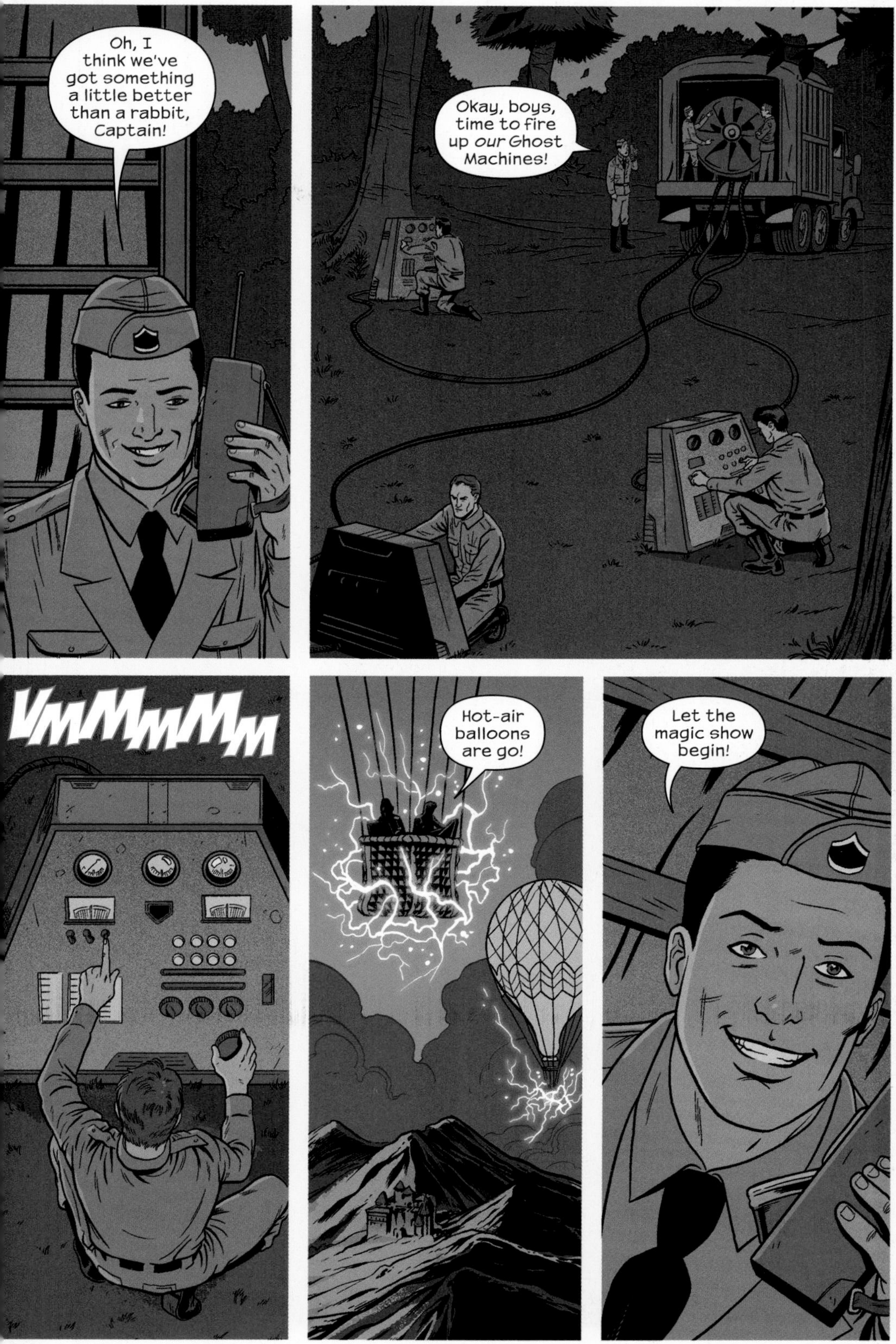
Oh, I think we've got something a little better than a rabbit, Captain!
Okay, boys, time to fire up *our* Ghost Machines!
VMMMMMM
Hot-air balloons are go!
Let the magic show begin!

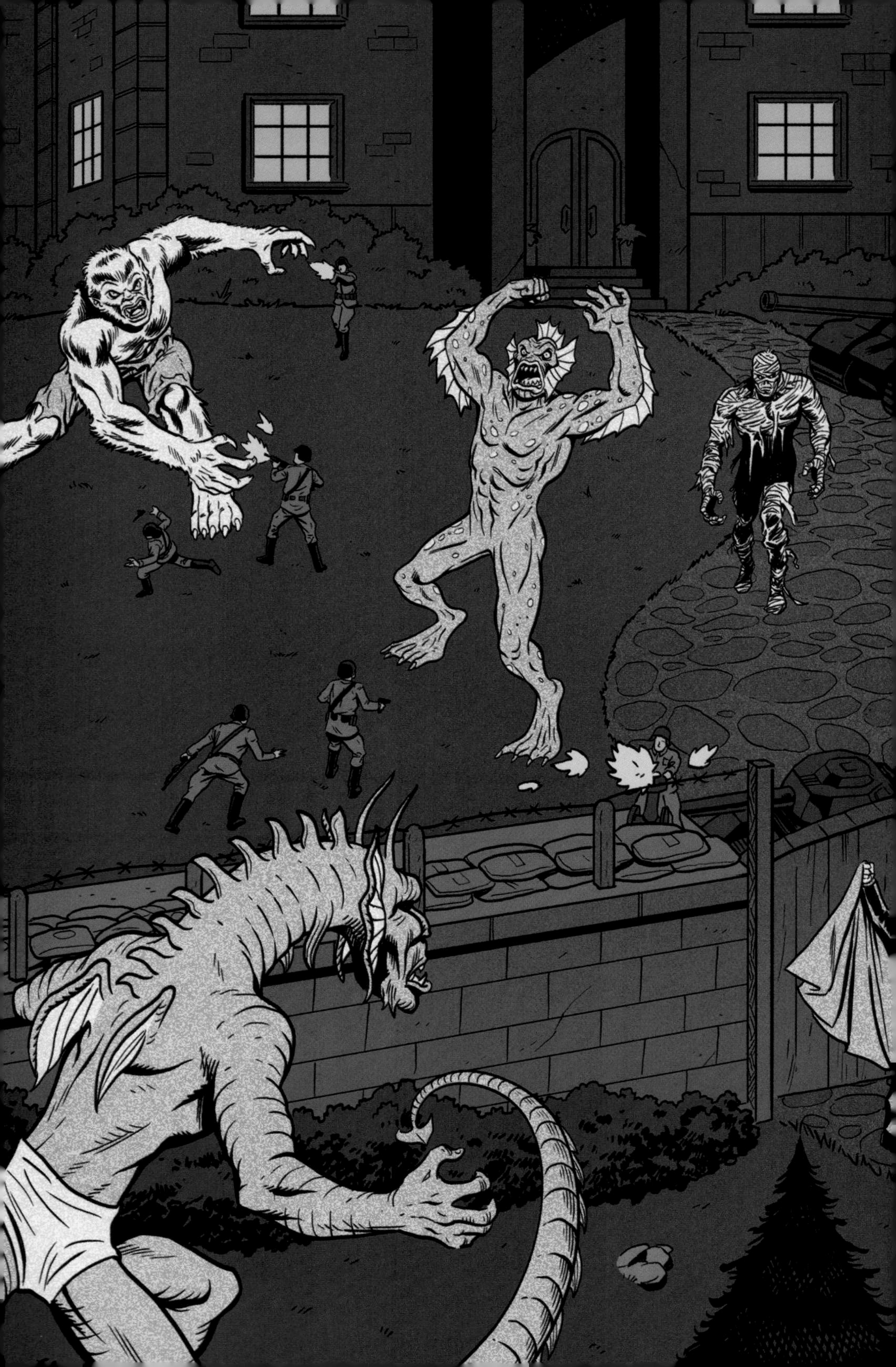

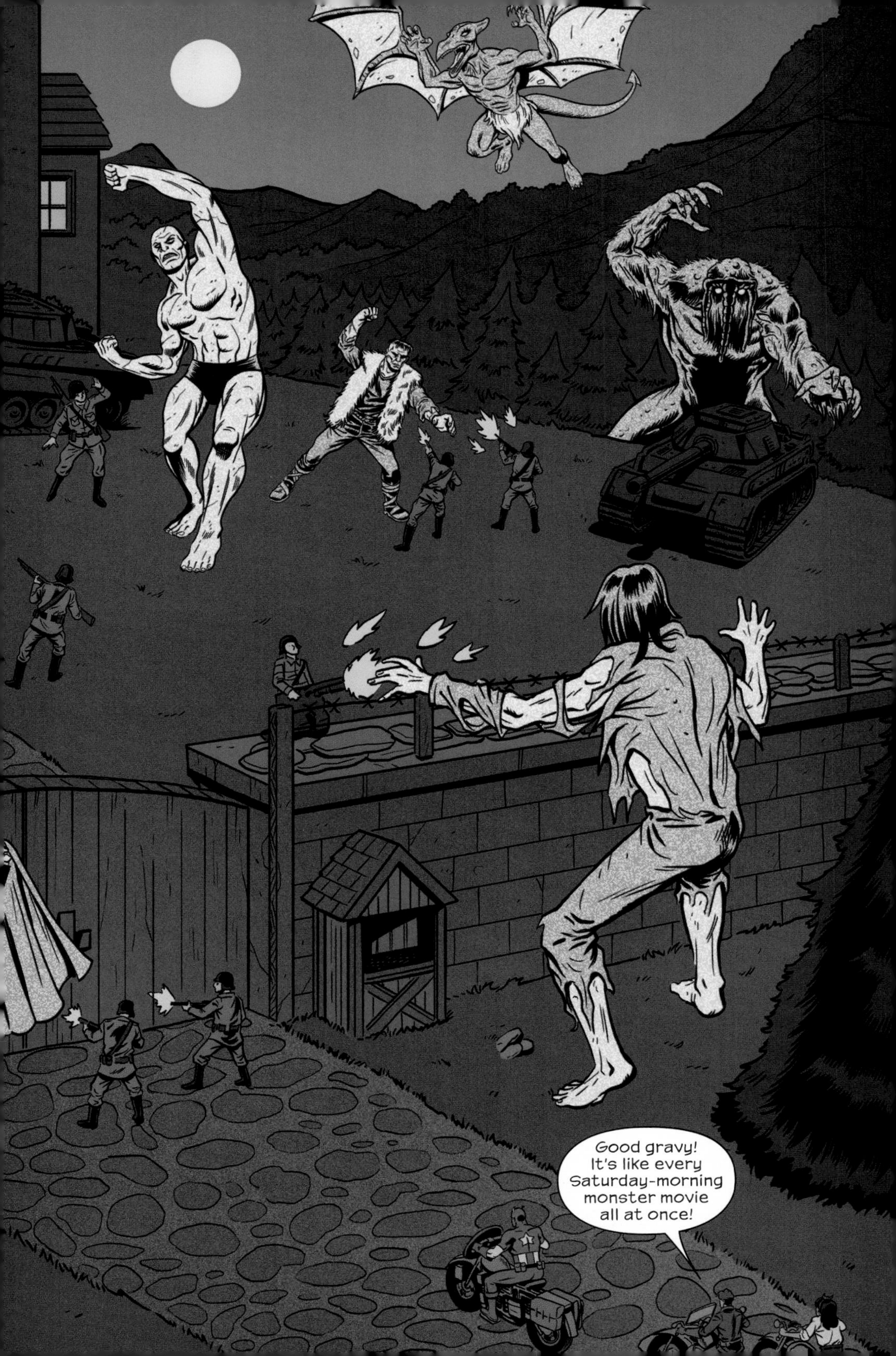
Good gravy! It's like every Saturday-morning monster movie all at once!

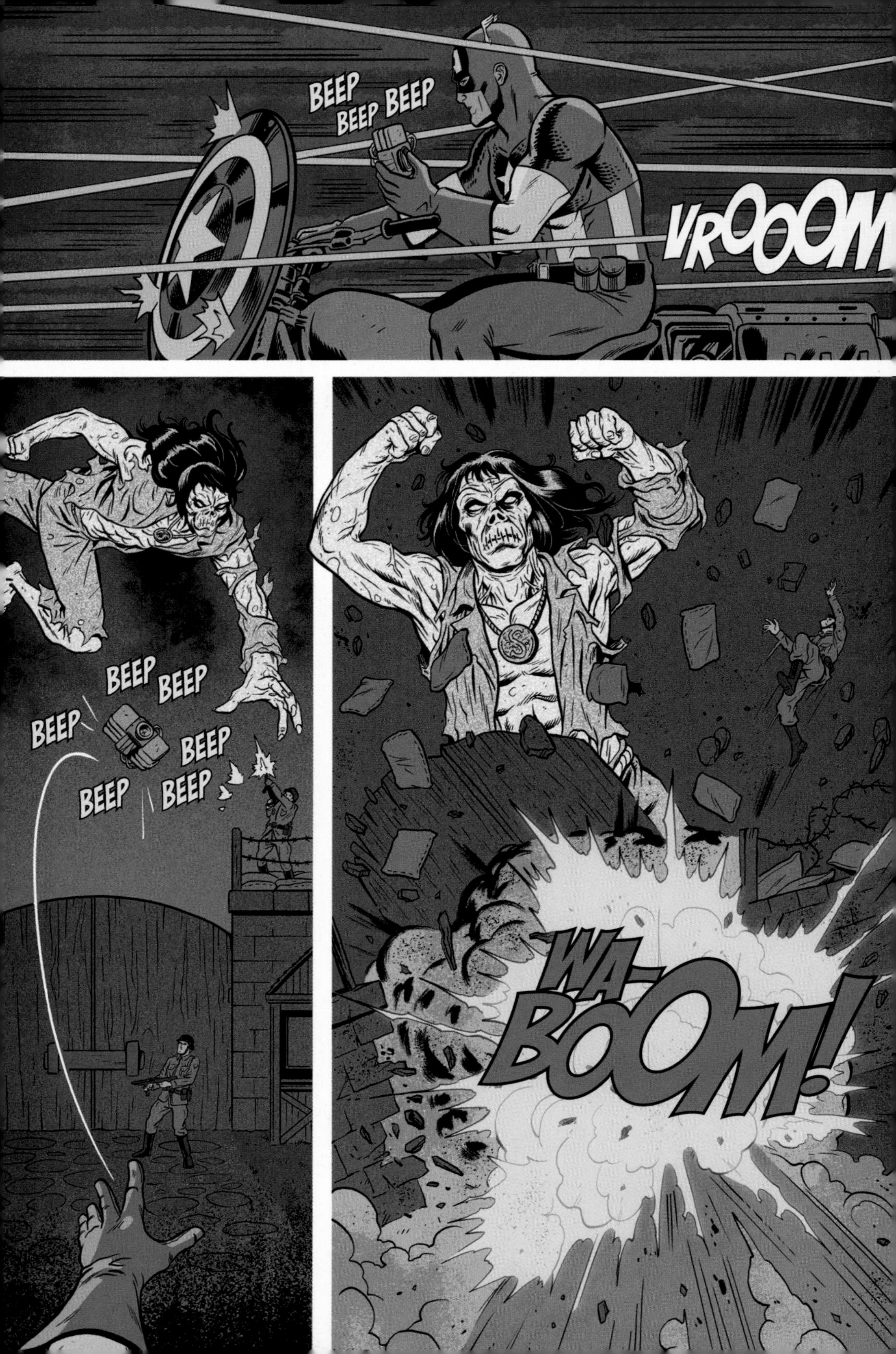
BEEP
BEEP BEEP
VROOOM
BEEP BEEP
BEEP
BEEP
BEEP BEEP
WA-BOOM!

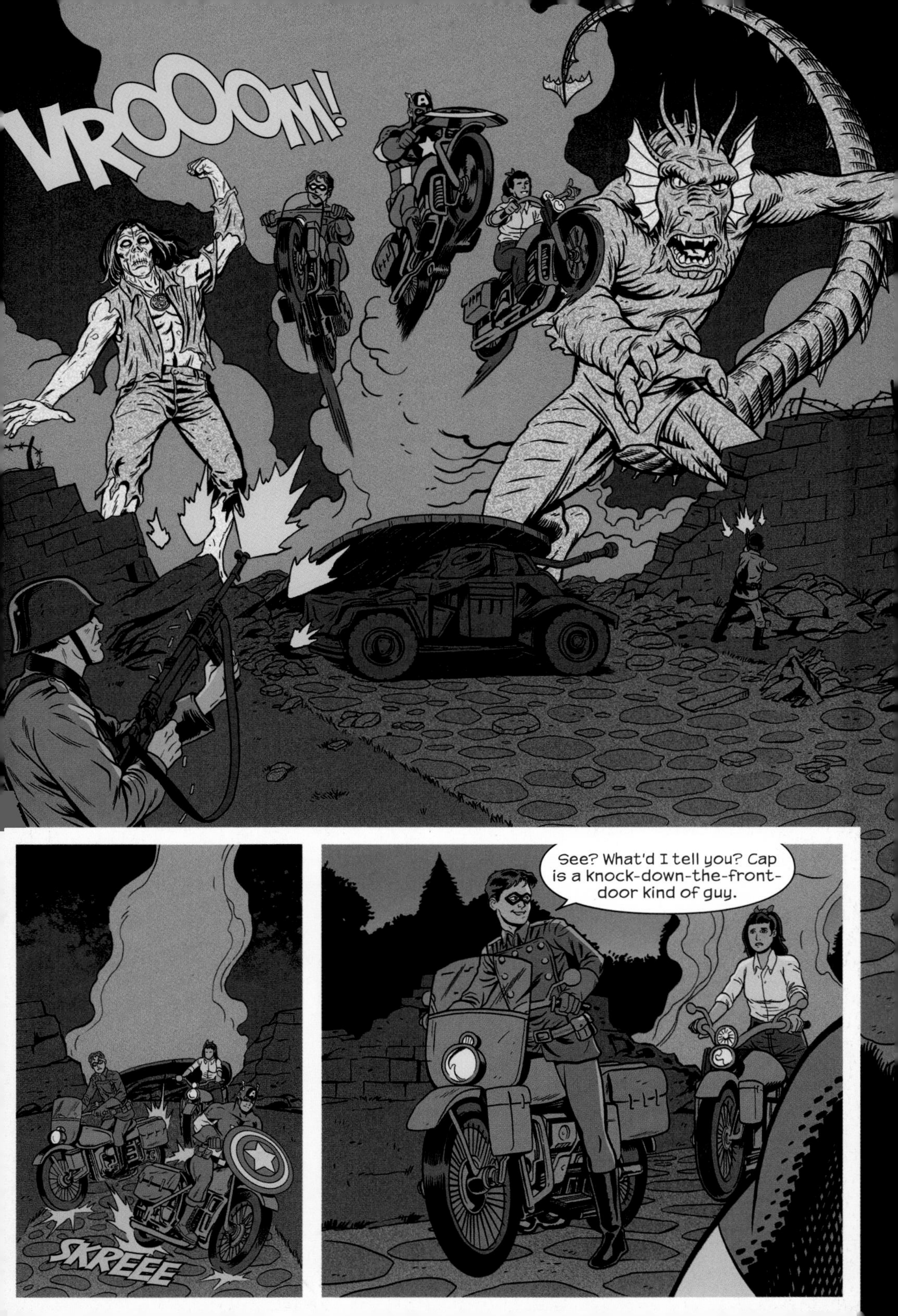
VROOOM!
SKREEE
See? What'd I tell you? Cap is a knock-down-the-front-door kind of guy.

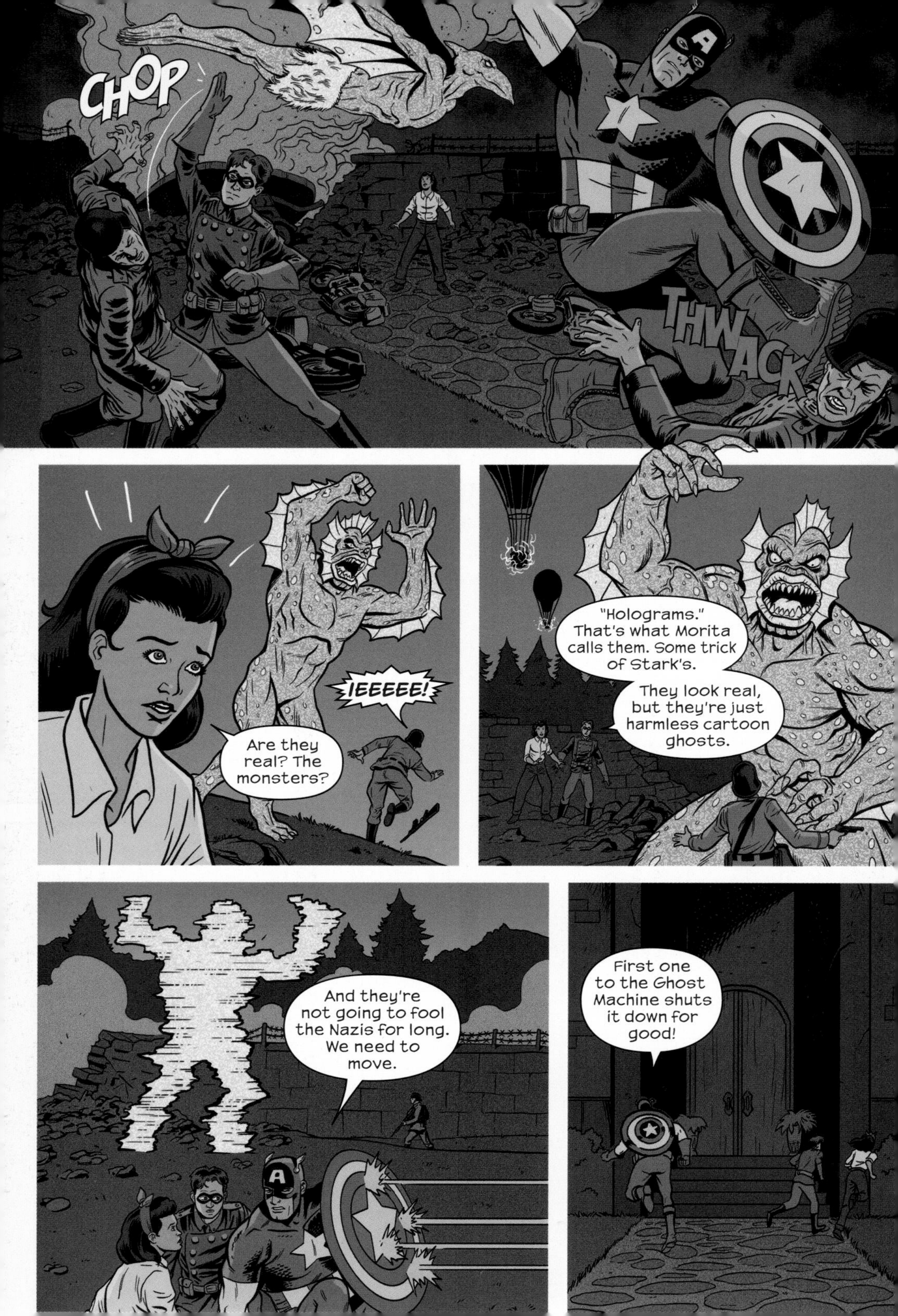
CHOP
THWACK
Are they real? The monsters?
IEEEEE!
"Holograms." That's what Morita calls them. Some trick of Stark's.
They look real, but they're just harmless cartoon ghosts.
And they're not going to fool the Nazis for long. We need to move.
First one to the Ghost Machine shuts it down for good!

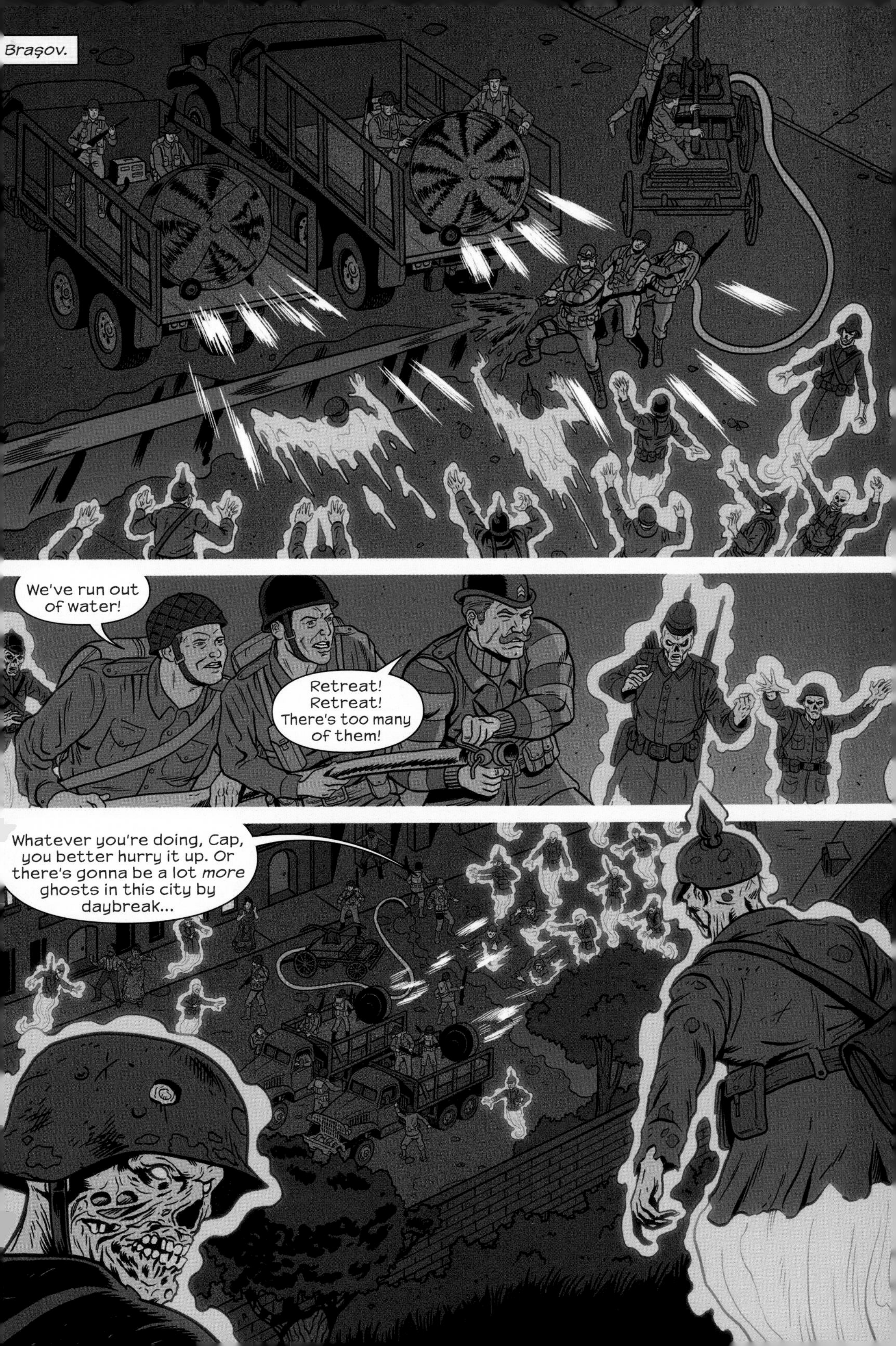
Brașov.
We've run out of water!
Retreat! Retreat! There's too many of them!
Whatever you're doing, Cap, you better hurry it up. Or there's gonna be a lot *more* ghosts in this city by daybreak...

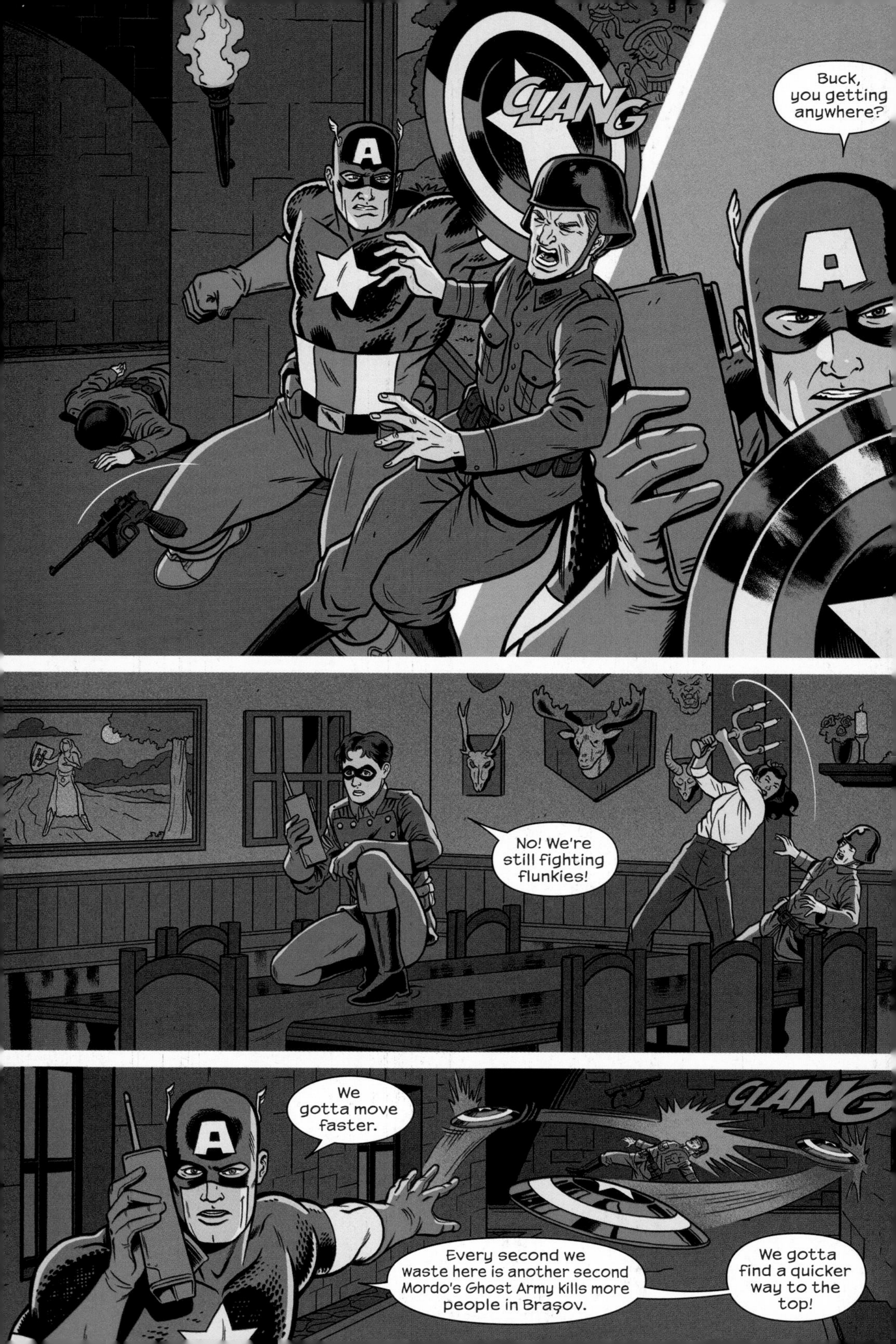
CLANG
Buck, you getting anywhere?
No! We're still fighting flunkies!
We gotta move faster.
CLANG
Every second we waste here is another second Mordo's Ghost Army kills more people in Brașov.
We gotta find a quicker way to the top!

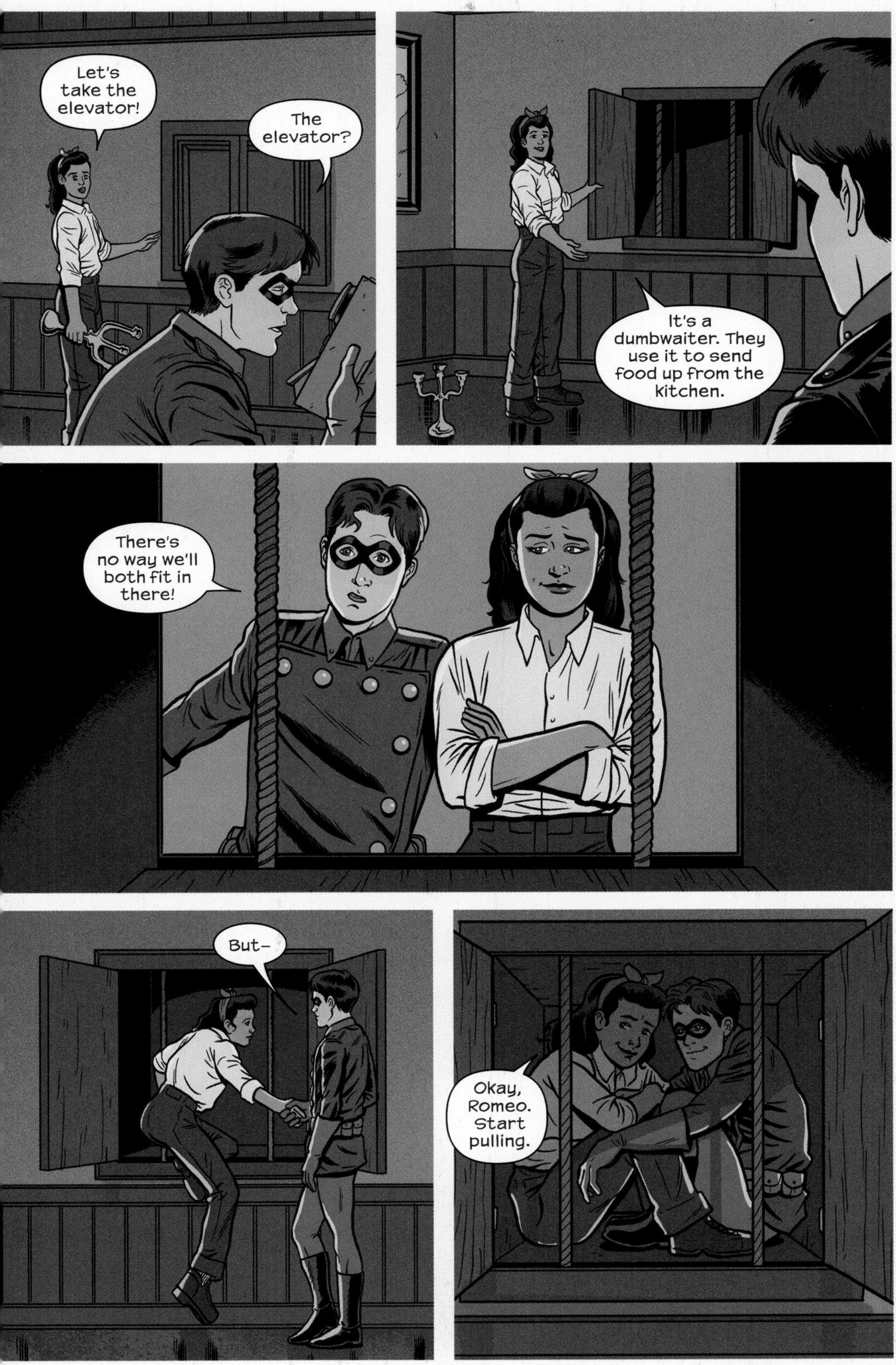
Let's take the elevator!
The elevator?
It's a dumbwaiter. They use it to send food up from the kitchen.
There's no way we'll both fit in there!
But–
Okay, Romeo. Start pulling.

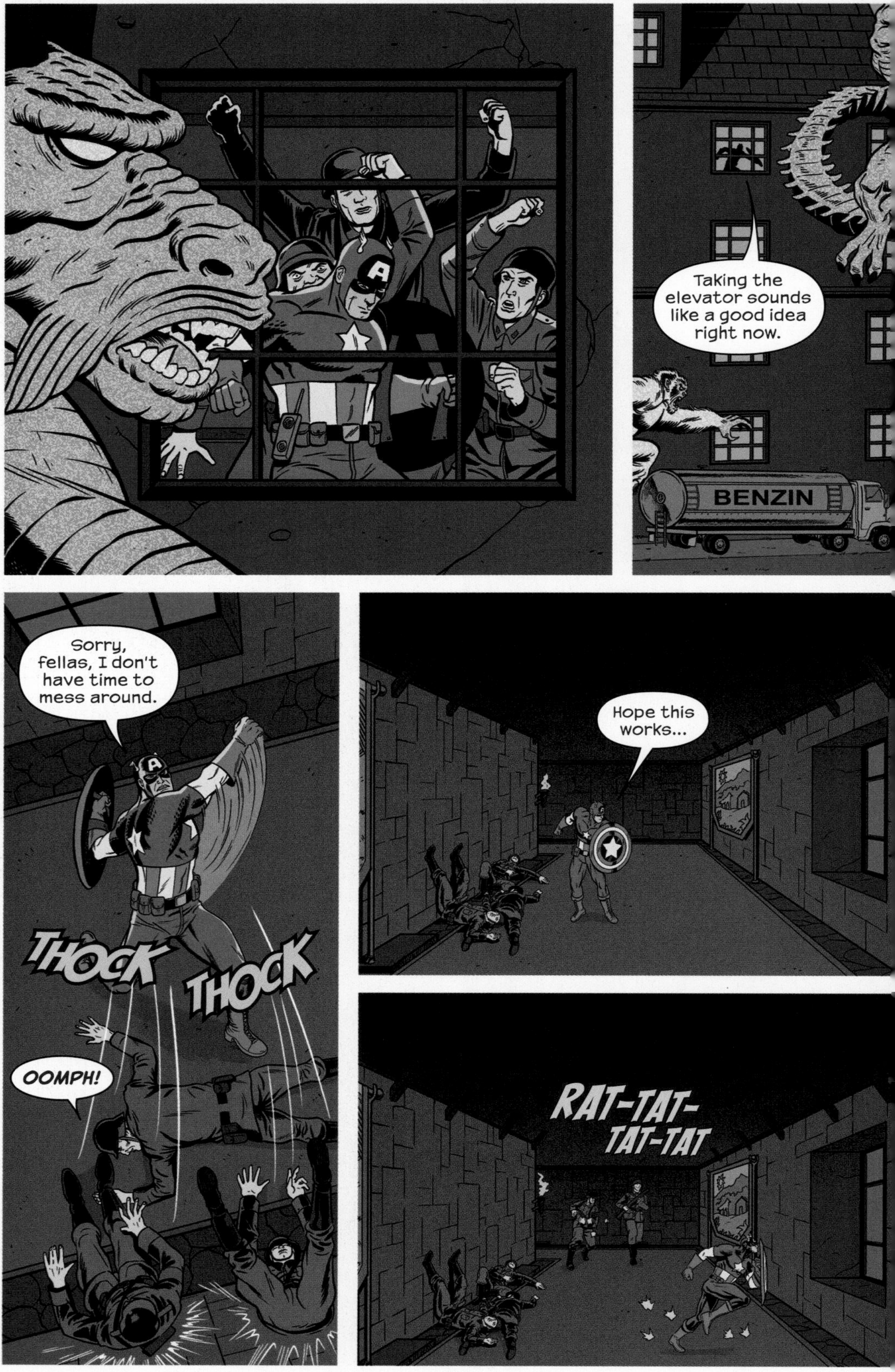

Taking the elevator sounds like a good idea right now.
BENZIN
Sorry, fellas, I don't have time to mess around.
THOCK
THOCK
OOMPH!
Hope this works...
RAT-TAT-TAT-TAT

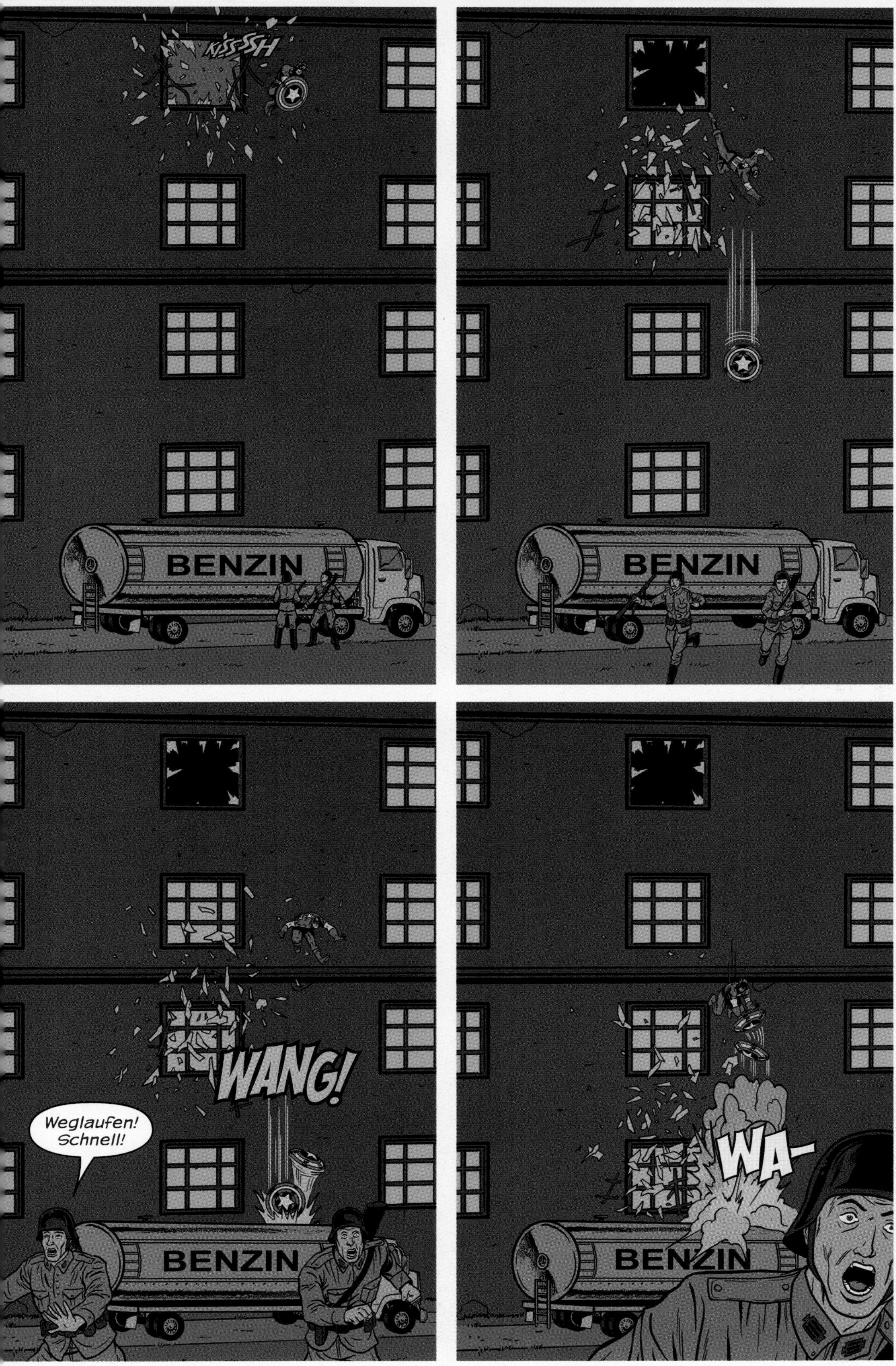
KISS-SSH
BENZIN
BENZIN
WANG!
Weglaufen! Schnell!
BENZIN
WA-
BENZIN

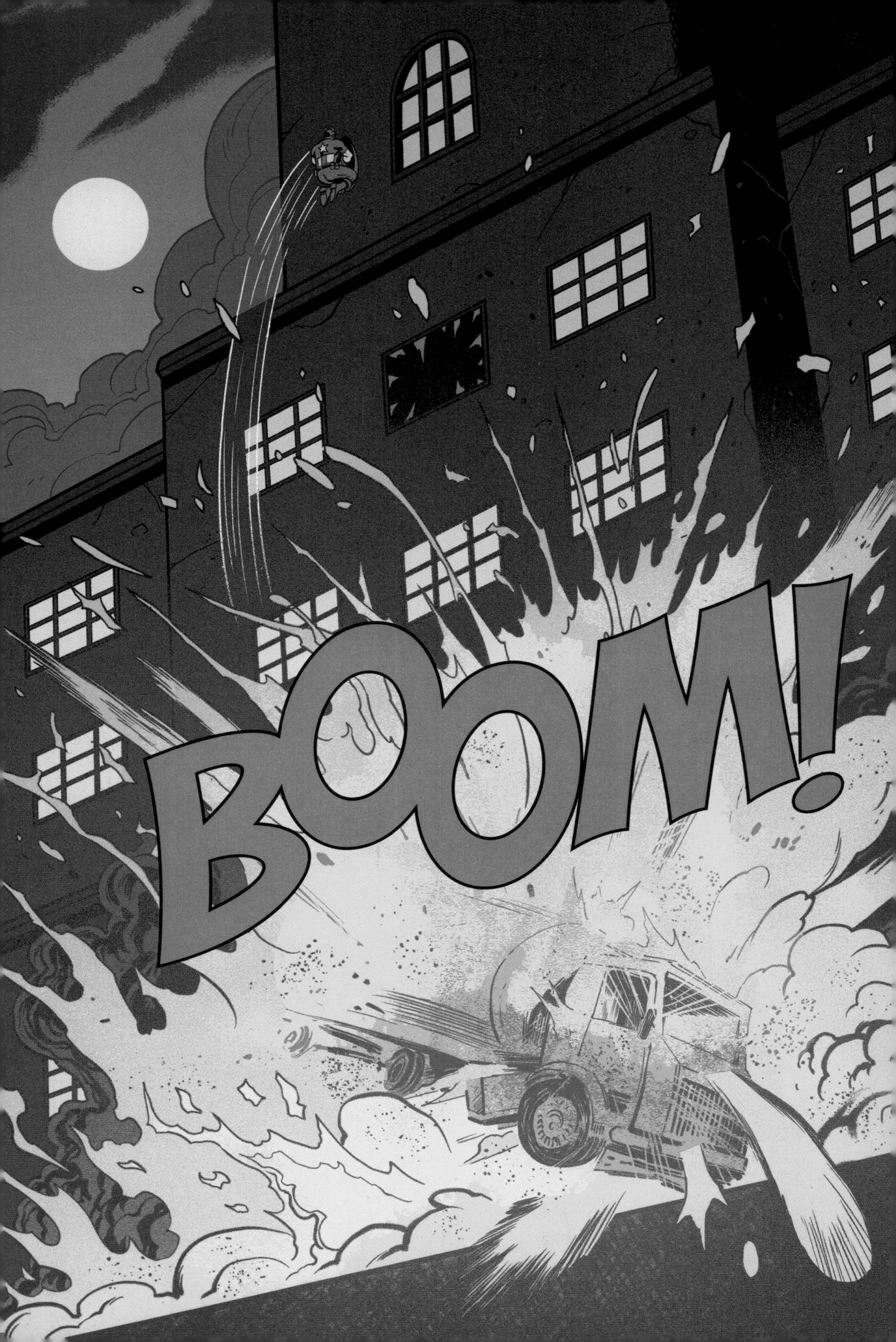
BOOM!

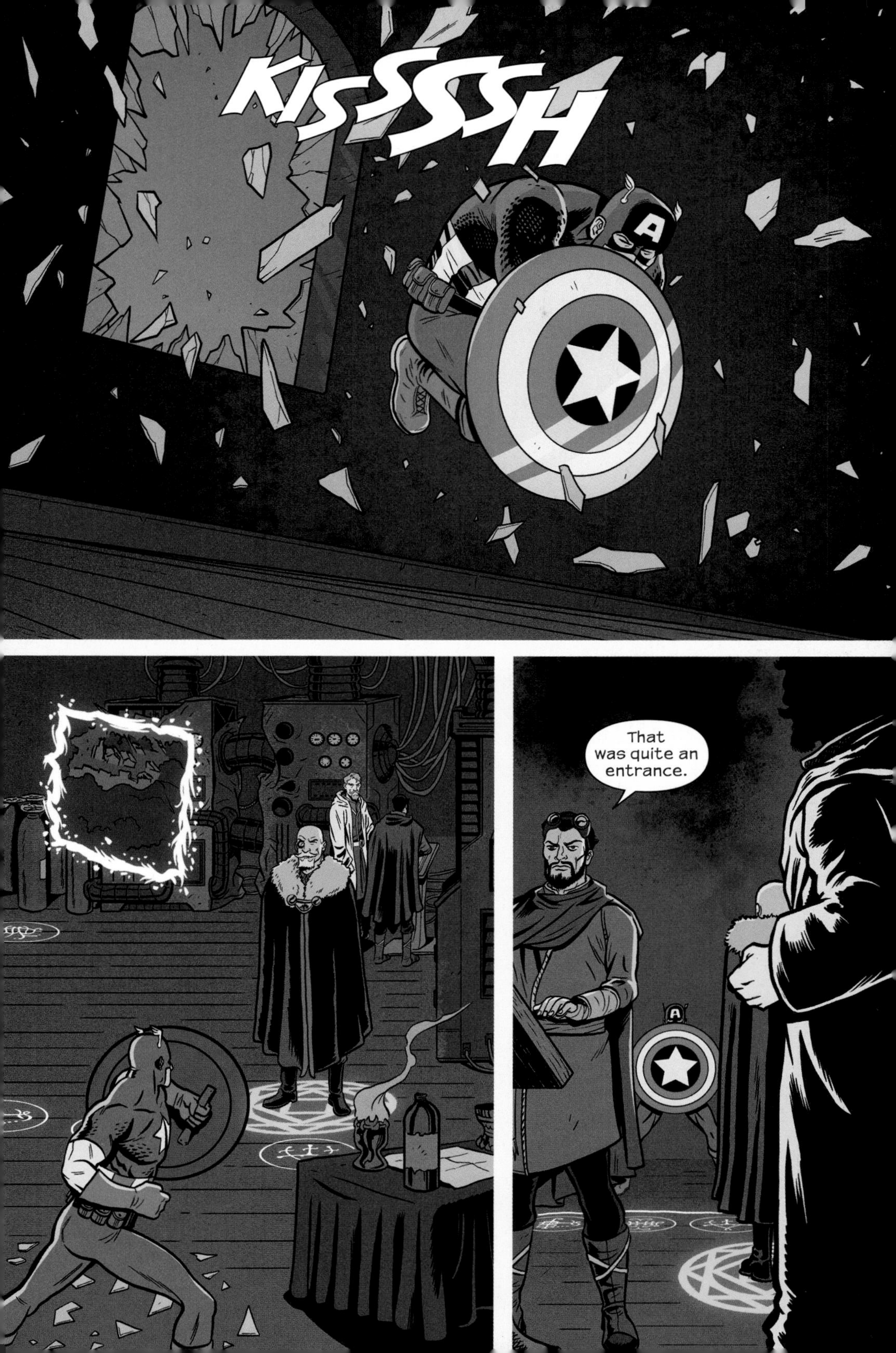
KISSSSH
That was quite an entrance.

WOM

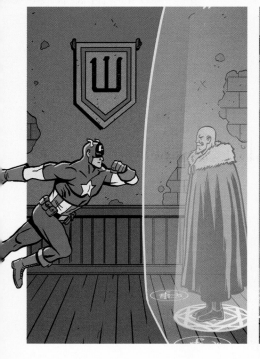

No bullets, no bombs—not even your amazing shield, Captain—can penetrate this magic barrier. You have lost.

FOOM

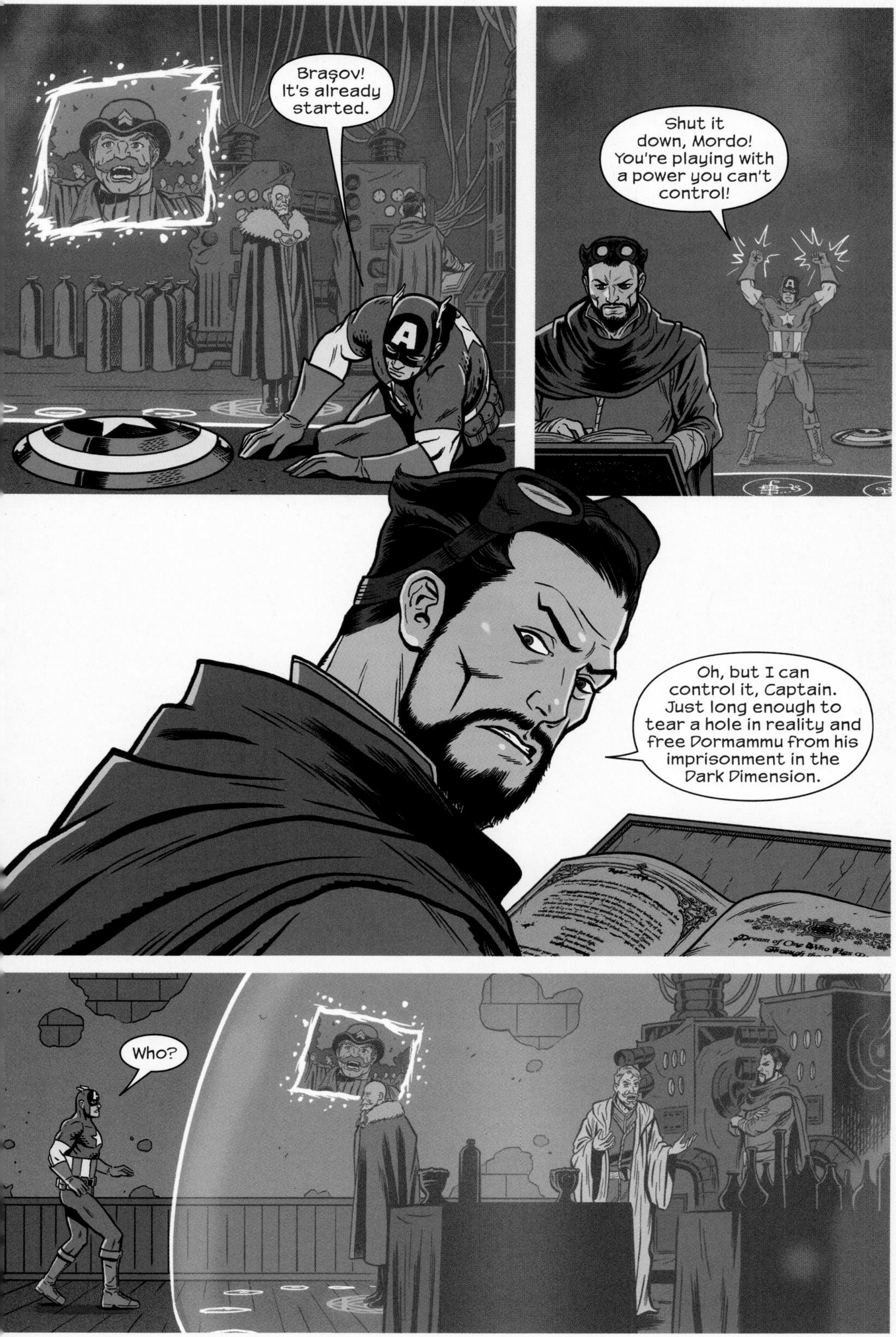
Braşov! It's already started.
Shut it down, Mordo! You're playing with a power you can't control!
Oh, but I can control it, Captain. Just long enough to tear a hole in reality and free Dormammu from his imprisonment in the Dark Dimension.
Who?

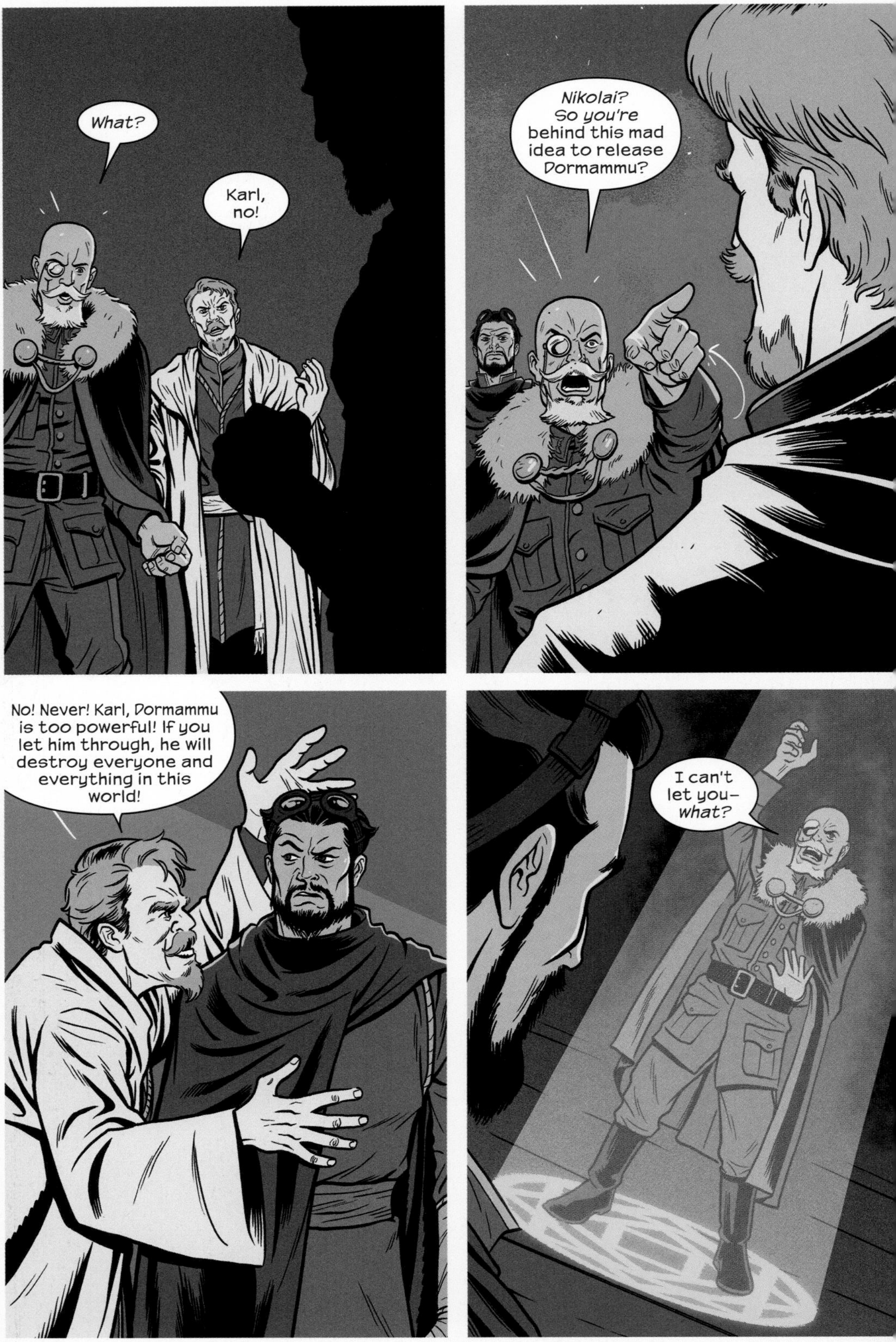
What?
Karl, no!
Nikolai? So you're behind this mad idea to release Dormammu?
No! Never! Karl, Dormammu is too powerful! If you let him through, he will destroy everyone and everything in this world!
I can't let you—what?

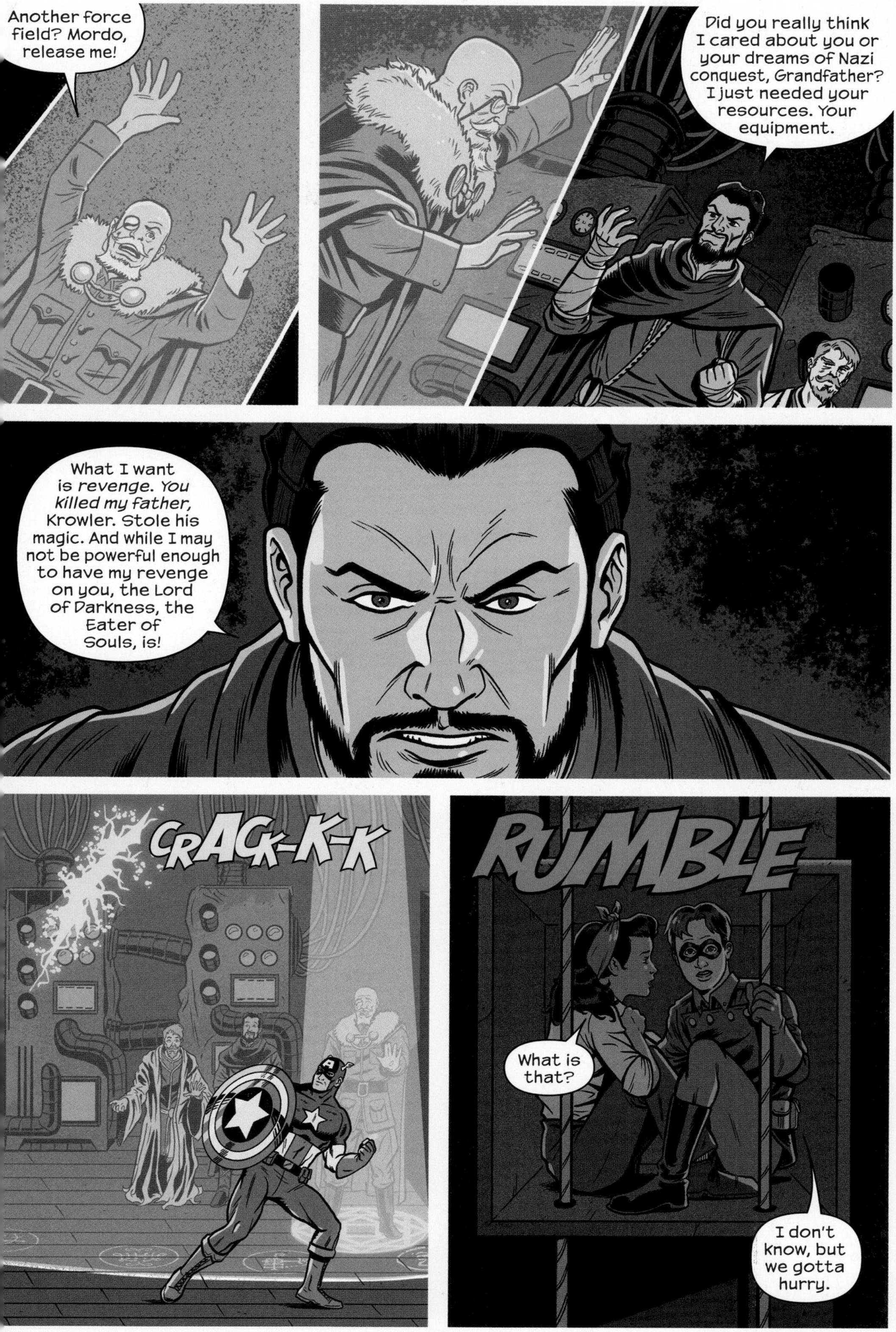

Another force field? Mordo, release me!
Did you really think I cared about you or your dreams of Nazi conquest, Grandfather? I just needed your resources. Your equipment.
What I want is *revenge*. *You killed my father*, Krowler. Stole his magic. And while I may not be powerful enough to have my revenge on you, the Lord of Darkness, the Eater of Souls, is!
CRACK-K-K
RUMBLE
What is that?
I don't know, but we gotta hurry.

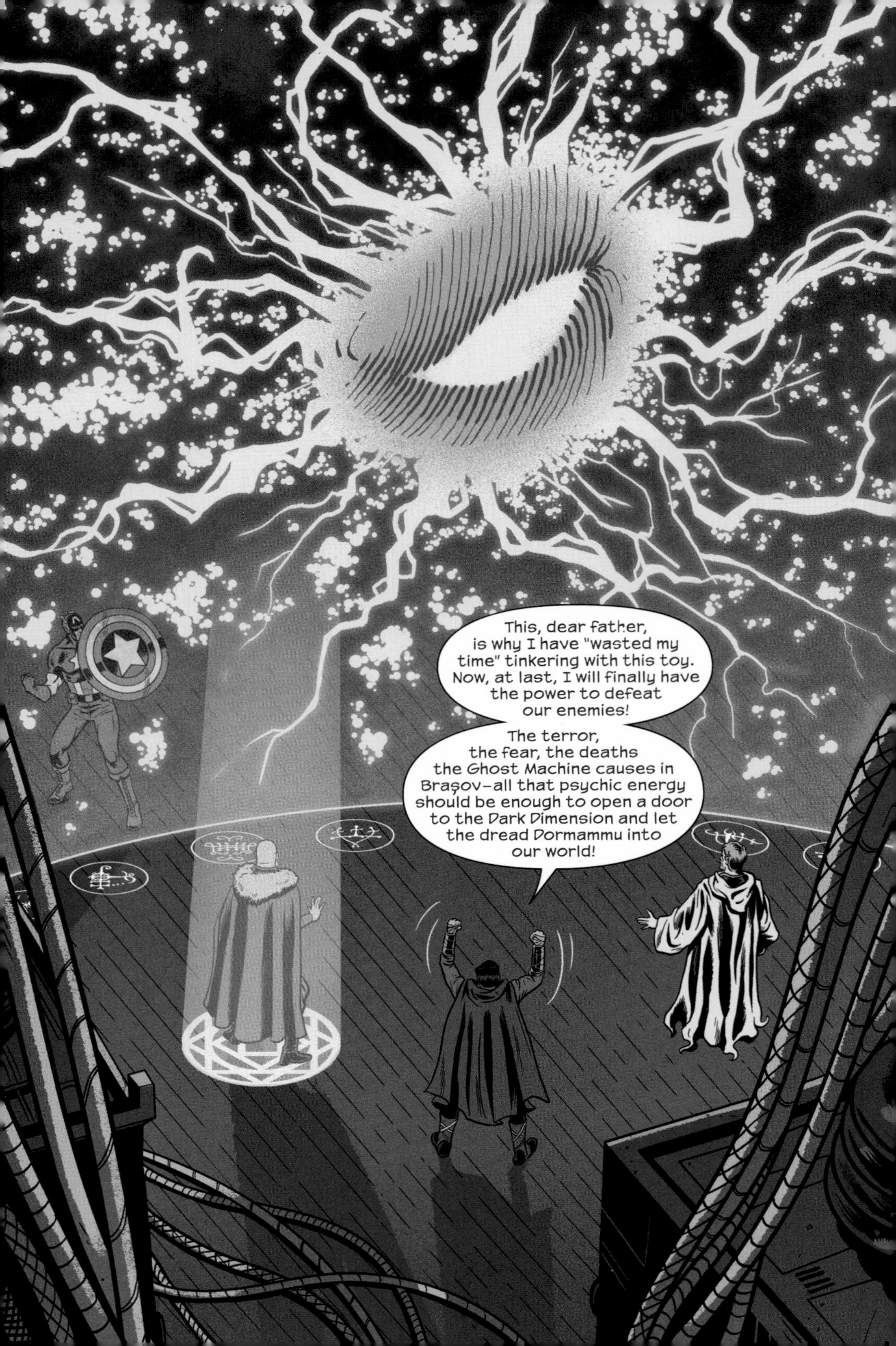
This, dear father, is why I have "wasted my time" tinkering with this toy. Now, at last, I will finally have the power to defeat our enemies!
The terror, the fear, the deaths the Ghost Machine causes in Brașov—all that psychic energy should be enough to open a door to the Dark Dimension and let the dread Dormammu into our world!

CHAPTER EIGHT
REVENGE

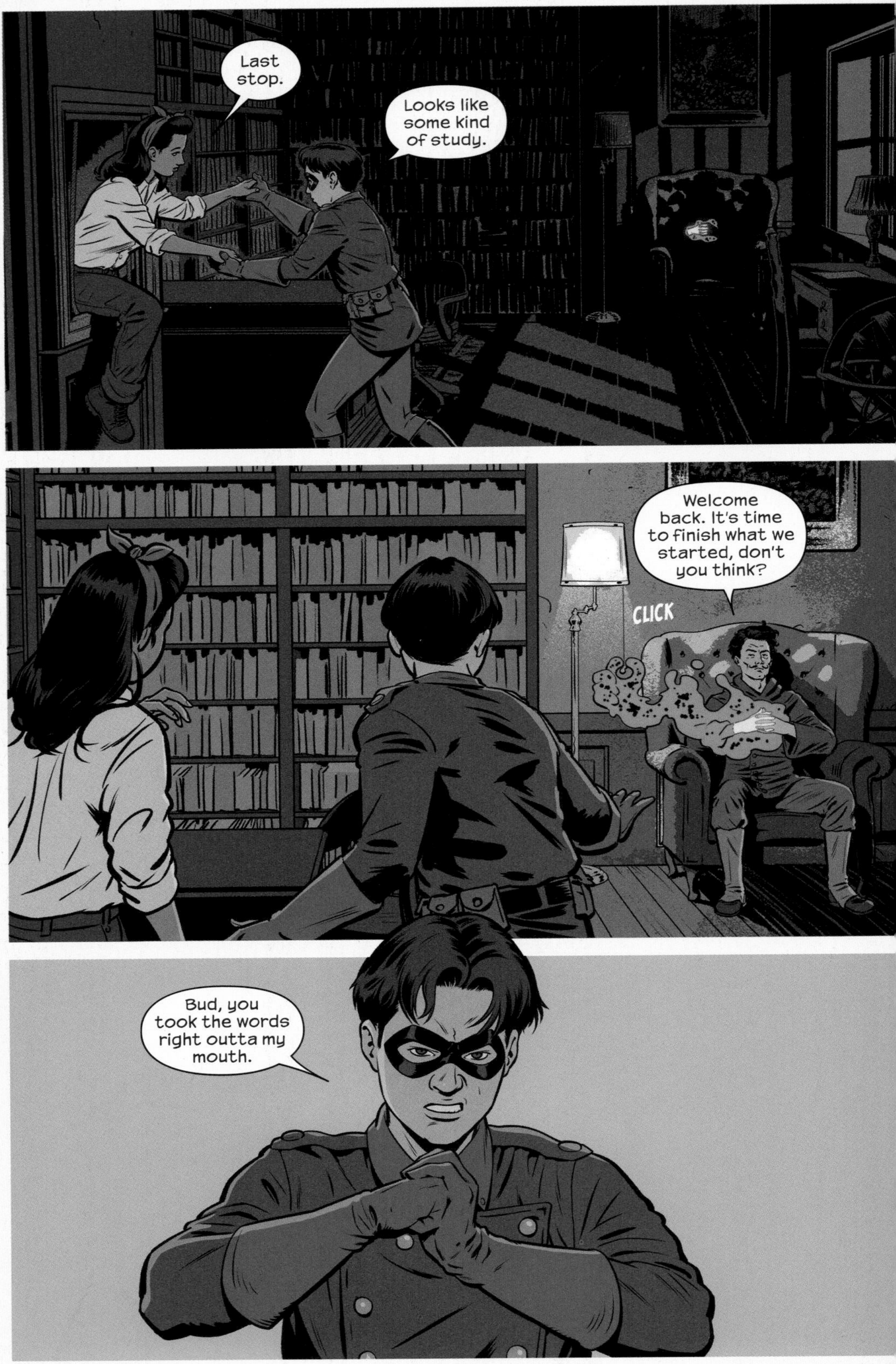
Last stop.
Looks like some kind of study.
CLICK
Welcome back. It's time to finish what we started, don't you think?
Bud, you took the words right outta my mouth.

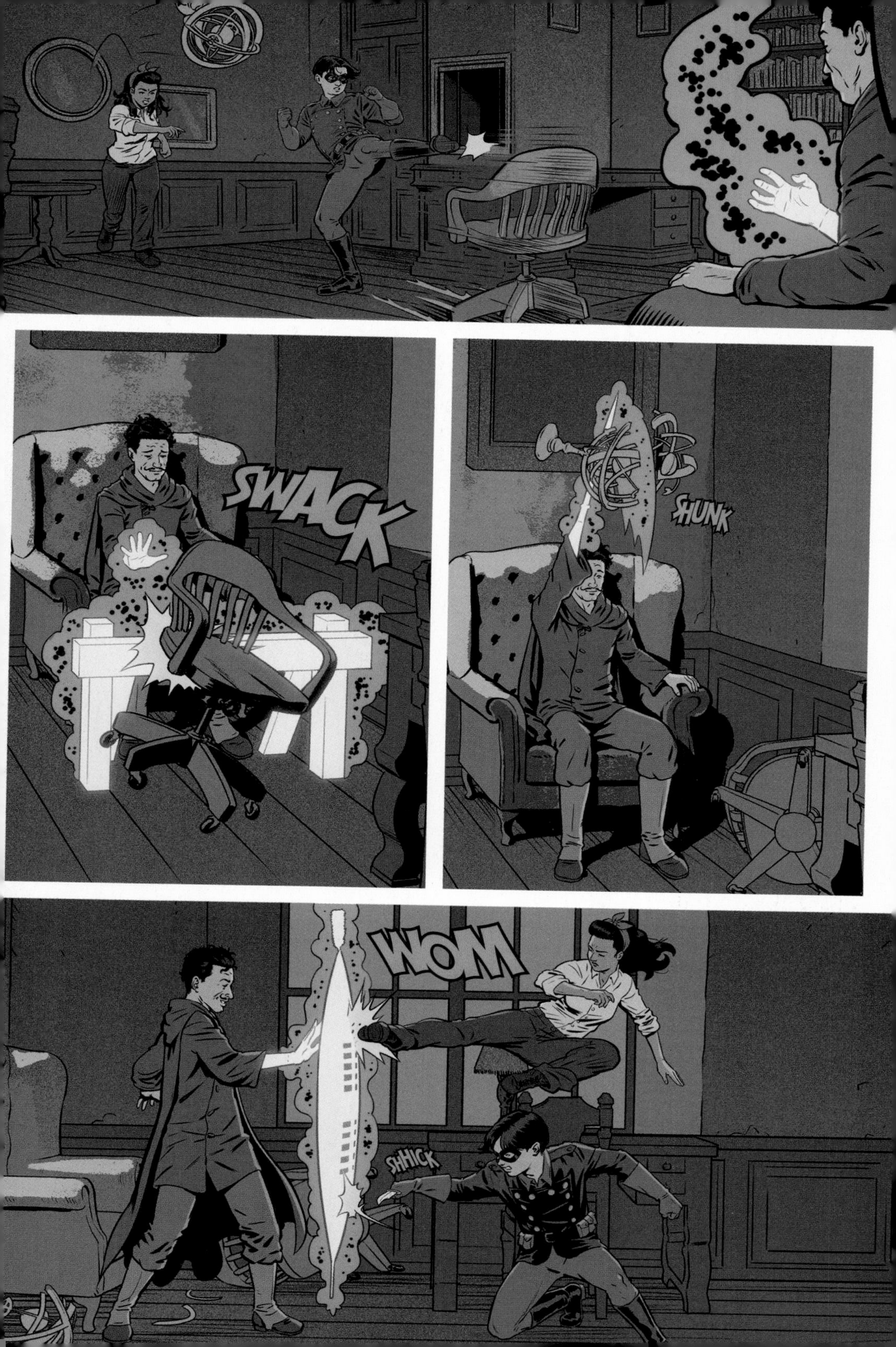
SWACK
SHUNK
WOM
SHHICK

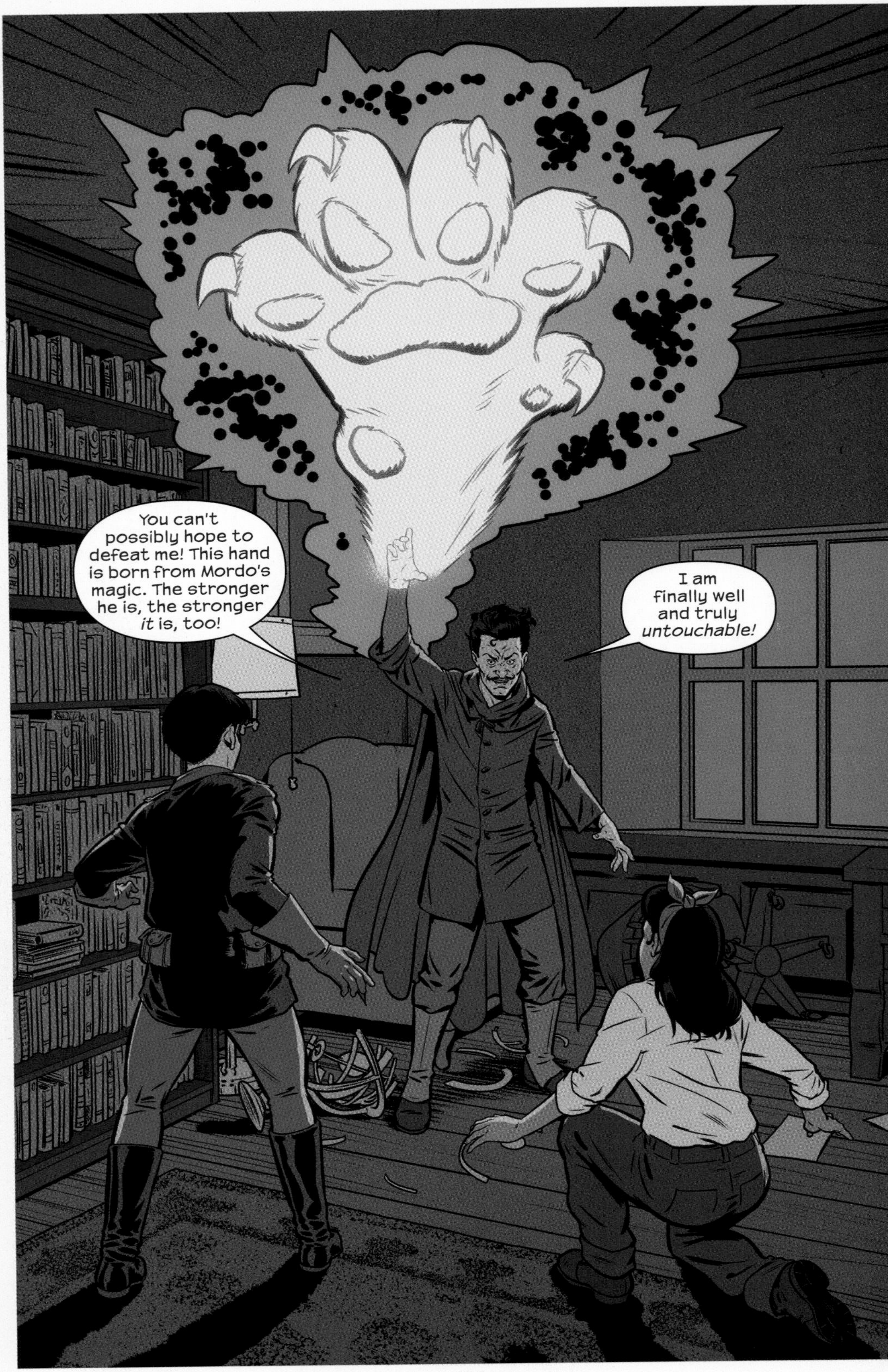
You can't possibly hope to defeat me! This hand is born from Mordo's magic. The stronger he is, the stronger *it* is, too!
I am finally well and truly *untouchable!*

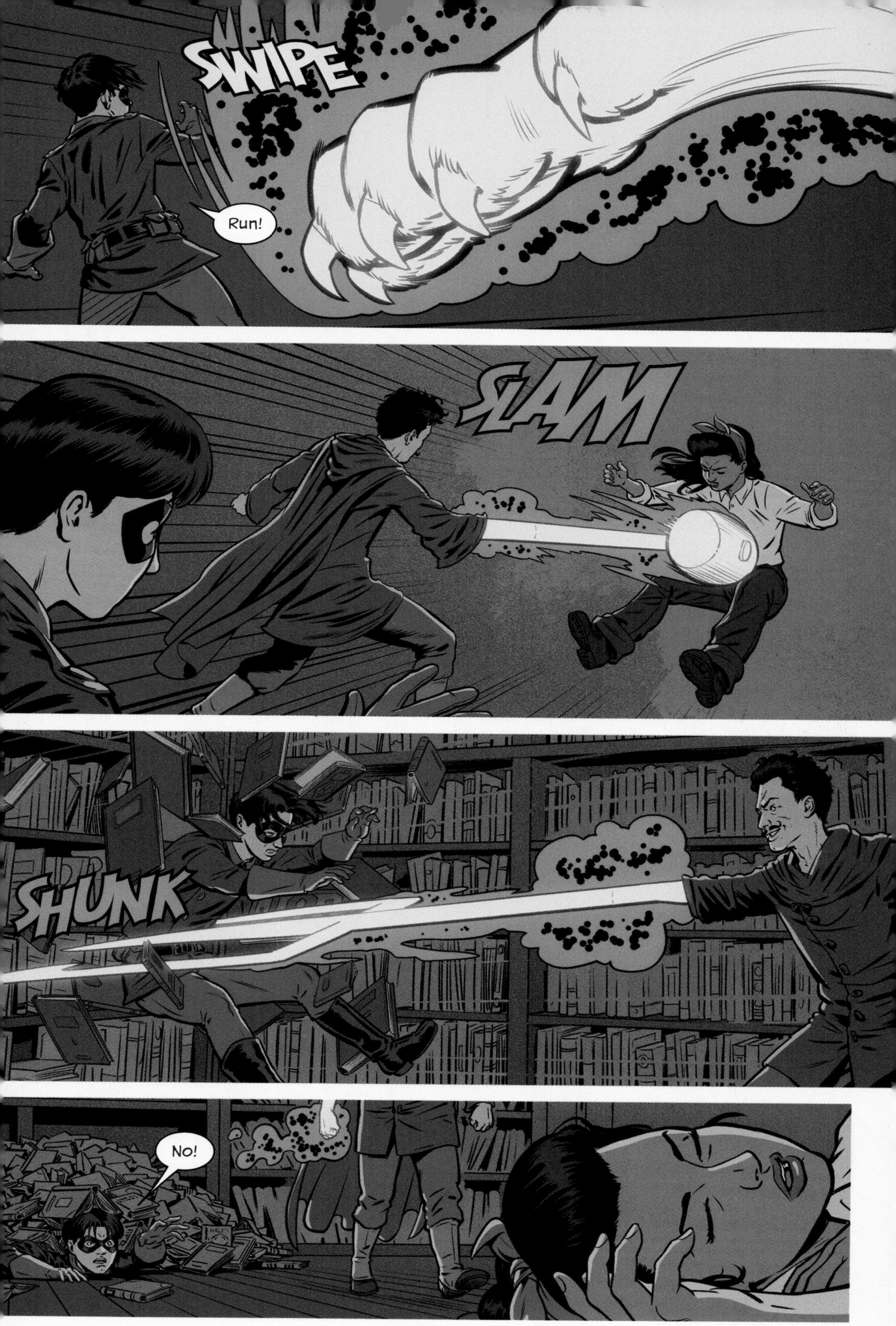
SWIPE
Run!
SLAM
SHUNK
No!

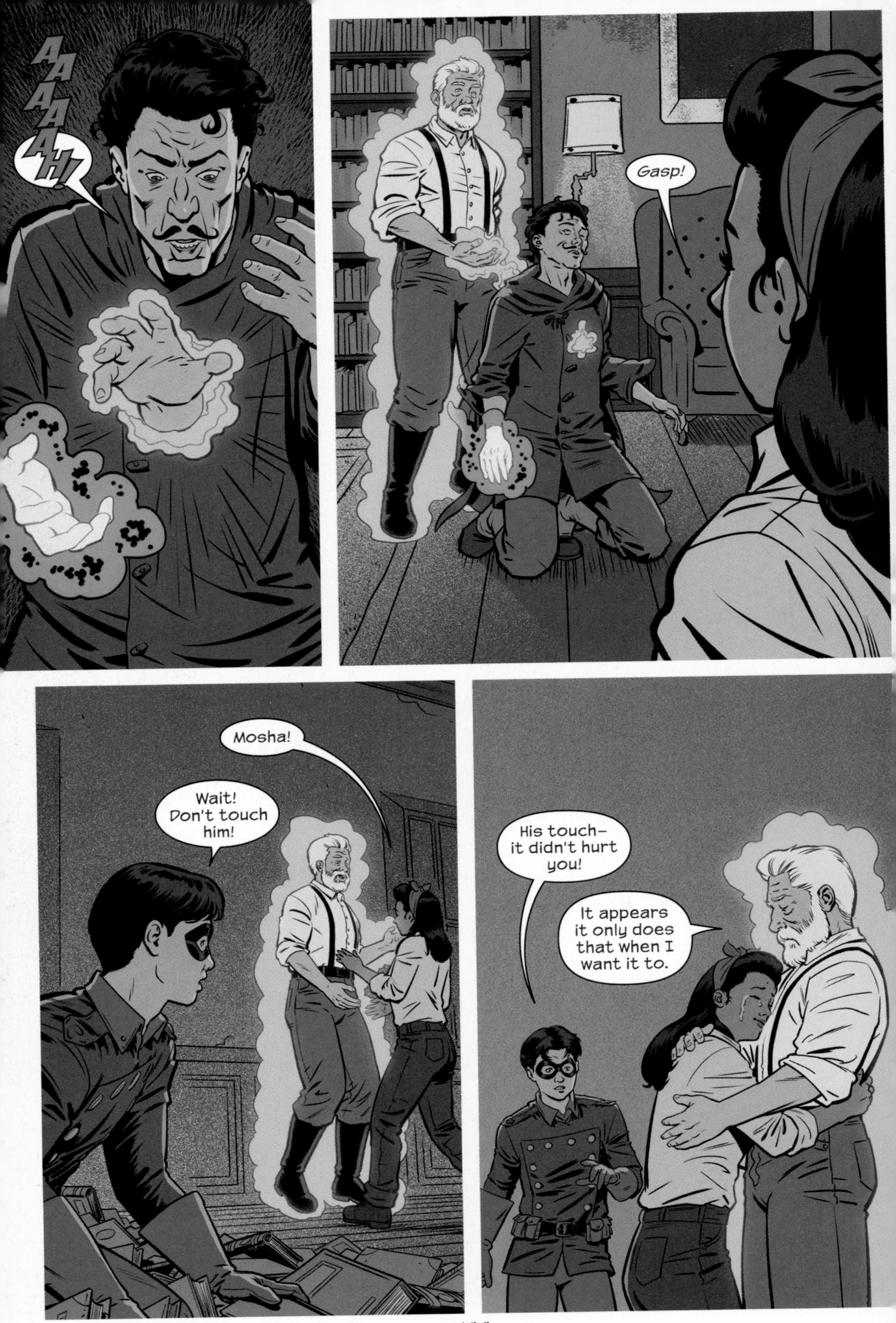
AAAAAH!
Gasp!
Mosha!
Wait! Don't touch him!
His touch— it didn't hurt you!
It appears it only does that when I want it to.

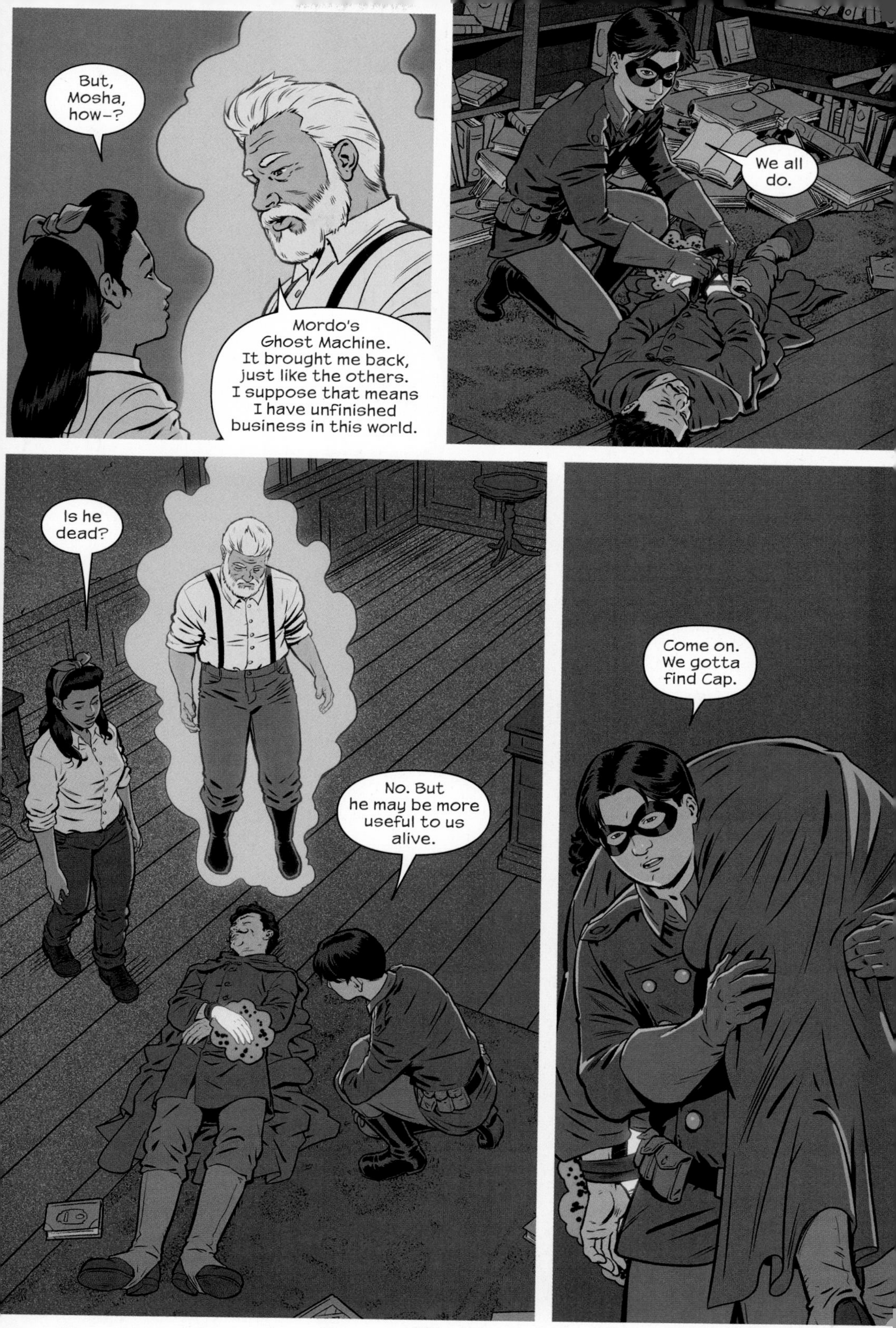
But, Mosha, how–?
Mordo's Ghost Machine. It brought me back, just like the others. I suppose that means I have unfinished business in this world.
We all do.
Is he dead?
No. But he may be more useful to us alive.
Come on. We gotta find Cap.

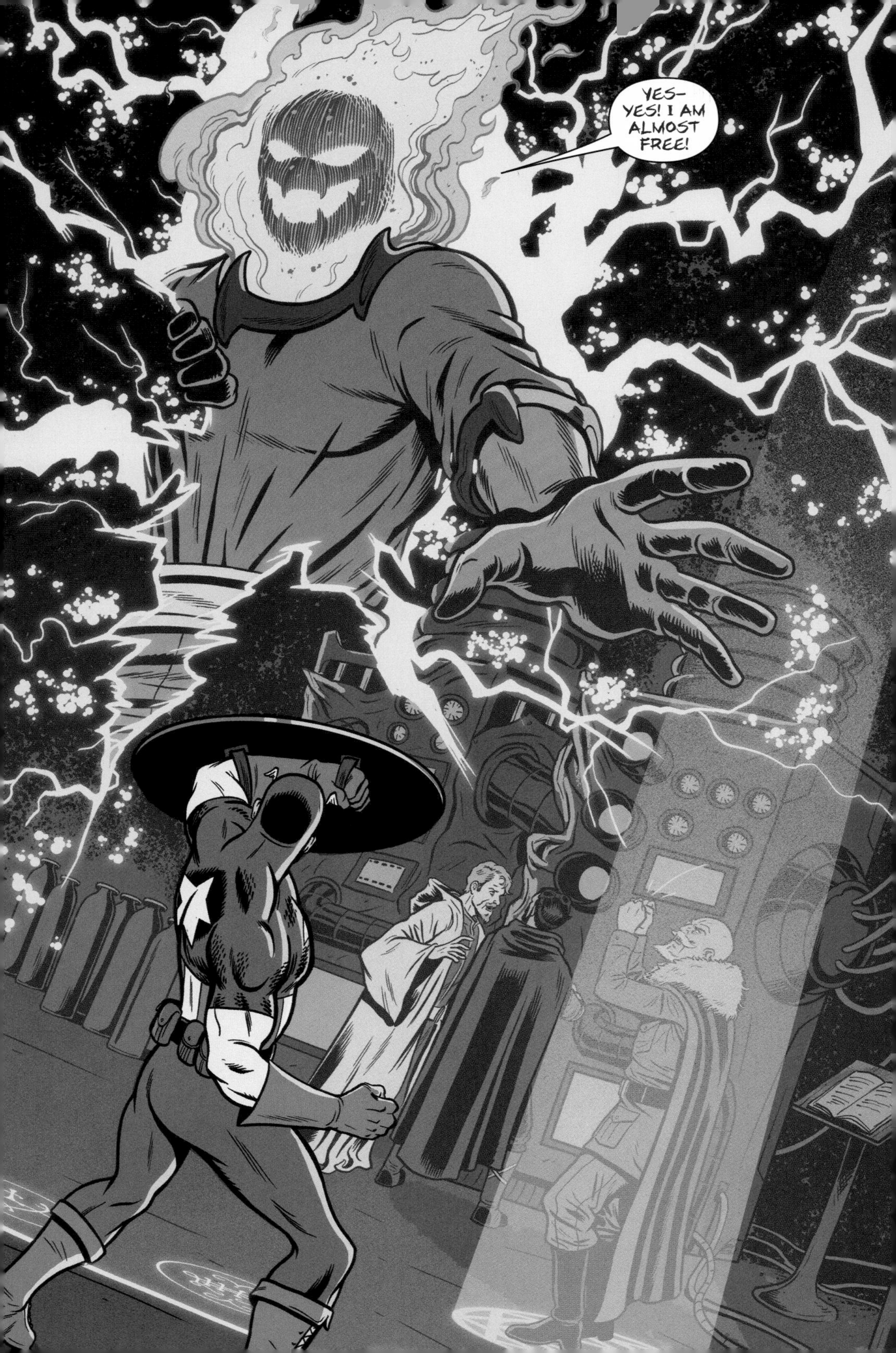
YES-YES! I AM ALMOST FREE!

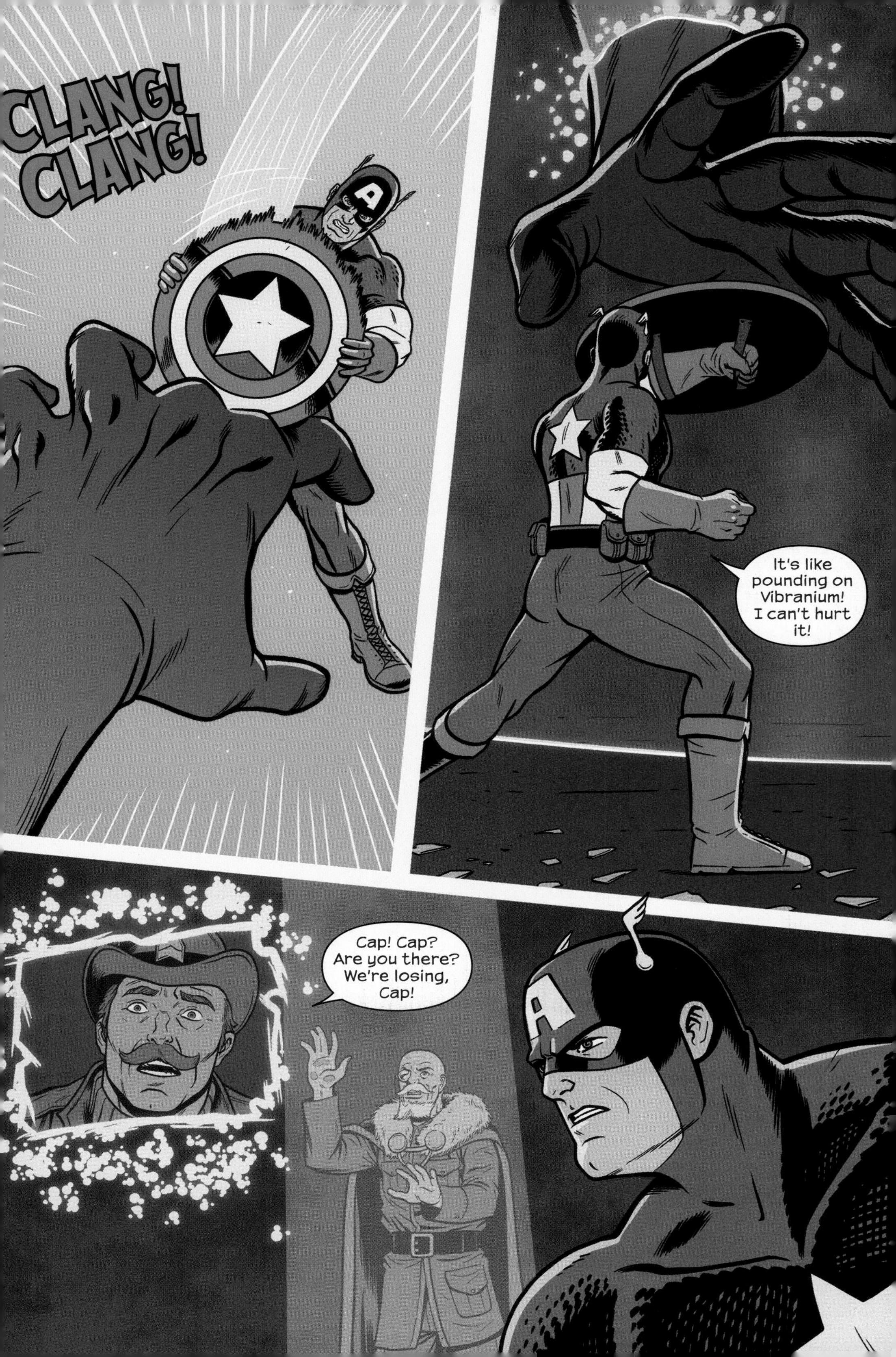
CLANG!
CLANG!
It's like pounding on Vibranium! I can't hurt it!
Cap! Cap? Are you there? We're losing, Cap!

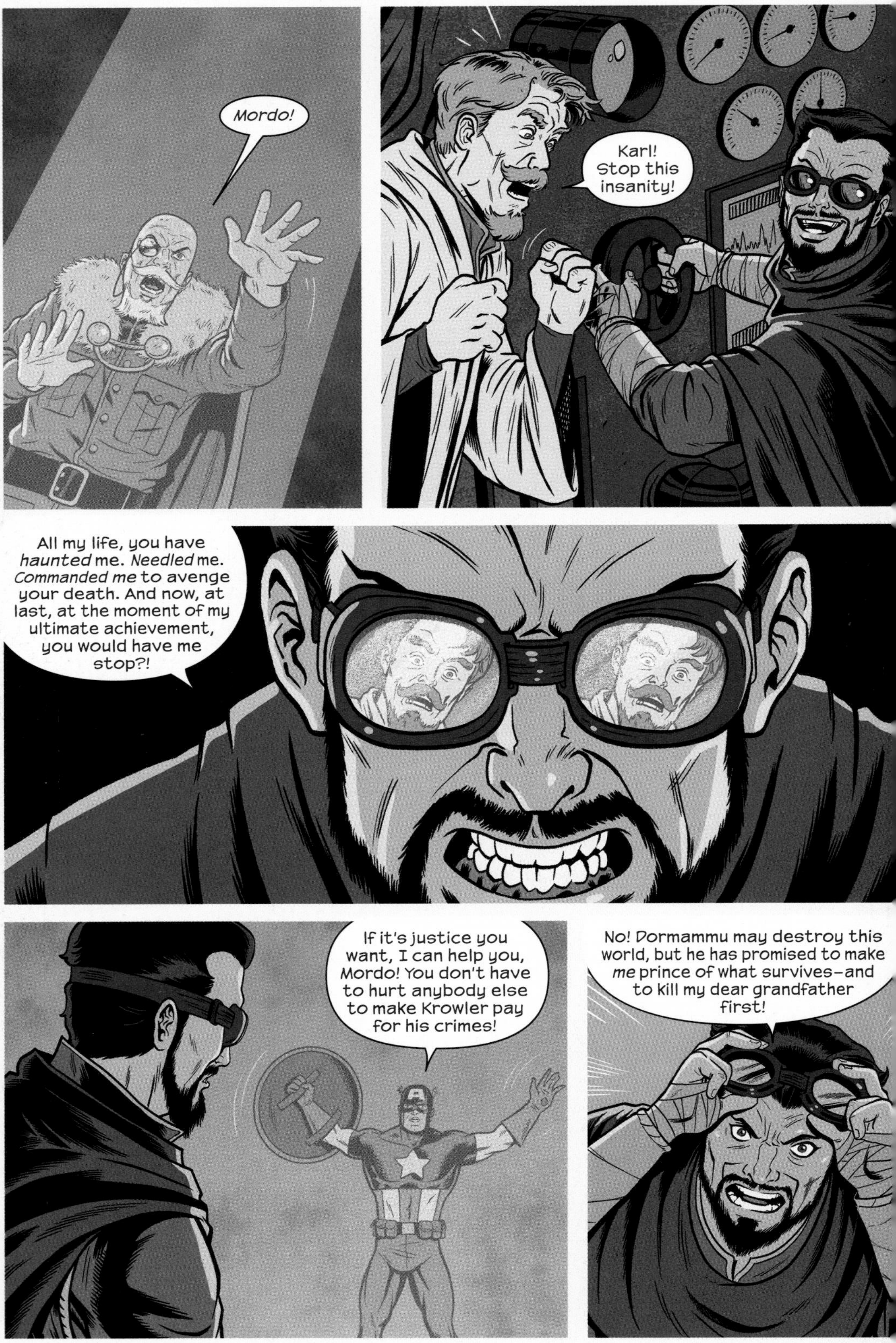
Mordo!
Karl! Stop this insanity!
All my life, you have *haunted* me. *Needled* me. *Commanded me* to avenge your death. And now, at last, at the moment of my ultimate achievement, you would have me stop?!
If it's justice you want, I can help you, Mordo! You don't have to hurt anybody else to make Krowler pay for his crimes!
No! Dormammu may destroy this world, but he has promised to make *me* prince of what survives–and to kill my dear grandfather first!

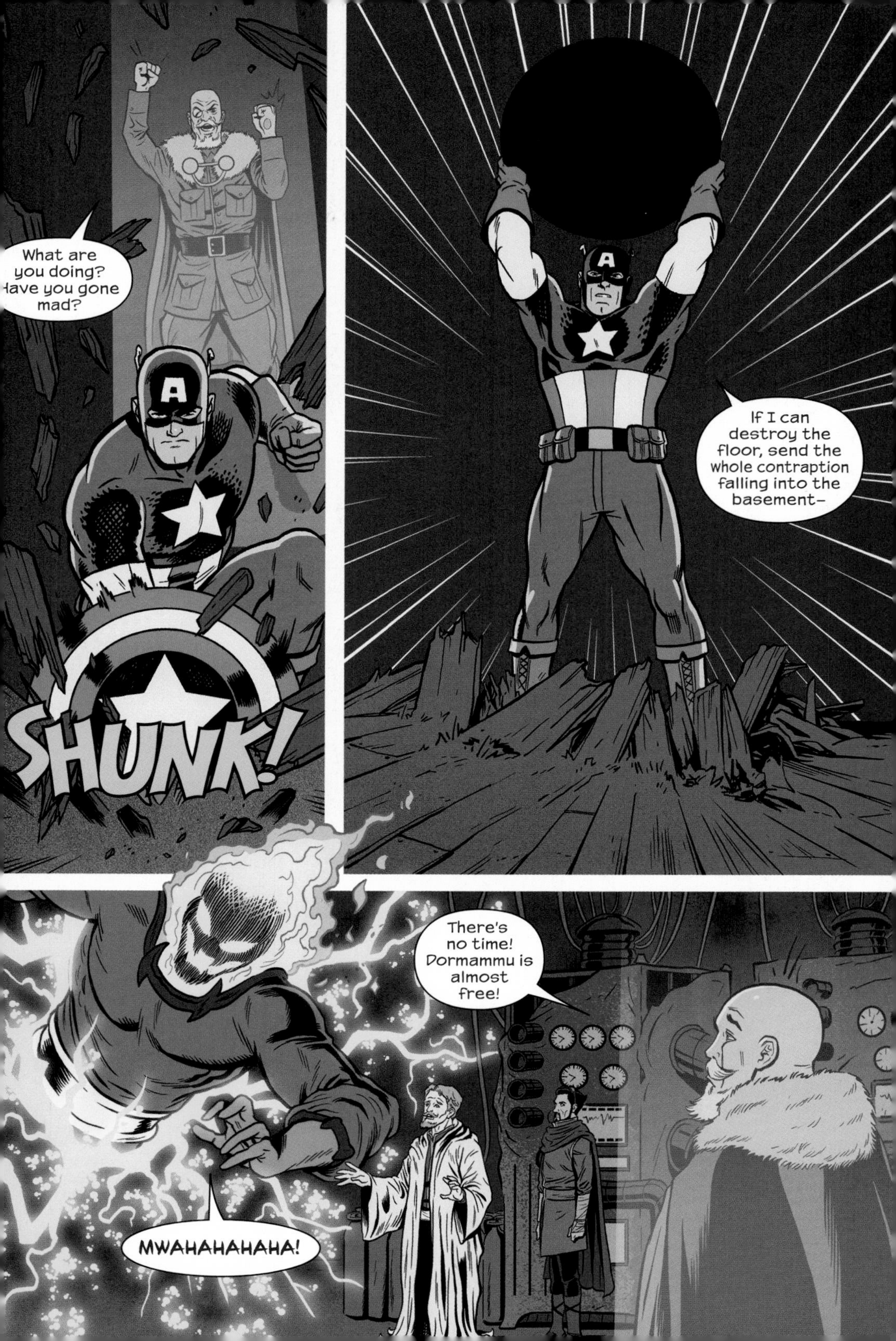
What are you doing? Have you gone mad?
SHUNK!
If I can destroy the floor, send the whole contraption falling into the basement–
There's no time! Dormammu is almost free!
MWAHAHAHAHA!

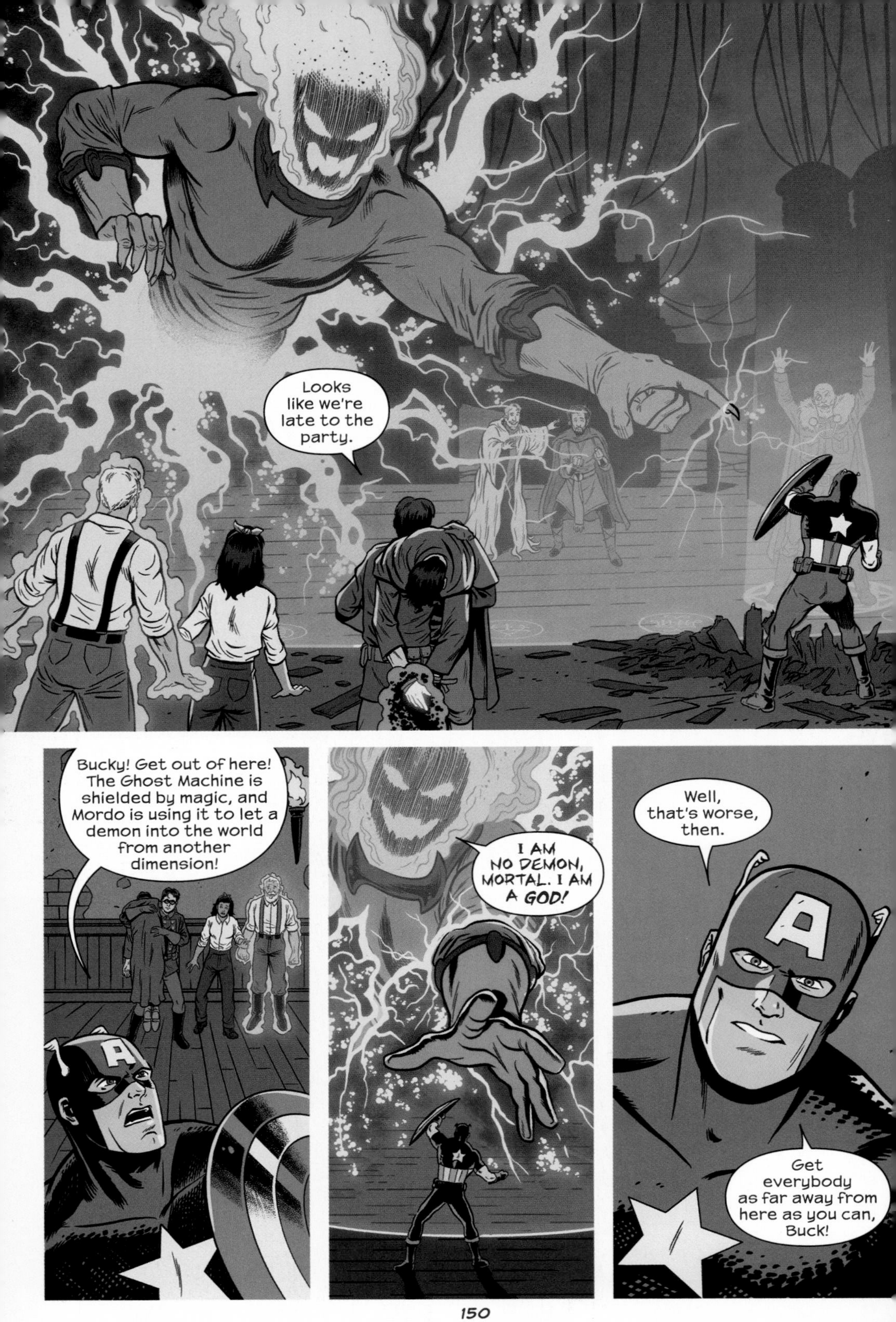
Looks like we're late to the party.
Bucky! Get out of here! The Ghost Machine is shielded by magic, and Mordo is using it to let a demon into the world from another dimension!
I AM NO DEMON, MORTAL. I AM A GOD!
Well, that's worse, then.
Get everybody as far away from here as you can, Buck!

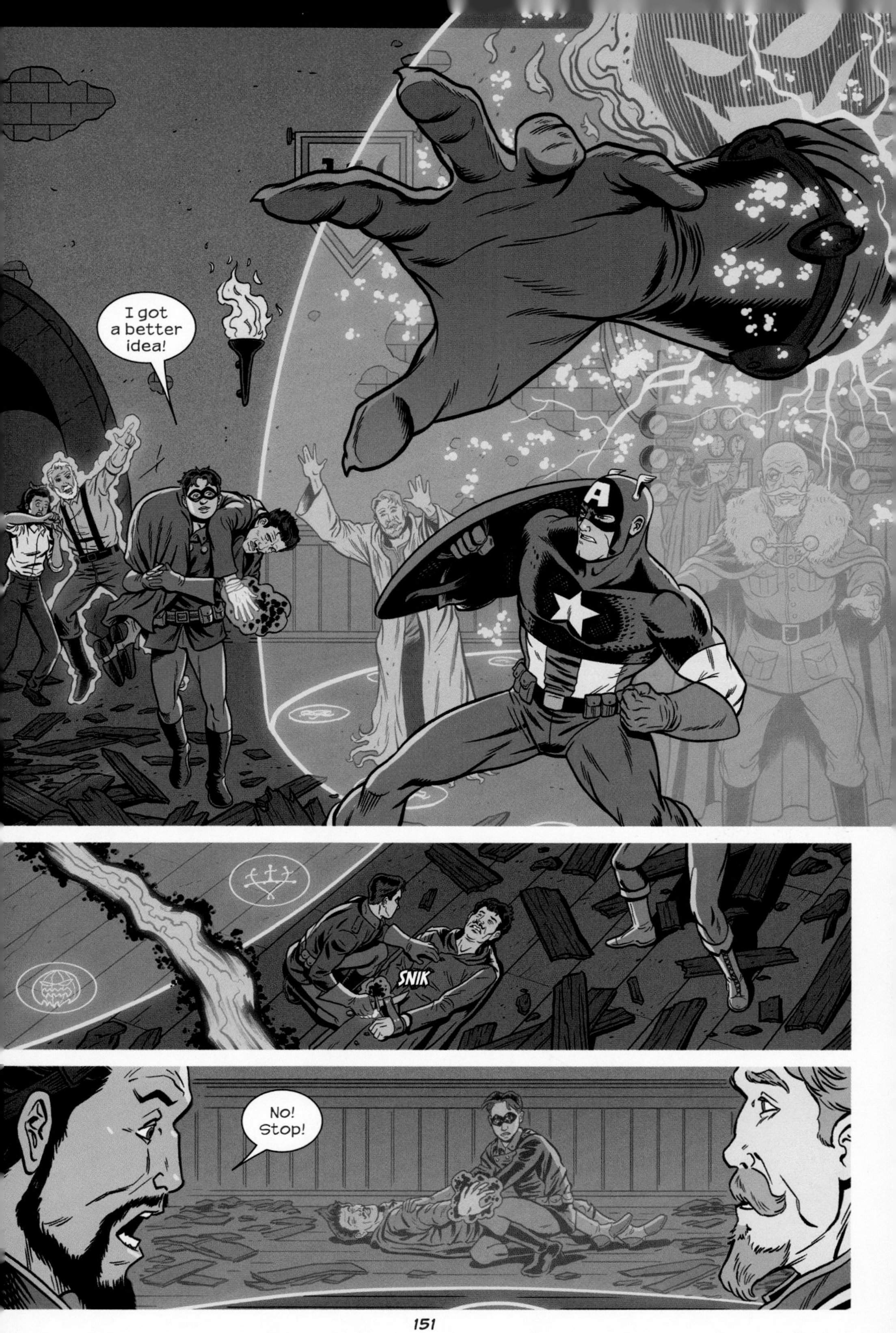
I got a better idea!
SNIK
No! Stop!

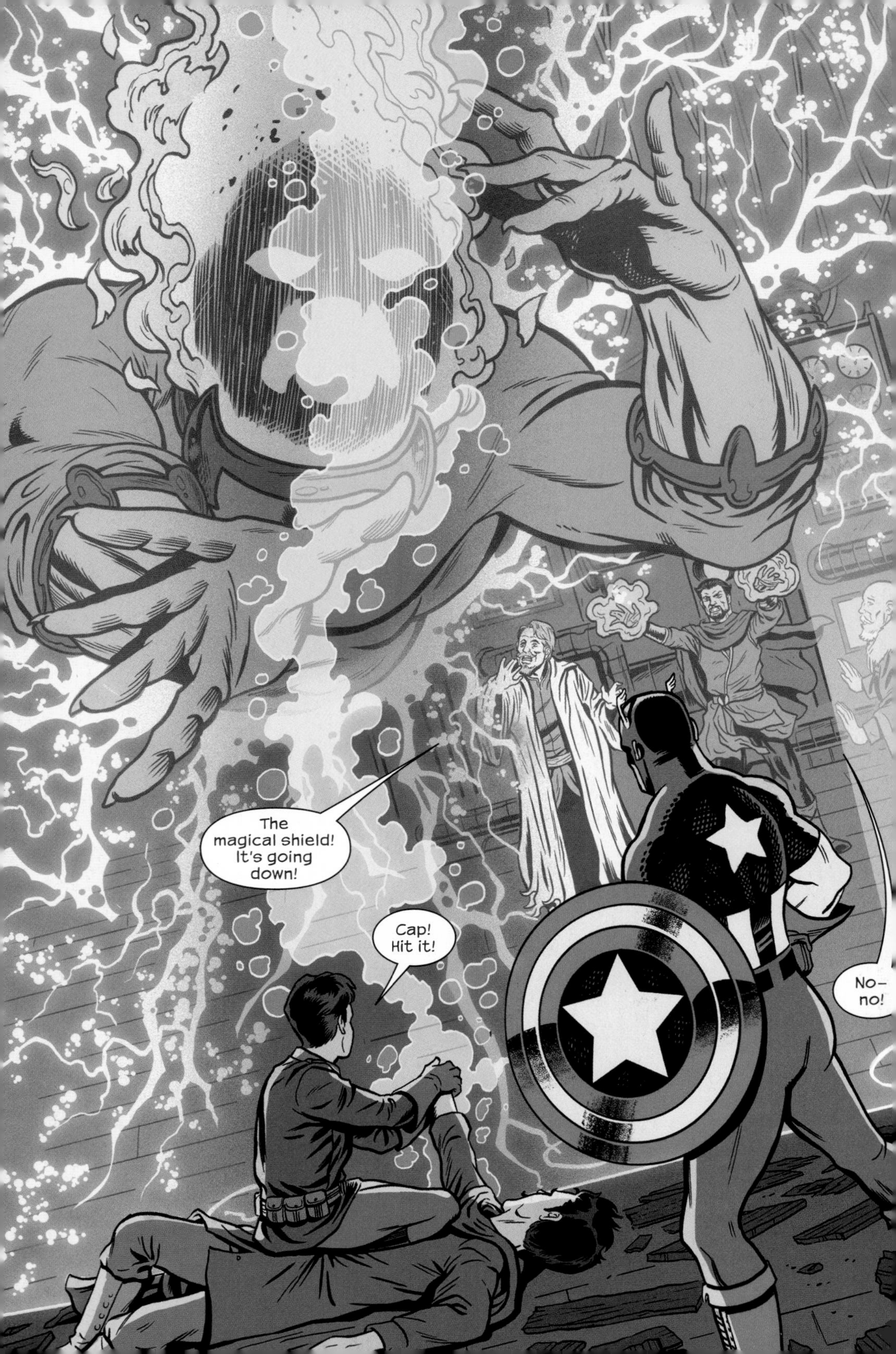
The magical shield! It's going down!
Cap! Hit it!
No— no!

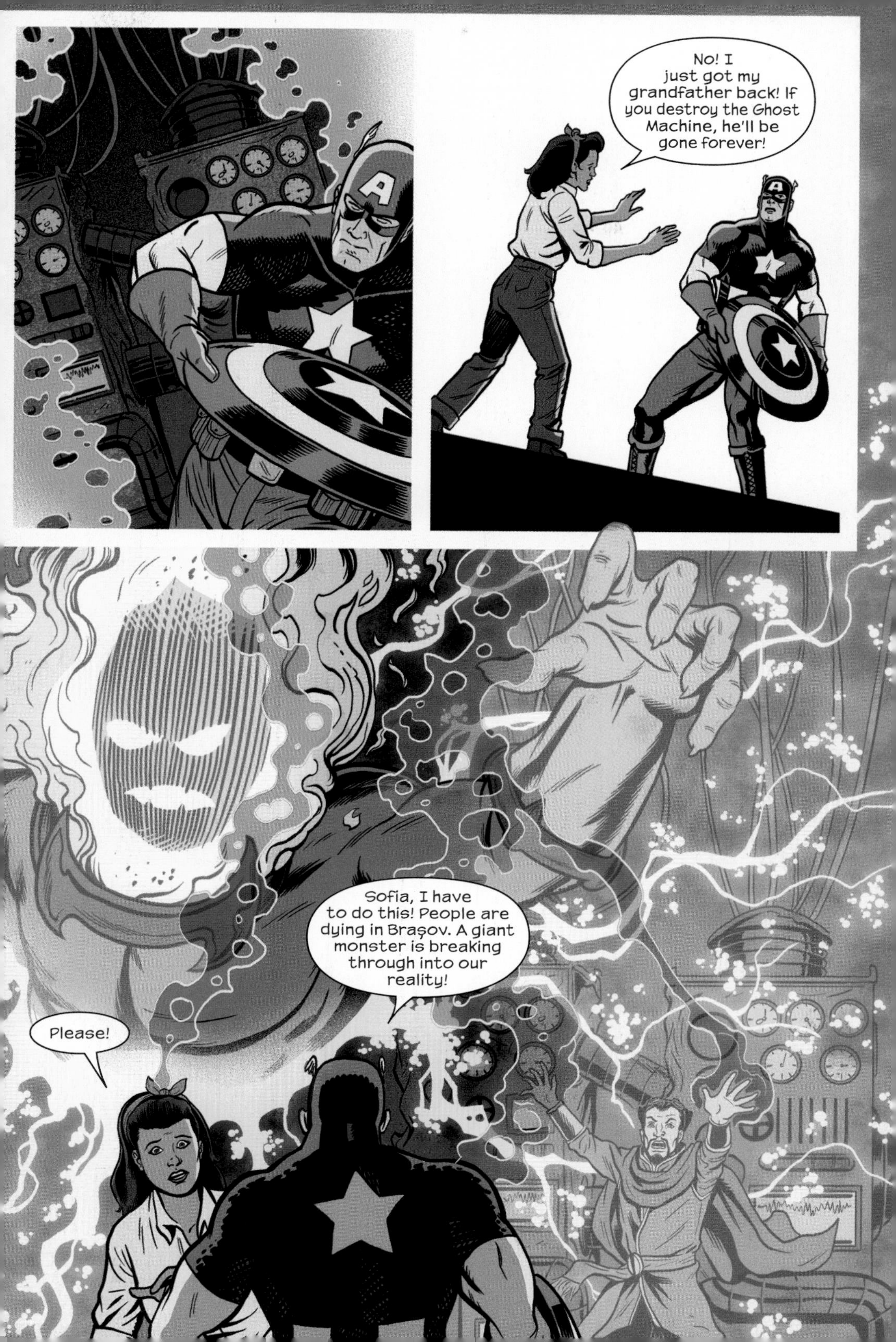
No! I just got my grandfather back! If you destroy the Ghost Machine, he'll be gone forever!
Sofia, I have to do this! People are dying in Brașov. A giant monster is breaking through into our reality!
Please!

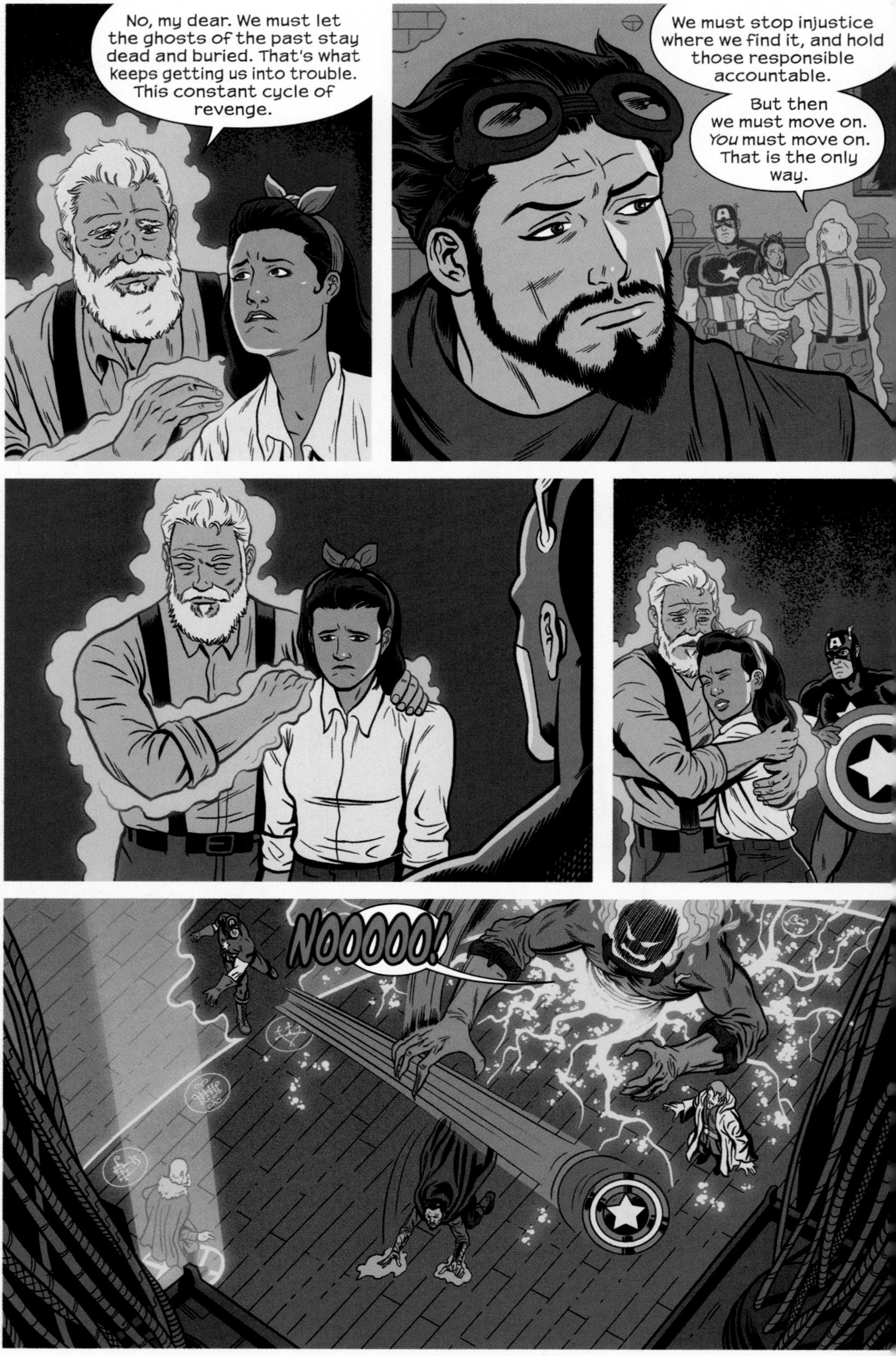
No, my dear. We must let the ghosts of the past stay dead and buried. That's what keeps getting us into trouble. This constant cycle of revenge.
We must stop injustice where we find it, and hold those responsible accountable.
But then we must move on. *You* must move on. That is the only way.
NOOOOO!

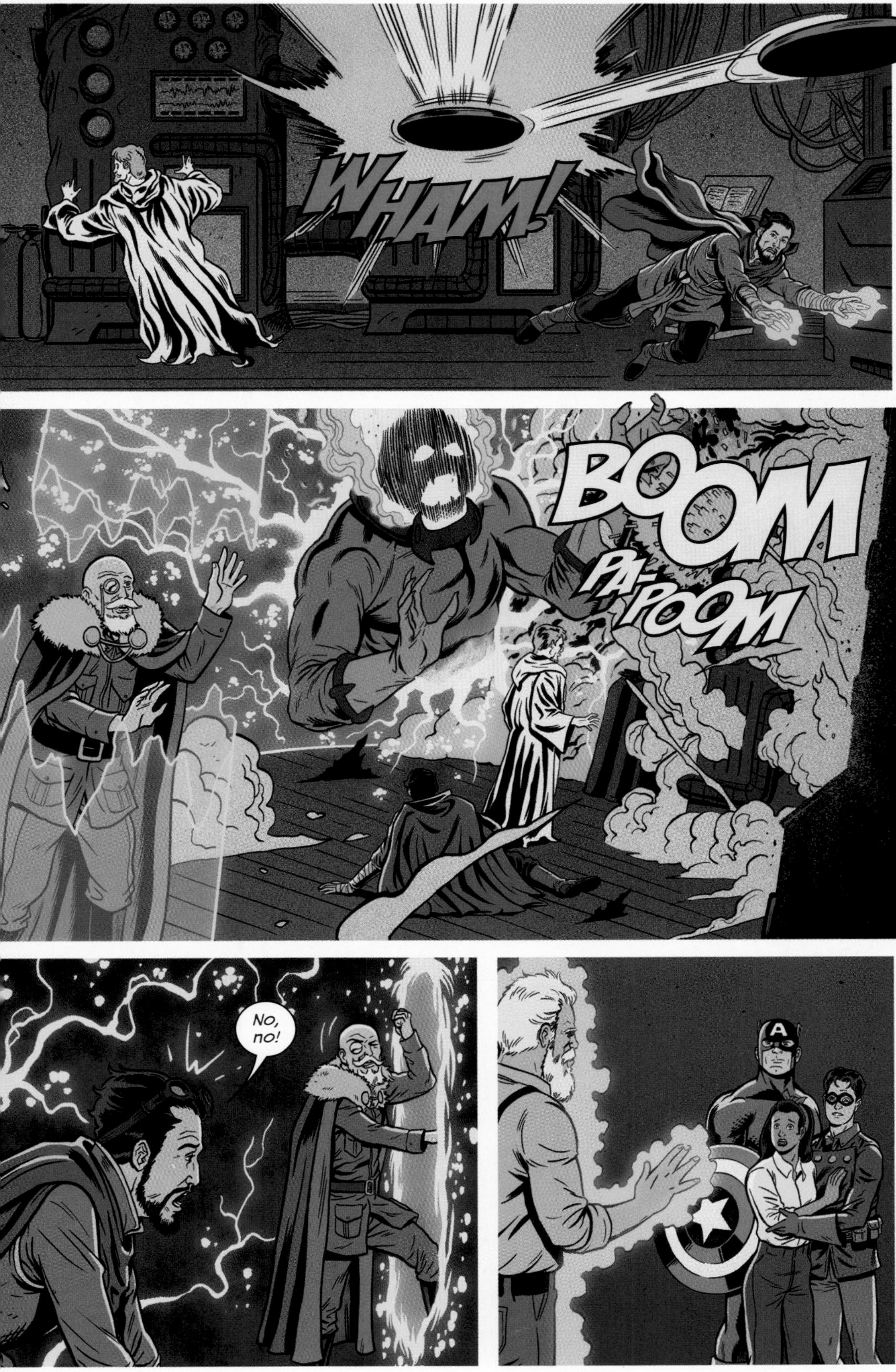
WHAM!
BOOM
PA-POOM
No, no!

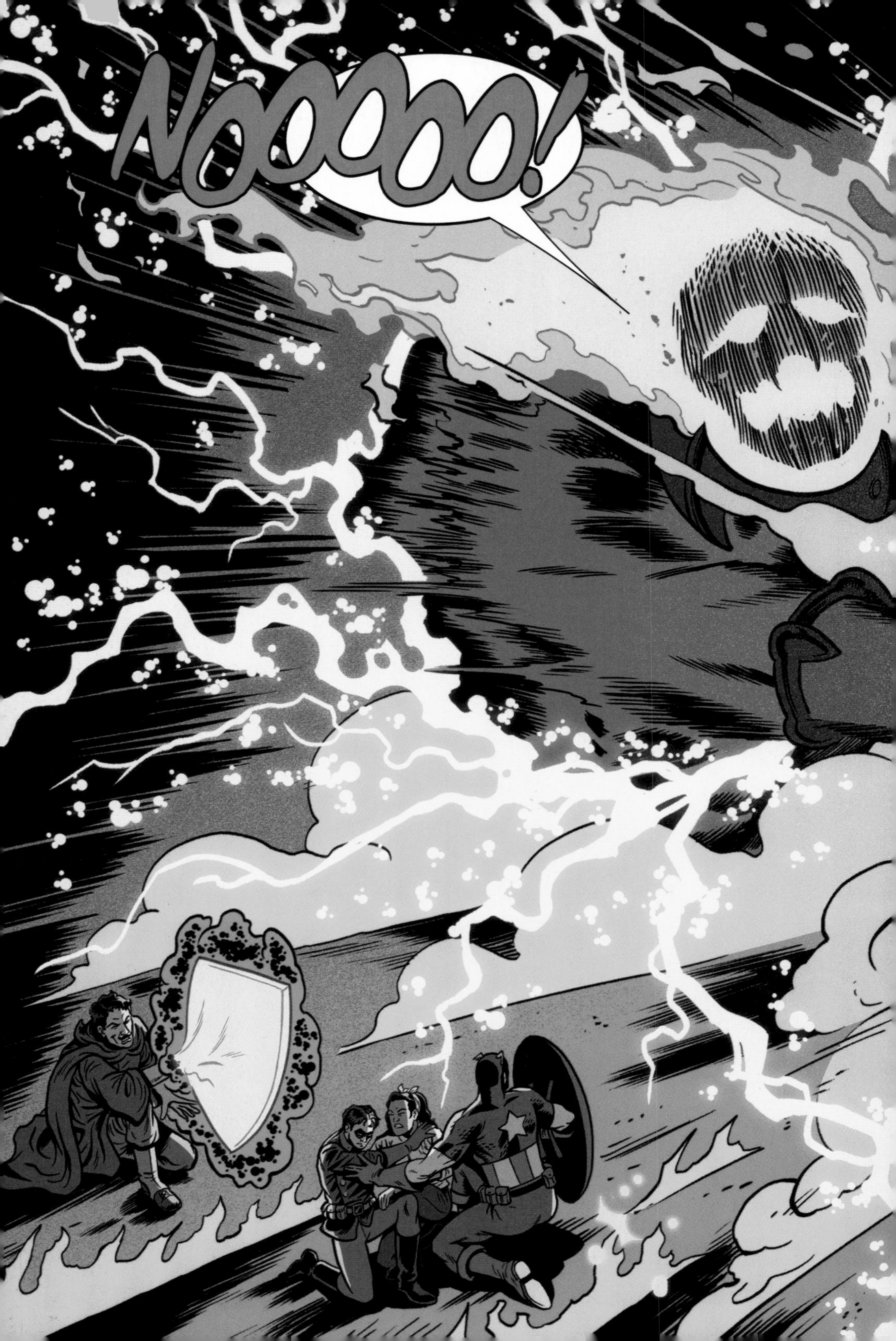
NOOOOO!

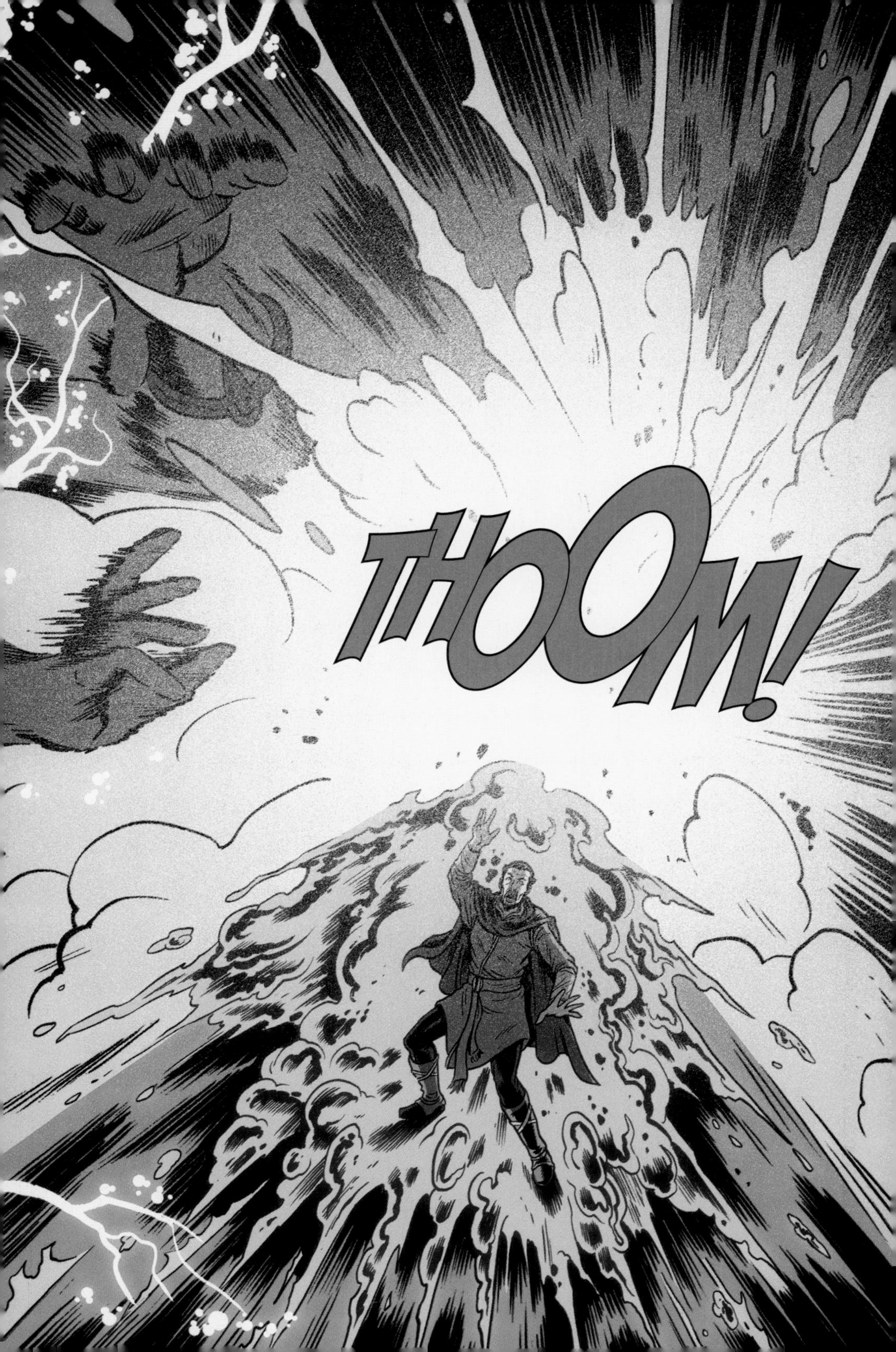
THOOM!

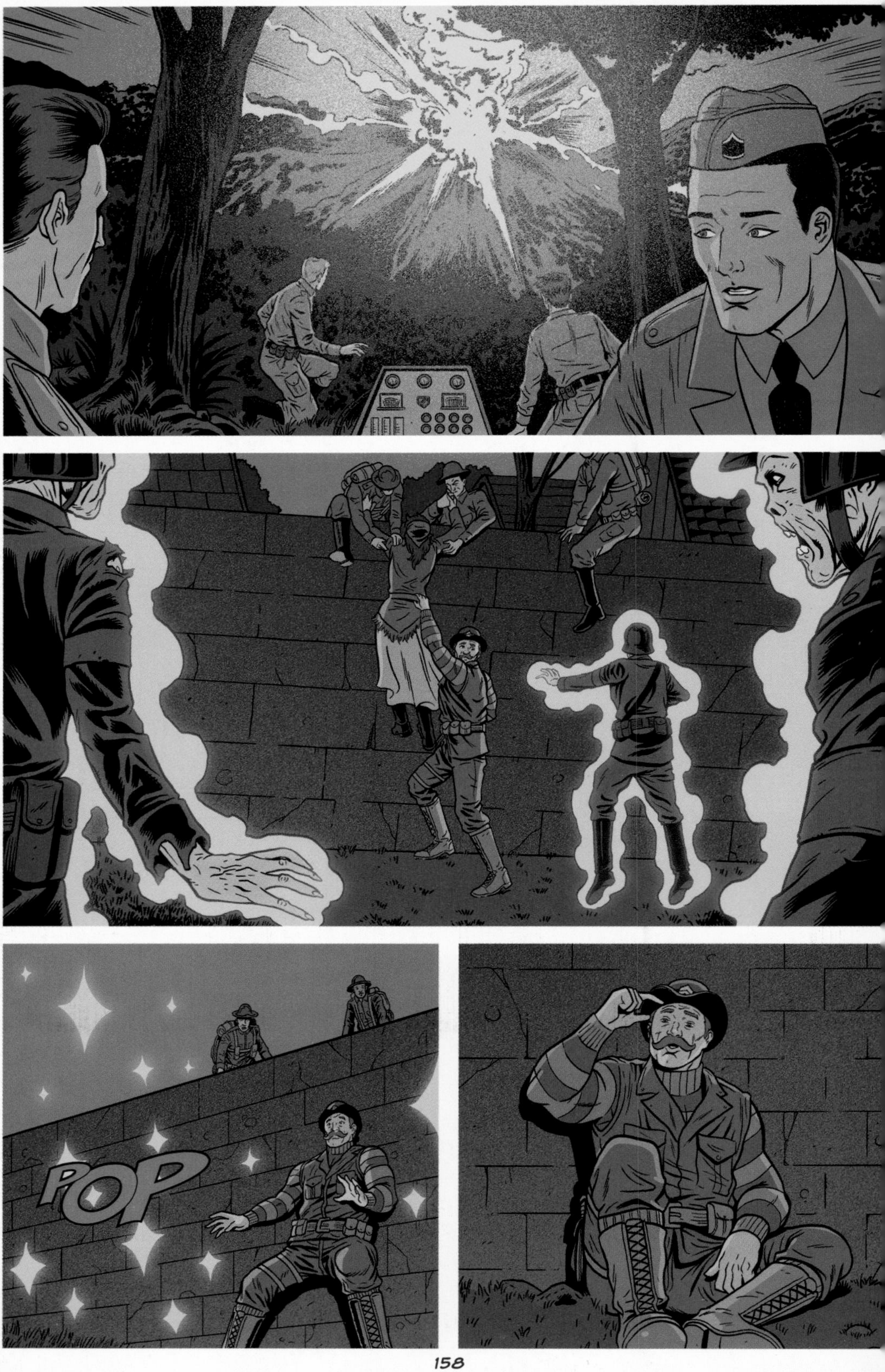
POP

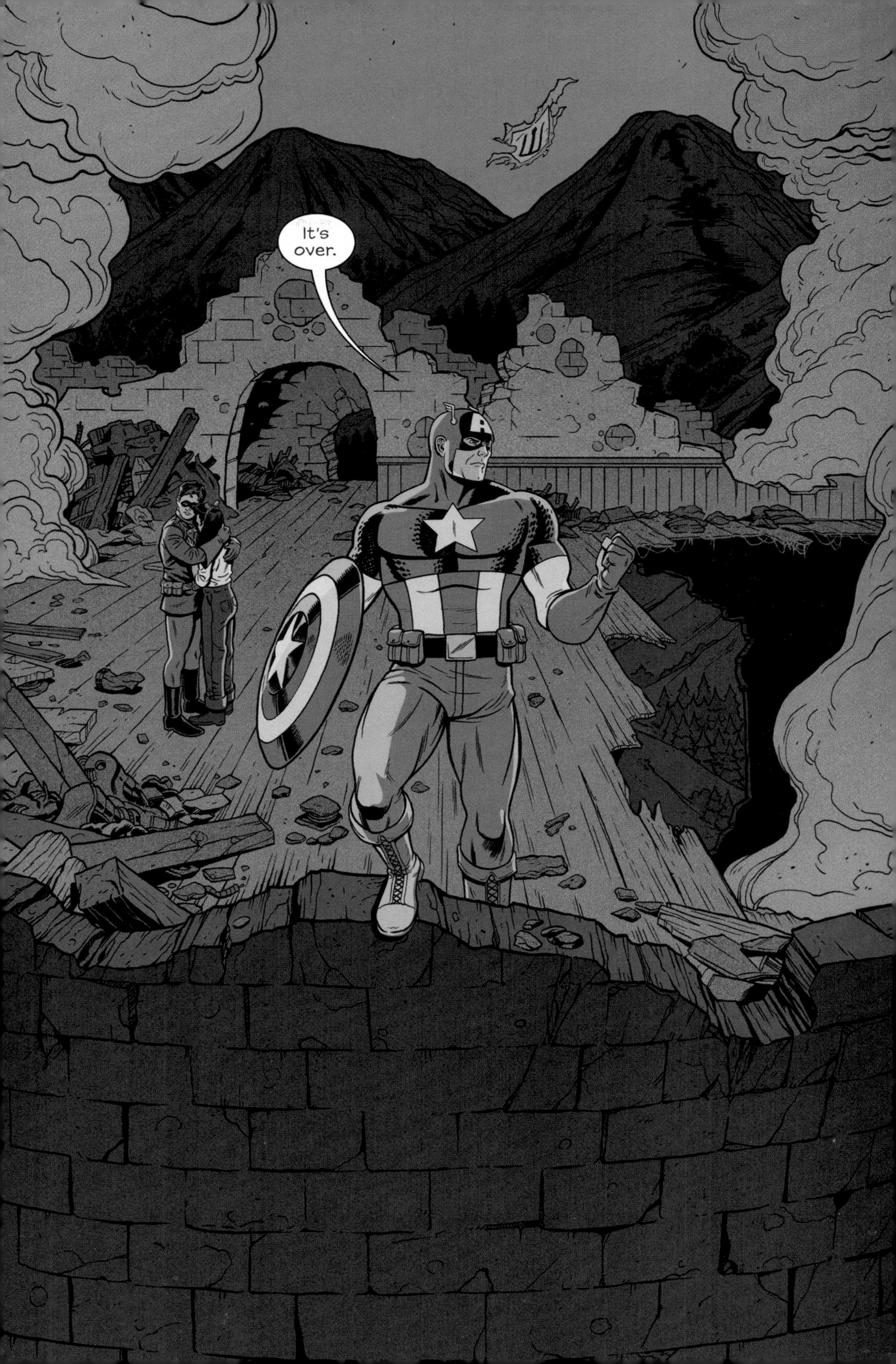
It's over.

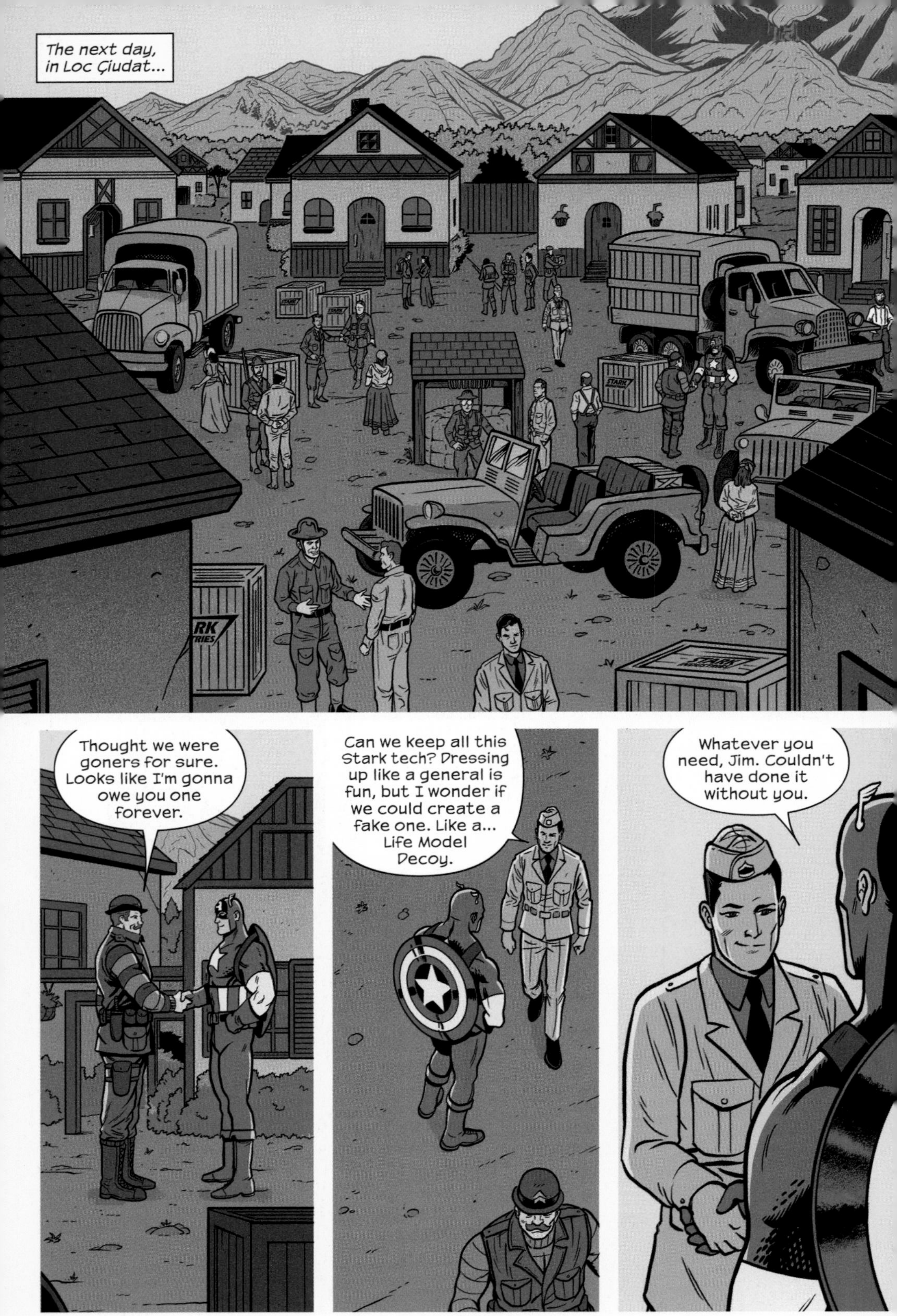

The next day, in Loc Çiudat...
Thought we were goners for sure. Looks like I'm gonna owe you one forever.
Can we keep all this Stark tech? Dressing up like a general is fun, but I wonder if we could create a fake one. Like a... Life Model Decoy.
Whatever you need, Jim. Couldn't have done it without you.

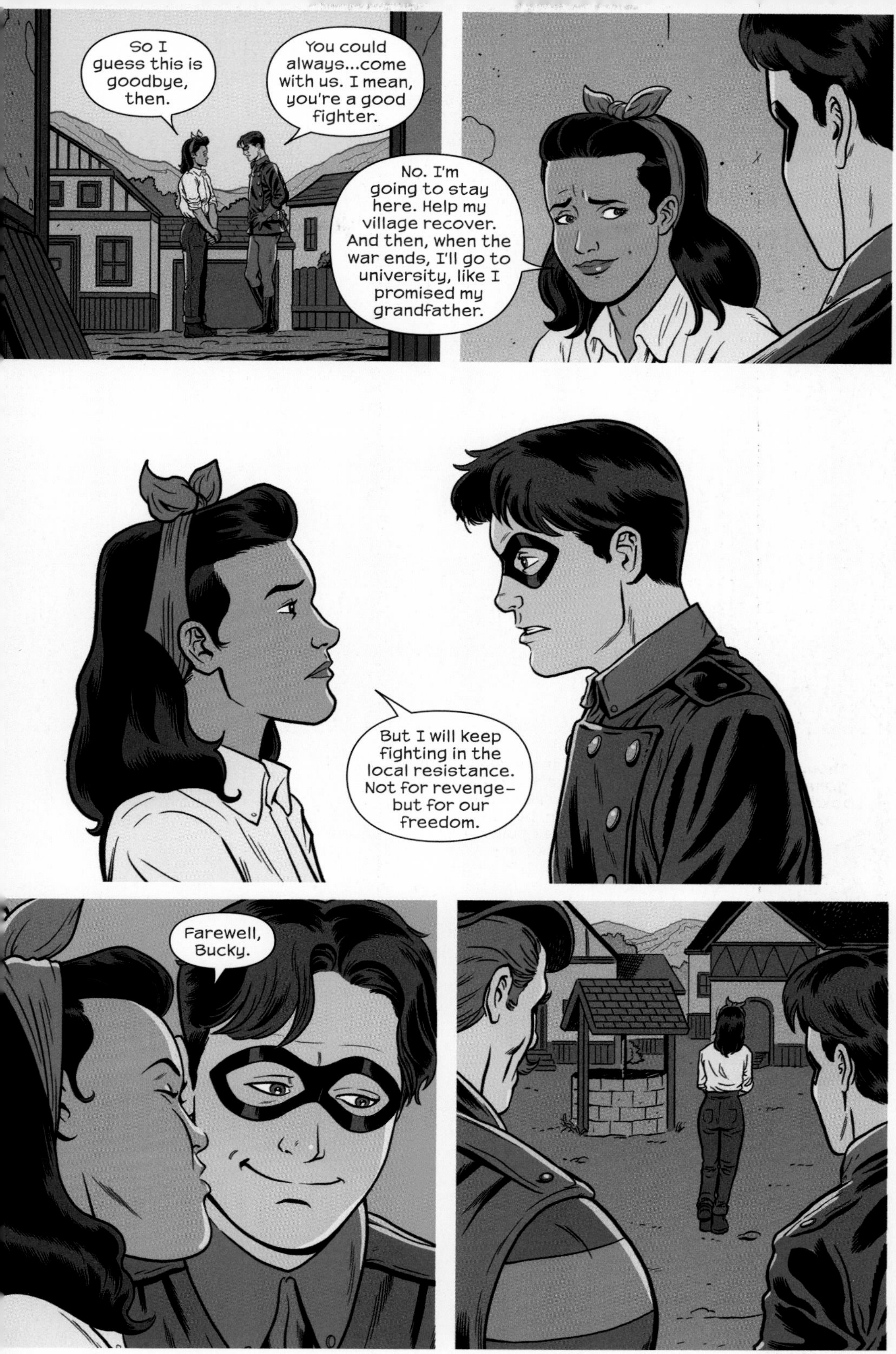
So I guess this is goodbye, then.
You could always...come with us. I mean, you're a good fighter.
No. I'm going to stay here. Help my village recover. And then, when the war ends, I'll go to university, like I promised my grandfather.
But I will keep fighting in the local resistance. Not for revenge– but for our freedom.
Farewell, Bucky.

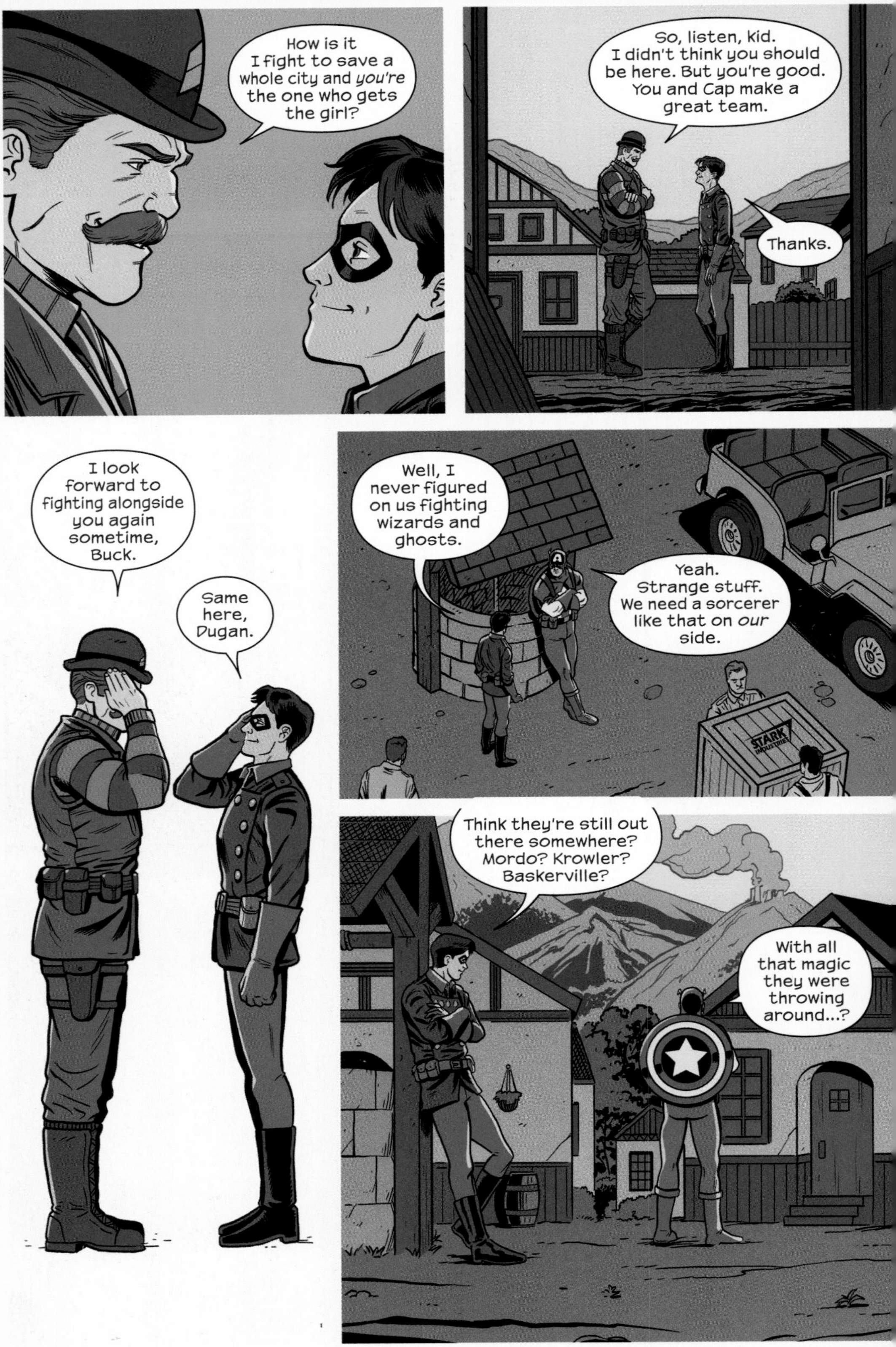
How is it I fight to save a whole city and *you're* the one who gets the girl?
So, listen, kid. I didn't think you should be here. But you're good. You and Cap make a great team.
Thanks.
I look forward to fighting alongside you again sometime, Buck.
Same here, Dugan.
Well, I never figured on us fighting wizards and ghosts.
Yeah. Strange stuff. We need a sorcerer like that on *our* side.
STARK INDUSTRIES
Think they're still out there somewhere? Mordo? Krowler? Baskerville?
With all that magic they were throwing around...?

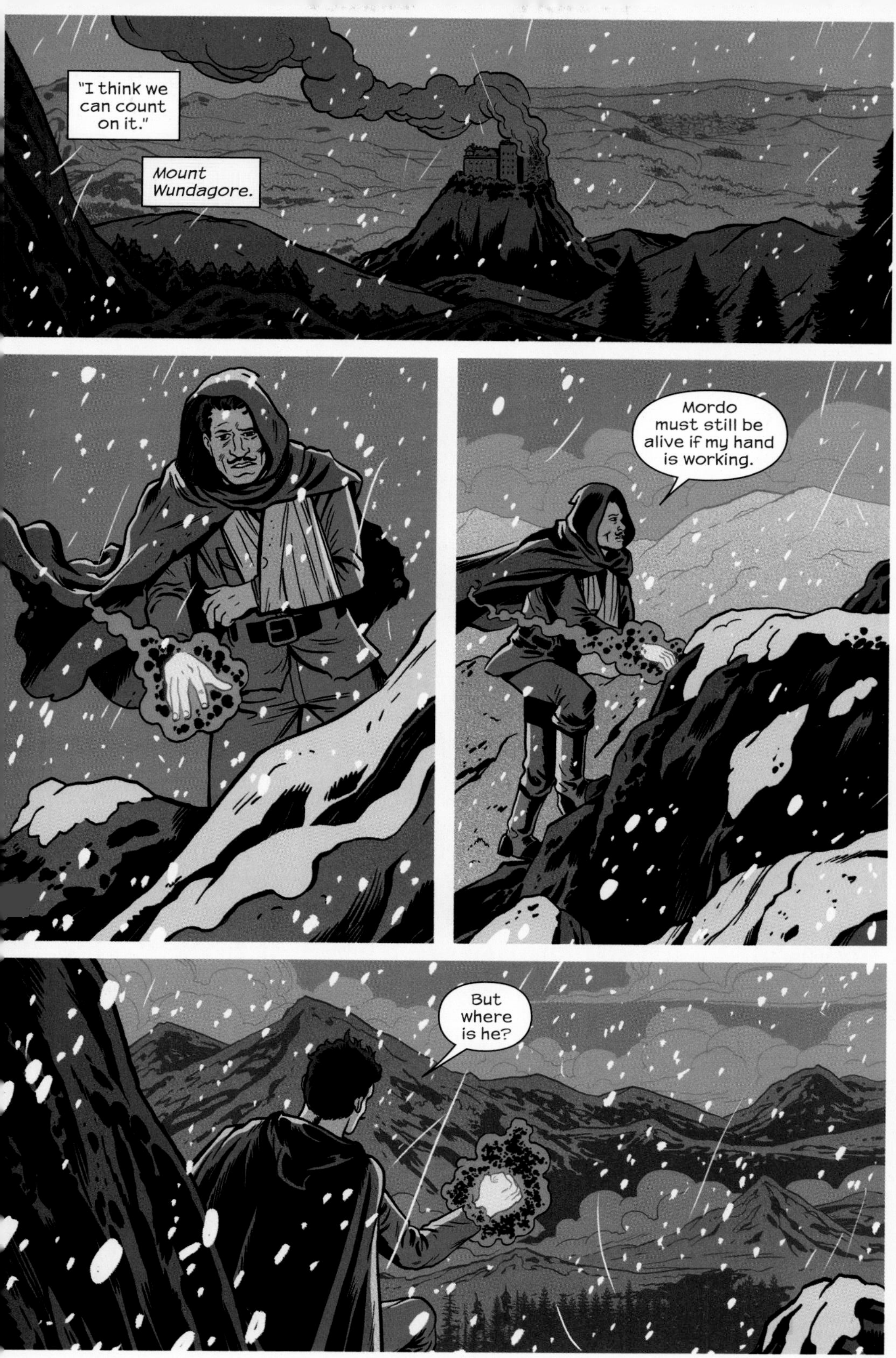
"I think we can count on it."
Mount Wundagore.
Mordo must still be alive if my hand is working.
But where is he?

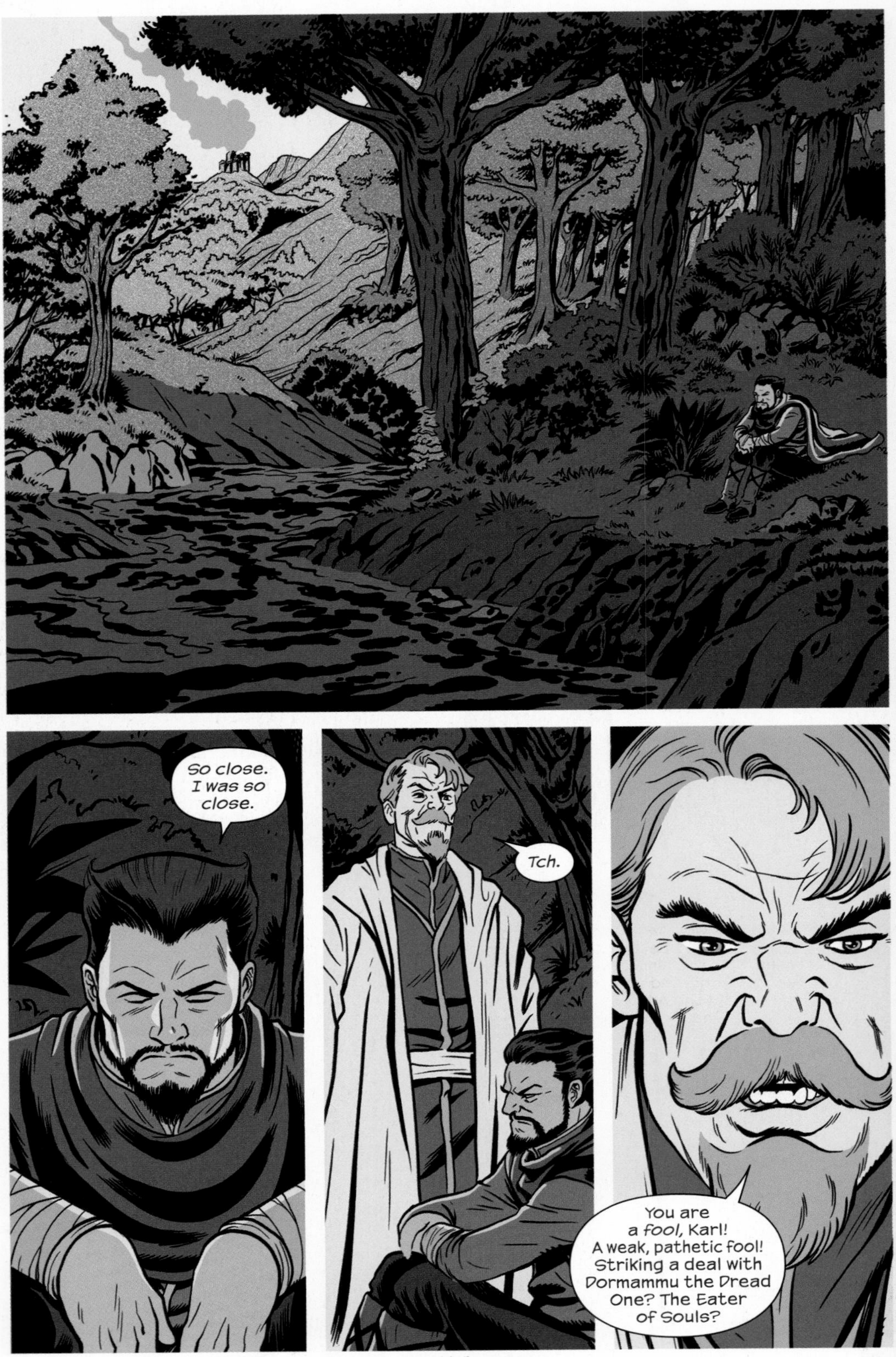
So close. I was so close.
Tch.
You are a *fool*, Karl! A weak, pathetic fool! Striking a deal with Dormammu the Dread One? The Eater of Souls?

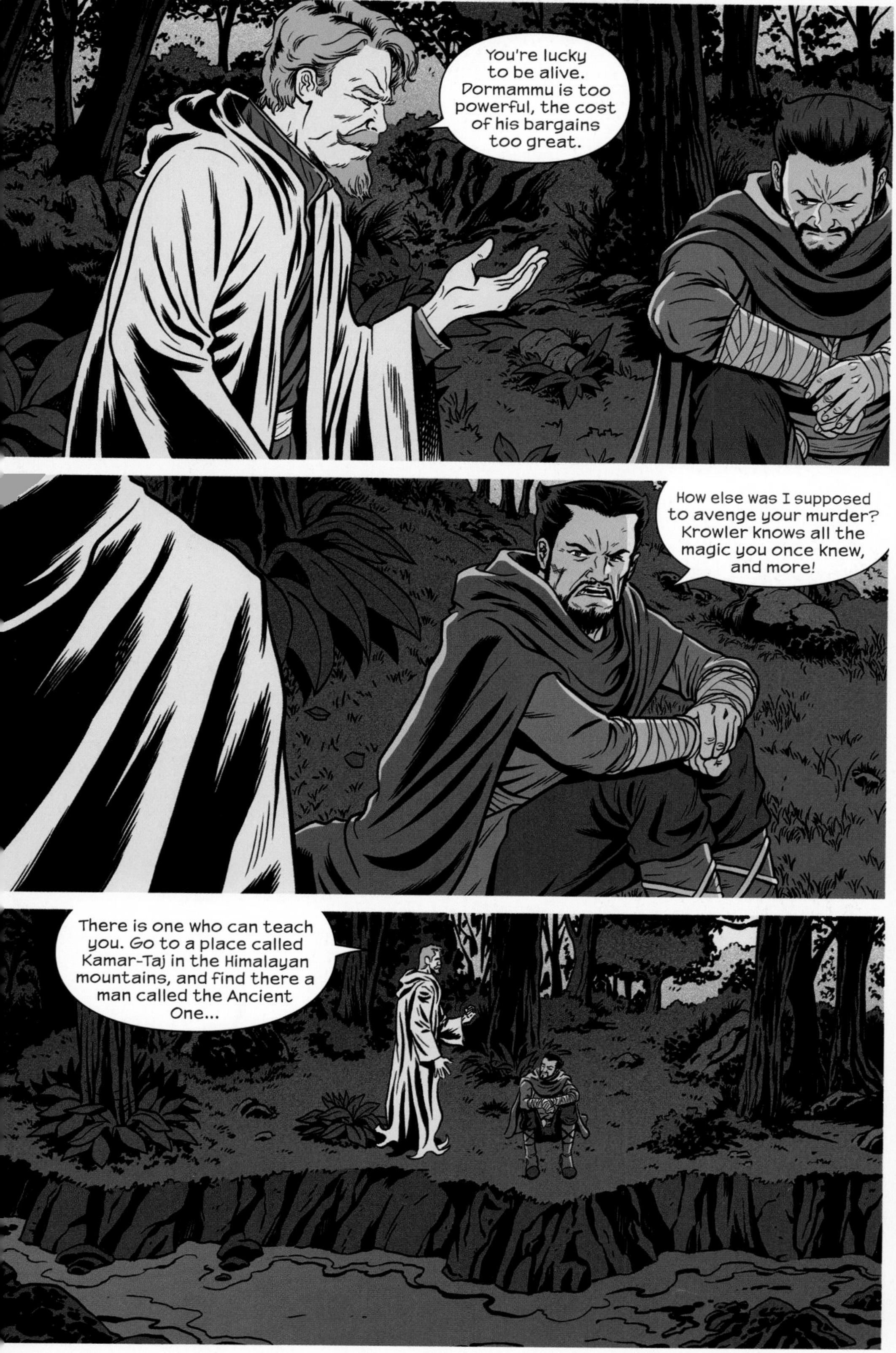
You're lucky to be alive. Dormammu is too powerful, the cost of his bargains too great.
How else was I supposed to avenge your murder? Krowler knows all the magic you once knew, and more!
There is one who can teach you. Go to a place called Kamar-Taj in the Himalayan mountains, and find there a man called the Ancient One...

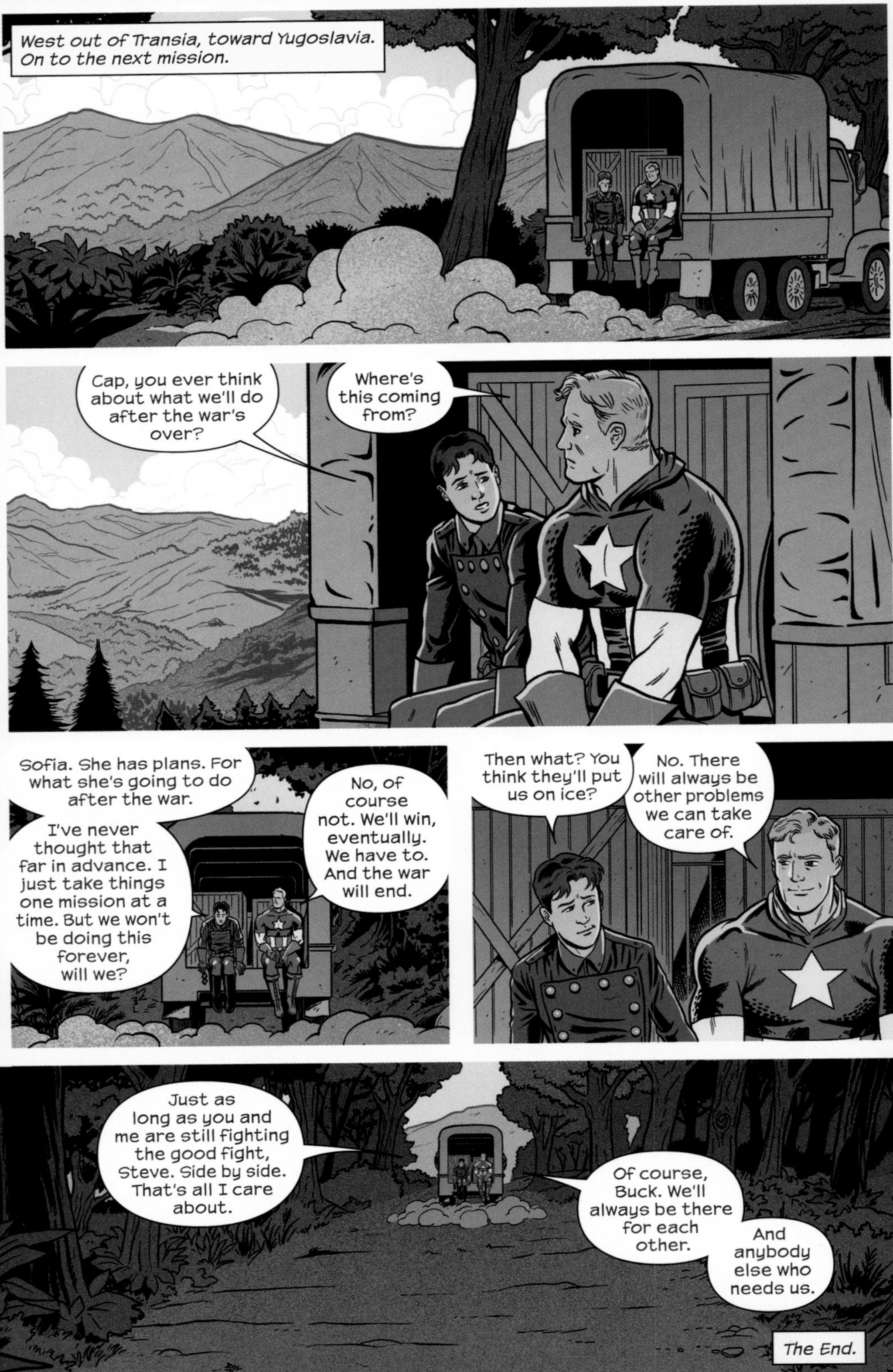
West out of Transia, toward Yugoslavia. On to the next mission.
Cap, you ever think about what we'll do after the war's over?
Where's this coming from?
Sofia. She has plans. For what she's going to do after the war.
I've never thought that far in advance. I just take things one mission at a time. But we won't be doing this forever, will we?
No, of course not. We'll win, eventually. We have to. And the war will end.
Then what? You think they'll put us on ice?
No. There will always be other problems we can take care of.
Just as long as you and me are still fighting the good fight, Steve. Side by side. That's all I care about.
Of course, Buck. We'll always be there for each other.
And anybody else who needs us.
The End.

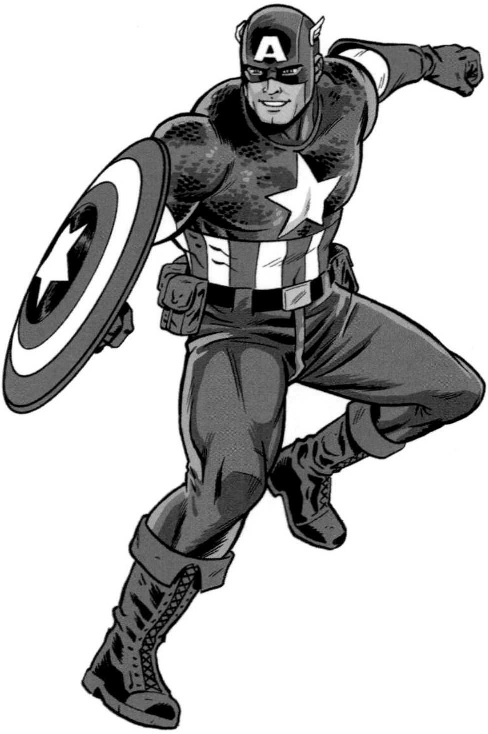

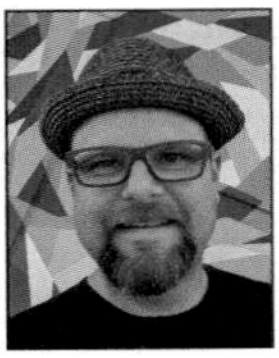

ALAN GRATZ is the #1 *New York Times* bestselling author of several acclaimed and award-winning books for young readers, including *Refugee*, *Allies*, *Ground Zero*, and more. A huge fan of comics and video games, Alan lives in North Carolina with his wife and daughter. Learn more at alangratz.com.

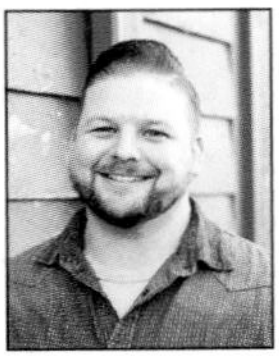

BRENT SCHOONOVER is a Midwestern-born illustrator who works in the fields of comic books and commercial art, having done projects for clients such as Target, Continental Airlines, Mayo Clinic, and the NFL. In the field of comics, Brent has worked on several creator-owned projects like *Devil's Highway* from AWA, as well as on well-known characters such as Batman and Superman at DC Comics, and X-Men, Ant-Man, Captain Marvel, and Black Widow at Marvel Comics. He currently lives in Minneapolis with his wife, Nicole; two daughters, Millie and Josie; and their bulldog, Agatha.

CHECK OUT A SNEAK PEEK OF

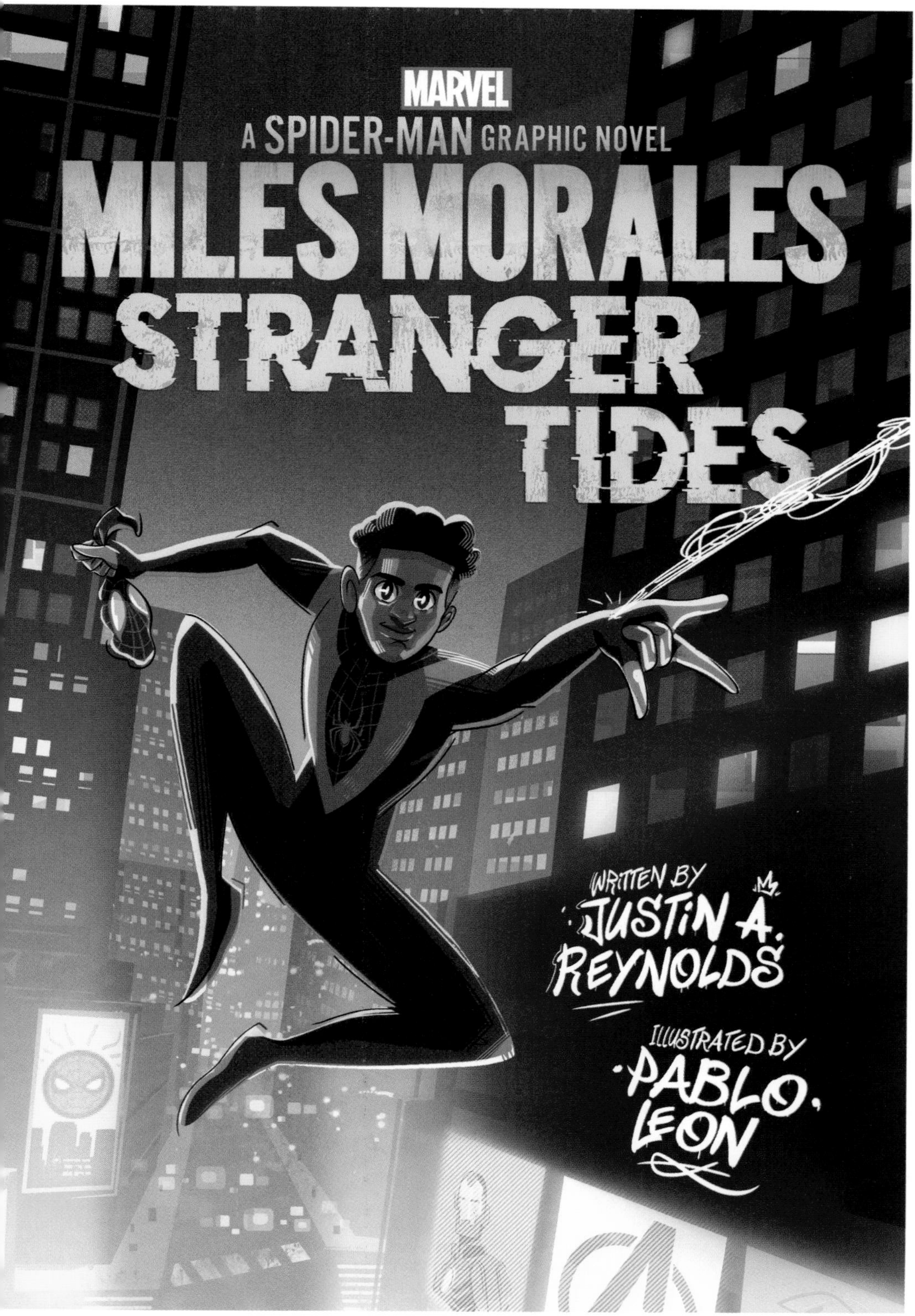
MARVEL
A SPIDER-MAN GRAPHIC NOVEL
MILES MORALES
STRANGER TIDES
WRITTEN BY
JUSTIN A. REYNOLDS
ILLUSTRATED BY
PABLO LEON

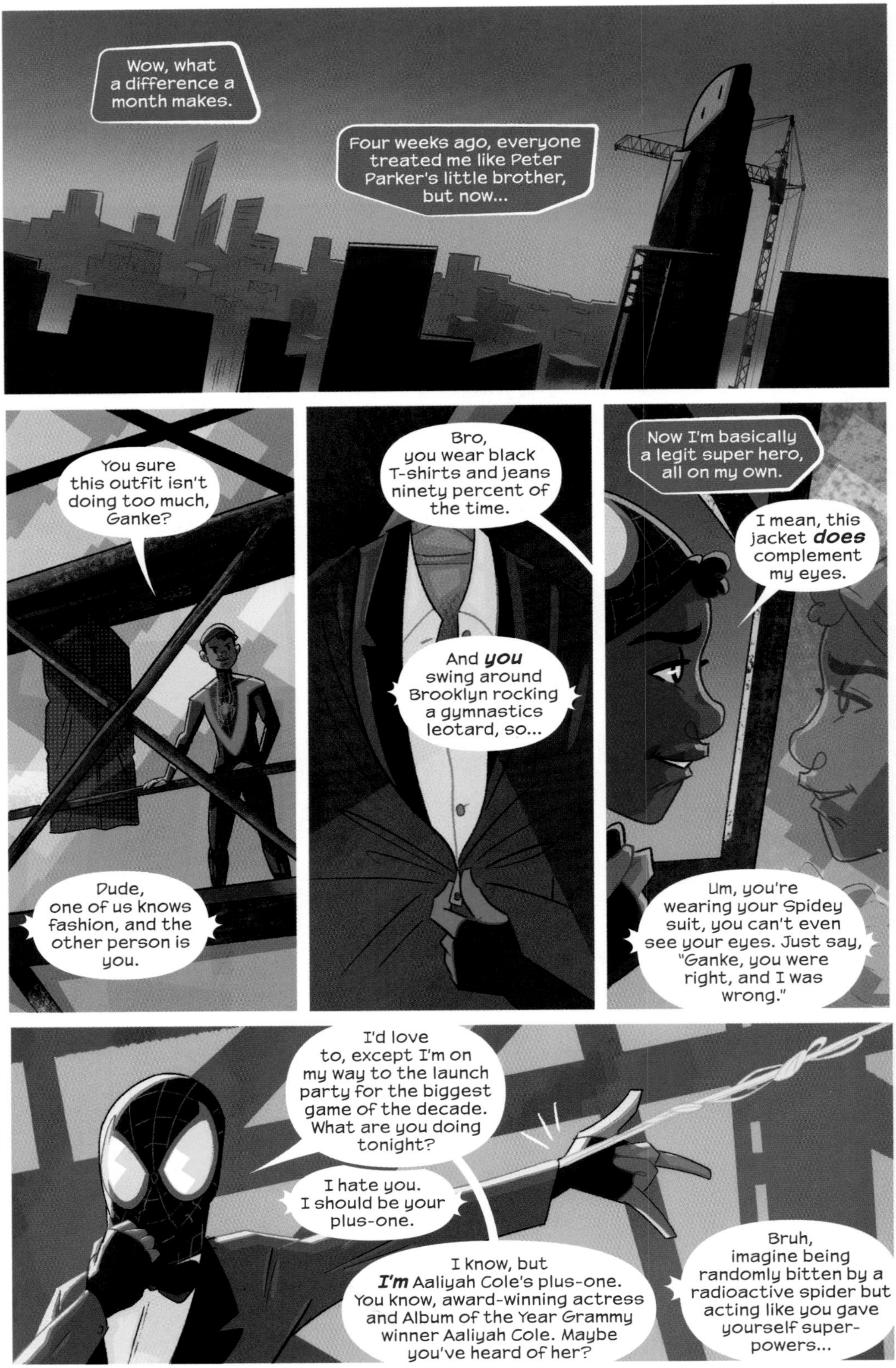

Wow, what a difference a month makes.
Four weeks ago, everyone treated me like Peter Parker's little brother, but now...
You sure this outfit isn't doing too much, Ganke?
Dude, one of us knows fashion, and the other person is you.
Bro, you wear black T-shirts and jeans ninety percent of the time.
And *you* swing around Brooklyn rocking a gymnastics leotard, so...
Now I'm basically a legit super hero, all on my own.
I mean, this jacket ***does*** complement my eyes.
Um, you're wearing your Spidey suit, you can't even see your eyes. Just say, "Ganke, you were right, and I was wrong."
I'd love to, except I'm on my way to the launch party for the biggest game of the decade. What are you doing tonight?
I hate you. I should be your plus-one.
I know, but ***I'm*** Aaliyah Cole's plus-one. You know, award-winning actress and Album of the Year Grammy winner Aaliyah Cole. Maybe you've heard of her?
Bruh, imagine being randomly bitten by a radioactive spider but acting like you gave yourself super-powers...

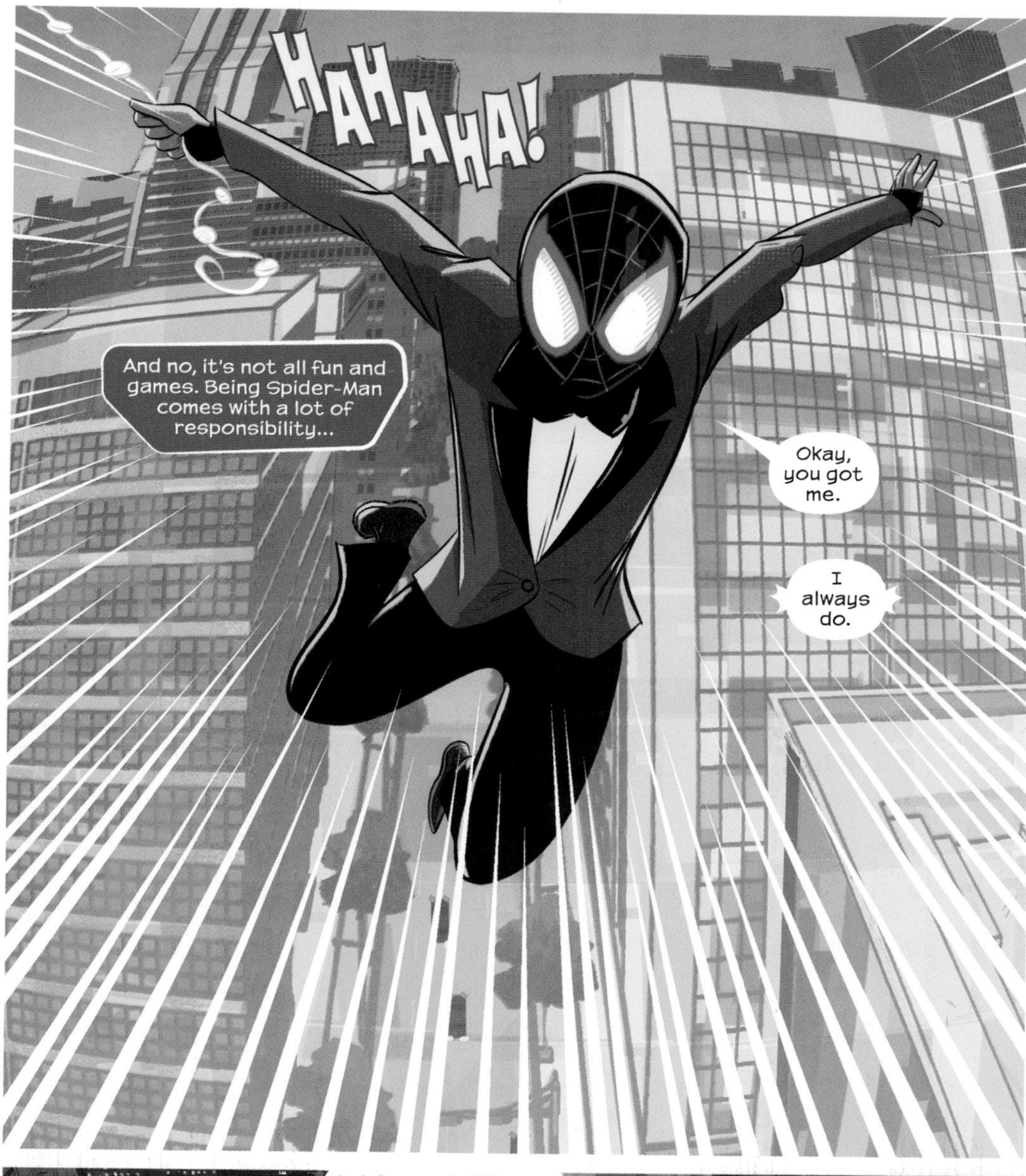
HAHAHAHA!
And no, it's not all fun and games. Being Spider-Man comes with a lot of responsibility...
Okay, you got me.
I always do.

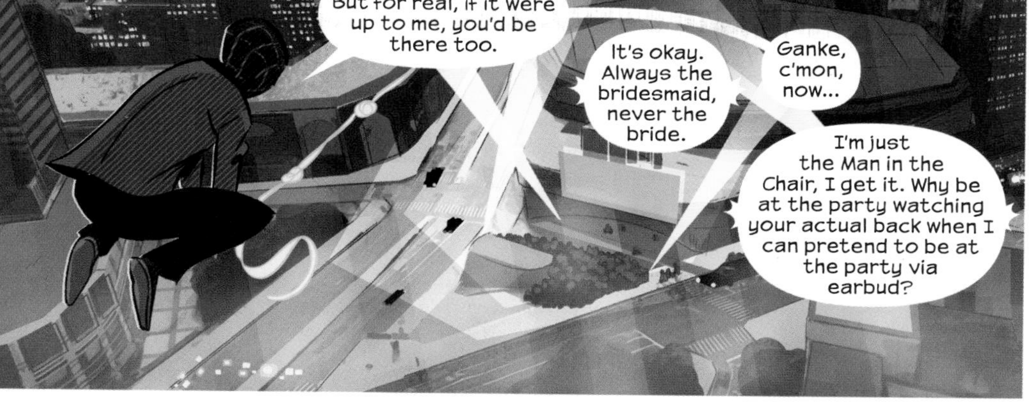
But for real, if it were up to me, you'd be there too.
It's okay. Always the bridesmaid, never the bride.
Ganke, c'mon, now...
I'm just the Man in the Chair, I get it. Why be at the party watching your actual back when I can pretend to be at the party via earbud?

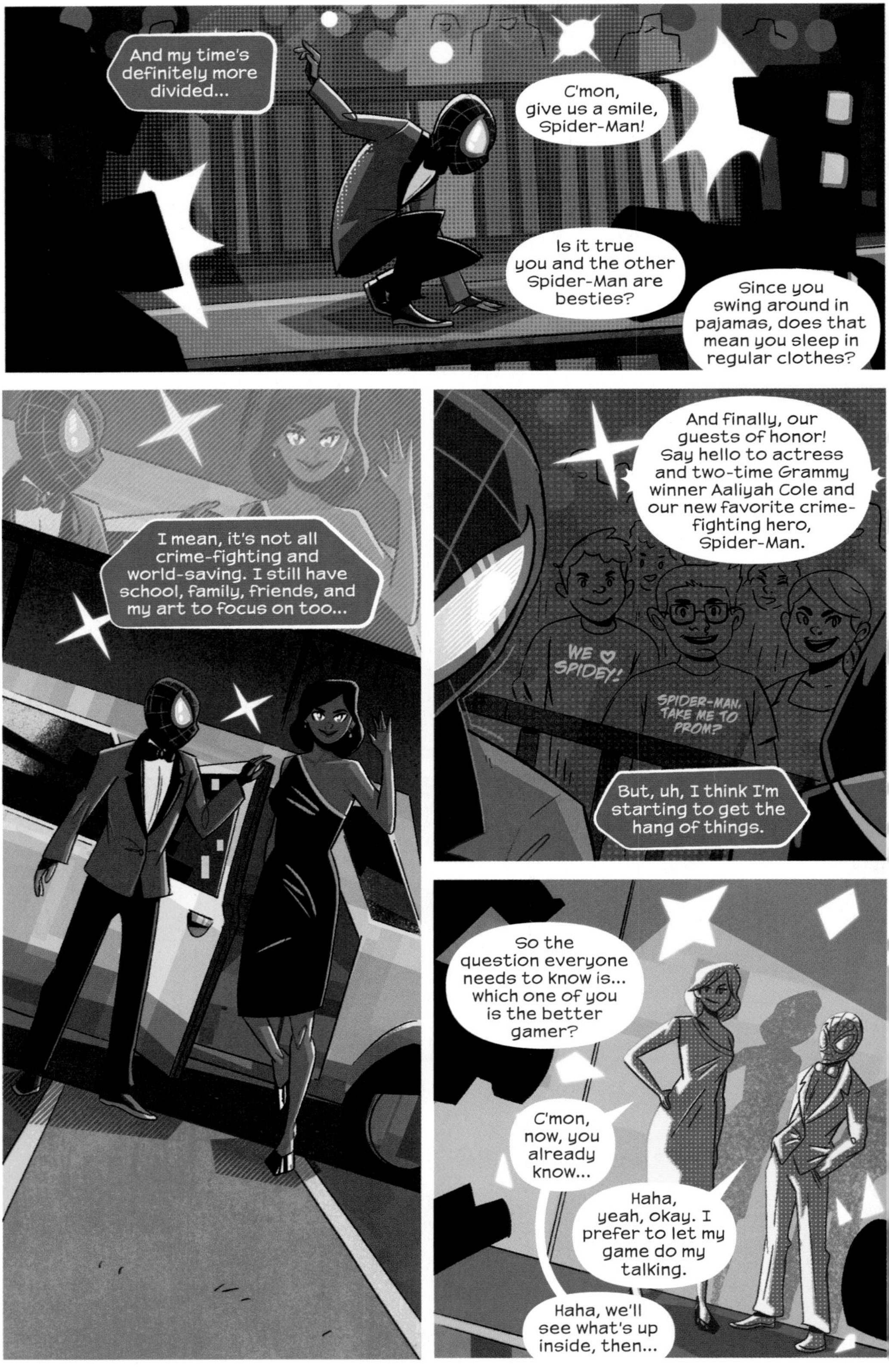
And my time's definitely more divided...
C'mon, give us a smile, Spider-Man!
Is it true you and the other Spider-Man are besties?
Since you swing around in pajamas, does that mean you sleep in regular clothes?
I mean, it's not all crime-fighting and world-saving. I still have school, family, friends, and my art to focus on too...
And finally, our guests of honor! Say hello to actress and two-time Grammy winner Aaliyah Cole and our new favorite crime-fighting hero, Spider-Man.
WE ♡ SPIDEY!
SPIDER-MAN, TAKE ME TO PROM?
But, uh, I think I'm starting to get the hang of things.
So the question everyone needs to know is... which one of you is the better gamer?
C'mon, now, you already know...
Haha, yeah, okay. I prefer to let my game do my talking.
Haha, we'll see what's up inside, then...

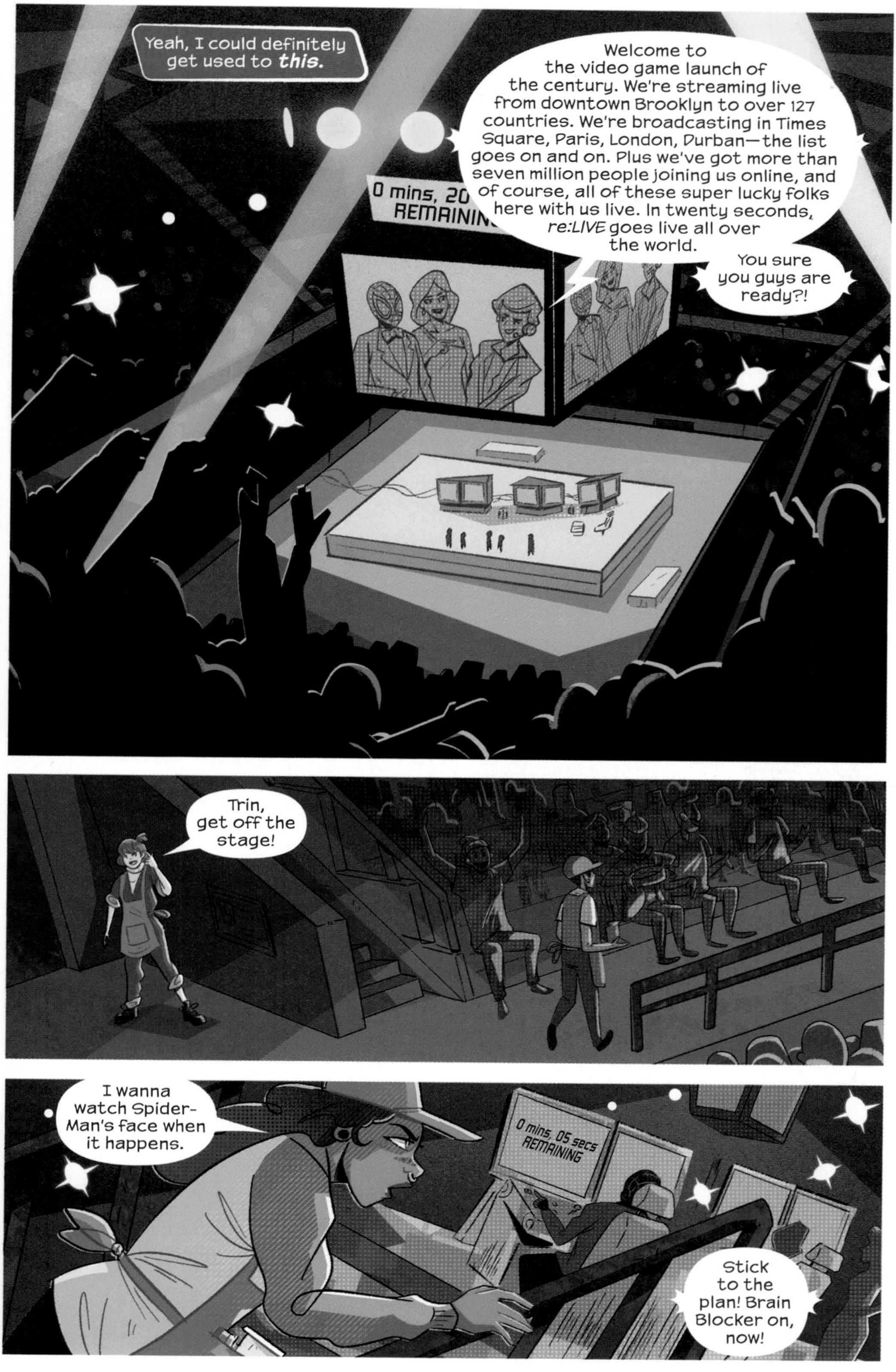
Yeah, I could definitely get used to *this.*
Welcome to the video game launch of the century. We're streaming live from downtown Brooklyn to over 127 countries. We're broadcasting in Times Square, Paris, London, Durban—the list goes on and on. Plus we've got more than seven million people joining us online, and of course, all of these super lucky folks here with us live. In twenty seconds, *re:LIVE* goes live all over the world.
You sure you guys are ready?!
Trin, get off the stage!
I wanna watch Spider-Man's face when it happens.
0 mins, 05 secs REMAINING
Stick to the plan! Brain Blocker on, now!

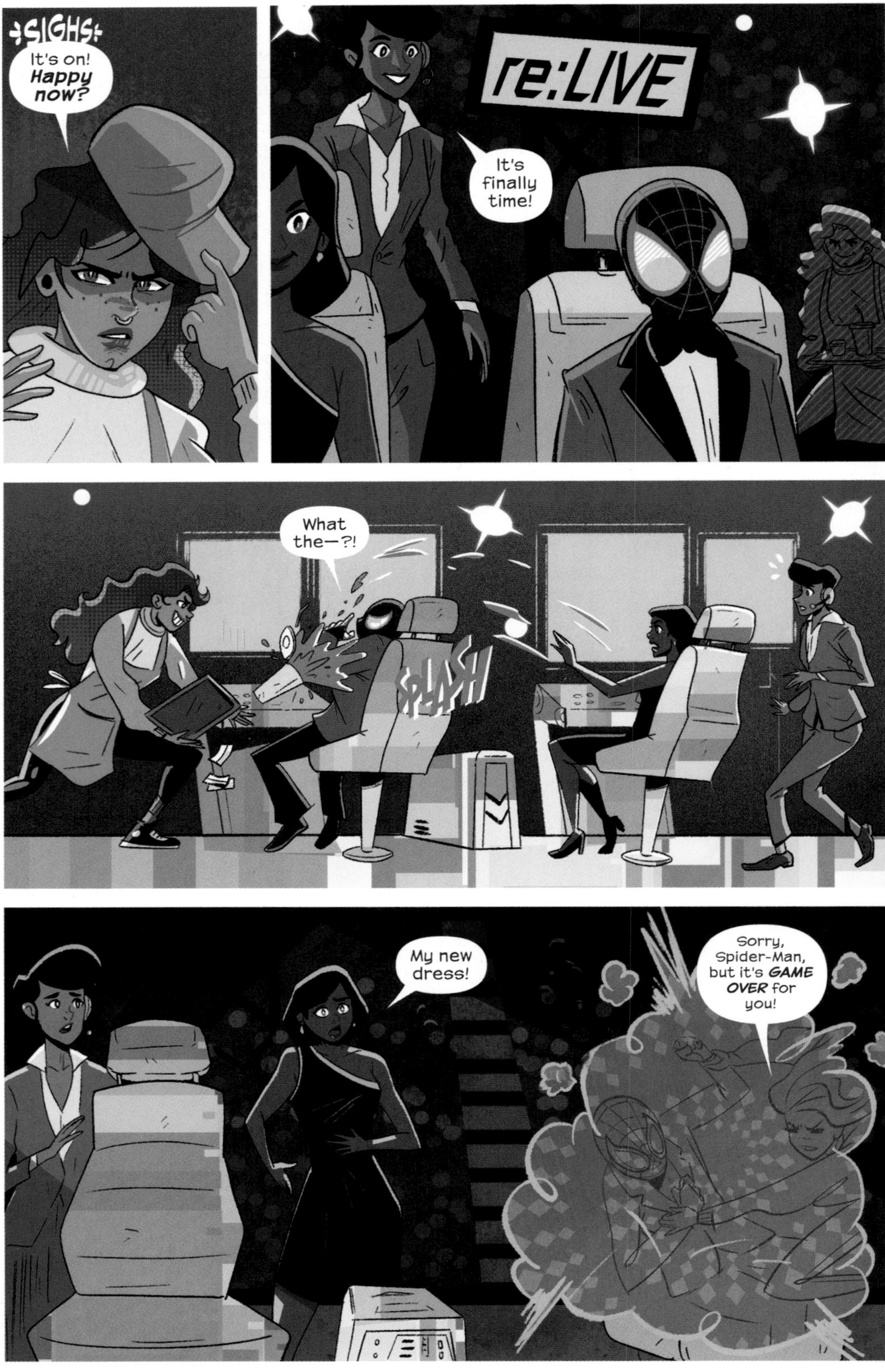
SIGHS
It's on! **Happy now?**
re:LIVE
It's finally time!
What the—?!
SPLASH
My new dress!
Sorry, Spider-Man, but it's **GAME OVER** for you!

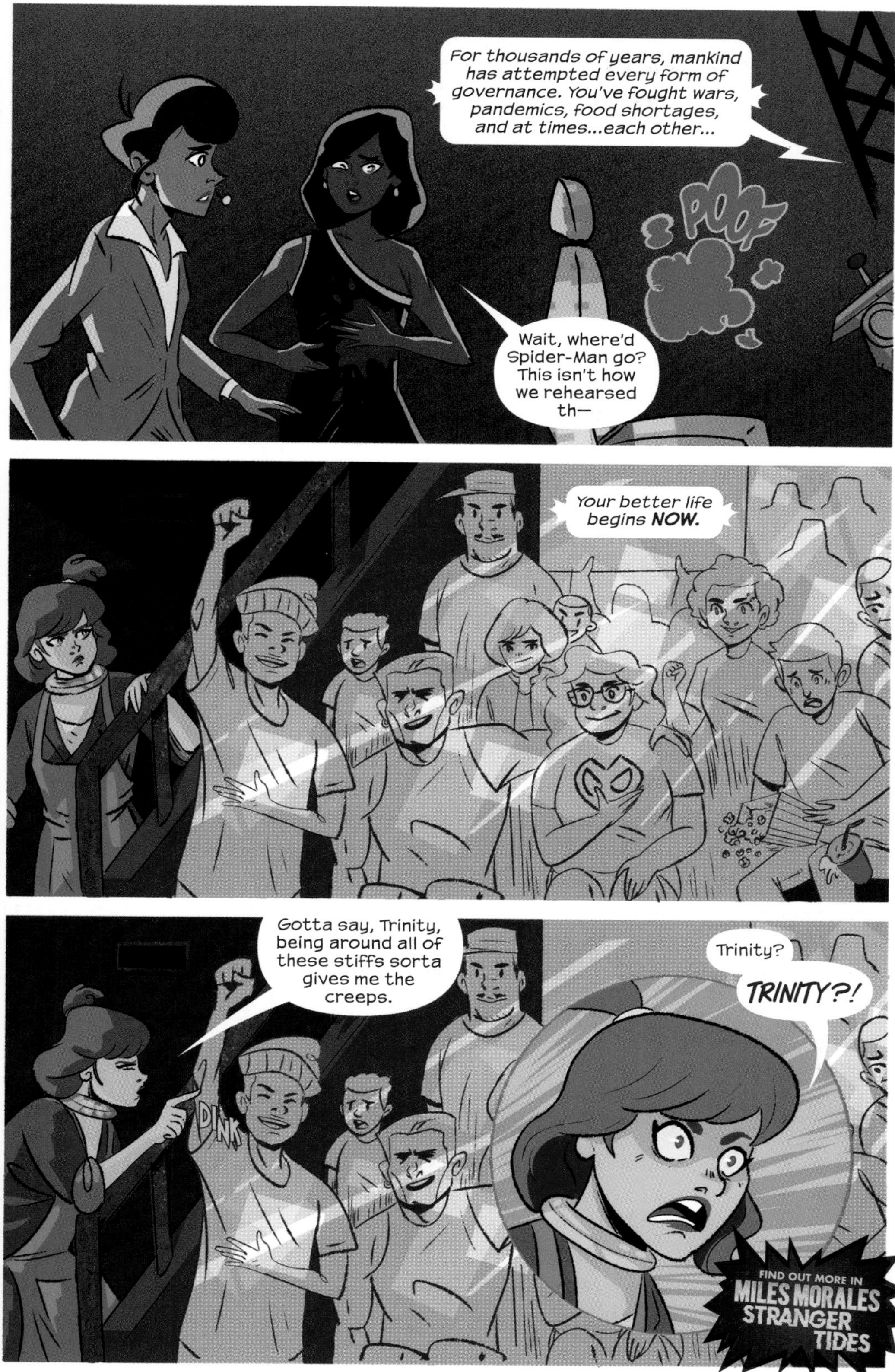
For thousands of years, mankind has attempted every form of governance. You've fought wars, pandemics, food shortages, and at times...each other...
POOF
Wait, where'd Spider-Man go? This isn't how we rehearsed th—
Your better life begins **NOW.**
Gotta say, Trinity, being around all of these stiffs sorta gives me the creeps.
DINK
Trinity?
TRINITY?!
FIND OUT MORE IN
MILES MORALES STRANGER TIDES

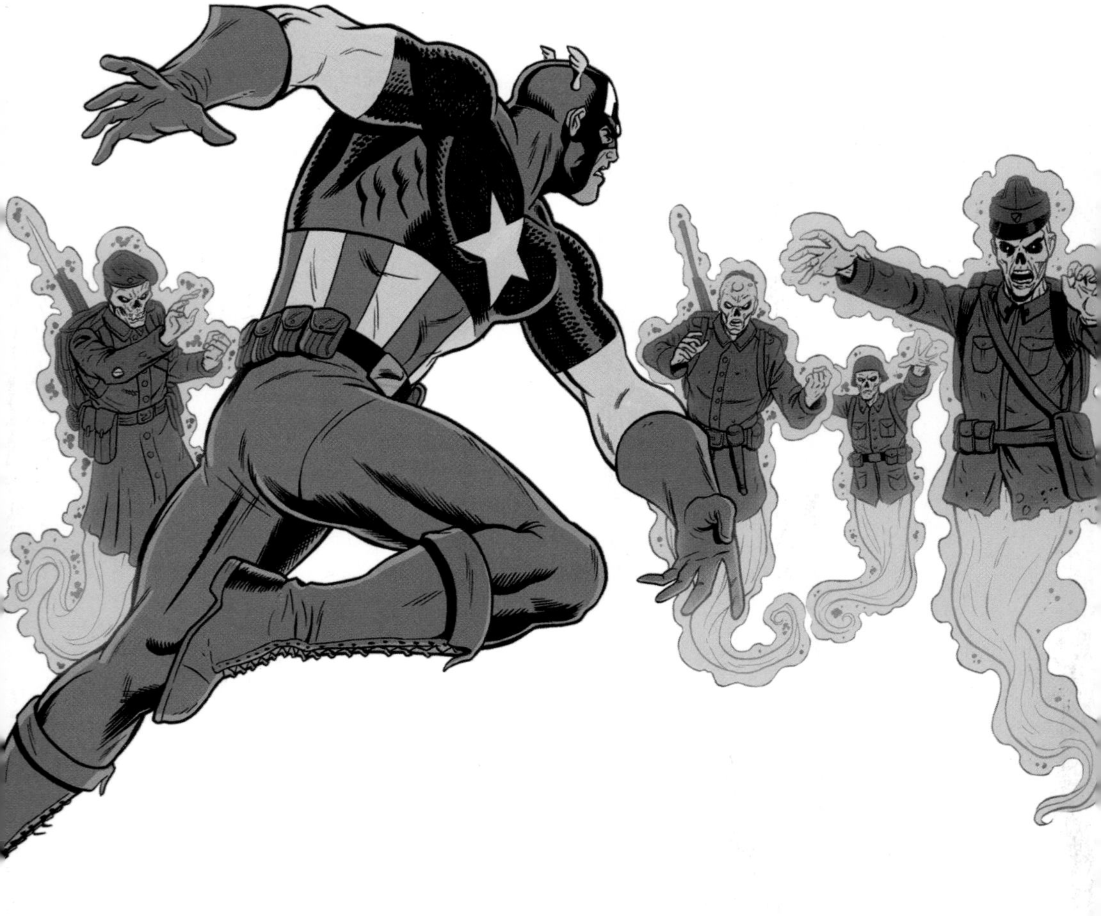